CELINE L. A. SIMPSON

Just My
LUCK

Copyright © 2024 by Celine L. A. Simpson

All rights reserved. No part of this publication may be reproduced, stored or transmitted in any form or by any means, electronic, mechanical, photocopying, recording, scanning, or otherwise without written permission from the publisher. It is illegal to copy this book, post it to a website, or distribute it by any other means without permission.

This novel is entirely a work of fiction. The names, characters and incidents portrayed in it are the work of the author's imagination. Any resemblance to actual persons, living or dead, events or localities is entirely coincidental.

Celine L. A. Simpson asserts the moral right to be identified as the author of this work.

Celine L. A. Simpson has no responsibility for the persistence or accuracy of URLs for external or third-party Internet Websites referred to in this publication and does not guarantee that any content on such Websites is, or will remain, accurate or appropriate.

Designations used by companies to distinguish their products are often claimed as trademarks. All brand names and product names used in this book and on its cover are trade names, service marks, trademarks and registered trademarks of their respective owners. The publishers and the book are not associated with any product or vendor mentioned in this book. None of the companies referenced within the book have endorsed the book.

First edition

ISBN: 978-0-6451611-7-5

Editing by Joeli Woodrow
Illustration by Ashley Quick
Cover art by Murphy Rae

This book was professionally typeset on Reedsy.
Find out more at reedsy.com

Mama,
whenever I wonder if I can do something, it's your voice in my mind that I hear say,
'yes you can, chook'.
This book, like all the others, exists because of that 'yes'.
Because I am my mothers daughter.

Prologue

Lucky Peters was the bane of my existence.

She sat in front of me in class, as she always did, and I knew she could feel my stare burning a hole in the back of her head. Long, golden waves and all.

It was a show. I'd learned that in a very slow, humiliating, and painful way. She wasn't quite as the world expected her to be.

Lucky was cunning. She was strategic and calculated and for all the luck she claimed to have, she worked her ass off as well. I could admit that. She had this desperate, obsessive need to outdo me at every turn, casting me in her shadow at every opportunity.

I hated her for it.

Lucky reached up to tuck a strand of hair behind her ear, following through with the movement and casting her gaze back at me, meeting my eyes that hadn't moved from where they rested on her since the moment we sat down in this class. Her eyes narrowed as she took the end of her pencil between her teeth, a small smile pulling up at the corner of her full lips before she sent a wink my way and turned back towards the teacher.

That bit—

She knew she had everyone in the palm of her hand, and she couldn't help it. It was like she *enjoyed* seeing me come second place. It was like she *worked* to make sure I would forever be known as 'that kid that was almost as smart as Lucky Peters'.

"—and Luck? The next element is?" Mr. Langem spoke from the front of the class, snapping my attention to him with the jarring reality that I had paid absolutely no attention to what was being spoken of in today's science class.

Did it matter? Nope. This was the last week of classes before school finished and left me a high school graduate, sights set on bigger and better things. A world without Lucky Peters busting my ass at every turn.

"Roentgenium," she called back without a moment's hesitation. Her voice sent a jolt down my spine.

Mr. Langem's attention cut straight to me and I knew I was fucked. Well and truly fucked.

"Mr. Thompson?" he asked, looking at me expectantly.

I leaned back in my seat and crossed my arms.

"Let me guess," he went on, the entire class turning to face me, "you have no idea what we're doing?" He lifted an eyebrow at me.

And it didn't matter, this class was a filler. All the important things we had to learn had come to pass. I wasn't the only person *not* listening in this class right now.

"Not a clue," I answered him truthfully with a tight lipped smile, only at the last second dropping the mask of acceptable agreeance I wore to school, letting him see, briefly, the cold and calculated emptiness that lived beneath my skin.

The class around me let out a string of whispered laughs and quiet coughs, none of them the wiser as Mr. Langem's face lost all its colour and a slight shake took hold of his outstretched hand.

He recovered well, I'd give him that. What surprised me most was the courage he possessed to deliver a retort. I'd done a very good job of hiding my demons, but when I let them out those who had been unfortunate enough to witness them didn't fare so well.

"Well," he cleared his throat, "if only you listened to me as intently as you stared at the back of Miss Peters' head, you might have made that number one spot for the year. Hmm?" He lifted his eyebrows further as everyone lifted the damper on their volume levels. Releasing a string of curses amongst other sound effects that highlighted how much his comment was intended to 'burn' me.

But my eyes travelled back to where lucky little Navy Grace Peters, or 'Lucky' as she'd always been called, sat. Her head still facing the front of the class like what had just happened was the last thing she had wanted. Like seeing me fall a little farther behind her didn't get her rocks off.

She didn't turn around again and when the bell rang, everyone, teacher included, couldn't have removed themselves from the classroom any faster if they tried. It was always the case. This was the last class on a Wednesday and usually it was just me left behind. I didn't see the point in throwing my crap in my bag only to have to reorganise and figure out everything later.

So, I took my time.

Putting hand-outs and papers where they needed to go, regardless of their uselessness now. Closing my textbook properly, I placed it into my bag with the sort of care that any piece of literature deserved.

I was methodical. I'd always been methodical. Process driven and strategy focused.

That's how you got what you deserved in the world, by working hard for it.

There was a Roman philosopher named Lucius Annaeus Seneca who had said luck was simply the point at which opportunity met with preparation. It was the only version of luck I would ever rightly admit to existing.

I packed up my things slowly, pretending not to notice when Lucky walked by my desk. Her skirt just barely touched the back of my hand that gripped my desk. I had the sudden urge to reach out to her then, like my hands had all of a sudden developed a mind of their own.

I didn't know what they'd do if they reached out toward her, but only knowing that I needed them to remain exactly where they were, gripping my desk as if my life depended on it.

She smelt like jasmine. Like wild berries. Like the outside world. Like the woods, and cool rain and fresh air. It suffocated me.

I counted to five, knowing that she would reach the open door in only three seconds and would be well on her way with the following two. I gave myself five seconds to collect myself knowing that it was only a matter of days before I'd never have to see her again, hating that my gut twisted with the relief of that reality as well as the dread of it.

Five seconds had passed and the sound of the door to the classroom clicking shut, quietly startled me. There were two options. She was either on *this* side of the door, or the *other*.

I picked up my bag and slung it over my shoulder, determined to keep my face in the very same expression regardless of what I turned to find.

Lucky stood with her hand on the doorknob, her back to me.

Her shoulders lifting with the steady rhythm or her breathing, at ease and unhurried.

I didn't think as I walked up behind her, close enough to be completely consumed by the scent of her again.

"What are you doing, Lucky?" My voice came out harsh. Weathered by the emotions that turned my mind into utter chaos at merely the thought of this girl.

She turned suddenly, immediately stepping back into the door having not expected me to be so close. As she took her step back, it was instinct for me to follow her, not allowing any more space between us.

I could see her pulse fluttering along the smooth expanse of her neck, right in the spot where her neck sloped down into the smooth expanse of her shoulder. I could see her pulse racing in a mimic of my own rapid beats. A mockery of them.

"I—," she hesitated, her eyebrows furrowing slightly, bringing a crease between her bright blue eyes. "I wanted to apologise for the way Mr. Langem called you out. I know you weren't looking—"

"I was looking," I cut her off and for the second time today let my features fall into their natural setting.

"Okay, well I just felt bad he made it seem like..." She didn't look away, didn't even flinch.

"Like what?" I pressed, my voice remaining in the same tone as when I first spoke to her.

"You know what? Nothing." Her eyes shuddered but didn't drop from mine, a spark of anger igniting in them that hadn't been there before.

"Oh, what is it, Lucky? Conflicted on whether or not to rejoice in me dropping another peg or two against the infamous Lucky Peters?" I crooned. "Please," I scoffed. "It was the highlight of your day."

She pushed away from the door, her body pressing against mine, making me step back once. Twice.

"You're seriously screwed in the head, you know that, Cole? It might surprise you to learn that everything I do is not simply to best *you.*" She pointed one of her delicate fingers right into the middle of my chest. "Besting you just *happens.* I don't *try* to outdo you, I just *do.*" She shoved her finger against my chest again, stepping once more and forcing me back another step.

Her chest was heaving now, deep breaths passing through her frame to try and ease the anger that I saw steadily building in her eyes.

"Liar," I said between clenched teeth.

"What did you say?" She had the audacity to look shocked.

"I called you a liar, Lucky" I stepped up to her, my chest once again flush with hers. "You ache for it," I said, my lips so close to hers I knew she felt the air move across her skin. I took another step.

"You look for me in a crowded room, only to make sure I'm already looking at you. Already aware that you're ahead of me. That you've outdone me. That you've somehow managed to do *more.*" Another step, until her back was once again firmly pressed against the door to the classroom. "You may do well, but you strive to do better if only so I don't. But I will outdo you, one day." I let my mouth lift slightly into a smile. Not something kind and gentle, but a dark, twisted thing. A promise. Another hint at the truth of who I was underneath.

"There will be a moment where I am the one that comes out on top, and I will look for you in that crowded room, only to find *your* eyes already on *me.* And I will love every minute of your downfall. Every. Single. Second." I was barely a hairsbreadth from her lips now. She would only need to move a fraction to touch them against my own.

Slowly, I moved my hand around her waist, her breath caught as her eyes became unsure even as she did nothing to put more distance between us. She was completely and totally at my mercy and I let my mind imagine it, just for a second. The way it would feel to wrap my hand around her throat, to see her pretty blue eyes fill with tears, to hear my name fall from that sharp tongue of hers in a sobbing plea.

Instead, I grabbed onto the door handle and stepped to the side as I pulled it open. My eyes didn't leave hers until she was forced to move to the side, dazed and speechless.

I strode out of the classroom. My heart beating at a calm and unaffected pace, like just the *thought* of her on her knees was enough to satiate the beast inside me, long enough to walk away from her at least.

My hands were shoved into the pockets of my jeans, as causal and unaffected as my heart while I walked for the doors at the end of the hallway, not looking back even though I could feel her looking at me. Feel the questions in gaze.

I left the next day for college.

That was the last time I ever saw Lucky Peters.

Content Warning

Violence.
Sexual Assault.
Blood.
Gore.

1

Lucky

I was always a lucky girl, until I wasn't.

"Come on, Navy," I murmured to myself as I heard Mrs. Backaratt descend the stairs in her sprawling manner, fixing my uniform and making sure my toque blanche was sitting straight on my head.

If I had a dollar for every time I blinked in all my twenty-eight years of life, I *still* wouldn't have enough money to even employ a gardener to tend to a house like the one I was working in the kitchen of. It was gloriously beautiful.

The first time I walked in to see the granite counter tops with metal hardware made of brass I sort of wanted to scream, dance and cry all at once. Yes, because of its beauty but also because – *oh my god*, the cost of fixing something from merely breathing on it the wrong way would be detrimental to my soul. I mean, the sleek and modern cabinets that looked like a solid, uninterrupted piece of tinted glass only opened when you *waved your hand in front of them.*

I'm talking about a *Falcon Classic Deluxe* range cooker in black and chrome. Henckels knives and a pantry akin to a small grocery store.

I'd never been surrounded by so much luxury and it made the reality of my situation sting a little more bitterly than it had this morning, and if I was being honest, every morning before. Especially when I dragged myself out of bed yet again to cook breakfast for someone else before even considering feeding myself.

"What in God's name is that smell?" Mrs. Backaratt's voice was a shrill croak that drilled into my skull in all the worst of ways.

"Good morning, ma'am." I couldn't sound more like the embodiment of sunshine if I tried. "This morning we have Eggs Florentine with salmon, as requested. However before plating I thought I would—"

"Florentine? I don't think I approved that meal."

I didn't know why I thought I'd be able to finish my sentence before being cut off and put firmly back into my place. People had no respect for those working in temporary positions. Mrs. Backaratt here, for example, thought I was a good-for-nothing deadbeat through and through. She didn't even look at me as she clip-clopped in her kitten heels through her ginormous house to her *breakfast* dining room (yes, she had more than one), and didn't even look to see if I followed when she continued speaking over her shoulder.

"Do you have any experience making that dish anyway? It sounds a little complex for someone of your station," she went on, snapping her napkin and tucking it into the front of her blouse as she sat down at the table.

I barely stopped my eye roll when she pulled her legs to the side, crossing her ankles like the fucking Queen of Genovia. I'd bet all of my best and happiest memories that she wouldn't know *my station* if it sat on her face.

The movement sent a gust of her overly floral perfume right into my breathing space, so powerful it absorbed the smell of the meal I had made and curdled my stomach.

"Yes, ma'am. Plenty of experience. Would you still like it with salmon? Or perhaps ham?"

I also didn't know why I bothered trying to do more for her than the bare minimum. The only explanation I had for myself was that it was an ode to the life I had before this one, an attempt to reach into the dark and grab the tattered remains of its existence. Let that be a lesson that no such tattered remains existed at all.

Her face scrunched up before I was able to get the pleasant words that tasted a lot like acid out of my mouth.

"*Ham?* Is this your attempt at humour, Janice? Because I am not amused."

My name wasn't Janice, but I'd corrected her at least half a dozen times since I started this gig a week ago and, honestly, if it was *Janice* copping this shit then I had some hope of one day blocking it from my memory, so Janice I would be.

I darted back into the kitchen and quickly plated the meal before walking it back out and placing it in front of her, knowing that she would completely disregard the spread of freshly baked pastries, fruit and other continental breakfast options that were spread out in front of her but also knowing that if they weren't there, there would be hell to pay.

I learned quickly that the need for the vast selection of food she wouldn't touch was a way to reassure the old woman that she still, in fact, had the money to waste on perfectly good food that she would never eat. It made my stomach roll, and I liked to think that it was because I was a good person and not a total sociopath.

Standing at attention while she took her first bite, it was all I could do not to let my face fall into a scowl.

She chewed a few times before flicking her wrist in my direction in what was a very clear dismissal of my presence.

Bowing politely, I walked back in the direction of the kitchen while mentally flipped her the bird.

Whether she liked the meal or not, I didn't care to know. I knew it was probably the best Eggs Florentine she'd ever catch but I also knew that she'd never admit it.

I had a few menial tasks left to do before I would leave this place, where all my dreams came to die at the ass crack of dawn every morning over the last seven days. I made a point to arrive early enough to cook everything that would be needed for meals plus snack options over the course of the entire day, all of which was planned and given to me by the keeper of the house.

Yes, that's right, *the keeper of the house.*

There were kitchen support staff here that worked with the regular full time chef, so they were able to prep and tend to any of the requests that the old bat demanded of her staff where food consumption was concerned. They were kind and good people, and didn't turn their noses up at my presence in the same way that pretty much every single person I cooked for over the last nine months did.

"Alright, I'm out of here Wren, thanks for your help. You really didn't need to come in." I pulled off my little white hat that was the topper to my chef's ensemble and shoved it into my backpack before flinging it over my shoulder.

"Are you kidding me? Thanks for letting me shadow you while you worked. I appreciate it and if things ever turn around..."

"I have your details, yes." I smiled at the young guy who couldn't have been more than twenty-one.

I won't lie and say that an appreciation of the skills I honed after years of working to get myself where I had been before my world came crashing down wasn't appreciated. You know what? Fuck it. I was a peacock preening herself in the presence of an admirer, unabashedly basking in the radiant light of his words.

It would last all of two minutes and when they were no more than an echo in my mind I would fall back down the two-dozen pegs that they had lifted me up from and be faced with my reality all over again, so I did myself a favour and lived in the moment.

Saluting him farewell, I navigated the maze of small hallways that were intended for the staff to use, pulling my hair out of my low bun and collecting it all into a ponytail on the top of my head.

The gravel of the drive crunched under my boots as I made my way to my pride and joy; Bessy the Beetle. My car was the only consistent thing I managed to keep a hold of. The VW Beetle had been with me since I was high on the optimism of life as a shiny eighteen year old, ready to take on the world.

Sliding into her comforting embrace, the worn and faded four-leaf clover and acorn printed blue car seat covers welcomed me like the old friends we were. My siblings had gotten them custom made for me as an ode to my name and I would sell a kidney before I agreed to ever part with them.

I closed the door and sat in the silence that pressed in on me from all angles, taking a deep breath before leaning down to kiss the steering wheel in greeting of my most reliable four-wheeled friend and companion.

"Take me home, Bess."

I stuck the key in the ignition and immediately settled when she rumbled to life beneath me, knowing that for all the luck I'd lost, the dregs that remained were woven tightly into the fabric of Bessy's mechanic soul.

2

Lucky

It was only seven-thirty in the morning, so I assumed that everyone in the house was still asleep. Everyone being my parents and my three nieces who had spent the night while my sister and her husband had some time to themselves.

I wasn't all that prepared for human interaction when I walked into the kitchen to see my father sitting at the dining table, sipping on his morning coffee and flicking through the day's paper.

He looked up at the sound of my dragging feet and my heart hurt a little at the way his eyes lit up, still swimming with the pride he had shared so freely over the course of my entire life.

"Lucky." He smiled as he took his glasses off and set them atop his paper.

I dumped my bag on the floor and walked over, leaning down and melting into the hug. "Hey, Dad."

I stayed slouched there for a heartbeat too many and wished for all I was worth that I could go back to being a kid. Years before I realised that, hey, guess what? Life *can* turn into a flaming turd left on your doorstep by the neighbourhood rascals. Something I would have never, *ever* thought of in my most wildest of dreams.

With a deep breath, I pulled myself from my father's embrace and dragged my weary soul to the coffee machine.

"I didn't think you were going to be up. Tough night with the girls?" I poured myself a big steaming cup of black coffee, holding the pot up in question if he needed a refill.

He peered in his glass and held it out to me in acceptance. "Mmm, little Janey just can't quite master her sleep yet, but we'll get there."

I grunted in agreement.

Jane was the middle of the triplets that belonged to my sister, Addie. The kicker here was that Addie was also a triplet. Yes, believe me when she told the family it was all screaming and crying and a number of different renditions of 'you have to be kidding me' all layered on top of one another.

I couldn't be happier for my sister, but I totally got the 'one and done' mentality.

I was the youngest of seven and we'd all seen the chaos that ensued with my parents trying to wrangle the lot of us. The eyes-bulging-out-of-the-head looks that a lot of people gave when they heard how many of us there were wasn't something new. Seven seemed like a lot of kids for modern day families, but there were only so many of us because my parents had gone the route of IVF after struggling to conceive on their own for the first six years of their marriage.

Their first round of IVF didn't work, but the next one did,

where they welcomed my brother, James, into the world. The next additions sprouted the first and only set of twins of the Peters' family, my brother Oakleigh and my eldest sister Riley, who were adopted at the fresh-as-a-daisy age of three weeks old.

After my brother James was conceived, my parents were told that if they wanted to try for another round of IVF that they could transfer all three of their remaining embryos at once. It wasn't a common thing to recommend, but because all three were a lower grade of embryo (something I still find so weird that they *grade* your unborn babies), they were advised by all their doctors that the transfers may not result in even a single viable pregnancy.

Well, that was a load of horse manure because all three girls - Addie, May and Kate - took. Coming out happy, healthy and screaming (according to my father).

That was it. They were done, done, *done.* No more embryos and six little rays of love, light and mess running around. Then the unthinkable happened. The unexpected, the never-in-their-craziest-dreams moment when for all their struggles, they found out they were expecting lucky number seven, and it happened the ol' natural way.

Navy Grace Peters, lovely to meet you. The seventh and last daughter of Philip and Meredith Peters. Born on the seventh day of the seventh month, 1994. The very same year where the first genetically engineered tomatoes were approved for sale and Lisa-Marie Presley married Michael Jackson. Or, as I've been called my whole life—

"Lucky?" My father looked at me over the top of his coffee mug.

"Mmm?" I sipped my own.

"How was work?"

It was a casual, lighthearted question that could be considered vague enough if there wasn't an ulterior motive, but of course there was one.

That was my cue.

I stood up, coffee in one hand and swiping up my stuff from where I'd dropped it on the floor with the other before I headed for the stairs that would lead me back to my childhood room. The very room I moved out of at eighteen, and moved back into ten years later.

"It was great, Dad." I gave him a small smile, "Loving all the experiences of working at so many different places." I kept that smile in place as I looked at him over my shoulder, and prayed my tenth grade drama class skills were shining through. "I'm going to go shower. Gotta be at the temp agency by nine."

"That's good, that's good." He smiled to himself in parental satisfaction before slipping his glasses back on and focusing back on his paper. "Your mother and I are off after Addie picks up the girls, so we'll see you in a week."

That stopped me in the doorway. "A week?" I frowned at him, taking another sip of coffee.

"We've got the cruise, remember? You're watching the house for us." He peered at me over the top of his glasses, his coffee cup half raised to his mouth.

"Oh, right. Yes, I remember." I hadn't remembered, not even a little bit. And of course I would be watching the house, I was sleeping upstairs for crying out loud. "Well, have a good time, send me lots of photos and love to Mum if I don't see you guys before you go."

"Thanks, Luck." He was already re-immersed in his paper

by the time I reached the set of stairs.

I bound up them two at a time, yearning for the warm embrace of a very hot shower. In the forty minutes I had taken (two of which had been with hot water, thirty eight of which had been cold as balls), I drank my coffee in the shower (don't you dare judge me) and shaved every part of my body, a once a fortnight task that I loathed.

Wrapped in a towel and wrinkled so badly I resembled a pool noodle, I padded down the hall back to my room. The house was quiet in an empty sort of way and I ducked my head into the room the girls had been sleeping in, only to find it empty and littered with unfolded bedding.

"Hello?" I called as I got to the top of the stairs.

Nothing.

"Anyone?" I waited a minute. Also nothing. I was alone, for *once*.

I exhaled in a way that *I* could even hear the heaviness I carried and continued my walk to my bedroom. Closing the door, I flopped onto my bed, staring at the ceiling fan that rotated in the mundane, repetitive way it always did.

Never one to not take advantage of a moment of complete and utter *alone-ness,* I reached over and rummaged through my bedside table drawer. Right at the very back where prying eyes of over-interested parents and small children looking for craft supplies could accidentally stumble upon it, I pulled out my single source of joy (aside from my car and my best friend, and no they were not one in the same).

I looked at my vibrator as I tried desperately to ignore the vintage early 2000's barbie bedding that adorned my bed.

"Hello, you hunk-of-lovin'."

3

Lucky

1 year 6 months ago

"Order up!" I tapped the bell, knowing that it was the only sound that would cut through the voices and music layered so thickly on top of one another you could practically see the sound vibrations hovering in the spaces between tables.

"Thanks, Chef," one of the waitresses called out into the kitchen while grabbing the plates of food and dashing back off into the madness that was *Seven*.

This was our busiest location, right in the centre of the city, so much so that the people currently sitting at the bar and tables enjoying their evening made these reservations likely over three months ago. Of course, there were the lucky few that snagged a booking off the cancellation list, and those people had dropped all their previously made plans to fit in an hour or two spent here.

That was the *Seven* way. It was simply the place you wanted to be. It was high end, exclusive, it wasn't just going out for a beautiful meal and a mouth watering cocktail, it was an *experience*.

Dreams didn't get more real than this. From where I was standing, every wish I had thrown out into the universe came to be. As weird as it might sound, luck had always been my *thing*. I was just a lucky girl and I tried desperately to never take it for granted, knowing that it was lucky to be lucky in a weird sort of way. It was as much a part of my life as waking up in the morning and I'd never known anything different.

Right from the moment I was conceived - lucky number seven - to the very moment I was born.

7:07 p.m. on the 7th of July, 1994. (People conveniently ignored the year and its lacking amounts of seven's).

It started off just as a fun coincidence, my parents always said, whenever they shared the story with anyone that would listen. I usually found somewhere to hide, whenever it was time to talk about *lucky number seven.*

Try having your cheeks pinched by a multitude of strangers letting you know how adorable it was that you were who you were, and tell me how much that gives you the warm and fuzzies. I could still feel them all groping my face now.

Eugh. Nothing lucky about *that*.

But the name stuck, to the extent that even on forms where you have to put in your full name and then your 'preferred to go by', 'Lucky' started being pencilled in.

There was something to it, though. Because luck followed me everywhere I went. It was finding things that had been lost, like my preschool teacher's engagement ring. Or guessing the exact amount of jelly beans in the jar at school to win the brand new bike with the basket on the front.

It was the car of my dreams and finding that exact make, model and colour for sale the very next day. Being late but hitting every green light. Walking down the street and finding a hundred dollar bill with no one around to hand it back to (I donated it that time, and the next day I found another one). It was having my sights set on the best culinary school there was, only to be called and told I was eligible for a scholarship I didn't apply for and it was just luck that someone knew someone knew *someone*.

It was like never getting a cold growing up, or breaking a bone, or missing out on food poisoning when I ate the same meal as everyone else.

The thought made me smile to myself as I wiped the bench down in front of me, knowing that the kitchen was closing soon as the clock ticked closer to 10:00 p.m. and that the last minute dessert orders were bound to start coming through.

Right on cue, three waitresses all at once handed in two orders each. A few crème brûlée's, a few dark chocolate tortes and the remainder were an even spread of mousse and sticky date puddings. The best part about the dessert was that they're already good to go, prepped at the start of the evening. All we had to do was plate and heat up the warm components.

"Frankie! Can you handle the torch for the crème brûlée's?" I called out to our newest Junior Chef, who was equal parts puppy-like enthusiasm and grumpy-oldman-seriousness.

Frank had only been on for a few months, brought in from the program I had set up with *August Eclair School of Culinary Arts.* The same school that I had graduated from, top of my class. The program provided the top two graduates with a junior position at both of my restaurants for twelve months, to give them the experience and expertise to learn what they needed to learn in the real world.

"On it, Lucky!" he yelled across the kitchen.

"Frank, we talked about this," I called back, still wiping the surface in front of me, trying my best not to let my smile creep into my words.

"Shit. Yes, Chef!" he threw over his shoulder as he hurried in the opposite direction. His profanity was followed by the soft chuckles of the rest of the kitchen staff. "Thank you!"

"Have you got this, Chels?" I asked my Sous Chef, knowing that I had a butt-tonne of paperwork to do before I could head home for the evening. It was the end of the week, so I was going to be here late, taking stock and writing out what we needed to order for the week ahead.

"You know it, Chef." She winked my way, and headed in the direction of the cold room.

I spun on my heels and walked the other way towards my office. My ass had barely hit the chair, not even a full minute had passed since I'd literally walked out of the kitchen when Chelsea was standing at the threshold of the office with a pained look on her face.

"What is it?" I was more curious than anything, maybe a little concerned.

The only time I'd seen a look like that before in my kitchen was when someone sneezed while julienning. It wasn't pretty and three separate people ran from the kitchen into the back alley to empty the contents of their stomachs.

"Something's been sent back," she passed the words on to me like the words themselves would invite unwanted energy and vibes into our space, and I was all about vibes.

"What do you mean?" I frowned at her.

Something was sent back? That made no sense. Nothing had ever been sent back to the kitchen at either of my restaurants.

She just looked at me, visibly swallowing before repeating herself. "Something was sent back."

The offending plate in question had already been brought into the back area of the kitchen as part of protocol. We had a system for this, of course, but it was never something that had to be implemented in the entire four years this restaurant had been open, or in the two since I had opened the other *Seven* across the city.

It was a beautiful dish, aesthetically it looked perfect. It was clear where the patron had started, eating a few of the thinly sliced wafer-thin potato slices that we had seasoned lightly in salt and pepper, fried to perfection, that literally melted on your tongue. The little dots of our in-house garlic aioli had been swiped through. The perfect accompaniment.

And then they had sliced right through the middle of their piece of perfectly seared swordfish, this week's special.

I picked up a set of utensils and opened up the fish.

It was raw. Just completely, totally raw.

The outside looked perfect. Coloured in a way that let me know it had to have been on the pan for the right amount of time, but not necessarily placed into the oven with the rest of the fish steaks. And there were dozens that went out tonight, more than dozens. There was no way to know how it happened, when it happened, or who had let it happen.

I had a firm hold on my expression, not letting anything slip that I had any sort of worry that this could have been intentional. Who would do something like that? I knew my staff like the back of my hand.

"It's raw," I said out loud, hearing my own swallow. "What did we do to compensate the customer?"

Chelsea replied immediately, "They were given their meal for free and a voucher for the next time they wanted to come, with an assurance of a spot within three days of booking regardless of waiting time." Her voice was still low and shaky, like she was worried the rest of the customers would hear. Nervous.

"And their reply?" I prompted.

"Gracious. Very understanding and pleased with the compensation," she said, equally as quietly, equally as nervous.

I turned on my heels to face the kitchen staff, faces pale and unsure. "Alright, this isn't the first time someone has sent back a meal in the history of fine dining, but it is the first time it's happened at *Seven*." I kept my voice light, but with the air of authority that the situation demanded. "Starting tomorrow, before removing any fish steaks from the oven pan, a thermometer will be inserted into each individual portion and the temperature will be confirmed. Frankie, I'm going to ask you to take charge of that job. Can you confirm the temperature we're looking for?"

"Yes, Chef. 135 degrees Fahrenheit or 57 degrees Celsius, Chef," he responded without hesitation.

"Perfect, nice recall." I nodded at him, truly impressed, "This was a once off folks, no need to lose our cool. We're lucky it wasn't worse. Let's learn and move forward. Back to the desserts and then clear up and get out of here."

"Yes, Chef," every team member called back in unison, dispersing immediately.

The mood of the kitchen had shifted to a muted version of what it had been before.

I walked back to my office, closing the door behind me and throwing the tea towel that I had rested on my shoulder over the single chair that faced my desk. I took a second to get my head straight before rounding the desk and taking up the same position on the other side.

My work space was relatively orderly but it had taken on an air of disarray. I had been here until late last night, and the night before, and the night before that, trying to figure out what had gone wrong. Chelsea had taken charge around six months ago on managing all our incoming orders for produce, on data input and tracking our spend on things in the back end. At the end of every month she would send me through a review and play by play on the figures from the month and, honestly, everything had been going well.

Better than well, actually. From the looks of things, I was still on track for restaurant number three.

I'd always preferred to keep the accounting for both restaurants in-house, knowing horror stories of outsourcing something so important, and it was only after many, *many,* conversations had I handed over the day-to-day ordering to my staff with Chelsea overseeing them. In the end it had come down to simply needing more time. More time and energy to plan and prepare and meet with the sort of people who could make a third *Seven* location become a reality through the day. So that I could split my time between both our current locations through the week of being present and accounted for, to show face.

I'd reviewed the last handful of reports, cross checking invoices that had been paid and filed away just to keep myself up to date on everything finance related after no longer really being involved with it. I'd run the numbers a hundred times but I was missing something. It was small and in some ways it was barely noticeable. It would be easy to brush it off as a simple miscalculation at one point or another and assume that if I were to redo things then the numbers would add up. But they were off, slightly.

They were *off*.

And they were off for the last three months to where looking at it big picture? There were tens of thousands not accounted for.

I'd called Chelsea in a panic and had her pull everything, and I mean *everything* to show me where the drop off had happened. We'd sat down together and she'd ended up finding the issue that we'd doubled up on payments for a number of different invoices.

In an effort to give herself some extra support she'd worked with a junior chef at our other location where both she *and* Chelsea had paid the same stack of invoices for all three of those months. Chels had emailed me this morning with a statement from the bank showing everything back in order and I'd almost cried.

Since it all happened though, I couldn't stop the nagging feeling in the pit of my stomach, something I'd never experienced before.

I huffed a laugh at myself purely for the absurdity of the thought that raced through my mind, and I shook my hands out to dispel the rest of the heaviness.

I could have sworn that for the first time in twenty-six and a half years that how I'd felt, even for a second was...unlucky?

4

Lucky

Present

I looked straight down the barrel of my fishbowl cocktail, my face slowly slipping through my hands that propped up my head.

"I wish I was small enough to just live in this fishbowl of wonder-water," I pouted.

"Wonder-water? That's new." Melody raised her eyebrows at me in a way that said '*I love you but you're losing it*'.

Taking a sip from her own gloriously under priced and overly-sweet drink, she shook her head with a small smile. "So, how was the temp agency today?"

I groaned, my head slipping completely out of my hands and my forehead smacking onto the table with a hard *thump*.

"Ow," I moaned before lifting up my head, only barely managing not to gag as I felt my forehead *peel* off the sticky table that had likely never had a proper clean in its entire existence. "I got the day wrong, it's tomorrow."

I grabbed my fishbowl with both hands as I leaned back and fell against the bright red booth we had claimed as our usual spot, tucked far into the dirtiest corner of our favourite bar.

Helga's Hell Hole was actually a somewhat tame multi themed diner bar that specialised in southern fried chicken wings and turkey jerky, of all things.

We started coming here because we thought it was so weird that it was actually cool, and we still came because we maintained that opinion completely and without a moment of veering from its perfect truth.

Our first visit was at the ripe age of sixteen after finally daring to enter on one of our walks home from school, and we had always had these very same fishbowls, except that back then, they were made with mostly pineapple juice and a little blue cordial.

"Oh, Luck." Her brow creased in worry with a little bit of pity.

"No, no. It's fine, Lids. See, we have fishbowls." I leaned forwards and held mine out proudly across the table, almost like it was my own little Simba, my lion cub, destined to change the world that I knew.

She held hers out and clinked it with mine. "To the fishbowl."

"To the fishbowl!" I yelled a little too loudly and slouched back into my previous position.

"How are your folks?" she continued with her usual routine questions.

Melody and I caught up as much as was humanly possible for two adult women doing life and living not overly close to one another.

She was wise beyond her years, an old soul (so everyone always said) and it wasn't hard to believe it the moment she set her gaze upon you. She looked at everyone like they meant something. Like they mattered. Even if they didn't feel it, you could tell she did. She was also gentle, and soft and I had always made it my mission to protect her at all costs.

"Oh, you know, tanning on a boat somewhere," I grumbled, only because *I* wanted to be on a boat somewhere.

"The cruise?! I didn't think that was for another week."

"You knew about the cruise?" I frowned. I hadn't known about the cruise.

"Of course, I spoke to Meredith last week." Lid just waved me away like I was a fly in her face. But then her gaze softened, and the concern that was there every time I saw her poured out of her eyeballs like goopy lava.

"I'm honestly doing great, you don't need to look at me like that." I waved my pointer finger in her face

"Lucky—," she started but I shook my head as I swallowed another too-big gulp of my wonder-water.

"This is *so* temporary. I'm just getting my shit together, finding my feet and I'll have another restaurant up and pumping in no time."

My stomach dropped a little even at the thought.

"You've been at your parents house for a year," she pointed out, not in a 'you're a massive loser' sort of way, but more like a 'are you sure you haven't just stopped trying?'.

"A minor setback, I assure you. It's all coming together, I feel it." I wiggled my eyebrows at her desperate need for me to give her assurance that everything wasn't grey clouds and sad faces where my current position in life was concerned.

"Well, if you *feel it,* who am I to question?"

When she caught my attention again, her smile had begun to fade. I dipped my chin, raising my eyebrows in a '*come on, now*' look.

I reached across the table and gripped her hand and she immediately held mine back so tight I swear I heard my bones squeak.

"Hey, look, it will be *fine*. After all, what's my name?" I smiled at her, still gripping my fishbowl, pressing my cheek to the cool glass.

"I just worry, sometimes I look at you and feel like I'm not really seeing you." Her voice wobbled a little at the end, her lip started to quiver, showing her tender heart and all the worry she insisted it carry for the people around her.

I got up and walked around to sit next to her, pulling her against me.

Was I stoked about the situation? I would say I was as thrilled as one would be to find their toilet seat replaced with a cactus, but luck was my *thing.* I would find my way around this, or rather, the way around this would find me. Eventually.

She gripped my arm tightly and sniffed loudly. "I'm making this about me, aren't I?"

"Absolutely." I squeezed her tightly and she swatted me. "I just need to find my feet," I said softly, and even though I was hugging her, I let it be a little for me too.

I was constantly reminded in moments like these how pure my friend was. I couldn't be all out of luck to have managed to keep her by my side.

"You can still move in with me and Brian?" she offered quietly after a moment.

"I thank you profusely for your offer, but I will quite literally never do that." I gave her temple a kiss, only after needing to pull aside her mass of big, beautiful black curls that made her look like a disco goddess, and shuffled back out of her side of the booth to take back my spot across from her.

"What's so wrong with Brian?" she huffed, swirling her straw around her still half-full glass.

I lifted my eyebrows in accusation. "Brian has never said the words 'please' or 'thank you' a day in his life. I have fallen into your toilet one too many times because of his lovely little habit of leaving the seat up. He is a man-baby that doesn't deserve you. *Plus* he calls me Lenny. He's lucky I haven't put itching powder in his underwear."

I gave her a deadpan look while she pressed her lips together and closed her eyes in an attempt to not laugh at that.

"*Lenny*, Melody. He calls me *Lenny*." That was the straw that broke the camel's back. A big, rocketing snort erupted from my friend that had me clamping a hand over my own mouth.

"He's not that bad," she mouthed at me as she wheezed.

"He smells like parmesan. I don't understand how you can have sex with him." I scrunched my face up, sure that I was beginning to smell the sharp tang of his signature scent surrounding us.

"Lucky!" she chastised me with a yelp, reaching into her glass for a piece of ice to throw at me.

I attempted to catch it in my mouth and missed, but that

was no surprise. I'd clearly misplaced my luck at present, and it seemed even the littlest of things weren't immune.

"You know that he works at a dairy farm."

I honestly couldn't even reply to that one, she was making it too easy.

Rolling her eyes she took three massive gulps of her drink before replying, "Yeah, yeah. He's a good guy. Don't knock it 'til you try it."

"And work? How's work? And Belinda?" I asked, moving further down the list of questions of our question rotation.

"Mum's good, she passes on her love, and I have five different weddings this week. It's going to be wonderful."

A smile, free and unrelenting, broke across my friend's beautiful face and it was the exact thing I needed after enduring Mrs. Backaratt for a whole week and my vibrator running out of battery halfway through our meet and greet this morning.

Melody was a florist, and it suited her down to the ground. She said she loved being the cherry on top of people's most special occasions, but also being the silent support in their hardest moments. It never stopped to amaze me how she saw the world.

The night gradually morphed to the point where I convinced her that line dancing had always come naturally to me, ever since our first visit to *Helga's* and proceeded to teach her a series of completely made up steps I swore up and down I'd seen online (I hadn't). I made them up on the fly and she was impressed when I tried to teach her a move where you jumped, turned a full three-sixty and landed on the heel of one shoe and the toe of the other.

By the time the sun was coming up, I'd made sure that

Melody had gotten into her Uber and was safely on her way back to her cheese-man and I started on the walk back home, grateful that my parents lived only a few gruelling blocks from the bar.

It could have totally been the alcohol, but as I turned the key in the lock and let myself into my childhood home, doing my best to ignore the pressing quiet of the too-big house for just a single person, I actually looked forward to the meeting at the temp agency, even though it was in - I checked my watch and squinted through my spinning vision - three hours.

"Shit," I mumbled to myself, kicking my shoes off as I tripped up the stairs, simultaneously asking Siri to set me an alarm.

I'd come to the conclusion that there was just still too much luck left around me for my lifelong streak to have ended so suddenly. Whatever was coming tomorrow was going to be a game changer, and I was ready for it.

5

Lucky

My head pounded with the unrelenting rhythm of a drum that could only be the signal of my impending lack of employment if I didn't get my shit together.

I sat in my car for a full twenty minutes trying to figure out if I was going to throw up. I tried my best to push the roiling waves of water and electrolytes back down before I pulled myself together and walked into the temp agency. I knew that Bessy would've never forgiven me if I soiled her fresh interior.

All the remaining optimism from the night before was slowly being extracted from my soul as I tried to only breathe through my mouth, and not experience the bouquet of incredibly offensive scents that seeped from the bodies around mine.

It was too early for any of this to be happening to me.

"Navy Peters," the receptionist called out my name, weird to hear it in all its stunning legality, and peeled myself off the little plastic chair that had an alarmingly small amount of back support.

"Thanks Nora," I waved to her as I walked by, moving my sunglasses to the top of my head.

"Look alive, Navy," she said to me with a stern expression.

Nora used to serve in the armed forces. Doing what? I have absolutely no idea. When I did ask her on one of my many visits to this very fine establishment, she just stared me down so thoroughly I thought the woman had fallen asleep with her eyes open.

"Got it." I offered her a couple of complimentary finger guns, which she continued to not take well, and made my way to the office she guarded with fierce pride.

I liked Nora. She had gumption.

Denise was on the phone and waved me in while mouthing an apology. That was also the exact way she greeted me every time. I *still* didn't know why she insisted on calling people in when she was so clearly in the middle of something. The only conclusion I came to was that it was some weird sort of power move.

The entire ordeal was made even more exciting because she was always having the same conversation with a range of men with names from the 1940's; Ronald, Gary, and some guy named Kenneth. I tried to make this entire experience as exciting as it could be, so I assumed they were her trio of lovers and let my imagination just run wild.

"Thanks Gary, speak soon."

Ah, Gary!

She hung up the phone with an exaggerated huff. "Sorry

Navy, it never ends!" she chuckled, giving me a look that said '*you know how us boss-ass women are*'.

I laughed back with a look that said '*you said it sister*'.

"Alright, how did we go with Mrs. Backaratt?" Denise started flicking through some files in her desk before pulling one out with my name on it and opening it to rifle its contents.

"It was great, the staff at the kitchen there were wonderful to work with."

I smiled politely, looking at my plain manilla folder she had set to the side and reached for it while simultaneously wondering if anyone had ever given a true recount of their experience at a temp position. I certainly didn't.

"How are things going on the other end of life? Are you still working on the re-brand? The rebuild? The relaunch?" She flicked her eyes up at me.

In a power move of my own, I decided to grab a pen from her pen pot and proceed to decorate my lonely little temp file with a four leaf clover.

"I'm still planning it out, but I have all the overarching plans right here." I pointed to my head with the pen before continuing my doodling.

"Investors lining up yet?" she volleyed back like it was the most interesting conversation she'd had all day.

I resisted the urge to narrow my eyes at her candid snooping, instead I shrugged like I was the most casually cool person to ever walk through her door.

"Ah, yes, sort of. I know a few people who I might approach but it's still very much in the planning stages, so I'm not quite ready to sit down with them yet."

"It must be some project. How long have you been planning this? Since you started to see me right? Nine months ago?"

Sweet grief.

If I was a weaker woman I would've broken under the pressure of her inquiry and let her know the flaming hot truth of it all. That I'd done sweet, sweet nothing in the last nine months to rebuild what I had lost.

I wasn't down and out. Was I epically baffled that I'd lost it all? Yes. Did I spend many a night sitting on the floor of my parents shower, crying while Jesse McCartney played loud enough that I could feel it in the wall at my back? Well, *yes*. But I'd pushed through the darkest parts of it all. I *wasn't* down and out.

"Yeah, about nine months." I placed the pen down and leaned back in my chair, suddenly very eager for Denise to put a sock in it.

These questions came from every angle, I mean, it wasn't like I was *nobody*, and I guess because of that, people thought they were entitled to know my deepest and darkest thoughts.

Seven had been really something, featured in magazines like *Food & Wine*, *Bon Appetit*, and *Better Homes and Gardens*. The last one was a bit random, but the article did surprisingly well.

When I walked in here and told her who I was she was firstly very excited and then shocked that I was sitting in her office. I was flattered by both responses.

I had gotten my first temp job just days before news hit of my initial 'gradual demise' and then suddenly, a very quick downfall of the same story littered the pages of newspapers and online blogs. Many favouring to go for the classic and completely unoriginal headline of '*Seven*; *not such a lucky number after all*'.

My stomach turned a little at that, the knowledge that my

luck had up and fled for the first time in my life.

"Ah, here it is. Alright, now don't get too excited because I know you're working toward your re-brand and all that, but I have a semi-permanent position that you would be perfect for." She was bouncing in her seat with excitement.

Semi-permanent was just an incredibly uninventive way of saying *'if you aren't shit, we'll keep you around!'*, but I let my face light with elation anyway, because whether Denise had a shocking sense of self awareness or not, a job was a job, and that meant only good things for me.

See? I *knew* something was coming.

"There is a prominent member of society who is also sort of in the hospitality business, though more on the investor side of things," she winked at me, "and he's looking for a personal chef!"

She looked up at me, eyes wide and a real, true show of excitement on her face. "It would be Mondays, Wednesdays and Fridays, with an early start running to midday and returning for dinner and cleaning up."

She passed me the job ad and my eyes almost fell out of my head. "Holy crap, that's what they're paying for three days a week?" It was a small fortune compared to the action my bank account had seen since I'd moved back home.

"What do you say?" Denise sounded authentically pleased.

I'd already forgiven her for her previous transgressions, knowing that she couldn't have known just how much I wasn't ready to talk about the lack of movement where sorting out my shenanigans was concerned.

I wasn't complacent, maybe just a little lost?

"I say hell yes, Denise." I sent a smile her way that was as real as real got these days.

Still not entirely sure what I was looking for, but I gripped that feeling with both hands, that one that spoke directly to my stomach where my intuition lived.

"Wonderful, because you start in the morning!"

6

Lucky

1 year 4 months ago

"This is going the complete and total opposite of well," I mumbled to myself.

There were empty tables in my restaurant. There'd *never* been empty tables in my restaurant.

The clock that sat on the wall of the kitchen told me it was 9:45 p.m. and we were two shakes shy of closing the kitchen for the night.

I took a deep breath and let it out slowly, casting my eyes back out through the pass to look over guests, still enjoying their meals though there were less of them.

Since the incident a couple months ago, the moment with the raw fish that we'd all been trying to learn from and forget simultaneously, things had been more or less normal.

Nothing as serious as that hullabaloo, but there had been a misorder here and a broken glass there. Both unusual but also nothing to write home about.

We'd had another two menu changes which were both great successes. We had built a reputation for serving flavours that everyone and their mothers would love, while letting them experience it in ways they never had and likely never would experience again.

We were classy, we were creative, and we were also clearly dying in the ass if the vibe on the restaurant floor was anything to be believed.

I closed the door to my office behind me quietly, sitting at my desk and taking in the stack of invoices from our range of different suppliers. That little issue from only a couple of months ago hadn't gone away, and the double paid invoices seemed to be the least of our worries. I'd even begun forking out my own money to cover our bills while I figured out what was happening but I was at a complete and total loss.

What should have been landing in the accounts was just simply not landing in the accounts.

I hadn't told anyone, not even Melody, determined to find the issue on my own. This was *my* business. *My* life's work. I would figure it out and things would return to the way they were. I just needed time.

I'd ended up cancelling all the work cards and ordering new ones because that was the only thing I could think of, that someone had gotten my banking information.

And to make matters better, we had three misdeliveries this week. *THREE*. Like I'm talking, we ordered a butt-load of fish and Gerard, the delivery man, brought me ham hocks. I cannot stress to you enough the literal lack of relation those two things have to one another.

It started as a situation that may cause you to go prematurely grey, but in classic *Seven* fashion, we whipped together a soup that was to die for. Frankie decided to call it something fancy and French and it was our most popular dish of the month, selling out within the first couple hours every night of the week.

It was the sort of win we needed. But, that's where it had stopped in a rather abrupt way.

I couldn't *not* ignore the fact that something over the last couple months had shifted. Like the room felt different when you walked in. Like the kitchen didn't have the same sparkle, and the sounds of people enjoying their nights weren't so much joyful and so-loud-but-so-fun, but rather like you're cupping around the back of your ears, just trying your best to be a part of the conversation in a sort of 'what-did-you-just-say?' and 'Kevin?-Did-you-say-Kevin? -Who's-Kevin?' way.

I let my head fall into my hands, giving myself a moment to wish for a pillow to scream into and maybe a plate or two to smash. This wasn't something I had experience with, the whole 'things not going to plan' stuff. I was a planner, a mastermind at the execution. But problem solving? Nope.

I could argue with myself like a lunatic and say maybe it was Gerard the delivery guy's fault? After all, he was the one that unloaded the ham hocks and had me sign a sheet that clearly said something about fish, but I doubted very much it was his fault. He was just a guy who loved his goldfish in a weirdly intimate way to the point where he had a photo of it in his wallet that he'd shown me many, *many* times.

I'd reached my quota on the pity party for one and had

begun hoisting myself out of the shallow hole I had started sinking into when my computer lit up with an email from our feedback form online.

I clicked on it, needing to hear the sweet caressing words of those who treated dinner at *Seven* like a religious experience.

Ha! Let me ask you a question: do you know what happens to a Chef who's kicked while she's down?

The review read:

"*Spending money at* Seven *used to mean you'd get the best of the best. It felt like I was eating some squirrel I'd charred over a campfire.*"

I stared at my screen with my mouth hanging open. "We don't even have anything that resembles a barbeque on the menu," I grumbled to myself before reading on.

"*Maybe they should change the name to Way-ven, because I will be Way-ven goodbye as I walk away and never come back.*"

It had been submitted just four minutes ago by someone who had typed in 'Fresh RevYouz' in place of their real name.

In a moment of pure frustration, I yelled at my computer some sort of insult pertaining to its inability to function without power and pulled the plug directly from the wall, proceeding to press both of my middle fingers firmly against the black screen. I kept my fingers pressed there, willing all my bad juju to move from me and into the monitor before me.

So, what happens to a Chef who's kicked while she's down? Well, she wonders first why the hell her kitchen floors are so dirty, and also where she can put her hands to hoist herself back up without touching something hot, grabbing the sharp end of a knife or flipping a bowl of pasta sauce all over her head.

I let my head fall to my desk in a loud *thump*, my hands falling from the screen in a dramatic flurry. Pondering if this metaphorical pasta sauce would turn the natural blond highlights of my hair a weird orangey red that would never come out. If that accidental change would mean I'd always have to look at myself and be reminded of my mistakes.

7

Lucky

I was nervous. Of course I was nervous.

If not for the fact that this could be something a little more stable, then for the other fact that this could be the *thing* I had been waiting on. The *thing* I had felt.

If I was being honest, I wasn't going to put too much into that 'feeling'. The one that pulled you towards or away from certain things. It had been a bit hit or miss for me as of late, as literally anyone that was awake with the use of any and all of their senses could deduce. In fact, I was certain you'd be able to see the shit storm of bad luck trailing me even if you were heavily sedated.

I sat in Bessy, discussing with her the pros and cons of the situation. Psyching myself up and knocking myself down a few pegs in a repetitive motion that gave me a little motion sickness before finding the ovaries to remove myself from her supportive embrace.

"Pro's?" I mused aloud. "Well, semi-permanent, though a C-grade way to advertise a job, it was a positive. Following that was the schedule. Sure, it was early mornings and late nights, but there was a whole five hours in the middle of the day that I wasn't required to be at the place of work. Did someone say work-life-balance?"

Bessy rattled a little from her stationary position beneath me. "You're right Bess. The pay. *Oh,* the pay."

Those sort of figures were spank-bank material for at least the next month, and only for three days a week?

Sure, that meant cooking extra, meal prepping, labelling, yadda-yadda-yadda, but it was a full time paycheck for only a part time job. Dare I say that sounded a little...*lucky?*

No, I'm going to take that back. That would jinx it, and though I had never been one to think of things like that before, I sort of was now.

In the words of Taylor Swift, Karma was indeed a cat, but it wasn't my lap she was purring in, and I had absolutely no idea at this stage of life if she loved me or hissed at the very mention of my name. I would currently go with the latter.

"Cons?" I pondered. "The man had his secretary send me the *code* to his *level of the building.*" I scoffed a little. This man owned a level of a whole damn building, and all I could see beyond the paycheck was a male version of Mrs. Backaratt and her opinion that ham was peasant food.

So, speaking plainly? He could be a dick. He could be a real, honest-to-god asshole and knowing how the cards were predicting my future at present, it was entirely likely that this *looked* like a taste of the good stuff but really, it was you in your best dress with a boxed wine clutched tightly in your arms, only to be told after missing two trains and taking the stairs you weren't even on the list to the party.

"Navy. Who are you?" I asked myself, grabbing the rear view mirror and angling it towards myself, looking right into my own eyes. "You're Lucky, that's who."

I started to nod at myself slowly, and if I strained hard enough I could almost hear the slow crescendo of the inspirational drum beat spurring me on. Could almost *feel* the uplifting natural breeze, pushing my hair from my face, and ignore that it was just the air conditioning in my car.

"You are Lucky Peters. World class chef, impromptu line dancer, modern-day-take-on-classic-car collector and self appointed badass."

Bessy groaned beneath me as her engine continued to support the car being on while being idle, but I took it for what it was: a car version of a *'hell yeah, you go girl'*.

"Thanks Bess." I patted the steering wheel and leaned in to give her a quick peck. "Wish me luck and don't antagonise any parking inspectors. We've simply had too many tickets already. I've checked the times, I've done my part, okay?"

Turning off the car, I grabbed my tote bag from the seat beside me, complete with two different types of appropriate chef's uniforms and made for the revolving door of the building.

I repeated the six digit code aloud to myself while walking through the elegantly decorated lobby and beamed enthusiastically at the two security guards who were stationed behind the desk just beside the elevators.

"Good morning." I held up a hand in a wave I was hoping was subdued enough for quarter to six in the morning.

"Morning, miss," one of the guards said around a yawn,

looking at me sheepishly in an apologetic manner after forgetting to cover his mouth altogether.

"Hello!" the other said probably two or three levels of jovialness up from where I had been.

I altered my path from direct-to-the-elevators to direct-to-the-guards and ended up reaching out my hand maybe a second and half too early to shake theirs. It meant that I ended up walking the last two steps with my arm suspended directly out before me.

Wonderful.

"Lovely to meet you both. I'm just on my way to a job interview so we may be seeing a lot of each other. Fingers crossed." I smiled as they both shook my hand in firm but friendly grips.

Was it weird to introduce myself to the early morning building guards? I guess so, but it wasn't particularly out of character for me and it felt like they would be a real asset to have in my corner, just in case.

"It's a pleasure—," the one with a more rounded stomach and full beard began to say.

"Oh, sorry. I'm Lucky."

"Lucky. That's different," the older man next to the first guard said, only to receive an elbow to the ribs by Mr. Round-Belly.

"I'm Jim, this here is Abe." Jim (rounded belly man that looked alarming like Paul Blart the Mall Cop) gestured to Abe next to him, and it could have been the fluorescents but the man sort of looked like Sylvester Stallone.

"Nice to meet you," I smiled, "hopefully I'll be seeing you every Monday, Wednesday and Friday." I sent them a couple finger guns, and I knew by the way they were well received they were my sorts of acquaintances.

"Good luck!" Abe called out just as the elevator doors opened and I stepped in.

It was 5:53 a.m., I would be a little early, if not arguably on-time, considering every employer measured work ethic on how much extra work you did for them that they didn't have to pay you for. Something that ground my gears on the constant and never enforced strictly when I had a staff of my own.

I wasn't all that prepared for what I was greeted with when the elevator doors opened. It was lavish beyond anything I would have ever been able to imagine in my own head.

The foyer was all marble floors and glass chandeliers, with a Grand Piano in this dark, rich mahogany set off to the side. Pillars were set on either side of the elevator, one holding a sculpture and one holding a vase, both probably worth more than anything I'd see in my lifetime.

My shoes were squeaking loudly in the most appropriate display of just how out of my league this place was as I walked out of the elevator.

The deeper into the foyer I went the higher on the toes of my shoes I walked in an attempt to minimise the squeaking, turning as I went. There were paintings and even an elegant little bench that looked like it had never seated a single person.

Just as I was completing a second turn, my back bumped into something. I turned so fast I was even a little impressed with myself, throwing my hands out to grab onto what I was sure was a priceless crystal statue that I definitely had *not* seen on account of the fact that it was pretty much invisible. My hands hovered around the perimeter while I watched in horror as it continued to rock side to side.

All hope lost on maintaining any semblance of propriety, my shoes squeaked like never before as they scurried in the way you might scurry from left to right when defending a goal from an opposing team. Arms stretched wide, and a face with an expression of determination with a touch of fear.

I threw myself at the statue which was more than a foot higher than my own height where I stood at five foot nine, and gripped it in a bear hug. Moulding myself to it until it stopped rocking, and once again stood steady on its own base.

That was how my new future boss' assistant found me. Groping a crystal statue of - I leaned back to finally look at it - a man? *Perfect.*

Clearing my throat, I righted myself and hoisted my tote bag further up my shoulder, turning to face the woman who stood shell shocked, for lack of a better phrase. My shoes let out their loudest squeak yet which made her flinch enough to snap out of whatever had gripped her.

"Hello!" I smiled at her, holding out my hand as I took the couple steps needed to close the distance between us.

Why did I keep doing that?

"I'm Navy Peters. Lovely to meet you."

She frowned, holding out her hand to shake mine at the same time she checked the clipboard she'd been holding in a white knuckled grip. "You're not Lucky? The Chef?"

"Yep, that's me. Sorry, Denise sends through applications sometimes under 'Navy', sometimes under 'Lucky'." I pulled my hand back from hers and held tight to the tote on my shoulder.

"Ah, I see." She pulled a pen from the top of the clipboard and made a note on something. "Alright. My name is Felicity,

I'm Mr. Thompson's assistant. We corresponded via email. I should point out that Mr. Thompson isn't aware that it's you who has been selected for this morning's breakfast trial," she spoke as she finished writing, only flicking her eyes up to me at the end of her sentence.

"Since his previous chef moved on, I have been trying to find the equivalent in skill and knowledge, which is where you came in. I was surprised to receive your application but I think this will be a good fit." She smiled at me in a way that I could tell she was trying to be as warm as possible, but her eyes flicked to the near-invisible statue behind me and a flash of doubt passed through her expression.

"Yes, no, absolutely. I think I'll be perfect for the role. I'm looking forward to demonstrating that this morning." I smiled at her with all the confidence I could muster.

If there was one thing I could do, it was cook.

If there was one thing I had, it was skill.

"Alright, let me show you where you can keep your things then to the kitchen. Mr. Thompson is currently at the gym. You have an hour and fifteen minutes until he will be sitting at the dining table."

Felicity turned to walk further into the apartment as she began speaking (can you even call this an apartment? It was a flat, single level mansion). Her heels snapped, crisp and clean, on the marble floor while I trailed right behind her, squeaking sneakers and all.

She told me about all the time-frames and needs where mealtimes and food availability were concerned. Mr. Thompson's favoured list of foods and meals that she had already prepped in a folder and placed in the kitchen.

He preferred to eat at home for lunch, and did so because

he enjoyed having some space from work in the middle of the day. And then dinner was usually around seven-thirty in the evening. But that did vary and depended on his own schedule which meant that I would need to be free and available to wait and remain here for whenever he would arrive home.

On the days I didn't work, I would need to leave careful and clear instructions to the household staff on how to prepare his lunch and dinner, but he didn't have breakfast here on Tuesdays and Thursdays, or the weekends which was why I wasn't required.

All instructions needed to be typed up and placed in the kitchen before I left.

"I don't have a computer with me," I said as I placed my bag in the small room that she had shown me to, coming to realise why the paycheck for this job was so big.

The room I was shown to had a door that was the same colour as the walls. I had *no* hope of finding it again, I knew that much.

"Also, should I change?" I asked her before she could take off in another direction.

Felicity looked me up and down in my jeans and shirt. "That's not necessary. You will be wearing an apron and must have your hair tied back. Mr. Thompson has never felt it necessary to enforce chef whites in his home. And you may use the computer lab we have here."

"Computer lab?" I gawked.

Felicity didn't even bother to reply to me as she strode off, heels clipping and me squeaking on behind her.

I made a note-to-self to wear some different freakin' shoes.

She wove around the floor, taking two rights before she opened a door to where five different computers sat on five different desks, all equipped with printers, lamps, stationary. It was like a mini office.

"Is this where Mr. Thompson works from when he's here?" I asked while peering around the room.

Felicity snorted. "No. This is for staff only." She frowned and glanced my way fleetingly. "There are a couple of his employee's that are studying and require computer access during lunch hours. He wanted to support them in every way he could, so this is a new instalment that you're also welcome to use."

She closed the door and turned with vigour where she stood, swiping me in the face with her long brown hair that smelt like strawberries.

I was teetering on whether or not Felicity was a good egg (if not a little uptight) or a bad egg (and doing her best not to be a raging bitch at work). Either way, her hair smelled wonderful.

As she led me back through the maze that was this apartment-mansion, probably knowing full well I wouldn't be able to find that room again with ease, let alone the room I left my stuff in, I had to think that someone who cared for their staff like that couldn't possibly be as much of a wet noodle as Mrs. Backaratt.

It gave me hope.

We pulled up to the kitchen that was one of the sparkliest, cleanest, nicest spaces I'd ever seen, and I'd seen some pretty fan-dangle kitchens.

It was a completely different style to the kitchen at Mrs. Backaratt's mansion but just as new-age and high end in its appliances. I wanted to hug every surface, and let this place know I'd treat it well, that it would be safe in my capable, well trained hands.

"Right." She looked from the kitchen to me then back to the kitchen. "If you need anything just tap my name on the call button on the screen next to the fridge, but if there is nothing else, you have," she looked at her watch, "fifty-five minutes until breakfast."

She didn't even give me a chance to thank her before she twirled again, hair flipping out in what I was beginning to think was her signature move, and striding off deep into the maze that was this rich man's home until I couldn't hear her shoes tapping against the floor anymore.

"Right." I took a deep breath and peered at my watch. Fifty-four minutes.

The folder was, thankfully, right in the middle of the bench and I allowed myself ten whole minutes to familiarise myself with the list of meals and food that were 'household preferred', as it was listed at the top.

Lucky for me, there were about fifteen different pages of things that would go down a treat. So, he wasn't picky. That was a plus.

I dug out the apron and pulled my hair to the top of my head, securing it in a tight ponytail before wrapping the long length into a bun.

Finding what I needed for an omelette, I now had about twenty minutes to get this man his breakfast before all the knowledge I mostly failed to absorb from Felicity would be made redundant.

I slipped the perfectly cooked omelette beside the most expertly buttered piece of toast with a little garnish to finish. I stood waiting, double checking that I had everything I needed prepped and ready to make him whatever coffee he requested.

I heard footsteps that could only be the result of the long strides of a tall man echoing around me, growing gradually louder until they stopped.

There was silence for a beat, a little too long to be normal before he spoke.

"Good morning, Lucky." His voice was smooth but with a calloused edge that hinted to something a little rougher.

It sent a jolt through me, something I felt at the tip of every finger, and at the root of every hair that sat upon my head.

I turned slowly, sure that this couldn't be happening.

Mr. Thompson.

Surely not.

Absolutely not.

I closed my eyes for the majority of my turn, and only when I had rotated the full one-eighty-degrees did I dare to open them.

My stomach dropped right out of my ass.

I swallowed as I beheld the dumb founded, completely and totally taken unaware expression of Cole Thompson before me, wearing a suit that had been cut to fit every part of his body.

A *man's* body.

Not the boy I had gone to high school with, who had promised me that he would be the very reason for my downfall, that he would relish every moment of it.

Well, that's just my fucking luck.

8

Lucky

I fumbled the plate in my hands before tossing it haphazardly to the counter in front of me, settling on *that* being a better alternative to it being Picassoed all over my shoes.

I was staring right into the face of Cole Thompson.

I mean, *this* was the boy who made it his personal mission to try and drag me down. To show me up, to make me *less*. Not that he'd ever succeeded.

"Who...*what*?" I looked at him, wondering if those two words translated into the more accurate '*What in tarnation are you doing standing right before me right now at like twenty past six in the morning in this apartment-mansion you stalker lunatic?*'.

He was still staring at me, but the look of shock and bewilderment had disappeared almost in the same moment it had flashed across his features.

Cole slowly dragged his eyes from my face down the length of me, and my entire body stilled under the weight of his perusal. His green eyes snapped back up to mine the moment my breathing hitched. The darker shade around the outside made the lighter colour towards the centre seem to glow.

His hair was still black as night, well kept and pushed off his face in the respectable sort of way you would expect from a businessman. A little shorter from the last time I saw him (which was - oh my *god* - over a decade ago? *Dammit* I was getting old), but it still held the same slight wave.

His eyes though...they had changed.

"Lucky Peters," he crooned in the same way that I remembered and a shiver went down my spine, causing me to hold the counter in front of me in a bruising grip.

Cole took slow, measured steps towards me, his eyes never leaving mine, his figure becoming more and more imposing with every step he took until I was looking up at him.

Another difference. He had grown. *A lot.*

"What," he started, placing his hands on the counter that sat between us and leaning in towards me, "pray tell, are you doing in my kitchen?"

The corner of his lips hiked ever so slightly at the obvious shock across my face, expertly deduced, I was sure, by my eyes almost falling directly out of their sockets.

"Your what?"

Wow. Lovely and intellectual, Navy. Way to stick it to the man.

"My kitchen, Lucky," he said again, leaning closer still. "You're standing in my kitchen."

I wasn't entirely sure what his endgame was here, but I would be *damned* if I waited around to find out. I'd gone through years of this boy's - *man's* - shit in my hay-day and I didn't need it. I didn't need it then, and I sure as hell did *not* need it *now*.

"Your kitchen?"

"My kitchen."

"No I'm not." I hastily untied the apron from around my back, pulled it over my head and threw it down next to the omelette I had prepared. I had even garnished the stupid thing. *Garnished it.*

I gripped the plate and pushed it towards him, watching as it slid across the smooth surface between us and stopped only because it hit his hand.

He pulled his eyes from mine for the first time since I had turned to face him.

"Enjoy. I retract my application."

I pulled my hair from the tight bun that I had scraped it into, withholding a groan from the utter relief of freeing the strands, and turned on my heels eliciting the loudest squeak my sneakers had produced to date.

My departure would have been all the more better if I knew where in the sweet heavens I was even going. I needed my bag. My keys, my phone, my wallet.

Felicity really should've given me a map, at the very least.

His footsteps immediately began to follow me, but not in a rushed sort of way, but in a slow and leisurely way a predator might toy with his prey.

"Where are you going, Lucky?" He didn't even raise his voice.

It echoed around me just fine and I spared a glance behind me to see just the shadow of him come around the corner.

"I'm getting the hell out of this fun house. I can't believe I didn't put it together," I replied, though I didn't particularly care if he heard me or not. I also had no idea how I even *would* have put it together.

He did hear me though, because his laugh rumbled through the space around me, low and taunting.

I flung myself around another corner and found a door I thought looked a lot like the one Felicity had instructed me to leave my things in, but opening it proved only to be one of the billion linen closets in this place.

"Mother of shite," I grumbled, closing the door with more force than necessary and willing my thundering heart to calm.

"Where are you going, Lucky?" The words sounded lazy coming out of his mouth, like he had all the time in the world despite the fact that I'd been briefed on his insane schedule and I knew that these were precious minutes he wouldn't be getting back.

Cole Thompson from high school's *home?!* What sort of mixed up, losing my mind, alternate reality crock of shit joke was this?

"I'm *trying* to find my bag that your assistant made me put in some room that I would never in a million years find again so I can wash out my eyeballs with vinegar and clean my ears with sand," I snapped, having to turn back the way I had came but I didn't run into him.

He knew I was going to hit a dead end and he'd obviously gone another way. He was toying with me.

"You know what Cole? Why don't you just do the gentlemanly thing and show me the way?" I stopped walking, having no idea where I was now even in reference to the kitchen, placing my hands on my hips and scowling.

"Oh, I don't think I'll do that." His voice was getting closer and it was coming from behind me.

I whipped around just in time for him to stroll into the little space I found myself in, making it feel about a thousand times smaller.

The picture of absolute ease and arrogance.

His hands were tucked into the front pockets of his slacks, and somewhere along the way of his little predator-prey routine, he'd unbuttoned the top of his dress shirt as well as his blazer. His hair, though it still sat nicely, no longer looked styled into place but rather like he'd run his hands through it a couple times.

"You're saying you *won't* help me find my things so I can leave?" My voice rocketed up a couple octaves at the end there and I was starting to feel like I was never going to see my family again. All at once I was grateful I didn't have some beloved pet at home that would be waiting on me for their dinner only to learn that I was never coming back.

He walked towards me and didn't stop, instead he continued to make his way around me. Circling me.

"You're not going anywhere." His tone had some bite to it that made the hair on my arms stick up and by the time he came back to stand in front of me I was certain the rest of my organs had followed my stomach on its departure from my person.

When he reentered my line of sight my breath caught in my throat. I hadn't anticipated he would be so close. A little *too* close to be casual. The type of close intended to intimidate. To make me realise just how much smaller I was than him. Just how much lower to the ground I was.

"Are you, or are you not in my employment?" His eyes lit with a sick satisfaction of having me under his thumb.

I wasn't oblivious to the fact that he was more than likely aware of my situation. That he knew every little detail of how my life had fallen apart. The man before me was holding himself in the sort of way that *oozed* victory. Like this moment had been something he had wanted for years, had dreamed of. Probably even whacked one out once or twice to the mere whisper of a possibility of this exact situation coming to fruition.

And I will love every minute of your downfall. Every. Single. Second.

The moment the memory flowed to the forefront of my mind I knew he thought of it too. I knew he was remembering the very moment we had last seen each other, and the promise he had made to me then.

I was getting the feeling that the man that Cole had become was not the kind who made idle promises. He wasn't the kind to say things he didn't mean no matter how long ago they had been spoken.

"I'd like to leave. *Now*," I said between gritted teeth, clenching my hands at my sides so I didn't do something like strangle that stupid smug look off his perfectly symmetrical face.

He had *not* looked like this when we were growing up...had he? I mean, we *had* grown up from the kids we had been, eighteen and on the doorstep of adulthood.

It was hard to remember what he had looked like when backyard barbecues and movie nights were plans we both scheduled into our weekend calendars. But I did remember what he looked like when we both did our best to pretend that we had never shared those things to begin with, and it wasn't *this*.

"I can see that. And though I am sympathetic to your situation, there is still the small, very little, *teeny-weeny* thing that is me being your boss." His smile widened a little. It could have been beautiful but if you looked too long you'd see it was all teeth. Feral, almost. Like he'd been starved and presented with his first meal in days.

"I quit." I lifted my chin, not backing down one bit.

"Denied." He flung my four letter word back to me with a six lettered word of his own.

I jolted like it had smacked me right on the forehead. "*Denied?* You can't *deny* my resignation."

"You're right. But if you do quit, I will be forced to personally call the agency that sent you here, and let them know just how displeased I was. Not only with the language that came out of your mouth, but the quality of food you presented."

"You son of a bitch." The words fell out of my mouth with the same quiet bewilderment my face held, just before I found my backbone again. "You haven't even *eaten* my food."

"Oh, I've eaten your food," he tossed back nonchalantly at the same time he turned on his heels and strode in the direction the kitchen was in.

"You came to my restaurant."

"Did I?" He asked lightly, like if he had, it hadn't been memorable. I knew there was no way *Cole Thompson* would have walked into my restaurant and I didn't know about it.

"I thought you didn't like liars," Suddenly even more furious than I was before and desperately hoping the squeak from my shoes was driving him bonkers as I followed. I still wanted I was not going to risk starving to death after getting lost in his TARDIS that was his penthouse.

He didn't even deign me with a response as the kitchen and dining space opened up before us.

Cole continued to stride right to where the omelette sat on the counter, maintaining his arrogant grace the entire time, and took the plate to the table. He sat down so fluidly it was like he floated into the seat.

"I'll have a cappuccino this morning, thank you, Miss Peters," his voice was calm in a pleasant, conversational way that made my blood boil.

"I'm not making you coffee. I told you, I quit." I was seething.

Cole picked up his knife and fork, only angling his head in my direction but not even giving me the courtesy of looking at me.

"If you walk out of this apartment, it will be the last job you ever have. Any hope of rebuilding everything you've lost will not only be a smaller possibility than the already minute one it currently is, but it will cease to exist altogether. You may not know who I am now, Lucky, but I know you. And all the people *I* know, know *you*. I have more power here than you could *possibly* dream of and so if a future is something you want for yourself, you will put that apron back on, put your hair back up, and make me a fucking cappuccino."

Fury like I'd never known before exploded through my entire body until I was sure that if I opened my mouth it would spurt fire. My whole face ached with the effort of holding in the hot, heavy tears I knew wanted to escape me. I had never been so furiously humiliated in my entire life.

But he wasn't done, even though he had so thoroughly won and we both knew I was going to make him that bloody coffee.

He finally deigned to look at me, his eyes no longer bright

and lit with mischief or the taunting victory of before. They were cold and empty, like bottomless pits of nothing. His gaze was piercing as he watched me from underneath heavy lashes.

"You're mine now, Lucky Peters."

9

Lucky

"I think I need you to tell me everything again from the top. Maybe a little slower." Melody was looking at me so intently her eyes looked like they began to cross periodically.

"*Heavens*," I rolled my eyes and shook my head before taking another massive bite of my burger.

Melody hadn't even touched her food yet because I couldn't contain the word vomit that spilled out of me the moment our asses hit our familiar bright red booth at *Helga's*.

As soon as I finished preparing lunch for *he who shall not be named*, I called Felicity on the fancy house-screen-phone thing to insist she come find me in that hell-hole of a kitchen and take me to my things before leading me to the elevator.

I had lost all of my fucks to give so I had probably lectured her for a minute too long on the very real issues I had not only with her employer, that in future the name of the employer should *not* be withheld from the potential employee under any circumstances and also that she needed a map to hand out upon arrival.

Jim and Abe were both absent as I was leaving, but the *New York Times* sat unguarded on the top of their little desk which I'd been on my way to get anyway, so I grabbed it and called my best friend with a code red and twenty minutes later, there we were.

"No matter how many times I tell you," I said around a mouth full of food, "it's not going to be any less mind blowing than the first time you heard it." I shrugged a shoulder and loaded another few fries into my already too-full mouth.

"Cole Thompson?" she asked, her mouth hanging open a little.

"Yep." I nodded, popping the 'p' and trying to not let the conversation affect my appetite.

"The same Cole Thompson you used to have naked swim dates with in the backyard of your parents house in your bright pink *Barbie* pool and matching arm floaties?"

"Why would you bring that up? And we were absolutely not naked." I scowled at her, taking another bite of my burger. It didn't deter her in the slightest because she just railed on through without a care.

"The same Cole who you wanted to hate-shag in high school?" She had placed both hands on the table now and leaned further towards me.

"I actually don't think you could have *paid* me to –"

"The same Cole who you were obsessed with beating at *everything*?"

"Is there a point to your trip down memory lane? But. yes to point one with the addition of clothes and yes to three.

Point two is as accurate as those *Flat Earth* brochures at the bar. Also, who says '*shag*'?"

"You're deflecting." She pointed at me with one of her chips before dipping it into her sauce and shoving the thing unceremoniously into her mouth to hide the smile I knew she was battling to keep under control.

"I'm not deflecting. I have the worst luck in the world right now and somehow after not seeing him for ten years, I have become his snack bitch," I grumbled into my burger, shoving the last bits of it into my mouth and licking all the sauce off my fingers.

I slid the paper I had grabbed from Jim and Abe's desk out of my bag and pushed my plate off to the side before opening it up in front of me. I flicked through the pages lazily, in no rush to get to the section of the paper I was really after.

"So..." Melody said after finally taking a bite of her own burger.

My eyes snapped up to hers in a silent prompt for her to spit it out.

"Was he hot?"

"His face has nothing to do with his rotten character or absent soul." I flicked to the next page in a show of my quiet rage, scanning but not reading anything.

"So that's a yes. Interesting." She ate another chip and tilted her head to the side quizzically. "And you say you tried to quit?"

"And *he* threatened to not only ruin any chance of me being able to rebuild my reputation. I am basically a hostage and the ransom I must deliver is my service."

"This is sort of crazy, Lucky." Melody had this crazed look in her eyes that told me she was prepping to sit back and enjoy the show whilst simultaneously being worried about my well-being.

"Yep. Just when I thought things couldn't get worse, they did." I flicked to another page.

"You're giving up?" She sounded incredulous.

I scoffed. "Ha! No." Meeting her gaze so that she could see I wasn't so easily broken. "But it's a curve ball I didn't see coming and certainly didn't need. Or want. Or appreciate."

"You really have to go back?" Her voice dropped now like she was, just for a second, really as upset about the entire ordeal as I was. *Yeah, right.*

"I do. But I won't be going quietly. Mark my words," I said as I finally got to the part of the paper I had been looking for. "Alright, are you ready?"

I sat up a little straighter and so did Melody, like seeing me do it reminded her that her posture had drooped too.

"Hit me." She rubbed her hands together before picking up her burger again.

I snapped the paper out before lifting it a little closer to my face to read the article written by *Acquired Taste*.

"Okay, it reads;

'*I am picky about Japanese food. I like what I like and, after being to the country itself and eating the real thing, it's true that very little can compare.*

There is something special about being immersed in the culture of the food you're consuming that makes the experience better tenfold.

'Bullet Train' is a new restaurant that's opened on the East Side of the city. It's chic, stylish and high class. This establishment has been open for four and half months and that's precisely how long it took me to finally get a seat at their table. Perhaps if they had

more seating, they wouldn't have such a long wait list. There is exclusive, then there is a little preposterous.

Unfortunately, I can't say it was the only thing that let me down.

The idea was there, if not fully formed. The menu is broad, and offers a range of different dishes and flavours. The meals I got were presented beautifully, but the flavour was lacking. If time had been taken to properly season the meal in the same capacity time had been taken to plate it, things might have been different.

It also could have been the quality of the products. It was clear to me that perhaps some corners were cut in order to provide a bigger serving? To make more per dish? Either way, the price of the portions is not a reflection of the quality of the ingredients.

Aside from the above let downs, the experience wasn't the worst I've ever had, but it's unlikely I'll be back.

My menu is listed below.

Star Rating: 2 stars.

Purpose for deduction: interior seating and space, quality of produce, flavour and seasoning.'"

"Well slap my ass and call me Melody." Melody's eyes were glued on the paper in my hands, her voice in awe. "That was painful."

"Not the worst, though," I chimed in, and Melody bobbed her head in agreement. "I mean, as far as *Taste's* reviews go, it wasn't so bad?" I stared from the paper in my hands to my friend and then back.

It was bad. I cringed, knowing that we would still try and eat there. We always wanted to give every restaurant they featured a go, it was sort of our tradition.

Acquired Taste was the world's most renowned and successful food critique. They hosted a quarter page spot in the

New York Times and Melody and I had been obsessed since the reviews had begun posting five years ago.

Their critique was gospel.

I had seen restaurants fall and crumble because of the words written in this paper, and I'd also seen establishments rise to fame and hold that fame still to this day.

The catch was, no one knew who they were. Was it one person? A team? There was no way to find out. And believe me, people tried.

There was an entire blog dedicated to unmasking this person about two years ago, but all they got were dead ends.

One led them to the bedroom of a small boy in Uruguay and the other, which the owner of the blog was actually quite vocal regarding their confidence of its accuracy, belonged to an old man named Bill who lived in a nursing home in Nashville, Tennessee, insisting he only owned a computer to play Tetris.

It was in fact *not* Bill, and after that everyone sort of gave up on the blog.

I closed the paper and let out a deep breath. The high of the review slowly faded as I slumped back into the booth and looked at Melody.

She pulled out her phone and checked the time on her lock screen, a frown blooming between her brows.

"That hour went very quick," she muttered, making the corners of my own mouth lift slightly.

"Thanks for making the trip out." I reached my hand out across the sticky table and she placed hers in mine. "I guess I'll let you know how it goes tonight."

"I need a play by play." She nodded. "And maybe we should have a code word or something so that if anything goes south of the border big time, I can call the police." Her face was stern and absolutely serious, so when I cracked out a cackle of a laugh, she jumped.

"I'll be fine, don't worry."

"Of course I'm going to worry." She went on as we scooted out of our booth. "I mean, if this was a movie or something totally not real I'd be so all over it, but you're being essentially blackmailed into keeping a position with someone who quite literally hates you and is likely going to make every waking moment of your time there miserable. I bet you won't even be cooking. He's probably going to make you lick his toilet clean and scrub his dirty underwear by hand."

Melody crashed right into the back of me as I stopped walking. A small *oomph* sound left her before I turned around to face her, my expression incredulous.

"Why," I put my hands on either side of her face, squishing her cheeks, "in the world would you say that?" I grabbed her shoulders shaking her with fervour.

"Sorry, Luck," voice distorted from the shaking. "It just all came out. I'm sure that won't happen, though. Obviously."

I flicked her forehead in retaliation before leaving the bar.

"Get back safely, but I am totally not speaking to you right now," I called over my shoulder.

"I understand and respect your decision," she yelled back at me as we continued to walk in separate directions. "But I think your safe word should be pineapple, okay?"

I held my middle finger up over my shoulder and heard the tinkling sound of my friend's laughter as I refused to dignify her with a response.

10

Lucky

20 years ago. Aged 8.

"Are they here yet?" I asked my mother, tugging on her shirt while she tried to finish whatever meal she was making in the kitchen.

"Oakleigh?" she called out to my brother before looking down at me. "No, Lucky. No one's here yet. Just be patient, okay?"

She pinched my chin gently before leaning down and kissing my cheek. "Why don't you get your pool ready? I'm sure Cole will want to swim as soon as he arrives."

My brother walked into the kitchen just as she'd finished speaking, walking by me and pulling on my ponytail before collecting a tray of meats mum had put to the side for the barbecue.

We were having lots of our neighbours over from our street and the one over. We did this sort of thing once a month and every family hosted, this time it was our turn again.

In the backyard my *Barbie* pool lay upside down from the last time I used it with one of my sisters.

With a heavy sigh I dropped the hose and attempted to drag the pool a little further out onto the grass and away from the fence to flip it over. It barely moved at all.

The last time I used it, James had helped me fill it up and he'd held it on its side to spray it off first. It looked pretty easy so with a shrug of my little shoulders I tried doing the same thing. I wanted everything set up so it was ready for when Cole got here.

I kept the hose in one hand as I tried to hoist the pool up and onto its side. It took a little time but I managed to slowly get my body under it, using all the strength in my legs that I could to get it up. I took a couple of big breaths, trying to find a balance in holding up the heavy thing grinning like no one's business that I was doing it on my own.

Pulling the lever on the spray, I frowned a little as nothing came out. I squeezed the handle back a couple more times and still, nothing happened.

I craned my neck to have a look at the hose, wondering if maybe something was stuck on the end, or if I'd forgotten to turn on the tap but the way I was holding the pool meant I couldn't really do that. I tried one more time, turning the spray head towards me and squeezed the handle again.

This time, water shot right into my face and I lost my grip on the pool I was trying to balance against my body. I managed to move out of the way just in time before it smacked me on the head, landing on the ground with a loud *thump*.

It was then that I heard the roaring laughter of a boy from behind me.

I turned in the direction of the sound and wiped the water from my eyes. Cole was standing with his foot a little too close to the hose, wearing a grin that took up half his face.

"Cole!" I yelled at him from across the yard and pointed to the fallen pool. "That could have hit me on the head."

"No way, Luck," he said, walking over to me, already wearing his swimmers. His black hair was a little shaggy and his green eyes bright with mischief. "I knew you'd be fine." He stood right in front of me, still wearing his grin.

"Liar." I dropped the hose and crossed my arms in front of my chest, letting him know I meant business.

"Take it back or I'll spray you." He grabbed the hose and ran back a bit.

"That's not fair. I'll tell!" I yelled again, wishing that sometimes he wasn't such a *boy* and would actually enjoy playing my games with me instead of scaring me and spraying me with the hose.

My threat to tell on him made him lower the hose a little and look over his shoulder even though I'd never really do it.

"Okay, okay," he said in an exasperated voice.

A little smile crossed my face at the feeling of victory, like I had somehow won that round. "I'll take it back if you help fill up my pool." I pointed to the bright pink thing still upside down next to me.

"If I help fill it up we have to play that water fight game your brother taught us last time," he said, his face lifting in a hopeful way.

"Half water fight and half water-land tea party?" I raised my eyebrow at him.

"Lucky," he whined, "I don't want to play tea parties with you. We did that last time."

I started walking before he was even finished, taking exaggerated little stomps back in the direction of the house. "Fine, then I don't want to play at all."

I'd made it two steps past him before he sprayed me with the hose and I let out an ear piercing shriek. It was cold and had completely taken me off guard. We were the only ones outside so no one saw him do it.

I watched as he did his best to hold in his laughter, moments from breaking when my mum stuck her head out the back door.

"Lucky? Cole? What's going on?"

He quickly moved the hose behind his back before we both called back in unison, "Nothing!"

She eyed us both with the right amount of suspicion that she knew we were likely up to no good considering I was soaking wet, Cole was dry and the pull was still upside down and empty. "Lucky?" she asked me, raising an eyebrow.

"Nothing, we are going to play water fights then tea party," I said quickly, looking over at Cole who was nodding his head furiously.

My mum looked between the two of us before the crease between her eyes smoothed and a knowing look crossed her face. "Do you need help filling up the pool?"

"I'll help her Mrs. Peters," Cole said, which earned him one of my mothers loveliest smiles.

"Thank you Cole, I know you will. You always do! Behave the two of you," she said in a final warning that held absolutely no weight behind it before heading back inside where more families had started to arrive.

Cole and I turned to face each other before bursting out into a fit of laughter that made my cheeks hurt.

He eventually held out the hose for me to take. "I can hold it up while you spray it first?" he said as I took the hose from him.

"It's heavy," I said, trailing behind him back towards the pool.

"I know I saw you trying to lift it. I won't drop it on you, Luck," he mumbled as we both reached down to lift it onto its side before he held it on his own.

"Promise?" I double checked with him as I got ready to spray the twigs and leaves off it.

All it took was that single word for Cole to drop the pool altogether, walk over and hook his pinky finger with mine.

Our version of a pinky swear was different to most.

I had insisted that there was no risk in kissing the back of your own thumb when you made a pinky promise. I had seen other kids do it at school. They would hook their pinkies, press their thumbs together and then seal their promises by kissing their *own* thumbs.

It made no sense to me, where was the risk in that? It was your own thumb, it didn't mean diddly-squat.

So, when I told Cole he told me he understood what I meant, and that it would make more sense to kiss the other person's thumb. That doing that would be a pretty big deal, that's how you knew that they meant the promise they were making, and they knew you meant it too.

"Promise." He nodded back, leaning in to kiss the pad of my thumb before I leaned in to kiss his.

I knew without a shadow of a doubt that he wouldn't let the pool come toppling over me.

He didn't drop it on me, and we even played water-land tea party first.

11

Cole

Present

The bell of the elevator rang through the entire apartment like a gong.

I had snapped my head in that very direction at least five times in the last twenty minutes, jumping at every little noise and sound that echoed through the apartment.

Navy Peters. Navy *fucking* Peters.

Lucky.

I'd never wanted to think of that name again from the last moment I walked out of the god-forsaken doors of my high school.

Firstly, because she made me feel so many things all at once, the strongest of those feelings being hate, and I was trying to move on with my life after finally being granted the opportunity to move out of my brother's shadow and my mother's disapproving, downcast and brutal gaze.

Secondly, because initially the distance actually helped. Out of sight, out of mind and all that. Or that had been the goal.

Even though I'd removed myself from everything and everyone I knew, Lucky still managed to touch my life. Even as I meticulously picked every thought that had to do with her out of my brain, it was futile to some degree when I saw her face on every magazine she had featured on the cover of, and read every article she'd been interviewed for.

Coincidental or not, she'd made quite the name for herself in the very industry that I'd made a name for *my*self in.

I eventually could think of her and continue to feel...well, nothing. I had long since moved past any of the feelings I had towards her, namely the ones that had me staying up late at night and using every ounce of remaining energy I had to hope that something, *anything*, would happen. That I might see her face fall with the reality of having someone, *me*, beat her. Be better, just be *more* than her, the way that it was always drilled into me.

If I tried hard enough I could pull the words being spat at me in my mothers voice from the dregs of my memories, *'Why can't you be more like your brother, Cole? Or Lucky Peters? Why can't you be more like her?'*

The moment I saw her standing in my kitchen I felt everything which was so different to the gnawing emptiness that usually resided in the very centre of me. I felt anger and sadness. I felt relief and excitement, and then I felt mad. I felt *mean* and furious and like I wanted to scream until my throat was bloody.

When it had all passed and I was left still standing there

somehow still completely in one piece, a single thought floated into my mind; That fate, or whatever fucking mystical workings of the universe finally gave me my opportunity.

Lucky Peters was dropped right into my lap as a present for everything I'd endured, everything I'd earned.

I should've let her go. Maybe even pretended not to remember who she was, though that would have been near impossible. She was intertwined in almost every year of my life up until that day I left.

You're mine, Lucky Peters.

I dragged my hand down my face.

"She's right, you are a fucking jackass," I mumbled to myself and felt about as sane as I'm sure I looked at that moment.

That didn't change anything though. I *couldn't* let her go.

Stalking her through the hallways of my home had been a quiet thrill I wouldn't soon forget. The way she'd lifted her chin in defiance only to crumble when she saw that I held all the cards...I knew of her downfall.

Had it been a real dick move to use that against her? Absolutely. Was I above that? Usually, yes. But where Lucky was concerned, I was throwing every rule out the window.

She smelt the same. Like jasmine. Like the woods after it rained. Like wild berries in the winter. I had seen the way her pulse fluttered at the base of her throat and knew I had pushed myself as far as I could go.

Refusing to think about how my cock twitched when her breathing had caught. How she had leaned into me without even realising it.

I stood up from my desk and buttoned my jacket while adjusting myself in my slacks. It only made me hate her more, in an unhinged sort of way I had never known before. The thought draped over my mood, souring it just as I made unhurried strides back to the kitchen after swept up in my own thoughts for the last hour and completely losing track of time. The clock had struck quarter past seven in the evening. I made my steps slow, taunting, a wicked smile splitting my features simply anticipating how her heart rate would spike. Wondering if it was excitement, or dread, or fear that she would be feeling right now as I slowly, lazily, made my way towards her.

I'd gone the long way, finding too much pleasure in toying with her, and finally walked into the open plan kitchen area that spread into the dining space.

The table had been set, a bottle of both red and white wine had been placed to the side of my table setting. Salads and accompaniments of varying colours scattered before me as I took my seat, snapping my napkin out before draping it over my knee.

I heard her intake of breath at my arrival and relished in the knowledge that I'd taken her off guard. That she hadn't known from which way I was coming, only that I was moving closer.

She didn't speak to me and I hadn't even so much as looked her way. I kept myself from doing so while desperately wanting to know what would happen when I did. Sounds had started coming from behind me as Lucky began to plate my meal, my body relaxed and unworried as she stopped just to my side.

"Dinner tonight is pan seared barramundi with a number of entrees and accompanying mains. We have a traditional bruschetta, as well as zucchini flowers. There is a fresh garden salad along with seasonal roasted vegetables." Her tone was clipped. Her words came out short, neither kind nor bitter.

Lucky placed the plate in front of me.

"Mmm." I leant forward and inhaled.

It smelt incredible and I was hit with another sick sense of satisfaction that she had prepped all of this for me. Even as I was sitting down and she was standing before me, I looked up at her in the same way my mother had always looked down at me, with a quiet resentment and I let myself relish in the power of our situation.

"Thank you, Lucky," I murmured, my voice husky with the swirl of emotions that had been raging in me all day.

My eyes tracked the way her throat worked when she swallowed, knowing she was biting her tongue on a snarky come back and doing all I could to challenge her to release her hold, to see what might happen if she spoke her mind.

She didn't.

Lucky didn't smile at me, but she didn't scowl either, only nodded her head once in thanks of her own.

As she was turning to leave I couldn't help myself, "Lucky?" My voice held a feigned innocence that I knew she could see right through. Its only purpose was to stoke the raging embers that had already been lit inside of her.

Her eyes held the rage I knew they would when she turned to look at me. There hadn't been enough time to compose herself and I savoured seeing her emotions come to the surface.

She didn't say anything as she held my gaze, even when my smile from earlier creeped back into my features. Not so much a smile as it was a slash across my features. Cold and jagged and harsh.

"I'll have a glass of the white wine, if you'd be so kind." My eyes flicked to the bottles that she had left on the table, assuming I would pour it myself. And usually I would have, I wasn't *that* much of an entitled prick. I wasn't one at all actually, but you wouldn't know that looking at me now.

Her eyes tracked mine as they too flicked to the bottle. In what looked like the most painful task she'd ever undertaken, she walked around to the other side of the table and opened the wine, pouring it with the class and standards you would expect of a chef and hospitality worker of her calibre. The perfect amount. No need for guidelines or an inquiry with me if it was too much or too little.

I lifted the glass, swirling it before inhaling and then finally taking a sip. I angled my face in her direction after placing the glass back down, but didn't meet her gaze. "That will be all, Miss Peters," I murmured before picking up my knife and fork to eat. My entire body was buzzing at the reality of this situation, at something I'd only ever *dreamed* about. The feeling like I'd finally, *finally,* beat Lucky Peters.

I couldn't decide if it was the worst or best part of it all, that I had no idea how I would ever be able to let her go.

12

Lucky

I'd slept fitfully all night, half waking from restlessness and half waking from a deep seated need to enact the ideas my unconscious brain had concocted.

I didn't dream of being stalked through elegant hallways, or deep seductive laughter that echoed around me, only to find myself falling through the floor with the last face I saw being Cole's cool, calculated cruel one like I thought I might. No, I dreamt of stalking *him*. Of my footsteps haunting *him*. That *I* was holding the cards. It might have been a dream but it sparked something in a part of me I thought had been a casualty of my downfall.

That's exactly what was running through my brain nonstop as I parked Bess and made my way into Cole's building to cook him something undoubtedly delicious in his mammoth kitchen that lived in his mammoth mansion-forward-slash-apartment.

Thinking through my previous approach, I did that thing I always did and went above and beyond to try and give him the best experience possible. I did it for Mrs. Backaratt and I did it for every job I had since temping. Like I needed to *prove* something.

This one was different, though.

For starters, I hadn't been blackmailed in any of those other positions, and I also wasn't serving food to someone who clearly wanted the very worst for me. Still, I called out all the names of the meals I prepped, going so far as to prepare *two* side dishes and *two* entrees.

I was going to play the most fucked up game of 'chicken' that Cole had ever seen. That's at least how the plan came together in my head.

I'd pictured us in a baking aisle of some random convenience store and I would stand right in front of the metaphorical shopping cart that was Cole, and I wouldn't blink an eye. I would stand tall and strong and I wouldn't flinch or falter. If he insisted I was going to have to remain in his employment like some...some creepy, super successful, incredibly beautiful businessman, then I refused to just bend over.

What I meant was, I wouldn't just lie down and take it.

For the love of all that's holy, I *meant* I would just grab this bull by the balls...wait, was it balls? Bull by the *horns*...? No, I was pretty sure it was balls. But that didn't matter either, I wouldn't be going anywhere *near* his balls.

"Lucky!"

I had never been so thankful to be pulled from my spiralling thoughts. Jim called out a jovial greeting from his spot at the desk. I would have to re-approach those thoughts later, and straighten them the hell out.

"Hey, Jim." I smiled at him warmly, resting my chin on my arms and leaning on the front reception security desk. "No Abe today?" I nodded my head to the empty seat next to him.

"Oh, no, he's here. Nature called, though." He shrugged in the way that said '*When you get to our age, there's no testing the limits. No pushing the boundaries. If you think something is coming on, you don't question it*'.

I lifted my hands up in front of me. "Ah," I nodded in a general sense of understanding, "Say no more." I backed away slowly, noting the time and not wanting to be any later than right on time.

"You're working for Mr. Thompson now? That's gotta be a great gig, hey kid? He's a good man, he'll treat you right." Jim nodded to me in the gruff sort of way older men tend to do when they're super sure of the truth behind the words they've spoken.

I wonder if Jim knew that Cole had stalked me through his apartment and threatened to take a dump on what was left of my reputation. Colour me intrigued.

"You know him well?" I stopped in my tracks to the elevators and tilted my head to the side, waiting for his reply.

"Mr. Thompson has owned the building for the last four years and we've never had a better boss."

"I'm sorry, did you say *owned*?"

"You bet. Really did wonders for the building and the staff. And of course the people that live here."

"He *owns* the *entire building*?" I was gawking.

"That doesn't surprise me that he didn't mention it. He's a humble man." He nodded in that way again.

I wanted to hold his head still and let him know that it was clear we were speaking about two totally different men. But Abe walked back in at the exact moment I was about to word vomit all over poor Jim and snapped me from my outrageous shock.

"Hey, Lucky," Abe said, smiling kindly at me as he sat back down at his desk. I tried very hard not to picture the man running for the bathroom with the fear of God in his eyes.

"Hey, Abe." Lifting my hand up in a half hearted wave, peeking at the time on my watch as I did. "Oh, crap. I'm going to be late." Turning on the spot I rushed for the elevators and tapped the button like my life depended on it. "I'll see you guys later!" I called back, hearing their replies being tossed back to me in a similar fashion.

I couldn't very well stick it to the man in the way I planned if I was *late*. That thought made me pause, because on second thought, perhaps that *was* sticking it to the man.

My frantic button tapping stopped immediately and I straightened my back, taking a deep breath and letting go of all the people-pleasing energy that surrounded me. The elevator dinged before me but instead of walking in I leaned around the door and tapped a random number before stepping back out and watching the doors shut.

A small mischievous grin split across my face as I watched the time on my watch turn over to a single minute passed six in the morning.

"You're late." His words were clipped.

I fucking *loved* it.

I'll be honest, it was just this side of terrifying. The more I looked, the more the casual stance of his body became accented with the effort of holding back a quiet rage that I had seen only once before.

In a move totally not like myself, I pulled on my tenth grade drama lessons and let my face crumble which caused a flicker of surprise to cross his features.

"Oh my god. P—please Mr. Thompson, don't fire me. Don't—" I stopped abruptly and walked out of the elevator, shoulder checking Mr. Apparently-Humble before turning around in the middle of the entry room, careful not to smack into his crystal statue this time.

He turned to look at me, a hint of amusement in his otherwise stormy gaze, but it flickered in and out of existence until it disappeared completely, like he had battled for control and the side of him that hated every single thing about me gave in.

"Considering your experience, I thought you would have known that the first rule of keeping your job is to show up on time." He took measured steps towards me until he only needed a single stride more to bring his chest flush with mine.

"It would be, if I actually *wanted* this job. Or have you forgotten that you denied my resignation and you're blackmailing me to be here?" I turned on my heels, flicking my hair for added impact and, regardless of my good intentions, almost ran directly into the invisible statue man.

"I'm so sorry," I mumbled, holding my hands out in front of me and moving around the stupid thing before taking the hallway that Felicity had led me down the last time I was here.

It was my second day, but this was the third time I'd been here and I was relatively confident I could find my way to the staff-bag-room. I kept up a strong pace, knowing that Cole was behind me, tracking my every step and likely figuring out what he was going to say next that would pack as much punch as possible.

"Lucky," he snapped from behind me, and I felt a brush of air at my back like he was moments from grabbing me. Like he definitely could have gathered my shirt in his hand but stopped himself at the last minute.

I ignored him dutifully and continued on my way.

"*Lucky.*" My name was a growl off his tongue and it took all my self control to stay on my path. It was guttural, that sound. Like it was full of all the emotion he was constantly trying to push down.

"Jackpot," I breathed as I flung open a door and found the very room I'd been looking for.

I threw my bag down unceremoniously, riding the high of my first effort of 'sticking it to the man' that I hadn't heard him come up behind me. Hadn't heard his rapid breathing or taken in his stance. I didn't even marginally hear what he'd begun to say when I turned on my heels, propelling myself with so much force that when I smacked right into his chest I heard the audible *crack* of my nose.

I was flying backwards, I knew it was only a matter of moments until my ass was shining his lovely marble floors and I would be left never, ever, wanting to stick it to the man ever again.

Right about the moment I knew I should have been eating shit, strong hands snapped out and gripped me tightly, righting me just as the pain of my nose set in.

"Ow, ow, ow, *ow.*" I grabbed my face and started hopping on the spot, certain that doing so would ease the stinging pain and pressure. My eyes cut to him, sharper than glass, needing to channel that pain somewhere before I started bawling my eyes out.

"You did that on purpose!"

"I made *you* run into *me* on purpose? Are you clinically insane?" He almost laughed. *Laughed.* "Ever thought maybe you just lack all the self awareness of a regular, decent human being?" He snapped at me, voice strained like it was an effort not to raise it. Like he wanted to scream in my face instead of reprimanding me like a puppy who had tinkled on his carpet.

His grip on my arms remained just this side of too painful, and his face really said he wanted nothing more than to just leave me there.

"What the hell is that supposed to mean? I am *incredibly* self aware!" I yelled right back. "Why are you always standing so close? Don't you have any idea what personal space is?" I tried to shove him aside but he wouldn't budge. "Cole, get out of my way, I'm not kidding around."

He ignored me and I was moments from asking him what the fuck his problem really was when I noticed the blood on his shirt.

"Oh my god, oh my god, oh my god, *oh my god,*" I gasped, pulling my hands away and inspecting the blood that now covered them.

Cole swore under his breath and looked down at his own shirt before releasing another string of curses. "Fucking great," he said through gritted teeth. Then, so loudly I actually squeaked in shock, he bellowed into the apartment around us, "*Felicity!*"

"I'm so sorry, oh my god. I've never had a bloody nose before." I tipped my head back in an effort to try and stop the bleeding, thinking back to all the movies I'd ever seen as my source of absolute truth.

He completely ignored my apology, opting to instead call out for Felicity again. She was obviously not here and that reality only seemed to make him angrier.

Cole gripped my chin roughly and brought it back down to its regular, non-tipped back position. "Are you fucking kidding me?" he said, his voice and face both conveying quite clearly that he was seconds away from snapping. "That's a wonderful thing to do if you'd like to *choke on your own blood.*" The words left his mouth a second before his face contorted into the sort expression that said, '*actually, yes, go ahead and do what you were just doing*'.

He sighed, "God, you're really not that smart, are you?"

"What are you talking about? I'm trying to stop the bleeding." I batted his hand away and accidentally got more blood on his crisp white shirt.

"God dammit, Lucky. Just— fucking stop. You have a sublime talent of making things worse than they need to be."

He finally freed one of my arms to lead me back through the maze of his apartment-mansion. I immediately noticed its absence and was grateful for the reprieve.

I was all for protesting my position here by being a few minutes late but I had bled all over the man's likely thousand dollar suit and I was still a good enough person to feel shitty over that. Even though it technically wasn't my fault, no matter how much of a bastard he was.

"I'm really sorry about your suit, Cole." My voice was muffled from behind my hands, but I saw his face when his eyes snapped back to me. There was no kindness there.

None at all.

"Please— just stop speaking," he muttered, almost like a prayer to whatever wicked god he thought to spend his time worshipping.

Cole's legs were much longer than mine, so I was practically jogging to keep up with him which made my face hurt more, but I think he knew that. I think he knew that and *liked* it.

Before I could tell him to slow down or let me the hell go, we made it into a living room space that was spread out on a sunken floor you had to descend a couple of stairs to enter. It was full of charcoal's and black's with accents of dark blues, oxblood reds and deep natural wooden fixtures.

It was completely unlike the rest of the apartment. I loved it. Truthfully, I didn't want to like anything that belonged to him, but I did really, really like this room. The floors were still the fine, luxurious marble but it's like the room gradually darkened to this centre point of a massive, incredibly comfortable looking couch. The sort of couch you looked at and thought '*yes, yes I could nap quite nicely on that couch*'.

This room stood out as an anomaly to the three other rooms I'd seen in my time here, and so far it was my favourite. Even beyond the kitchen.

Cole's grip on my other arm had increased in pressure so much I was beginning to think he was playing his own twisted game to see how far I'd let him go before I tried to rip free of his grip. I was torn between relief and anger of my own when he released me, practically throwing me onto his couch.

"Lean forward and pinch the bridge of your nose. I'll be right back. Don't get any blood on this couch." He didn't look at me as he mumbled the words, but his distaste was no less clear.

All I could do was stare at the back of him, desperately trying not to remember a time in our lives where he'd looked at me like I was *something*, not someone who he hated with every fibre of his being.

My eyes burned a little with the emotion I was determined to keep in under lock and key. It would be a cold day in hell the moment that man saw me cry. This was why I'd outright refused to think of him in the last ten years. If he happened to creep into my head I pinched myself in punishment.

He was back quickly with tissues, a small bowl and a few little packets of what looked like alcohol wipes. He knelt in front of me and placed everything on a small table that was beside the couch.

Handing me the tissues, I replaced my hands with them and held out a bloody palm for more, to soak up what had covered my hands.

He obliged wordlessly, but not before opening one of the wipe packets and cleaning my hand as best he could. I would need to wash up, but still.

Cole's hand barely touched mine, just enough to tell me not to move while he tried to be as thorough as possible. From the outside you might have thought he was being gentle. I knew better. I was positive if he held onto me in the capacity he wanted, he'd crush every bone in my hand.

Once he seemed satisfied, he placed more tissues in my grasp and I snapped my hand back as fast as possible.

"Is there any blood running down the back of your throat?" He reached over to pick up a new little wipe packet as he asked, not meeting my gaze. His voice was still quiet, but in the sort of way that spoke to restraint. Keeping himself in check.

To anyone else, it might have even sounded *tender.* If I'd learned anything since coming face to face with this new version of the boy I had known, 'tender' and 'Cole' didn't belong in the same sentence.

"No," I answered quietly, my eyes never leaving him.

"Let me have a look." His eyes finally landed on mine, and there was nothing there but a cold and brutal clarity that this man truly hated me.

I had thought there would be something, a tiny shift even, just while I was prone to bleeding all over his clean and tidy life. But no. I was looking into the eyes of a complete stranger. They were not the green that I remembered, of sage and soft grass. They were instead the brutal cut of gemstones; hard and unyielding.

"It hurts," I croaked, leaning away from him, feeling a small trickle of blood still dripping out and into the tissue.

"Obviously, I know that, Lucky," he said, every syllable was clipped and short as he gestured to his ruined suit.

"Say you won't try to hurt me more. Say it," I pressed, feeling stupid, needing some reassurance from this man that clearly wanted all the bad things to happen to me but just in a way that meant he wouldn't need to do any cleaning up.

He tipped his head back and let out the most dramatic sigh I'd ever heard.

It caught me so off guard I had to stop myself from bursting out into laughter, but then he looked back at me and said, "I won't do anything that will make it hurt more." His face looked so sincere that it took me off guard for the second time in as many seconds, and the words fell out of my mouth before I could stop them.

"Promise?" I asked.

I swear he flinched at that word. But this man wasn't the boy I had known. He wasn't even the almost-man I had fought so hard against in high school.

My stomach still dropped as that single worded question was asked, and I really did try to keep any sort of pain from my face.

He looked at me for a moment longer before wordlessly nodding just once, his lips pulled into a thin line.

Slowly, I pulled the tissues from my face, keeping my eyes squeezed tight. "Is it broken?" My voice was a whisper. "It's all crooked and out of shape isn't it? I look like Owen Wilson don't I?" My rapid succession of questions were all asked very quickly and equally as quiet, but he didn't reply to any of them and the silence had begun to get heavy.

I did the only thing I could think of and just kept talking, because *that* was always a lovely idea.

"Not that it's a bad look for him. I actually quite like it. For me though? I don't—"

I was cut off by my own hiss of pain and it was a reflex to reach out and grip his hand in both of mine, bloody tissues and all.

"*Ow, ow, ow. Cole!*" I squeezed his hand even tighter. I didn't let go, even as he lifted the alcohol wipe and started to clean away some of the blood. I held my breath the entire time until he slowly unpeeled my hands from his and I peeked out of one clamped eye. He was already looking at me.

"So?" I asked, holding my hands to my chest. "Broken?"

"It's not broken, no. Just bruised." He started to move away from me, collecting everything into the little bowl he brought and I knew that this pseudo truce between us was on its last leg.

"Thank you for your help. And I'm sorry about your shirt." I still spoke quietly, scared that if I was too loud he would snap and I would be left needing to figure out what the hell to do around him, but that was it, because when his eyes snapped up to mine the burning hate had resurfaced and I hated how it made my chest hurt.

"You're an employee under my care, I have a duty to ensure your safety while you're in my home." He stood, looking down at me from his impressive height.

That was all I needed to remind me that the person in front of me was a complete and total stranger to me. What's more was this was absolutely not what I needed right now. I stood, my back rigid and muscles tight, expecting him to step back and out of my space. Figuring he'd learned a thing or two from the blood stains on his probably overpriced shirt, but alas he stayed right where he was.

I did my absolute best to ignore the way I was completely enveloped by his smell. It was mint, but subtle, intertwined with the comforting smell of clean laundry and something crisp and masculine, like the woodsy scent of fresh mountain air. I was about two seconds away from moulding my entire body into his when I remembered *who* exactly he was.

Why I was even here.

Regardless of whatever truce had been between us it was well and truly over now, and no matter how good he smelt I would *not* voluntarily press my chest to his.

I pushed against the chest in question in both an effort to steady myself and to put some distance between us. In the same move he had grabbed my wrists in an iron grip once again, like he needed to be reminded how much stronger he was than me.

"Let go of me." The words came out as defiantly as I could manage. I cast my eyes up to his and tried to move out of his grip, but he just held on tighter.

His height really caught my attention in that moment.

Cole stood at least a head and a half taller than me, which had unequivocally *not* been the case when I saw him last in the room of our senior year science class.

In a move so fluid you'd think it was practised, he pulled my wrists behind my back, giving me no option but to be as close to him as possible. Terror flickered through my body like a spark. Not igniting, but showing that there was potential for this thing to *blow*.

"Or what, Lucky?" He leaned down towards me, "You'll quit?" He didn't stop in his movement, and my heart beat riled up with every millimetre of distance he closed between us.

His nose traced my jaw, the contact making me jump and my chest began to move faster, like somehow taking in more air would push him further away from me. He traced the length of it before releasing a low laugh that had my stomach tightening.

I'd heard him laugh before.

It was throaty and mocking, and it had made my stomach tighten deeper for completely different reasons that were astronomically out of my control. But this laugh was different from the one he had let loose when he stalked me through his apartment.

This one sounded...*disappointed*.

I scoffed, trying with all my strength to pull my wrists from his hold, ignoring the pang that sent through me like his opinions *mattered.* And maybe they did once upon a time, but they hadn't for a very, *very* long time.

All I achieved was rubbing myself against him like some crazed cat-in-heat.

"Yeah, well, you're no oil painting either, buddy." I scowled at him, doing everything in my power not to headbutt his peck.

Cole's eyes flashed back down to mine, taking in whatever he saw in my expression. It was only a second that passed between that moment and the next, when he shut himself off completely and I couldn't even see the anger that he enjoyed parading about. This man was giving me some serious motion sickness from the way his emotions changed and shifted and shut off all together. If I threw up on his shoes, he would only have himself to blame.

"The next time you decide to test the limits of this position," he went on, pulling back and sending a chill through me as cold air replaced the warmth that had radiated from his body, "I will not hesitate to hand out the appropriate punishment as a consequence of those actions."

I couldn't decide which part he meant, the tardiness or the blood on his shirt. Either way, I figured it wasn't the right moment to ask for some clarity.

Cole released my wrists and stepped back which meant I finally took a full deep breath that was absent of *him*.

"I'll take eggs today. Scrambled. A side of mushrooms and spinach. Don't dry out the fucking eggs this time, Lucky. In my study in ten minutes. You've already wasted most of the morning with," he looked at me from head to toe, scrutinising me and then flourished his hand in my direction, "whatever this was."

He turned to leave and I was sputtering, at a loss that he would just *expect*— "I don't know where your study is!" I yelled at his back, so loudly my throat burned with it. So loudly I hoped he could feel the violence in my words that I felt in my body.

"Not my problem, Navy. Nine minutes," he called back to me as he made his way out, likely in the direction I had to follow but I was taken so off guard I didn't even think to pay attention.

Instead, I stood in his fancy as shit living room, wondering what in the flaming pits of hell just happened, where the fuck the kitchen was, and how on *earth* any of what just happened would even qualify as sticking it to the man.

The worst part was the lump in my throat I couldn't quite swallow at the undeniable truth that my luck, whatever I'd managed to hold onto, had well and truly run out.

13

Cole

I tapped my pen rapidly against the notepad in front of me, knowing that even if I tried to enter back into the meeting I'd have absolutely no idea where we were at.

Lucky had been at the apartment last Wednesday evening, and it surprised me. I had expected her to call in sick, do or say something about what happened the morning before, or put together some excuse to get out of work for the day because of the whole bloody nose ordeal. Something that would mean I'd have to drag her ass from whatever hidey-hole she'd popped herself in after her less than graceful descent from the top.

But she didn't.

She wasn't even late and it made my teeth grind.

I'd arrived back at the apartment for lunch and went straight to the kitchen, keeping my steps light, so that she wouldn't know I had come straight for her.

It was sort of fucked up, but I'd wanted to catch her off guard. Instead, I found myself stuck in the shadows of one of the many doorways that led to that part of my home and watched her as she worked. She'd taken the time to clean herself up but she was in the same clothes as she'd been this morning. The only note that something had happened was the slight bruising that started to arise under her eyes.

I clenched my fist to stop it from flying through the wall beside me. I'd expected puffy eyes. A total inability to do anything, but there she was, moving about with the sort of ease and grace a dancer would have on stage. I half anticipated I'd catch her doing something to the food, something that would give me the opportunity to deliver the sort of punishment I had promised, but she didn't even double dip her tasting spoons.

Did this girl ever fucking give up? Her perfect attentiveness made a frustrated noise work up and out of my throat.

The noise caught her attention and her eyes snapped up and met with mine. But they couldn't see me, hidden as I was.

A slight frown marred her features even as her attention was pulled to another of her tasks. I knew that I'd thrown her off, that she might be feeling like someone was watching her, waiting, and the thought fed that same sick part of me that had salivated at hunting her through the apartment.

I didn't say a single thing to her when I finally strolled into the kitchen. She didn't speak to me either, only placed the meal down before me with a gentleness she hadn't exhibited the last time she served me, and went back to clean up. She was gone by the time I turned around.

When I arrived back for dinner her bruising had settled in

more under her eyes, but it wasn't as bad as I thought it would be, looking like it would clear in a few days.

To put it plainly, it looked like someone had clocked Lucky square in the face, and I wouldn't put it past her to try and one up me in any way she could. I knew her, and I wouldn't put lowering herself to that level past her. I *was* blackmailing her, after all.

With a quick message off to Felicity to make a note of what had happened, I took a seat, phone still in hand, and waited for her to serve me my dinner. I wanted her every waking moment spent paying attention to me, while never giving her the time of day. I wanted her nervous, on edge, unsure. I wanted her *scared* of what might come next, her palms sweating and stomach churning.

I wanted her to feel the way that I had.

I relished the dizzying thrill of power that still lingered every time I took a meal, the same exact feeling I had that first moment I saw her standing in my kitchen.

Her cooking was undoubtedly delicious. But I knew it would be. She was an incredible cook, and though my distaste for her was palpable, I couldn't apply the same sourness I felt towards her to her food. There was a reason she was who she was, why she'd developed the name for herself that she had.

That was a week ago.

And so here I sat, a week later, letting Lucky feel nothing but my very worst emotions on the two days she'd worked after the...incident. Trying so hard to pretend she didn't exist at all while hardly even tasting the food she had made.

Here I sat wondering why, on one of the two days of the work week I now looked forward to simply because they would spare me from her company, I was wondering what she was doing. It was pathetic.

It seemed wrong to me, now that she had been *dropped* in my fucking lap after all these years, after every attempt to remove her from my mind, that she experienced nothing but the same. I wanted her to be miserable. She deserved nothing more.

The way she got under my skin made me want to peel it off my bones just so she had nowhere to hide. I could picture the rapid rise and fall of her chest, hear the air moving past her lips as I dragged my nose along her jaw. As I felt the shiver wrack her body.

I wanted her to be faced with just exactly what I could do to her, beyond what I had already done. But to have that control over her, I needed to be around her and the last thing I wanted was to be was close to her.

That was a lie, and I hated her for it.

The pen I had been holding snapped under the pressure of my grip. As I found the blank note pad in front of me suddenly soaked with black ink and seeping into the cuff of my navy suit every head snapped to me.

"Mr. Thompson? Are you alright?" Felicity asked me from my right, her eyes on me along with every other member of the board.

Smart, respectable business men and women who assisted me in not only reviewing and analysing new potential investments, but also reviewing current investments and making sure that they were still performing in a way that was profitable to the business.

If there was a restaurant, club, bar, hell it could even be your grandmother's kitchen, if it was worth a dime in this entire country I likely had a hand in it, one way or another.

Thompson & Co was not only the door you wanted to get your foot into, but we were the people you wanted to impress. I had worked damn hard to build the empire that surrounded me and I was proud of it.

I pulled myself back into the present and willed the darkness from my features that I knew they were all seeing, knew they were all wondering what was *off* about me. Wondering what was so unsettling about me.

I took in the mess before me again, using it as an excuse to move the moment along. "Well, the secret is out. I, in fact, *do* have superhuman strength." I shrugged one shoulder in a gesture of knowing there was nothing I could do about being found out.

The members of the board released small chuckles, visibly relaxing. "It's nice to know our theories were correct, Cole," Drew, one of my many external advisers, chimed with a smirk on his face.

"You've made some of us very rich today," Sandra, the director of my company and quite literally one of the nicest people I'd ever met, added her two cents.

I gave them my best bored expression. "You're all hilarious."

My dry humour only made them laugh more until I adopted a small smile to soften my features.

"But in all seriousness, I will have to cut this one short. I'm sorry for not being completely present today, I—"

The rest of the sentence didn't make it out of my mouth, for no other reason than the fact that I literally had nothing to say to them. I mean, what? Imagine if I spoke the truth: *'I was distracted by a woman I hate so much I've actually blackmailed her - yes, me - into working for me because she was one of two reason for the miserable and outright shittiness that was my life growing up and she actively tried her best to always make it worse, to make me fail, to watch me fall, day in and day out for years and now...well, now that I have her exactly where I had always wished for her to be I'm realising that I would very much like to have her beneath me in more ways than she already is. I want her to hurt. I want her to suffer.'*

Ah, yes. Perfect. That wouldn't be alarming at all.

I cleared my throat, "If you'll all excuse me." Everyone stood with me, murmuring things about not needing to apologise, and that most of what we were there to discuss could wait.

Thanking them all one last time, I turned my attention to Felicity, "Flick, you can finish early today. I won't be needing you this evening."

"Are you sure, sir?"

"Quite." I smiled at her warmly, because she was really a great kid. Felicity was the daughter of one of my college professors, Fyn Bennett, or Benny as he went by. Someone who had taken me in and treated me like family. Who still treated me like family.

I remembered when Felicity was a kid, twelve years old and sitting in at the lectures her father used to do when they were after her school pick up. Front row and notepad at the ready.

She was working as my assistant now as a way to pay her own bills, while actively shadowing me, learning all the tricks of the trade and the power of investing. She was an incredibly bright young woman who had fast tracked it through high school and was now studying at university. She reminded me a lot of my older brother, Brooks, in that way.

The mere thought of him made me realise that it had been

well over a couple months since we last spoke. Even longer since I'd seen him. I'd eagerly ignored his last two phone calls and had made a point to forget to call him back.

Pulling the door open to the meeting room, I strode straight for the elevators. My phone was to my ear the next moment, calling my driver. That made me sound like a pompous prick but there's really no way to say you had a driver without sounding like you had a stick of relative size up your ass.

He picked up on the first ring, his gruff voice scraping through the line, "Sir?"

"John, I told you to just call me Cole. I'm pretty sure I'm about thirty years younger than you," I murmured as I stepped into the elevator.

"Appreciate you pointing that out once again, Sir," he shot back with the same dry sarcasm that made up my own sense of humour.

I barked a laugh and made a woman, who I hadn't realised was in the lift with me, let out a shriek. My head whipped towards her. "Sorry, I didn't see you there," I said to her, urging a look of apology onto my face.

Her face scrunched up like she'd all of a sudden smelt something pungent and as soon as the doors opened she strode out muttering something about incorrigible youths under her breath.

"I'm on my way out now," I said to John as a farewell before ending the call and sliding my phone back into the inside pocket of my jacket.

My shoes made a soft tapping noise as I strode through the lobby of the building and I slid my hands into the pockets of my slacks, nodding in simultaneous greeting and farewell to the staff. I'd made it a point to know the people that worked for me, no matter their job title.

"Afternoon Mr. Thompson," Maria, one of our lobby receptionists, called out as I passed by.

"Maria." I smiled before altering my path, taking the three long strides to the desk. "How did Alexandra's dance recital go?"

"Oh, she did amazing!" Maria beamed at me. "Thank you for asking. She's a lot younger than the other girls but has twice the stage presence," she went on, her words dripping with the obvious pride she had for her daughter.

"I'm pleased to hear it. Don't forget to take a break every now and then, alright? You guys work too hard down here." I tapped the top of the receptionist desk before lifting my hand in a final farewell.

Maria's quiet laughter followed me as I made for the exit of the building.

"Holding the fort, Frankie?" I squeezed the shoulder of our longest standing doorman. Frank had been at the building longer than I'd owned it, and was one of four gentlemen that stood at attention at its doors every week. Some people might have thought doormen were outdated, but they added the sort of personal touch that major corporations lacked. I wanted people to feel at ease when they arrived at this building, at any of my buildings. No matter the city, state or country.

"Absolutely, Sir." Frank tipped his hat towards me.

"Cole is fine, Frank," I corrected him, pulling open the door. "Have a good one. I'll see you later," I called back as the door shut behind me.

The weather outside had turned and the first drops of a storm had begun to descend as I kept my unhurried pace heading for the car.

COLE

"John," I said by way of greeting as he stood under an umbrella with the car door open and waiting.

"Sir." He nodded back.

I couldn't help the lift at the corner of my mouth at the stubbornness of this man. He had been in my employ for the last five years and not once did he crack on the name thing. He always gave the classic response every time I asked him how many more times did I have to tell him to call me Cole - *'At least one more time, Sir'*.

The door closed with a soft thud and I pulled my phone out, my knee bouncing rapidly, as I flicked through my contacts and found my brother's name. Sucking in a deep breath and letting it out slowly, I undid the top two buttons of my shirt before tapping his name and running a hand through my hair. It rang three times before his voice poured over the line.

"Cole?" He said my name like a question, like he was sure the call was a butt dial or something equally more likely than me actually picking up the phone and intentionally calling him back.

"Hey, Brooks." My voice was soft and I could hear the faint echoes of a little boy's laughter somewhere on the other end of the line.

"I didn't think you would actually return my call," he huffed, a door clicking closed behind him, the laughter ending abruptly.

"Small miracles I guess." You could hear the smile in my voice, though I was sure I was the only one who knew it was forced.

I loved my brother, but he had always held the same expectations as my mother. Though that wasn't what got to me anymore. What got to me still was how he felt like he was responsible for my success. *All* of my success.

Brooks had a family of his own now. He had a couple of great kids and a beautiful wife, Laura, and I would have loved nothing more than to leave him to that life he had and never set foot in it again. But our mother passed away a few years ago and overnight he felt like it was his responsibility to make sure we didn't lose touch regardless of the fact that I hadn't spoken to her since the day I left our hometown.

I knew that he knew that but I went along with it because even though I hated him, I loved him too.

Riddle me that.

"Well, I'm glad. When are you going to come over for dinner? Soon? I know the kids would love to see you. Laura, too." He asked the question in the sort of way that didn't allow space for any other response than one that agreed with his assumption.

"Yeah, soon." I had no intention of doing that whatsoever. He had a really nice way of making me feel singularly alone, whether he meant to or not. Brooks was a good husband, and a good father. But a good brother?

I watched the buildings and people move by the window of the car, all rushing from one spot to the next in a desperate attempt to avoid the rain. "How are you?"

"I'm great, actually. The firm is doing well. We've won seven out of ten cases in the last two months, so no complaints there."

Brooks was a human rights lawyer and I'd made sure that whatever I had ended up doing with my life was nothing like the path he'd chosen.

"That's great to hear."

The line went quiet for a bit while we both tried to figure

out what else there even was to say, and I don't know why I did it, but Lucky's name first came to my mind, then fell out of my mouth.

"I ran into Lucky Peters."

I didn't *run into her*.

"You're kidding!" he bellowed in laughter on the other end and I pulled the phone from my ear slightly. "Little Lucky Peters, I haven't heard that name in years. God, she was a bit of a firecracker growing up, wasn't she?"

I frowned. "No."

I wasn't sure what I was expecting. Maybe I thought he would have shared the same sentiments as me? That he knew how clearly she had fucked me over? How much she'd loved doing it? Assuming that was stupid though, because no one had known.

"Yeah, you two always had a bit of a thing since you were kids, didn't you?"

"No." I clenched my hand into a tight fist, still looking out the window but no longer seeing past the water droplets as they made their descent down the glass.

"Yes you did. You two were thick as thieves whenever we would—"

"Brooks," I snapped in warning from between clenched teeth. I had never regretted anything as much as I had by bringing her name up in a conversation with my brother.

I hated that *he* was now thinking of *her*. I hated that he was thinking of her in the same way as everyone else. As someone to cherish, someone who had been worth the luck she had never earned. Mostly, I just hated that he was thinking of her at all.

"So, are you seeing her again?" he asked, like he'd sooner

have *her* over for dinner than me.

I remembered him being close with a couple of her siblings. It was that alone that drove my reply. It was stupid, and childish. Brooks was my brother, and happily married. But he needed to know that she was *mine.* Mine to ruin, mine to torment, mine to break.

"Tomorrow." *Fucking dammit, Cole.*

"Oh, hey! Got a date? So, no more bad blood between the two of you, eh?" He chuckled like this was some joke between pals and completely contradicting himself from his last 'thick as thieves' statement.

"Something like that." *Nothing like that at all.*

"You'll both have to come over then, I'd love to see Little Lucky Peters again! See how Oaks is getting on."

Over my dead fucking body.

"Sure thing, Brooks," I said, reigning myself in, looking at the last five minutes of conversation and wondering what had even gone on inside my own brain. Why it even mattered that he asked about her when I had been the one to bring her up in the first place.

"Anyway," I said when John pulled up outside my building, "I have to run."

"We'll talk soon! I want to hear how things go with Lucky." He sounded elated. I wonder if he'd sound so happy if he really knew how things were going with *Little Lucky Peters*.

"Sure," I said instead.

I ended the call, running my hand through my hair again. Well, no doubt about it, two months was nowhere near long enough between phone calls.

14

Cole

12 years ago. Aged 16.

The crack of my mothers palm connecting with my cheek assaulted my ears before the pain registered.

Crack. A second time.

Crack. A third.

I knew what to expect. The sting was sharp at first and turned into a burning that made the entire right side of my face feel like it was on fire. My eyes pricked at the sensation no matter how much I willed them not to. No matter how many times she hit me.

"You *stupid* boy," my mother seethed, spit flying from her mouth and landing on my face.

When I looked at her now I had to remind myself that she hadn't always been like this. That she had *loved* me once. She had tucked me in at night and pushed my hair from my forehead and told me I could be anything I wanted to be.

I think I hated both her and myself in equal parts for that. Her for saying it, and me for believing her.

"How many times have I told you? Don't leave your shit around the fucking house for me to clean up, you useless boy. I've been cleaning up after you and your brother all your lives. At least he had the sense to do something *good* with the opportunities I worked to give him. What have you done? *What have you done?*" She was heaving, her body small and too skinny with the scent of stale booze on her breath. "You disappoint me every single day, you know that Cole?" She gave a shove to my chest before she stormed off to a different room of the house, the flick of a lighter sounded shortly after, along with the sound of the television.

My mother used to be beautiful. I wasn't sure what she was now.

When Brooks had lived at home I would hear them fight sometimes. I didn't remember it being like this, but I also struggled to remember much from even the years he *had* been home. He'd always make me go upstairs before things got too intense, and sure, I knew that she had liked to drink at parties and barbecues, but never like this.

I didn't think it mattered as much, because she hadn't seemed so sad then. So *angry*.

I couldn't tell you what changed, but when Brooks left it was like something in her snapped. The only time she ever tolerated me in the last four years was when I showed any inkling of following in the footsteps of my brother, showed any potential at being more than what I was. He had fast tracked his way through high school, obtained every scholarship he had applied for and hightailed it out of here without so much as a goodbye.

I'd always thought he was just naturally smart, that he was one of those people that was born a genius. In the last four years I'd come to learn that maybe he worked his ass off to get the hell out of here because of *her*. Because even though I was only seeing this version of my mother now, maybe it was the version he'd always known and in the end, staying with me hadn't been enough of a reason to stay at all.

I looked down at the class roster in my hand, the entire reason for the exchange with my mother. It had been sitting amongst the papers of my homework that was scattered over the kitchen table and she had seen it on her way to the kitchen to refill whatever poison of choice was available today.

I could have worked in my room, I had a desk up there but I always needed more space. Space to learn more, to read more, to try and *be* more. Maybe if she saw me there, working my ass off every single morning and every single night that it might be enough. I didn't think she really cared, to be honest. I think that it was the only thing that she could latch onto that she could use against me.

What else could I possibly do with my time? I couldn't get a part time job because then I couldn't study. I couldn't do sports because we couldn't afford it. I couldn't have any friends because I needed to be here, cleaning up the house and making sure I was around in case she needed someone to scream at. Someone to hit.

It was a stupid fucking piece of paper and it made me want to claw my way up and out of my own skin. Lucky's name sat above mine, just as it had done every semester for the last four years. She was relentless in her climb to the top, and every single time she reached the end of whatever metaphorical race we were in before me she always looked back, always made sure to see that I was watching.

Her over-satisfied face was the last thing I saw every night before I drifted off to sleep. It's the very thing that mocked me in my dreams, chasing away the hope of getting any peaceful rest.

Peace.

All I wanted was some fucking *peace*.

God and she loved it. Her face lit up every single time I fell a little farther and for what? What point was she trying to make?

Sometimes I'd stare at her and wonder if she knew. If she knew just how badly I needed a win, how much I needed to succeed and I wondered if she did what she did because she wanted to see me fail. Because she hated me *that* much.

'Lucky Peters. Why can't you be like her, Cole?'

'The Peters' youngest is quite remarkable, you could learn something from her, Cole.'

Lucky, Lucky, Lucky, fucking Lucky.

My mother used to say it all to me when Brooks left. When she still went to the barbecues that our families attended together. When she would hear news about how Lucky was doing at school, at the strides she was making. The first time she'd said that to me I'd been devastated. I'd never needed to be anything but what I was, and then suddenly it was no longer good enough. It was like as soon as Brooks had left, there was nothing left to be proud of, nothing left to show for her own life except for her last son who wasn't quite making the cut of whatever imaginary bar she had set and refused to tell me how high it was.

I was twelve at the time and as soon as she'd said it I bawled my eyes out like a baby. I'd wanted to talk to Lucky about it, I'd *needed* her desperately. The safety of her presence and the solace I'd always found in her company. I was waiting for her, harrowed by everything I couldn't understand and knowing I just needed to *see* her, but the moment her voice sounded from behind me...it was the first time I'd ever felt rage. I'd never hated anyone so much in that moment because she'd always been loved, and she was the reason I no longer was. She'd always been praised, and for what? Being the seventh child born into a family that was arguably too big?

Be more like Lucky. Be better like Lucky.

It was the mantra that played in my mind on an infinite cycle.

Sometimes I would see her and I'd forget, just for a second, what she had done to my life. What she continued to do to me. I'd see bright blue eyes, long blonde hair, pigtails and a hot pink *Barbie* pool. I'd see her hand in mine in pinky swears. But it lasted all of a second before every memory I had of her was doused in gasoline and set alight.

How could she not know? How couldn't she fucking *know?*

My mother wasn't a big woman. She wasn't particularly strong or brutal, but every single time I thought about fighting back, be it with my hands or my words, I froze. Like a deer in headlights I just *froze*. My tongue wouldn't work, my body wouldn't move. I was completely helpless until she left. It was because of that that there were always marks on my body.

Always.

I hated myself every time for letting it happen, but I'd always hate Lucky more.

I had a calendar on the inside of my locker at school that

tracked the days left until I could leave, and then I would finally be just like my brother. I would leave and I'd never come back.

I wonder if she'd finally love me then?

15

Lucky

The sound of my alarm pierced my skull like an ice pick and I woke up in flight mode. With the blankets wrapped around me in some sort of Celtic knot looking contraption, I flopped unceremoniously to the ground, groaning like a labouring cow as the only things that softened my fall were my lady melons.

It had been a long two weeks.

Last night Cole hadn't returned home to receive his dinner until the early hours of the morning.

I'm talking *after fucking midnight*.

After cooking, I'd busied myself with reading the two latest articles from *Acquired Taste* that had come about unexpectedly and only a single week apart. I sent through my comprehensive feedback on it to Melody and eventually fell asleep on the kitchen floor only to be woken from a less than gentle kick to the thigh.

"Why are you sleeping on the floor of my kitchen?" Cole looked down at me with a scowl in place, and the light of the kitchen illuminating behind him casting him in complete shadow.

My hair had fallen out of the bun I had put it in and blonde strands fluttered down and around my face. I tried to pull myself from the groggy disorientation that came with falling asleep under bright lights in a crazy man's kitchen. Knowing that, it didn't surprise me at all looking back thinking that I was peering up at some beautiful silhouette of the devil.

"Who?" I mumbled, though I wasn't totally sure that's what I said.

"Get off the kitchen floor, Lucky." He took a step back and I rubbed my eyes and slapped my cheeks a couple times to wake myself up.

Reaching up to the counters, I groaned as I got to my feet. My eyes nearly fell out of my face when I caught the time on the fancy wall-touch-screen-phone thing..

"It's quarter past twelve... in the morning," I muttered to myself in disbelief, but of course Cole thought I was speaking to him.

"Mmm. So you can imagine how hungry I am, and every minute that there isn't food in my mouth is another minute overtime you owe me." He snapped a napkin out and placed it over his knee.

"*Overtime?*" I'm not proud of it, but I shrieked. I did.

He lifted his hand to swipe a pinky in his ear, likely to stifle the second shriek that followed the first.

"Are you kidding me? *It's literally the next day.* It's Saturday morning."

When he was sure I wasn't going to damage his eardrum further, he removed his finger and gestured to the table in front of him.

"You know," he said, like he was really about to share some enlightening, life-changing truth with me, "what I find so interesting is that there is *still* no food in front of me. What's more, is that you were also sleeping on the floor of my kitchen instead of prepping for my arrival and that you now owe me," he checked his watch, "about six minutes of free labour."

I stared at him and my hand twitched with the desire to slap him. I wanted to see a red hand print on his pretty face and see if he thought this entire situation was still entertaining then. I'd certainly find it about eighty percent improved.

But I didn't.

Ugh, my life story.

It hurt me to do it, but I cleared my throat, fixed my hair all as he sat there, staring at the table in front of him, still as a statue. I opened my mouth to kill him with kindness when he spoke over me.

"Seven minutes of free labour." He cut his gaze towards me before relaxing back into his seat, his legs spreading wide under the table like he had the biggest set of balls on him that had likely ever grown on a man.

"You're a real asshole, you know that?" I snapped.

"Oop. Let's make that eight minutes now for the loose tongue," he quipped, never moving his gaze from mine.

I can't say what exactly came over me, but I stomped my foot down like I'd seen one of my nieces do on many occasions and stalked back to the kitchen, knowing for the first time in my adult life why some people just never grew out of tantrums. I wanted to break every plate in this damned kitchen, and smash every pot against his stupid fucking marble floors.

I had made a creamy chicken pasta for dinner, with a side of garlic bread. It sounded delicious, and it had been...about six hours ago. I couldn't care less if it didn't taste fresh and all melty-in-the-mouth, and I couldn't care even *less* than that if the garlic bread was so tough that he had to rip at it like a rabid dog.

I reheated everything and stalked over to drop the food in front of Cole before heading straight to get my bag and get out of his weird little power-move makeshift jail.

The real cherry on top was how he so callously called out to me as I headed for the elevator, his voice settling over me like it crept along the walls and cast a web over my head, "Drive safe, Lucky!" His laughter wrapped around each syllable as I tapped the call button furiously and flipped off the apartment with both hands as the elevator doors closed before me.

That was only a single, painful example of just one night of every single day I had worked in the last couple weeks. Sometimes he was earlier and got in around ten, and sometimes, like last night, he arrived after one in the morning. I had a suspicion that he wasn't actually working late. That he was just punishing me for Gordon-Ramsay-fucking-knew what.

There had been one evening that he'd made me recook the entire meal. I hadn't even had enough ingredients in the fridge and then he had the audacity to tell me just how awful it was. He was making my life hell and loving every minute of it.

"Lucky!" My mother called from downstairs.

My parents had been back now for a couple of weeks and they were all Caribbean tans and optimism as the chilly start of October greeted us, and everything turned from flowers and sunny days in tank tops to pumpkin spice flavoured things (no thanks) and scarves that were also beanies (genius).

"Lucky, your brothers are here!" She called again.

It was Saturday and I'd slept all day. By the time I got home it was just past two in the morning and I had only the energy to kick my jeans off my legs before being consumed by my beautiful, deliciously soft bedding. With a final request to Siri to set an alarm for five in the afternoon, thinking I would be up well before then, sleep dug her enticing claws into me and dragged me down, down, down.

I groaned again, trying to yell back to my mother with something that resembled 'I'm coming!' or maybe 'one second!', but it could have been pig-Latin for all the clarity it held. I ended up just staying there, still tightly wound in the Celtic knot of my sheets and staring at the fibres in the carpet on my bedroom floor. I'd begun spiralling on the shocking reality that this carpet had been in this room since I could remember and I'd never once thought to clean it beyond a weekly vacuum when my bedroom door burst open.

"Oh, wow," my brother James, or Jamie as I'd always called him, said behind his hand as he leant on the door frame and tried desperately not to laugh, "how the mighty have fallen." He must have decided it was just too good to enjoy all on his own. "Oaks!" he called down the hall.

"Yo," Oakleigh sauntered up just as he was readjusting his baseball cap on backwards. "What's—Woah," he said, acknowledging my situation.

"You know," I started, moving my head so I could see them both clearly without straining my eyes, "I could have been naked when you burst in here. You both would have never been the same." I huffed, making no attempt to try and get up.

"You forget, Lucky Number Seven, that we," Jamie gestured between himself and Oakleigh, "used to change your dirty diapers."

"*Okay!*" I scrunched my face up. "Point made."

They both kept staring at me for a moment longer before Jamie spoke up again, "You alright, kid?"

Jamie was my eldest brother, sure, but he and I were also the closest. By the time I came along he was eight years old, but he had never been too cool to be my older brother.

"I wonder if the scene before you answers that question without need for a verbal response." I muttered, tucking my chin to my chest and trying to lift my blankets over my head without any success.

"Alright, that'll do it," Oaks said as they both walked into the room and pulled me up onto my feet. "Have a shower and come down, everyone's almost here and we're going to enjoy this Peters' barbecue like our lives depend on it," he said, not an ounce of sarcasm to be seen or heard.

I saluted him back in earnest, "Aye aye, Captain."

"At ease." Oaks flicked my nose and made for the exit of my room. "Catch you downstairs, Jamie," he tossed back to our eldest sibling.

"I'm good." I smiled my most toothy grin at him and gave him a single thumbs up while my other hand still held onto my blankets.

"Yeah, well I believe you about thirty percent. But I'll drop it for now because I think this conversation needs more time than the two minutes between now and your shower. I'll meet you downstairs and you can tell me all about this new fan-dangle job that Mum and Dad can't stop going on about."

"No one says fan-dangle, you elder." I smiled at the back of his head as he made his way out of my room and I trailed behind, aiming for the bathroom.

"They should." He started counting out all the points on his fingers, "It's unique, multi-functional, it's—"

"Alright, I get it. You're hip. One with the youth," I cut him off as he made it to the stairs and I kept going for the bathroom. "I tremble at the presence of your greatness, yadda-yadda-*yadda*."

I closed the door as his bark of laughter followed him in his descent to where the rest of our family had begun to arrive.

"Oh, you guys would have loved it. I really feel like a Peters' Family Cruise is in our future," my mother all but cried into her salad as she finished recalling for the umpteenth time just how beautiful their trip was.

"I'm not sure I'd do too well on the water," Riley said around a bite of her burger.

"They have all sorts of pills for that now, Riles. You'd be fine," Addie piped in while she cut up three burger patties into bite sized pieces for the triplets.

All while May's son, Jasper, just kept smooshing his hand into a puddle of tomato sauce and proceeded to lick it off. He'd been doing that since she'd put the plate down in front of him and no one questioned it when she just topped up the sauce and kept eating her own food.

"Needs must," she said by way of explanation anyway around a weary sigh. Both Kate and Addie nodded in unison and genuine understanding. It was weird when they did that triplet thing.

Riley cut Addie a scathing look that told her to can it. She just didn't like large bodies of water. "It's called Thalassaphobia, and it's a very, *very* real thing. Why do you think Arthur and I have kept our travels on the road? As in, *on land."* Riley educated us at every opportunity. She'd even made us do those online quizzes that tell you whether or not you had the phobia.

"How is Arthur, sweetheart?" my mum asked gently, nothing but love in her eyes. "I thought you'd bring him over." Arthur was Riley's cat, not her boyfriend, or husband, or life partner. Her cat.

Arthur was a rescue, he was also a Maine Coon which none of us had known until he just didn't stop growing and Riley was convinced he would turn into some small jungle cat and eat her. She conveyed this exact concern quite eloquently during a FaceTime call when she was somewhere on the opposite side of the country on a solo van tour and realised that she was sharing a bed with a cat that was taking up the same amount of space as a small human. She'd been frantic and Kate still had a video of the entire mental breakdown on her phone that she took over my shoulder. He was massive and the absolute best, most tame animal ever.

I wasn't a cat person but, my god, Arthur was magnificent. The cat did his business *in the toilet.* I'm talking, hands free, no muss, no fuss, no litter box. Arthur was better behaved than every child in this family, maybe except for Phoebe, who was the youngest of Addie's triplets. I had a soft spot for little Phoebs. I think we bonded over being the last arrivals of a large group and it was something no one else could quite grasp.

"That cat gives me hives. I'm glad she left him behind," Oakleigh mumbled into his burger. It was promptly followed by a "Hey!" as he was pretty much stoned with a hoard of burger bun tops, covered in a range of different sauces and cheese types. "What the fuck guys?"

He proceeded to take note of all the places sauce had stained his clothes while May pointed an accusatory sausage at our brother. "You keep those awful words out of this wholesome barbecue. Arthur is a family treasure and you know it."

"Amen," I said at the same time as Kate.

"Yeah, what the fuck, Oaks?" came from Addie.

"You bastard," Jamie said with a horrified look on his face.

"I'll thank you all to watch your language, please." Mum frowned at all of us, earning a chorus of poorly harmonised apologies.

We sat eating in a heavy silence for a while before dad rustled the paper, reminding us all that he was still in fact present. Peering over the top of his reading material, his glasses on the end of this nose. "Jasper!" he gasped in alarm at the six year old who was covered in tomato sauce, proceeding to scoop up more and gel his curly black hair into a mohawk.

"Sweet heavens," our mother gasped in horror and it was the final point to send us all over the edge into hysterical laughter and all but erased her previous reprimanding.

By the end everyone had dispersed and it was just Jamie and I left in the dining room cleaning up. And by cleaning up I mean that he watched on with a concerned look on his face while I was on the floor, trying to remove the dried sauce from the grout.

"I mean, would it kill you to help out?" I pouted up at my older brother.

"It very well could, yes," he responded without a hint of sarcasm. "Besides, it's always easy to talk about hard things when you're focused on something else."

That made me pause for a second, but I willed my hands to keep cleaning in hopes that I wouldn't need to explain my current life situation. It was a temporary 'owie' on my road to success. I would happily confess all the details when they had come to pass, but I was handling everything just fine.

"I have nothing hard to talk about, Jamie," I mumbled with my attention tracked on the floor.

"Oh, I beg to differ. Mum said you've been home midnight and onwards from work for the last couple weeks," he challenged.

"I have been working late, yes, but I fail to see how that's a bad thing?" I quipped back, determined to help the conversation come to a quick end as fast as I could.

"Navy Grace, I smell a lie on you," he chided in only the way an older sibling that acted like more of a parent could.

"You're totally not allowed to middle name me. This situation doesn't call for that sort of reprimanding," I scoffed. I sat on my heels and looked up at him, feeling like I was a six year old looking up at my teenage brother while he blamed me for the cookies I had eaten on his bed.

He took a deep breath and pinched the bridge of his nose. "Look, okay. I'll level with you. I'm worried." He looked down at me and took another deep breath. "You're all gold stars and happy days but your life changed almost overnight. And now, after a whole year, you're out into the early hours of the morning and—" he paused, "and I know about the bruises you had on your face."

"My *what*?!" I gasped in alarm and stood up. "How do you know about that?" My voice was all whisper shouting now, mindful that Oaks was just in the next room doing.

"Are you spying on me? Oh no." Horror now laced my words. "Are there *cameras* in this house?" I ended up regular-whispering the last bit, clutching onto my imaginary pearls.

"What? Lucky, no." He sounded exasperated. "Sophie saw you at the grocery store," he explained. Sophie, his very lovely, newly pregnant wife who was currently at home, sleeping off the morning sickness that had hit her hard, no matter the time of day.

"Sophie," I echoed, cursing myself for not thinking that I might run into that saint of a woman at the grocery store that was near my parents house. It was also coincidentally *their* grocery store. She was sensible, with her doe eyes and softly curled brown hair. Of course she would have seen me, likely clutching her *own* pearls and ran to Jamie in terror-stricken concern immediately.

"So, is there anything you wanted to tell me now?" He looked at me, knowing he had cornered me.

It was a sticky spot, yes, but I could work it. He might hand me my ass after the fact but I was still firmly on the need-to-know basis.

"Alright." I cleared my throat, "My new job has...weird hours."

"Weird hours?" He arched an eyebrow at me, letting me know that I absolutely needed to do better.

"Yeah, well," I tried to think about how to word this best, "I work for a very busy, very *important*," literally had to stop my burger from coming up at that, "...man."

"You work for a busy, important man who makes you work until the early hours of the morning?" he asked, his face slowly turning into a mask of horror.

"Yes, Jamie. I work weird hours for a very busy, important man." I beamed up at him. Nailed it.

"Oh my god, Lucky. Are you...are you trying to tell me that your boss is...he's *making you* stay late to...to..." His eyes were about to fall out of his head.

"What?" I frowned at him, and then it hit me. I had given Jamie the impression that this man's kitchen pans were not the only thing I was warming. "Oh, what? *What?!* God, Jamie, no! No. *No*," I sputtered, my face turning bright red.

"Lucky, no, this is okay. I can help you. What..who..." He was sputtering now while trying to remain calm.

"Oh sweet grief, Jamie. That is absolutely not what's happening. I have to stay late because my contract stipulated I must remain at the place of work until he arrives home to be served dinner. He works...late." There was no keeping the distaste from my voice on that one.

"Oh." He looked at me like this entire conversation had taken years off his life. I knew without a doubt that once he got his shit together he'd have marched right up to that stupid apartment and squeaked his own way right into Cole's personal space bubble. Maybe then the man in question would see just how important it was to not always stand so close to people.

But he didn't know it was Cole, though the idea of sending my big, scary older brother up there didn't sound too bad.

Jamie was about half a head taller than Cole, with the same blonde hair and blue eyes as me. He was a big guy and had made his living working as security for a number of high profile people and events before starting his own business that now provided the same service. He had some pretty insane stories to tell though. One of my claims to fame growing up was that he was security on not one, but *two* world tours for my favourite band, *Lady Luck.* He had Wyatt Smith's number in his phone. *In his fucking phone.* If I thought about it too much I'd cry.

"Oh," he repeated, slumping back onto a chair that was luckily devoid of sauce and cheese.

I mean, from his perspective I knew what this looked like. Bruised face, late hours, weird and choppy explanation. My own face softened at that and I walked up to my brother, reaching for his hand.

"Hey, sorry, I didn't mean to worry you. I *am* fine, really. It's actually great pay even though the hours are about as pleasant as being tasered. I had a 'Lucky Feeling' about this one, so I'm seeing where it goes."

He looked at my face for a while longer before a reassured smile ghosted his own and he stood, pulling me forward into a hug that turned very quickly into a headlock.

I was laughing so hard I almost peed as I tried every which way to get out of his hold. "Okay, okay I am going to piss all over your shoes, I'm tapping out."

Jamie grinned at me, that sort of pride knowing he could still outmatch his baby sister glinting in his eyes. I wasn't going to highlight that I was a third of his weight and the top of my head hit his sternum. "Who do you work for anyway?"

"If I just said a very busy and important man, would you

drop it?" I cringed, turning away from him.

"Nope." I could feel his eyes burning holes into the back of my head. I had wanted to avoid this, but I suppose it was the final piece to dropping it. Jamie would let the entire family know and they would make a massive deal about it. I just had to pray he didn't inform them until at least I had left the vicinity.

Turning back to face him, I squared my shoulders. "Cole."

Jamie frowned back at me. "Cole?"

"Cole Thompson." I clarified.

His face lit up like a freaking Christmas tree, "As in, your single-digits boyfriend turned high school sweetheart, Cole?"

"Um, I'm not sure where you got that information from but it's all entirely false. Yes, Cole as in Cole Thompson who I had made a small and fleeting friendship with during our many family barbecues. Who then descended to his rightful place on the throne of Hell, where he made it his life's mission to see me fail through our high school years. If that is what you meant by all of your lies then, yes. That's the one."

"Good to know you haven't held a grudge, Luck." He grinned at me, striding for the sliding door to join the rest of our family outside. "Well, well. This should be interesting."

"You better lose that smile, Jamie Peters. I am telling you this is only the case because it's convenient for *me*. I didn't even know he was going to be my boss until I arrived for the interview." I crossed my arms and conveniently left out the part where I tried to quit and then was blackmailed into remaining in his employ.

"Oh, sure." His voice was full of withheld laughter and I was moments away from trying to tackle him.

"Jamie, stop it." I practically whinge-cried out of serious frustration. "I'm serious. I actually can't stand the man. He's a total jackass." The last part of the sentence I muttered to myself but he heard anyway.

His laughter trickled through the almost closed sliding door. "Oh, of that I have no doubt."

The door closed between us and I knew what was coming. Every single member of my family knew about what had transpired between Cole and I in high school, I couldn't shut up about it on my daily recount to whoever had populated the kitchen when I walked in the door from school. Jamie might have been my biggest fan but that didn't mean he wasn't finding this entire situation as entertaining as the rest of my family were about to.

Their wild, unrestrained laughter hit me like a tidal wave, letting me know that he had spilled the beans.

"Oh, for fuck's sake," I muttered, quickly wiping up the rest of the sauce on the tiles and making a mad dash for my jacket and keys. I was *not* going to hang around here to be swarmed and interrogated by every member of my family.

Bessy's gentle embrace was exactly what I needed. Her engine purred to life and immediately began putting miles between me and all my problems, giving me at least some reprieve, some space to *breathe*, from the chaos that was about to engulf me.

16

Lucky

"Your mum called me to ask if you were sleeping with your boss," Melody said as she sipped from her takeaway coffee while we walked around our favourite park near her work. She said it so casually that I had to give her a double take.

"My *what*?" My feet stopped moving of their own accord and Melody was forced to turn and look back at me with...was that *pity*?

Cringing, she kept going, "She also called and asked that *last* weekend. I had to build up the nerve to tell you because, well, you know..." she trailed off, dropping her gaze and taking a big drink from her coffee.

Never mind that it was now almost an entire *week* after the disaster that was the Peters' Family Barbecue that I'd managed to escape only by the skin of my nose. Since that fateful day, I had avoided every phone call from every member of my family and refused to look either of my parents in the eye.

Of course I knew why she held off saying anything.

"Oh, probably because my entire family thinks I'm now sleeping with my deranged, criminally inclined high school nemesis turned employer, but *they* think the sun likely shines out his ass, so they called to ask *you* for the gossip?!" I did yell the last part.

"Yes, that's exactly right." Melody looked at me with sympathy. "If it helps, I got the impression that Meredith was actually quite happy about the reunion." She side-eyed me in the way you might side eye a pan on a stove that was too hot and spitting oil everywhere, trying to look without *really* looking, just in case some oil got into your eye.

"Can't imagine why." I rolled my eyes and released a groan before taking a sip from my own coffee.

That was a lie. I absolutely knew why.

I lopped my arm with Melody's and let my head drop back so that the sunshine was being absorbed through every pore on my face.

My entire family had been team Cole-and-Lucky when I was growing up. We were a duo that couldn't be un-duo-ed. If there was Cole, then Lucky surely followed and vice versa. Everyone had a 'person'. Whether they're your person in a super platonic sense, or your person romantically. Well, I guess you could say that for those formidable early years of my life, I had been Cole's person, and he had been mine.

My stomach turned into knots just at the very notion of those memories resurfacing. I would *not* go there.

"I said you were being incredibly professional about it," Melody snapped me back to the present and out of the memory hole I'd delved into, "and that there wasn't any friendship between the two of you. I also said I had no idea what he looked like and couldn't confirm or deny if he had, and let the record show I am quoting directly from your mother, 'grown up to be the looker that everyone knew he would be'."

My head whipped up so fast it cracked. "She didn't." My eyes widened in disbelief. "Tell me she didn't say that. That's *so weird*, Melody! My entire family is *so weird.*"

Melody reached over and stroked my hair, shushing me gently. "Oh, she did. And yes, very weird. May was also on the line and was voicing some supportive commentary on the entire ordeal in the background too. She said that the name *Clucky* would be making a comeback."

A groaned cry left me that was full of all the frustrated annoyance I held to this day. No one had ever believed that he was a pain in my ass. When I refused to go to any more barbecues after Cole had broken my little twelve year old heart right out of the blue, they thought it was typical children being children, not that he had been possessed by the devil and lost all his goodness.

His older brother, Brooks, had just left for university a couple months before, and we had spoken a little on how he had missed him, how his house felt a little empty and it was sort of weird that it was just him and his mum now, but he and I had been fine. Just like we'd always been.

I'd arrived at his house for one of our family get-togethers along with a couple other families on our block. He'd been outside and I didn't think twice as I ran straight out to him. I'll never forget the look on his face when he turned to face me. Like he *hated* me. I'd never been looked at like that before.

"Cole?" I had said, my voice gentle and full of every uncertainty and ounce of confusion I had felt in that moment. I never had any reason to be anything but a totally open book to Cole in all our years of friendship.

"I don't want you here, Lucky," he'd said, pointing a finger right in my face. "We aren't friends anymore." He turned away sharply, his shoulders rising and falling as he struggled to get a hold of his emotions.

"What?" I'd heard him just fine, but I was so confused.

Cole was my friend, my *person*.

"You have no idea, *no idea*, what it's like to work hard for something. To try your best and then be beaten by someone who's only doing better than you because everyone thinks they're some golden child. That's *you*, Lucky." He said it all while facing away from me but I took a step back like he'd shoved me.

"Cole." I frowned, and clenched my jaw tight, suppressing the immediate wobble to my bottom lip and fighting as hard as I could to not let the sudden storm of emotion overflow where it'd begun to churn inside me. "That's not true at all. Why would you say that? I—"

"Save it." He turned, his face cold and nothing like the boy I knew. This boy scared me. "At least I deserve everything I earn because I work hard for it. You'll never know what that's like. I hate you. Do you understand me? You act like you're better than everyone and I'm sick of it. *I hate you.*"

I didn't want to listen to another word that came out of his mouth. I turned and flew out of the house, running right by everyone with hot, heavy tears rolling down my face and still trying to understand what had happened to make me lose him like that.

My name was called by every person that I passed until I was out the front door and charging for my own house. It was only a few minutes until Riley had knocked on the door to my room, took one look at my face and wordlessly sat with me on my bed while I cried in her lap.

We didn't talk about anything, she just sat with me until the tears had stopped and then she sat me up and said, "If people can't see your worth, then they're not worth your time."

It was probably a quote from a magazine that she had read in all her sixteen years of wisdom, but I clung onto it as the sole reason for the end of my friendship with Cole.

That was one of the last times his mother hosted and shortly after they both stopped attending all together. I refused to think about that day again, channelling every ounce of hurt, pain and confusion into what I *could* control, which was beating him at everything and anything I could, and showing him exactly what hard work got me.

The trek down memory lane had dropped my mood to a sort of mellow, silent version of myself. This was why I didn't dwell. It left me feeling like *this*.

When I arrived back at Cole's apartment to prepare dinner, I headed straight for the staff computer lab, determined to write up and print out all the information needed for his house staff to prepare and put together the meals based on what I'd planned.

Autumn was in full swing and the sunlight that shone in, setting the entire space ablaze in golden hour goodness, was one of my favourite parts of the day. I might have wanted to kick the man in the family jewels but he'd certainly known what he was doing when he purchased the building. I would have done it too, if I could've, based on that view alone. It had been my own quiet rebellion over the last month that I made sure to enjoy every single one of them.

I was leaning on the kitchen counter when I heard the foreboding sounds of Cole's over priced shoes clip-clopping towards me. He did it every time he arrived. Sometimes it took him five minutes to get to the kitchen, sometimes it took him twenty. I knew he was just walking in weird circles hoping that the sound would taunt me. Like he could scare me into becoming whatever he wanted me to become in his presence.

I wasn't entirely sure what Cole *did* to be honest. What it was that made him work until the early hours of the morning. I knew from the temp agency that he worked within the hospitality industry, and I knew that he was likely very good at what he did (his apartment-mansion in the building he *owned* being example numero uno), but I'd never bothered to follow his career after our paths split ways.

I'd been there long enough to cook everything I needed to cook and clean everything I needed to clean when he made his grand entrance. He was wearing a dark charcoal suit with a navy blue dress shirt beneath, the top two buttons were undone as always showing a small expanse of his tanned skin. His black hair wasn't as styled as it usually was, but rather casually swept from his face in that 'just rolled out of bed and ran his hand through it' sort of way. His jade green eyes were on me, hard and full of all the sharpest emotions, just as they usually were.

He was relentless in his hatred, but at least he was consistent.

I looked at him long enough to take him in, and covered up a swallow with a sip of the tea I had prepared for myself, flicking through a cooking magazine I had brought with me. We didn't get on but I was still a warm blooded woman. Cole had grown into...well, he was sexy. And I had a brain and ovaries. Sue me.

The tea was the perfect thing to cover up just how the sight of him always made me feel off balance, like the floor was shifting and I needed to lie down, preferably with him on top of me.

God dammit, Lucky.

Someone on top of me? Sure. Him? Nope.

"Lucky." He spoke directly in front of me.

I'd ignored him so thoroughly that I hadn't noticed him eat up the rest of the distance between us.

I looked up at him with nothing but innocence. "Mmm?" I held my tea in both hands, leaning my hip against the bench and staring at him over the rim of the cup.

"That's fine china," he bit out like he couldn't believe the audacity.

I looked down at the cup then back at him. "This?" My eyes widened in feigned shock that I knew he saw right through.

I knew this was his fine china. I knew it was a part of a large, very expensive collection that Cole owned. I also knew that this particular piece of china I was using, which was actually *not* a tea cup and currently being used for the entirely wrong purpose, was Joseon Porcelain.

Before I'd decided to mess with him, I had taken the time to appreciate holding one of the more impressive pieces of porcelain that likely existed in the world today. It sat in the highest set cupboards at the far end of the kitchen and there was an entire section of his silly rule book that spoke to staff touching this exact item under no circumstance. I had to stand on the bench to reach the damn thing. It didn't even hold a respectable amount of tea in it.

I'm sure if I was anyone else he probably wouldn't have really cared as much as he did. What he *did* care about was that *I* was the one holding it. And that, ladies and gentleman, was precisely why I *was* holding it.

Like I said, the man was consistent, even if he was a prick.

"Yes. *That*." His hand twitched like he was torn between wanting to smack it out of my hands or grab it back into his own embrace.

"Oh, I had no idea!" I set the small bowl down with an unnecessary loud *clang*, and Cole jolted.

"Jesus, Lucky. Are you fucking kidding me? The value of what you're holding could—"

"Could what?" I levelled him with my most fierce glare.

"To put it plainly for you, as I'm sure there's no other way you would understand this, in its numerical value, it could do a lot of good."

I snorted, "You wouldn't know 'doing good' if it sat on your face, Cole."

I picked up the little bowl to take another sip, my eyes never leaving his. It was clear, the moment that he pulled in his anger and channelled it back out in the form of another mask.

A cruel smile grew across his face. "I'm not surprised, Lucky Girl. It's obviously the most valuable thing you've ever held in your hands." His words dripped with the sort of poison I knew he hoped would kill me slowly. "It must have been hard, no? Having built up quite the reputation for yourself, and then seeing it all fall down around you. Being surrounded by all the things you wish you had. Does it hurt? Does it *kill* you just a little to be faced so completely with how far you've fallen?"

My hands smacked down on the counter so loudly I felt the shock reverberate up through my skull. "Don't you fucking say a *word*—"

"Oh, it's not polite to interrupt people when they're speaking, Lucky. I wonder if I should add this as more minutes on our unpaid labour chart?" He lifted an eyebrow at me.

I didn't go for his bait, instead he'd just rattled the cage of my barely contained temper when I was around him. "You have no idea what you're talking about. Hard work? You want to talk about *hard work*?"

"Oh, good. I was hoping you'd finally let me in on your secret on how exactly you held so tightly onto the coattails of those around you."

I laughed. I actually *laughed.* "Around me? Whose coattails was I holding onto? I hope you're not referring to yourself? If I had tried to raise my standing by using *you* as a leg up, I'd have dropped farther in high school than I've fallen now."

His cruel smile dropped from his face.

Cole might have known how to get under my skin, but I was there too. I was there for every moment he was and I could just as well get under his skin.

"Watch it, Navy." He braced himself onto the counter before me, a small tremor making its way through his body.

"Oh, '*Navy*'?" I stepped around the counter and walked in slow steps towards him. "No more '*Lucky Girl*'? This must be getting quite serious if—"

The words were stopped in my throat by the hand that now gripped it.

"Not another word," he said with a lethal quiet that made me shiver.

I had no idea what was wrong with me, but with every enunciated syllable, a pulsing rhythm shot through my entire body, and ended right between my legs.

My body flushed immediately in a wave of heat followed by an immediate chill that caused my nipples to strain and pebble against my bra. The sensation of the rough material against the sensitive peaks pulled a whimper from the base of my throat. I swallowed it down at only the last second. Instead, favouring a small smile that I let play on my features while my tongue darted out to wet my bottom lip.

The idea was to try to drive him to the point of a potential mental breakdown, to where the thought of getting rid of me surpassed any other option he had considered up until this point, but his eyes tracked the swipe of my tongue and I saw his gaze darken in a way I never had before. Like he was hungry. *Starved.*

The act only seemed to make him squeeze my throat tighter and for some reason, my body thought the appropriate response was to squeezed my legs together in an effort to relieve the building pressure in my lower abdomen, but the only thing that achieved was releasing the moan I had trapped in my throat and propelling it through my lips.

I wasn't entirely sure that it was audible to anyone but me, but I also knew that I would likely *combust* over the very fact it happened once the moment passed.

The act caught his attention and his eyes dropped immediately. His lips parted a fraction, and if I hadn't been so absolutely focused on every move he was making, I would have missed the way he pulled me towards him ever so slightly before he pushed me back, releasing me like my skin was on fire.

Our bodies stood close enough that our heaving chests made contact. The mere whisper of a touch was too much for my heated skin. I needed a cold shower, or even just a fucking *fan.*

I'd have to have been blind to miss the very clear bulge in the front of his work slacks before snapping my eyes back up to his. The feel of his hand around my throat lingered long after he'd let go as we stared at each other.

I set my hand on the kitchen bench and let the cool bite of stone ground me. Let it chase away the heat that was still racing through my body. "I think I'll be handing in my resignation now, Mr. Thompson." My words were quiet but strong which surprised me.

There was no hint of the pounding rush of blood that was raging through my body. No hint of the racing pulse I felt rush right through my head, starting between my legs and soaking my panties as it continued to thrum. A pitiful gust of wind could send me over the edge at this point if I was being honest.

He had his hand wrapped around my throat.

If there was anything I needed to send this fucked up game of ours into a checkmate it was this. I let the small smile remain on my face as I moved past him, letting my hips swing a little more than usual, knowing my ass looked particularly good in the skirt I was wearing, and savoured the taste of my victory.

"I wish I could say it has been a pleasure, but, well, it hasn't. I will let the agency know to expect one hell of a recommendation."

My boots thudded as I walked away from Cole, still as a statue in the exact position he had been in when we had finally separated. I had made it just to the threshold of the doorway when he finally spoke.

"You should consider your next step very carefully, Lucky," he said from behind me.

I didn't turn but I could tell that he had now moved to face my direction.

"I had wanted to have this conversation with you at a later date, but I will admit that you've forced my hand on this one." His steps were relaxed as he made his way to me. "You assume that my impact on your standing would be within your agency, and then maybe a few media outlets once they got word of whatever creative lie I would have put together, and you'd be right. That would be just *one* of the very wonderful things that would come of you taking one more step away from me. But there is something else you should know, and I honestly expected you to figure it out by now, but I always knew you weren't quite as bright as you seemed."

Cole was behind me now. He grazed the tips of his fingers up my back, my entire body igniting once again under the mere idea of his touch, until he got to my hair where I had left it loose in yet another attempt at defying him.

Gathering the golden strands, he moved them gently to one side, exposing my neck to him. My breathing became rapid and my thighs clenched again on their own accord as he dragged his lips up the length of my neck before reaching my ear.

"Have you ever wondered what it is that I do, Lucky?"

I gave myself a second to swallow before I replied, determined for my voice to come out strong. "I know what you do," I murmured, doing my absolute best not to show exactly how much having his front pressed to my back was impacting me.

Cole grabbed my waist and spun me to face him, my hand flying up to land on his chest, didn't attempt to push him away.

"Mmm," he hummed in amusement, "do tell." A command, not even a question.

That pissed me off. "You're employed to stare at naughty children until they cry. I imagine you're also paid with vials of their tears—"

His grip on my waist tightened to the point of pain and a small cry left my lips.

He leaned forward until his mouth was by my ear again. "Have you heard of *Thompson & Co?*" he asked and it only elicited a frown from me.

Of everything I thought he was going to say, that sure as hell wasn't it.

My body was still pressed against his, his hands still on my waist and my panties soaked for reasons I would rather not admit until I was at home, in my bath, with a glass of wine in one or both hands.

Of course I'd heard of *Thompson & Co*, they were the biggest investment company in the country, nay, *the world*, where hospitality came into the picture. I had sent them a couple emails when I was setting up my own restaurant with never a reply. The majority of their investments were Michelin Star.

My face went slack just as a smile bloomed across his. He saw the realisation sink in. I had known of the business, yes, but I hadn't known it was *his* business.

"You're..." I stared up at him, seeing flashes of just how much further there was to fall with this man standing above me. Seeing for the first time the power he really held where the rest of my life was concerned, and exactly *who* he had built himself up to be. It was terrifying at the same moment it was awe inspiring, though he'd never hear that from me.

"Yes, *me*." His hold on my waist loosened but he didn't step away from me. "So you see, if you do take a step that isn't back towards that kitchen, all the fleeting remains of your time in the limelight will cease to exist. Every single person who you know that would be able to help you rebuild your life? I know them too. I know them *better*. So, by all means, go right ahead. Run away from me again."

Cole leaned in, pressing a lingering kiss to my cheek.

It wasn't kind, and it wasn't hopeful. It was a promise that he would see me fall and crumble entirely before he let me up from beneath his thumb.

17

Cole

My weekend was an absolute waste of time.

Every single moment of my time was consumed by thoughts of Lucky. Of my hand around her throat. Of the whimper that came out of her mouth and how my cock had hardened to the point of pain, until it was only because of the frayed remnants of my restraint that I didn't bend her over my kitchen counter and fuck every smart mouthed comment out of her. Until my name was the only thing left on her lips. In her head. Until the only thing she knew was the feel of me sliding in and out of her pussy. Until she was *consumed* by me in every way I was consumed by her.

"Fucking hell," I bit out between clenched teeth into my empty office, reaching up to pull at my hair before adjusting myself in my jeans.

What sort of maniac wore *jeans* around the house on the

weekend? The sort who's been sporting sporadic boners like a fifteen year old that'd discovered incognito web browsers on the family computer and was continuously stumbling onto porn sites. I needed something with a little more structure to keep everything...in check. I was alone but I still couldn't bring myself to walk around at full-fucking-mast.

No. *No.* Lucky knew exactly what she was doing. She had baited me, and what's even more infuriating is I had let her. This was *not* the way things were supposed to be. I still looked at her and felt every moment of what it had been like being cast in her shadow, but now there was something else. Something she had unlocked and I'd spent every hour of the past two days trying to shove whatever she'd awoken back into the little box it lived in well at the back of my mind.

I released a long breath, inhaling through my nose and out my mouth a couple more times before my heart rate slowed enough for me to think a little clearer. My desk was scattered with files and letters and reports. All things that required my sign off and all I could do was read the first sentence of one page over and over again. I still couldn't even tell you what I'd read, but I could tell you, in detail, exactly how I imagined Lucky spread out before me, a meal of a different kind but no less mouth watering.

"*Fuck!*" My voice ripped raw by the guttural yell as I shot up from my chair. The force propelled it behind me with a loud *thud* as it hit the wall. I needed something, *anything.*

It took me five minutes to make my way to my bedroom, change into some gym gear and head straight for the gym that was back on the other end of the apartment.

My entire body was locked and tight, my cock still hard in my loose workout shorts that made me eternally grateful that there were no staff here on Sundays.

I lost myself in the movements of every machine I used. Focusing on the strain of my muscles as I pushed myself farther than I usually would before running the rest of my energy off.

It had taken two and half hours and every single part of me was drenched in sweat but I had finally come back into myself. My body tingled from being pushed to its limits and it was a genuine relief to let myself lay in the middle of the floor until the sweat had dried and my body had cooled down, with nothing but silence in my mind.

It took some serious effort and a pathetic groan to eventually get off the floor. With my towel slung over my shoulder I pushed the door open, snapping off the lights as I went and thinking only of the pizza I would be ordering for myself for dinner, glad to have something plain and greasy. The absolute opposite of what I ate through the week.

I had barely taken a step into the hallway when the squeak of sneakers undid everything that I had just spent that last two hours working out of my system.

The door to the staff bag room was wide open, the light on and framed in its centre was a pert, jean clad ass that could only belong to one person.

"There you are!" Lucky called out victoriously as she shot up straight as an arrow. Her face was almost split in half with the smile she wore. And then she saw me.

"Cole." Her voice was quiet, her face softening and her eyes searching but looking for what? I couldn't say.

I made slow strides towards her, her eyes tracking the movements with her bottom lip caught between her teeth, cheeks flushed and hair tousled. Her eyes wide and unsure.

God. Maybe...fuck, I couldn't concentrate like this. I couldn't do *anything* like this.

I stopped before her, causing her head to fall back and look up at me. The very fact that she was forced to look *up* at me shot a sick sort of thrill through me and it was with the slow blink of her too-big eyes that the idea solidified.

Once.

I needed to taste her, touch her, *feel* her once. My problem was clear to me as anything ever had been before, I needed to get Lucky Peters out of my system.

As I let the idea settle over me in finality the ache in my balls worsened. I walked around her slowly, taking the opportunity to tuck myself in the waistband of my loose gym shorts. It did *nothing* but it was better than accidentally knocking her over with it.

I leaned in close, my lips grazing the shell of her ear, "What are you doing here, Lucky?"

"My phone," her voice cracked. Clearing her throat she tried again, "I left my phone." She held her chin up high and stood a little taller, as if I couldn't see exactly what I was doing to her. She wanted me just as bad, but she was stubborn. More so than even I was.

"Mmm. I see that." I grazed my lips down the curve of her neck, eliciting a shiver that wracked her entire body. "Are you cold, Lucky?" I teased her, making my way back around to stand in front of her.

Eyes hooded, she looked up at me again with as much conviction as I'm sure she could muster, refusing to give me a response.

"No?" I leaned in closer, looking at her now almost at eye level. "Why the shivers?" The side of my mouth curled up involuntarily. I couldn't help it, this was *fun.*

"You're an asshole, you know that?" Her words whispered across my lips, the smell of spearmint enveloping me.

It took every ounce of willpower to keep my face in the mask of careless confidence I held from the moment she noticed me. My hands twitched with the need to reach out and pull her into me.

"So you've said," I said, keeping eye contact.

I wasn't going to be the first to break, and I didn't need to wait long before she lost whatever silent battle she was having with herself.

Her hands shot out, gripping the loose fitting gym shirt I had on and pulling me towards her with more strength than I would have thought her capable of. It was all I needed though. For her to make that first move.

My hand slid around to the back of her neck, holding her to me while my other gripped her waist, hard enough to elicit a gasp from between her lips that I captured with my own. I slipped my tongue into her mouth, fighting for the dominance we were both after.

I won.

Lucky whimpered as she gripped my shirt in her fists in a way that told me how angry she was that she wanted this.

She pulled back from me suddenly, her lips already swollen and her face blooming with a deeper flush than before. But her eyes were bright. *Alive.*

"This changes nothing," she breathed, her grip on my shirt never lessening.

I moved my hand from the back of her neck to the front and applied pressure, "Obviously." My voice didn't sound like my voice. It sounded rough. Desperate.

"I still hate you," she said, with less conviction than her other words as she pulled herself back up towards me.

"Likewise," I breathed before crashing my lips to hers again.

This wasn't delicate. It was fuelled by the overflowing well of *everything* that there was and had ever been between us.

Fury shot through me like a bolt of lightning at the memories that surfaced in my mind and my grip on her throat tightened.

Her hands slipped into my hair, yanking harshly.

I grunted at the pain that took me off guard a second before my cock pulsed.

She was going to be the fucking end of me.

I lifted her off the floor, her legs immediately wrapping around my waist. My hand reached up between us, cupping her full breast and earning a moan that turned to a cry as I pinched her nipple hard, grinning against her lips as I absorbed every sound that left her mouth. My name fell from her lips and I hated the way it sent a rush through me. How in that single moment I felt my control slip, slight as it was.

I didn't know what I was doing, what I needed, what I wanted, because I wanted it all. I *needed* it all.

I dropped her to the floor unceremoniously, balancing her on unsteady legs.

"Beg for it," I said, my voice something I hardly recognised.

"No." She was defiant even as her legs shook with the effort of staying upright. She gripped my shirt in one tiny fist and yanked me forcefully back down to her.

I kissed her with every last shred of every ugly emotion I felt towards her and she gave as good as she got. Lucky kissed me back the way she approached everything, with the need to do it *better*. To do it *best*.

The thought pulled a growl from me and I pulled her bottom lip between my teeth, biting down roughly and felt nothing but satisfaction as the metallic taste of her blood entwined with our kiss. I swallowed the pained sob before soothing the sting with my tongue.

I wanted all of her cries. I wanted every fucking ounce of her pain.

It was a fraction of a second before I was diving back into the wet heat of her mouth with the fervour of a mad man. She was intoxicating and I hated how much I didn't care to fight it. My fingers deftly undid the button of her jeans and slipped into her panties. The tips of my fingers grazed her core, already coated in her arousal, causing her hips to buck up in response.

An involuntary groan tore from the back of my throat before I could get a handle on it, "Do you know how wet you are, Lucky?"

Her only response was a moan as I slid my digits along her folds before pinching her swollen clit between my fingers.

She yelped, my shirt stretched and ruined where it remained in her grip as she brought her lip between her teeth once more, eyes clamped tightly shut.

"Say this is because of me," I commanded, releasing the sensitive nub to rub light, slow circles. Not enough to take the edge off, but enough to drive her crazy.

"No," she whimpered, her fingers finally releasing my shirt only to dig into my biceps.

I lightened my pressure even more, "Say it, Lucky," I bit out between clenched teeth, challenging my own remaining control.

COLE

She met my eyes with clear, unrelenting fury of her own but she knew I had won. Her grip tightened on me as her breaths became more rapid.

"It's you." The words were barely audible as they left her mouth. It wasn't enough.

I don't know what ever *could* be enough.

"What?" I didn't change my pressure as my other hand snaked up her body wrapping around her throat once more.

She looked at me cold fury dancing behind her blue eyes, biting the words out between clenched teeth, "It's because of you, you fucking assho—"

I drove two digits into her before the words had finished leaving her mouth, the last one trailing off into a rasped scream as I pumped into her wet heat, my eyes never leaving her face.

Her hands reached out, gripping both my arms and digging in her barely there nails. I was sure that her grip might leave the smallest marks on me and I couldn't find it in me to give a fuck especially when I realised that she was holding me in place, not pushing me away.

It was driving me insane.

I added another digit and watched as her eyes rolled back and her mouth parted in a silent scream, my palm rubbing her clit as my fingers continued to sink into her tight pussy. I couldn't take my eyes from her, I couldn't even blink because there was no way I was missing a single second of watching her come undone.

"*Cole,*" she rasped, the sound barely audible with the pressure I had on her throat, but it was enough. It told me everything I needed to know.

"Come for me, Lucky." I leaned in, clamping my teeth hard

then sucking on the sensitive flesh between her neck and shoulder.

I felt as she gripped my fingers, the orgasm ripped through her hard and long, exhausting her of the last remaining strength she had until my hands on her were the only thing keeping her standing up right.

My name along with every other filthy word in the English dictionary left her mouth until all that was left was a mixture of pitiful, broken noises, my fingers still inside her, slowly coaxing every last bit of her release from her.

I watched her through every moment of her undoing, my eyes shifting only to watch my own hand that disappeared into her jeans where my fingers moved in and out of her as she rode the waves of her climax.

It was only when she could stand on her own did I pull my fingers from inside of her and step back. Watching her as she watched me bring the digits up to my mouth to taste her.

Her breathing caught, her eyes snapping down to the very clear and very prominent situation I had from the waist down.

I had never been so hard in my fucking *life*.

Lucky's throat bobbed with an audible swallow, her eyes remaining locked on my cock where the thin fabric of my shirt did nothing to hide the length of me. When her eyes flicked back up they heated and hungry with a shadow of uncertainty.

I couldn't stop the smirk that lifted the corner of my lips when her eyes tracked my every move, as I pulled my fingers from my own mouth only once I was satisfied that I had gotten every morsel of her off them.

"I'll see you Monday, Lucky." My voice was thick with emotion as the words filled the air with something besides our heavy breathing.

I made my way across the apartment to my bedroom where I'd deal with my own situation. The thought of using my own hand to pull the release that I'd been neglecting myself when I could have so easily had her on her knees was a decision I regretted immediately. But I hadn't really had a choice because that had been everything I knew it would be.

She had tasted, *felt*, better than I knew she would and I didn't know if once would be enough.

18

Lucky

Do you know how wet you are, Lucky?

I jolted in my car seat. My hand accidentally flying to the horn, the sound assaulting the night around me as my own thoughts rang through my head shrouded in the heavy rasp of Cole's voice.

"Fuck me," I mumbled to myself, my heart thundering in my chest. Nope. Nope, nope, *nope*. A moment of weakness. Another stumble. One I had conveniently forgotten. One I refused to think about.

Beg for it.

His voice speared through my mind, a wave of heat made its way through my body, making me press my thighs together as I tried to focus on my drive. Focus on the steering wheel I gripped in my hands and the rumble of the car beneath me, the vibrations pulsing through my pus—

No, actually I would *not* think of the rumble of my car.

What was happening to me? This was insane. He wasn't even *here* and he was ruining my morning.

"Sorry, Bess," I mumbled to my beloved car, holding the steering wheel with a more gentle hand and reprimanding myself that I would think of her rumblings as anything *but* mechanical.

Come for me, Lucky.

"That's it." I let out a loud, aggravated breath. "I'm not going to let this consume me. Do you hear me Bessy? I will *not* let him get under my skin. Who am I?"

The car said absolutely nothing, obviously, but I felt her vibes. "That's right, I'm Lucky fucking Peters and I came because *I* wanted to. Not because he...he...what? He commanded," I scoffed. "Right?"

There was no vibe this time.

"I'm going insane. I'm talking to my car and I'm going insane."

Cole's building came into view and I pulled up to my usual park across the street from the imposing structure. All sleek and shiny and impressive.

I huffed, blocking out every memory of his touch. Of his hands and his lips and his—

I rubbed my eyes. "Take my word for it, that was all me," I grumbled as I grabbed my things and hopped out.

Bessy let out a groan as I stepped onto the curb. The rattling went on for a little *too* long.

"Oh, shut up. You're a car." I slammed the door and turned with purpose to the wide glass doors of his building.

Cole Thompson had met his match in me from the very beginning. He may have forgotten, given the years that have passed, but now? It was time he remembered.

I had been successfully ignoring Cole for the last week.

I wasn't an idiot. Well, that may not be entirely true, but the part of me that wasn't a total idiot was aware that my ability to ignore him was not a one-girl-tango.

He was ignoring me too. Was I happy about it? No. Why wasn't I happy about it? Because *I* was ignoring him, and I wasn't fully able to do that to the best of my ability if he was also ignoring me.

I had started my days at four in the morning every single day this week. Five minutes, in and out, no unnecessary exposure.

He hadn't even so much as questioned my lack of presence at lunch times, which was in and of itself infuriating, because it meant it wasn't rubbing him the wrong way. That shouldn't bug me either, but even his attempts to ignore me were getting under my skin.

I slammed my shot glass down on the table, making Melody jump and cast her wide eyes on my less than sober face.

"I hate him," I mumbled. "I hate him and his stupid hands."

"His hands?"

"*His hands.* His big, stupid hands." I let my head thump on the sticky table between us at our usual spot at *Helga's*.

Melody reached over, lifted my head and slid a napkin between me and the table before letting my head thump back down unceremoniously.

"Thanks," I said, barely audible over the music that surrounded us thanks to the busy Saturday night.

"Don't mention it. Now, can we just run through this one more time?"

I lifted my head to stare at her, eyes narrowing in suspicion, "I think you like hearing about my sex life too much."

"First of all," she leaned down to take a big sip from her fishbowl cocktail, "I have a right to want a playback. That was probably one of the hottest things I've ever heard in my life. Ever."

"Don't condone his behaviour."

"Second, I'm trying to understand whatever fucked up dynamic you guys have that lead you both to the same conclusion."

"Which is?"

"You're both desperate to give one another orgasms."

"*Liddy!*" I scolded. "I'm cutting you off." I reached out to grab her drink but she slapped my hand away.

She stared at me for another solid minute before a whine tore from my throat and I let my head drop down to the table again.

"The harder you do that, the more brain cells you lose," she said around another slurp of her drink.

"Good," I mumbled. "Maybe I'll lose whatever brain cell it was that thought letting him put his hands in my pants was a good idea." I lifted my head and let it drop once, twice, three times.

"How about now?" There was a smile in her voice like she was getting a real kick out of this.

"I am still of the opinion that it was the best orgasm I've

ever had so the brain cell must still be there."

Liddy tipped her head back and released a howling laugh. "This is so wonderfully entertaining for me. You have no idea."

"You're supposed to be my friend, help me plan a way to end this...this...*torture.*"

"Torture?" she parroted, eyebrows raised and totally unconvinced.

My only response was a grumble.

"'*Ask for it, Lucky. Tell me how much you want my di*—'"

I flung myself over the table and covered her mouth. "Melody Amelia Harper, that is entirely misquoted," I whisper-yelled all while fighting a smile that was only being spurred on by the laughs causing her entire body to shake.

She held up the peace sign in a show that she would agree to a truce.

I slowly released her before flagging down a waitress and requesting two more fish bowls along with two more shots of tequila. I leant back into the worn red leather seat and ran a hand down my face, "I thought that once we...*collided*, that would be it. Whatever had been building would just, *poof*, disappear."

"And?"

"And it's only gotten worse. And what's even *worse* than what's gotten worse, is he's ignoring me too, as much as you can ignore the person who cooks your meals."

"I thought this was what you wanted? For him to just leave you alone."

"It was," I said, just before the waitress brought our drinks.

I grabbed the straw of my beautiful blue, incredibly alcoholic drink and stirred it, knowing what this conversation would expose and not being entirely ready to face the reality of the words I hadn't even really wanted to admit to myself.

"And now?" Melody asked, eyes on me. The joking twinkle that had flooded her expression now completely gone.

"*Now*," my voice was quiet, but I knew she would hear the words, "I feel him *everywhere*. I heard his voice in my head. It's like he's done this on purpose, like he *knew*. Like it wasn't enough that he consumed my life in every other way, now he needed to be in my head."

Melody was quiet for a minute before her brow furrowed slightly and lips pinched. This was her thinking face.

I took my straw between my lips and watched her, slowly sipping from my drink and determined not to disturb her while she did her best to solve my problems.

"I've got it!" She practically yelled in my face, both hands raised above her head in victory.

Her declaration made me jump, a little of the blue liquid in my beloved drink spilling over. But that didn't matter, not while I stared at her expectantly.

"Alright," she started, "we're both in agreement that you need to do something about your situation."

"Quite agreed." I nodded my head vigorously.

"And it helps no one to lie about how you felt about the situation, so give it to me straight. Rate the man out of ten."

My eyes rolled so completely that I saw my brain for a fraction of a second before giving in, knowing there was no way out of this. "On what grounds?"

"Fair point." She nodded, her expression entirely serious, "Let's break this down into categories. Internal and external. And internal will be broken into two subcategories of brains and heart. So, external?"

"Like his clothes? His smell?"

"So, what you're saying is you've spent a decent amount of time *sniffing* the man?"

"Well, I mean he's been *close* enough—"

"You saucy minx, Lucky-Lou!"

"You're making this out to be far more layered than it really is."

"Oh, please. Like you haven't drained the life out of every battery in your house beating the ever-living-life out of you vag—"

"*Okay!*" I yelled, my ass half lifted from the seat, hands raised in surrender. "Okay, I absolutely have received your point. There is no reason to bring Hunk into this."

"You didn't." Melody looked at me like it was Christmas morning.

"Melody I swear—"

"You named your vibrator *Hunk?!*" She threw her head back and released the most soul consuming cackle that made the blue liquid of my drink flood out of my nose. "*Why didn't I know about this?*" She could barely get the words out, and what she could was a wheezed delivery.

Both of our faces were frozen masks that looked like we were silently screaming, bodies convulsing as tears flowed freely down our faces. It really wasn't that funny. It was absolutely the shots.

"Oh, my." Melody wiped the tears from her face with a napkin, "*Oh, my sweet baby Jesus.*"

I wiped my own face. "This feels like an over reaction. Let's talk about *you*."

"Your attempt at a lane change is futile." She waved off my words and sat straight once again on her side of the booth, clearing her throat and proceeding like we didn't both almost piss our pants, "He's a high number isn't he?"

"Have you seen his face?" I deadpanned.

I was sitting right beside her when I finally permitted her to Google him at the start of the night. There actually weren't many photos of him online at all, we sort of had to dig to find it in the dregs of his company's website pages.

"Noted. External is a ten. Internal?"

"He's smart," I conceded. "Very smart. Annoyingly so."

"Alright, let's be realistic and say, nine?" she hedged, cringing a little even as the words left her mouth.

I just nodded. There was no point in denying it.

"But his heart?"

"There is but an empty, echoing chamber where a sad little husk of an organ sits. Now, it's probably where he stores all the little vials of children's tears he collects."

"Well, that's...vivid." Melody scrunched her face up, conveying just how disturbed she was but she shook it off quickly.

"Alright, we'll place 'husk' in that column, not to be confused with 'Hunk'." She winked at me, but promptly moved on before I could reach over and pinch her.

"What does that tell you?" I toyed the little glass between my fingers, looking at her expectantly.

"Oh, absolutely nothing. But you've been so tight lipped all night, I needed *something*."

"Melody, I swear to god—"

"Oh, hush and untwist your Cole-invaded-panties you little hussy, the answer is simple: *you* must do something." She beamed at me, clearly entirely pleased with herself, while I had just been faced with what felt like the biggest anticlimax of my entire life.

"Wow, the last time I was let down this bad was when Anthony Jenson stuck his hand up my skirt in tenth grade, came in his pants then thanked me with a fist bump." I scowled at her which she only rolled her eyes to.

"You're legally never allowed to place me in the same category as Jenson, you promised."

"Yeah, well...," I lifted my eyebrows and gestured towards her general area, hoping she would realise that she had really placed herself in that category.

"The playing field isn't *even*, Lucky. He's got into you - pardon the pun."

I reached out to shove her but she grabbed my hand and held it. "You need to take back control of the situation. One up him, outdo him, get under *his* skin."

I stared at her. "You're suggesting I..."

"Make a move. You need to pull down those big girl panties, grab that man by the balls and own the entire situation. Plus, it is also my humble opinion that you would benefit from a solid lay." She nodded, as if she were saying 'case closed'.

"Firstly, oh my god? And secondly...I'm sorry, you're suggesting that the way to make this all go away, is to what, bump uglies?"

"I doubt whatever you bump on that man would be ugly, but yes. He may have gotten a taste—"

"*Melody*—"

"Okay, *okay!* But really, he may have, but did you?" she asked, no trace of her alcohol fuelled bubbliness in sight, just straight to the point.

I swallowed, thinking of the way he had held my gaze as he pulled his fingers from inside me, and slid them into his mouth. I clamped my mouth shut at the whimper that got lodged in my throat, even at the memory of watching him do that, and how it wasn't hate that resided in his eyes in that moment.

"Did you?" she asked again.

"No." My voice was rough and husky and she was entirely right.

She lifted her shot glass up to me, "Here's to doing something about it."

I lifted my own, "To getting a taste."

I threw the shot back and slammed the little glass on the table and felt something I hadn't in a very long time; I felt like I had a plan, like I had control.

"Alright," I began, "now you. Does Brian still smell like cheese?"

19

Lucky

God this was a mistake.

This was *such* a massive fucking mistake and I was totally going to kick Melody's ass the next time I saw her for convincing me that this was somehow the answer to my problem.

I was here, yes, but I could just get a really early start on everything I needed to do today. There was nothing in the rule book that said I couldn't start work at three in the morning. Only that I wasn't allowed to arrive later than six.

Perfect. New plan, here we go.

New plan, new plan, *new plan*.

Gripping the strap to my bag so tight my knuckles ached, I started to walk on the balls of my feet in a way that would have ballerinas throwing their pointe shoes directly at my head. My pace was achingly slow and with the adrenaline that was pumping through my body, I began to sweat. It was the sort of sweat that had about a fifty percent chance of burning right through my natural deodorant of choice.

The bag room came into view and I'd never been so happy. Opening the door on quiet hinges, I placed my things down gently with every intention of just sitting in there for at least an hour and a half until it was a more appropriate time to enter the kitchen.

But then the room that sat directly adjacent to where I stood now loomed over me, mocking me and my plan like the rest of this apartment.

The doors to the gym were a mixture of frosted glass and black matte metal panels, with sleek handles of the same look and material that ran the length of the doors. They were like everything else in Cole's house; sleek, new aged, and cold. Clinical and *cold*. Like there was no colour. No life.

That day had been the first time I'd seen him in anything but his work clothes. The first time I saw his forearms, banded in corded muscle. Saw the expanse of his legs in nothing but his own golden skin and not the slim fit work pants that he favoured. The Cole that stepped out of the gym that day looked nothing like the man I'd come to know.

Now I found myself taking steps towards the very room in question, wondering what it was like. Wondering if it reflected the man I knew or if it rather represented someone else, a man that maybe I *didn't* know.

The metal bit into my palm as I gently pushed on the door. It gave easily, gliding open so that I could slip through and not make a single sound.

I was immediately engulfed with the smell of him.

He always smelt so put together. Fresh and clean. But here,

it was infused with something else. It was woodsy and rich. Darker.

I allowed my head to fall back and didn't stop the groan that burst from me, thick and husky and wanton.

I walked deeper into the room, the smell sticking to my clothes, my hair, the back of my throat. It might have been twisted, but the fact that I would leave this room with a piece of him that didn't seem to exist anywhere else gave me a satisfaction I probably shouldn't have felt. Like I was stealing something from him he didn't want to freely give to me, just like he was doing with me. With my time, my career, my life.

It was dark but warm in the gym, and I took stock of the machines that surrounded me. Picturing him on every single one before turning to the view that stretched before me.

A panel of windows overlooking the city. A view that was different to the one that could be seen from the kitchen which was on a different side of the building, but no less beautiful.

I was entranced. So completely consumed.

The smells, the lack of sounds, the total stillness and absolute deafening quiet that I hadn't been able to find anywhere else, even within my own head. And in the unlikeliest of places, it seemed I finally found a kernel of peace.

I exhaled slowly and resigned myself to heading back out. To just grab my bag and leave. I'd sleep in my car for a couple hours if I had to. I knew I just had to *leave* and hope that this part of my life would come to an end soon.

I turned on my heels and it was like every little bit of air that filled my lungs had been ripped away. My hand flew up to clutch at my own throat, the silence around me instantly replaced with the roaring of my own blood rushing through my ears.

Cole's black hair was dishevelled, sticking up every which way like he just rolled out of bed. He stood just inside the doors of the gym, his eyes bright and clear, filled for once with only curiosity and maybe something more I couldn't quite place. His chest was bare, the slopes and dips defined in the most incredible way by the light casting in from the windows.

In the moments where I had placed my hands on his chest when he had gotten too close, or when he had pressed against me, I had felt the hardness of his body. I knew that there was muscle beneath his clothes but, my god, I had not expected *this*.

He was beautiful.

He was so completely beautiful I didn't think I could look away. I didn't want to. And I knew he was watching me as I took him in, that maybe I should be embarrassed but I couldn't stop.

My breathing became shallow and I let my eyes wander, watching as his abdominal muscles contracted with each breath he took, loosening and tightening as my eyes continued their descent to his Adonis belt that disappeared beneath the band of his loose, low slung dark grey sweats.

My heart was beating so fast and I wasn't sure when I had blinked last but when I'd taken him in entirely, my eyes couldn't be pulled from the spot on the floor where he stood.

I couldn't do anything, especially when he moved, making a silent path towards me.

My body started to shake, my fists balling at my sides.

Control.

I needed control and instead I was losing even more of it.

He was so close now I could feel the heat rolling off his

body. I could see how the smell that surrounded me here was so completely him. How the version of him outside of this room that only wore suits and perfectly styled hair was just a single version of the man before me, the only version that he'd permitted me to see.

I was overcome with a wave of crashing, heart wrenching sadness because I couldn't understand *why*. Why was everything so perfect one day and so awful the next? Why he looked at me with such disdain? Not just since I came into his employ but every day of high school until we parted ways? Why his lips used to curl in disgust when I entered any room? Why did he look at me like I was the sole reason for everything going wrong in his life?

I pulled my eyes up from where they were still locked on his bare feet, placed close enough that if I took just one single step, we'd come chest to chest.

My eyes lifted all the way up his body again, greedily taking in every expanse of exposed skin until I reached his eyes once more. I expected them to be full of the hatred he felt for me but they were still clear. Clear and framed with dark full lashes that sat upon heavy lids. He was looking at me like he had been waiting for me, like he hadn't been able to stop thinking about me, like all of *his* unanswered why's were being answered right now.

So, I didn't flinch or back away or move a single muscle when his hand reached out to wrap around the back of my neck, holding me firm and in place. I refused to let out the small sigh that desperately wanted to escape my lips at the relief of his touch.

I didn't back down or look away as he pulled me closer, his eyes flicking from my eyes to my lips, and kissed me.

His skin beneath my hands was scorching, and I couldn't seem to touch enough of him. I was burning under his hold and I knew that if I died here, now, I'd be totally a-okay with that. I'd think about how wonderfully stupid this was later, but for right now, as his tongue swiped the seam of my lips in a silent request for me to let him in, I didn't feel embarrassed at the whimper that he pulled from me as his tongue delved into my mouth.

I was completely consumed with the feel of him. The taste of him. The *smell* of him.

His hand stayed in place at the back of my neck while the other wrapped around my waist and pulled me so firmly against him I couldn't move.

Cole's kiss was unrelenting. It was greedy and starved and my entire body erupted into goosebumps at the electricity that shot through me, making me feel the absence of his fingers between my legs, the absence of feeling him inside me. The hollow feeling at my core made me pinpoint the exact location of his hands on my body and how they were everywhere but where I wanted him.

He captured my bottom lip between his teeth, biting enough to hurt but not to draw blood before releasing me.

We were both breathing hard, the roaring in my ears had dissipated a fraction, and now every single one of my senses were focused on him.

Cole held me to him firmly, his lips red and swollen in what I was sure was a mirror of my own. His eyes had darkened but shone with the lust I could clearly feel with the length of him straining against my stomach, his lids half way closed and lips parted, taking me in just as I was taking him in.

Neither of us said anything. There seemed to be this fragile, thinly built truce that existed and I knew the moment words were spoken it would shatter. I didn't want that.

But I did want *this*.

Cole's hand moved from where he held me close at the waist and slowly travelled down the length of my body to where my skirt brushed my mid thigh. As one hand moved, so did his other, pulling from the back of my neck to what I was coming to learn was his preferred grip, at the front of it.

I had a second, *less* than a second, to decide. The moment that hand travelled anywhere else, anywhere higher, I was a goner, and I had come here with a purpose.

A reason.

Before his hands could move another fraction, I lowered myself to my knees before him. I cast my eyes up under my lashes, wanting to see if the view was exactly as I thought it would be.

It wasn't.

It was better.

The look on his face was priceless.

His hands that had gripped me were still suspended around the ghost of where I'd been standing and before I lost my nerve, I reached for the waistband of his pants and slowly pulled them down. I freed his erection easily, given he hadn't been wearing any boxers beneath the loose fitting sweats.

All I could do for a second was stare at the thick, hard length of him, a bead of pre-cum already gathered on the tip.

My mouth instantly dried. I mean, I'd given blowjobs before, sure, but never, and I mean *never*, to someone with anything that looked like *that*. I looked up at Cole again, finding he was already looking down at me, his face smug and his eyes lit with challenge and amusement as if he knew exactly the thoughts in my own head.

Well, fuck that.

Slowly, I eased him into my mouth, my eyes never leaving his, and the moment the swollen head of his cock touched my tongue his composure broke completely and a wave of pride washed through me.

He let out a hiss, a hand snapping out to grip my hair around his fist to steady himself. He didn't take control or push deeper, only gripped tightly.

I knew that I wasn't going to be able to take all of him, and when I stopped to swallow and settle around the invasion, he took the opportunity to press in as far as he could go, which still left a good few inches *not* in my mouth.

My eyes instantly began to water and I closed them as a gag worked its way out of my throat until I settled into breathing through my nose. I lifted my hands up, one to wrap around the base of his cock and the other to grip his hip in an attempt to steady myself, to remember that this was my moment to take control of, and that I would see *him* come undone because of *me*.

That resolve settled in as I once again lifted my eyes up to meet Cole's.

He looked down at me, a small grin spreading across his face that didn't remind me of pretty things. It was dark and dirty and the sight of him looking at me like that made a heaviness settle into my stomach.

"Mmm." His voice was rough and raspy. It was the first sound to break the silence that had settled around us. It didn't shatter our truce like I thought, instead, it set me alight. "Good girl."

My entire body erupted in zaps of pleasure and my stomach

plummeted. It was wave after wave of delight, pushing and pulling my need in every direction until it was almost too much to bear. My nipples tightening, aching, desperately preening under his praise.

I gripped him as hard as I could just to keep from sliding two fingers into my own wet heat. The very thought made me groan, the vibrations eliciting an involuntary thrust from Cole.

"*Fuck*," he bit out between clenched teeth.

I moved without a second's hesitation, pushing against the grip he had on the back of my head and keeping a steady rhythm while I hollowed out my cheeks. I worked him with my hand at the same time as I swirled my tongue around the head of his cock, the sweet and salty taste pushing another wave of heat to my core.

Drool cascaded off my chin, mingling with the tears that continued to fall from my eyes. Every time I took him further into my throat, further than I was able, the room around us filled with my gargled moans and Cole's heavy breathing. It was the dirtiest sound I'd ever heard and I was coming absolutely undone.

"*Fuck*, Lucky," Cole panted, his pleasure sending a surge of pride through me and I could already feel the proof of my own arousal coating my thighs. My pussy clenched around merely the thought of him being inside me, the pulsing need causing pressure to build behind my eyes, pulling a whimper from my chest.

I'd never felt this much need for another person before. It was without reason, without senses, without any bounds.

His hand tightened further in the back of my hair, his other moving around to my throat, his thumb resting at the base possessively.

"Do you know how much I've thought about this?" he grunted breathlessly, slowly overpowering my attempts to set the pace and taking over control. His grip on my hair tightened to the point of pain as he began to thrust even deeper into my mouth, down my throat.

"Do you know how often I thought about fucking this smart mouth of yours? You on your knees before me, *begging*—" He slammed in roughly to the hilt. He filled my throat so fully, so much more than I could manage or was comfortable, restricting my airflow completely.

"You take it so well, Lucky. I bet you're soaking wet, aren't you? *Aren't you?*"

God, I was going to come just by his filthy words alone. A sweat had broken out over my entire body and my hands shook with the restraint to keep from dissipating my own desperation and sliding them into my aching core, to pay attention to the throbbing at the apex of my pussy. It was maddening. I was so close and I knew it wouldn't take much to send me over.

I was going to do it, my self control was in tatters and I didn't care anymore. I *needed* my own release. I'd barely begun to move my hand but stopped instantly at his words.

"Touch yourself, Lucky," he commanded. His tone allowed no room for argument, the order delivered in a way that I knew the man before me likely didn't know what it was like not to get his way.

Fuck. No. *Fuck* no.

And if I was honest, it was purely because of that reason that I resisted. I wouldn't give him the satisfaction. I almost caved, almost relinquished the control I had come here to claim. Well, not today, Satan.

Cole attempted to slow the pace, knowing that he was close to his own release as he swelled in my mouth.

I gripped him tighter and moved my head faster, locking my eyes with his and daring him to look away from what was before him clear as day; I may have been on my knees but *I* was the one in control this time.

My own need built and built as I took him in, at what was happening because of *me*.

It struck me again just how beautiful he was. I know I've said it before, but it repeatedly caught me off guard. His face flushed in the dim light being cast in through the windows, his mouth parted slightly and a thin film of sweat coating his chest and stomach. I couldn't help myself as I reached a hand up to drag down the length of his chest, my nonexistent nails raking across his tanned flesh and feeling every defined ridge of muscle.

A moan ripped through me, the feel of his body spurring me on and I moved my other hand to cup his balls, squeezing gently.

"*Luck*," he grunted, looking down at me with not a single wall up to keep me out, not a single mask on to hide himself from me and it was the most vulnerable I had ever seen him. "Fucking touch yourself, *Luck*—"

His words were cut off as his orgasm hit him hard and fast with a final, brutal thrust into my mouth. His resounding growl filled the room around us.

I swallowed every bit of his release, easing him from my sore and aching mouth with a pop and a final lick up the length of him, base to tip.

I was sure I looked like an absolute wreck, but it was worth every moment as I stood up on shaky legs, my body still slick with sweat and the need for my own release. I took in a breathless, speechless Cole.

"Now, we're even." My voice was rough and husky and there was every possibility that I had a bruised oesophagus.

"I—"

"I have a job to do now," I said before he could say a single thing, striding for the gym door feeling utterly in control for the first time in a long time and maybe even a little dizzy with power at what I had just been capable of.

I left Cole looking after me. His eyes bright and brimming with confusion, breathing hard, cock out and with his world thoroughly, *thoroughly,* rocked.

20

Lucky

1 year ago

Jamie had called me this morning and told me to meet him at *Seven*. He was the only person I knew that I could trust with my concerns. Jamie had run and operated his own security business for years, all above board and successfully. So, when I had begun to have trouble – scratch that – when I came face to face with the reality that my business was likely going to go under, I called him.

Of course, the phone calls at the start were all the known variations of 'you're fine' and 'there's probably been a mistype somewhere. Do you know how many times I've put the wrong figure in? One time I thought I had lost a hundred thousand dollars but it was just because I hadn't formatted the cell properly with the correct formula'.

That's not what happened here.

What happened here is I had been fooled. I had been played and I didn't know it until it was too late.

Jamie sat at my desk with his head in his hands, he didn't move an inch even when I came in, closed the door softly behind me and dropped my bag to the floor.

There was a second reason why I asked for Jamie's help. His speciality was cyber security. I called my older brother thinking that everything would be fine.

Everything had absolutely not been fucking fine.

Jamie dragged his hands from his face and sat back, lifting his tired, blood shot eyes to meet with mine.

"Hey, Luck," he murmured, voice quiet and deflated with the weight of the defeat he so clearly felt.

My heart sank.

"Sorry I called you so early but," he took a deep breath, "my guy had a breakthrough last night." His eyes flicked to the pile of papers in front of him. It wasn't a very imposing stack, but it was thick enough that it stretched the manilla envelope in an uncomfortable way.

"What's that?" My voice sounded so hollow I almost didn't recognise it. Any time the reality of my situation floated through my head I just kept thinking *'this can't be real. How was I that stupid? This can't be real, this can't be real'*.

"Sit down, Navy."

"Don't." I held up my hand and pretended I didn't notice how it shook along with my voice, "Just tell me what it is."

He leaned forward again with his elbows on his knees, pointer fingers steepled just beneath his nose. "They're the undoctored account records."

Undoctored? *What—*

"What does that mean?"

"It means that what we found up to about six months ago, was that your account statements on anything and everything to do with both *Seven* locations were changed prior to landing on your desk or in your inbox. The numbers and figures that you were seeing were not real. There was enough money left in the accounts to allow the business to continue running relatively smoothly up until about a month ago."

"I don't— I never got any notification from the bank? Never even a phone call? Everything I had received came from the bank?"

"You'd been removed from all the accounts as a primary contact and it's not difficult to impersonate those types of emails if you know what you're doing."

"But when I logged in—" I stopped short because I hadn't been the one to log in. I had been stuck with my head in the physical, *paper* statements, in the spreadsheet, all while I asked Chelsea to pull up the accounts, relied on her support and her help and her knowledge of what was happening day to day.

"There's nothing left, Lucky." Jamie delivered the words as cleanly as I knew he could, but I felt them each like a punch to the gut.

I slowly lifted my eyes from the folder back to my brother, his figure slowly beginning to blur as I lost the uphill battle of keeping my emotions in check. I hadn't cried yet. Not once. I didn't even give permission for these traitorous tears to fall, though they did anyway.

"Chelsea?" I hated the way my voice cracked on her name.

"She's disappeared. So far all we know is that she's a ghost. All the identification details she gave you belong to a girl that lives on the other side of the country. She had no idea that her identity had been stolen."

The air between us hung thick with the reality of what his words meant.

Chelsea had stopped showing up to work a month ago. The first day she actually sent a text saying she wasn't well. She messaged to say 'Hey Luck, I've come down with something. Sorry! Be in tomorrow.'

The first statement I got after she left showed me in so much debt I almost passed out. *So* much debt, and not even debt I'd accumulated, but debt that Chel— whatever the fuck her name was, had accumulated under the guise of my business. She had drained every single penny that was invested and earned into and by the company and then did *more*, as if that wasn't enough.

Jamie had explained it to me. I'd understood at the time, but it was all getting away from me now, like smoke in the air. The moment I reached for it, it disintegrated in my hands and separated into even more pieces that it had been in before.

I finally sat down, and Jamie ran me through what the next steps would be in a super clinical way. He was moving from point A to point B to point C without skipping a beat because he *knew* there was a countdown on what was happening in my own head and that we had to do as many of the important things now as we could.

He kept on talking about needing to keep this as low key as possible. Given my status as a public figure, even when the business goes down, the details of why would never be known, that in time I would, maybe, be able to come back from this. I was lucky that I decided to keep the books all in-house in that regard.

Lucky.

I was *lucky* that we could even do some damage control.

It was the first time I hated my own name. I felt every tether of luck in my body pull away from me. I felt it snap, one thread at a time. Perhaps that was what I'd felt this morning when I woke up. Not dread like I'd thought, but the absence of this part of me that had been ripped away; my luck. Something I had never known a day without and now it had evaded me completely.

Everything from that moment on was a blur.

Heading out to explain to my staff that this would be the last night they would be under my employ. The only relief I felt in that moment was not having to paste on the fake smile I had carried around like a neon sign of my shame that only I had known of.

I'd driven with Jamie over to the second location of *Seven* on the other side of the city to inform the staff there too that we would be closing down indefinitely. I had to explain to those people that I didn't have the means to compensate them totally in their redundancy. That I could only offer them letters of recommendation, but knew that the praise of a washed up, failed chef was about as good as rain on a campfire.

I stood there and absorbed the questions of concern, the condolences on the loss of the business and the hateful, pained word of people who had relied on me to ensure they could support their families, and when it was done I went home.

I went home because there was nothing more I could do tonight. Tomorrow, I would make my way into the bank. I would call my lawyers. I would do those things and I would lose a vital part of myself with every paper I signed.

I looked around at my three bedroom apartment in the city, walking distance from what used to be the main location of *Seven*. I looked at the windows that showed the city around me, bright and full of life. The reading nook I had finally styled *just right*. I looked at the plants I had spent so much time and effort keeping alive because I had read the importance of clean and filtered air in your home. I had everything set up and organised in a way that brought me joy, brought me happiness because I'd finally been able to create a space that was mine.

I could only look around me now and see everything I was still yet to lose.

Dropping my things where I stood, I walked on autopilot towards my bed, tucked myself into a ball, grabbed a pillow and screamed into it.

I screamed and screamed and screamed until I had absolutely nothing left.

21

Cole

Present

I heard Lucky in the kitchen on my way back to my room, dazed as I was. And though it was only four in the morning, there was no chance in hell I was going to be able to sleep now.

Now, we're even.

I released a humourless laugh under the cold spray of the shower. Maybe there was a part of her that truly believed we were on even ground, now that I'd had my fingers inside her and she'd had her lips wrapped around my cock that this was where things stopped.

She couldn't have been more wrong.

Any semblance of restraint where it came to her was all but dust now. I didn't think she actually knew exactly what she'd done.

It was why I'd turned and walked away from her even as the taste of her climax still rested on my tongue like a drug I hated myself for needing a hit of. It was why I refused to give in to the stares that burned into the back of my head when she believed I was ignoring her existence for the last couple of weeks.

Now I wasn't sure what I wanted from her, but I knew what it had been before was no longer enough. It wasn't even *close* to enough.

Dressed in a black suit, black dress shirt and black boots, I secured my cuff links as I headed towards the kitchen.

Lucky was making enough noise to wake the dead, but I doubt she was oblivious to that. She had every burner on the stove going and the oven was on. Soft classical music was playing gently as she glided from task to task, refusing to look up as I entered. She simply cracked three eggs into a bowl to scramble and slid a couple of pieces of bread into the toaster.

"Your coffee." She set the cup down in front of me. It was only a couple of minutes later that she set down my meal with surprising gentleness.

Her murmured "Enjoy" was too gentle.

My teeth ached from the amount of sugar she poured into that word, and I knew she was floating on a cloud of self-satisfaction.

"I'd offer you to sit and join me," I started, picking up my knife and fork, my words stopping her in her tracks, "but I assume you've had more than enough to eat this morning."

Breakfast was plain eggs on toast. But even her attempt at a 'bad breakfast' was good. Of course it was good.

Lucky never did anything half-assed including scrambled eggs on sourdough. She even garnished my eggs. It was four in the morning and she *garnished my eggs*. My mouth lifted slightly in amusement before I caught myself and willed a blank expression into place.

"Actually," she started with a voice filled with barely masked fury, my fork full of food stopped halfway to my mouth, "it was arguably average."

Her words were delivered with the perfect amount of stern-seriousness that I had to clamp my lips together and compose myself before I set down my utensils, wiped my mouth with my napkin and turned to face her.

"*Arguably average?*" I lifted a quizzical brow.

"Has anyone ever told you how incredibly annoying you are? Like a little mosquito, buzzing around."

"You're deflecting in a very unimaginative way."

It was a testament to the control I had on my expression that I didn't smile at the way she scoffed, "You think you're more imaginative than me?"

I shrugged, "Can't be mad at a duck for quacking."

She looked dumbfounded. Utterly bewildered as her face morphed into something that told me she thought I was clinically insane. "Do you *hear* the words that come out of your mouth?"

"You said arguably average, Lucky. Do tell me more."

"You heard me the first time, you insufferable lizard."

COLE

"Oh, I love it when you talk dirty to me, Peters." I grinned at her, picturing just how she responded to the things I'd said in the gym. "And I heard you, and as much as I thank you for the venom, I just don't believe you."

She rolled her eyes and dramatically threw her hands up in the air. "Wonderful, you're one of *those* men. I mean, I already knew it but you're always so eager to hammer nail after nail into your own coffin."

A flicker of amusement trailed its way through my body, settling into my limbs with an unusual weight. I couldn't tell if it was uncomfortable or a perfect fit just yet.

"Pray tell," I started, standing up and casually tucking my hands into the front pockets of my black slacks while I trailed behind her, refusing to react to her aggressive strides back to the kitchen, "what *those* men are like?"

She couldn't stand still. I was making her nervous.

My amusement flared into satisfaction. Hands on hips she stared at me, a gentle symphony of bubbling, frying and string instruments surrounding us.

"I'd love to." Lucky held out her hand and began ticking things off, "You're an asshole, for one."

"Naturally."

"Your ego is so large you had to build a small town at the top of a building just to fit it all in." She made a weird series of hand gestures that to her probably amounted to *exactly* the point she was trying to make.

I held the smile back with a great amount of effort, ignoring *why* it was even something that required effort in the first place. "Observant."

"You're entitled, rude, short tempered, demanding," she continued counting, nose scrunching.

"How original." I slowly began walking around the counter that separated us.

"Let's not forget you're quite literally *blackmailing* me into working for you."

"Am I? Because it appears you've forgotten that little tidbit." I was standing right in front of her now, so close that she had to crane her neck to look up at me.

She met my gaze with her own. Unflinching, her blue eyes were bright and burning with the anger that she felt. With a rage that called to my own.

The realisation caught me so off guard I wondered if the shock registered on my face before I could cover it.

"No," she said through clenched teeth, her pulse a rapid flutter at the base of her throat that my hand twitched to reach out and clutch. It was why I loved to grip her there. I could feel the very beat of her heart right beneath the pads of my fingers and I fucking loved it.

Memories of my thumb resting on the very spot just an hour before made my own pulse race, my cock twitching with remembered want, *need*.

Oblivious to my thoughts she went on, "I have not forgotten exactly who it is that you are, Cole. There is one difference now though."

She waited for me to ask, but I wouldn't. I owed Lucky nothing. I merely stared at her, allowing the hardness I carried with me to fall over my features, the coldness to settle in. Reminding her of who I was before she forgot. Before I did too.

"I am not someone you can *scare* anymore."

"No?"

"No," she breathed, her back against the counter, her grip

on the edge white-knuckled.

I reached a hand out and dragged it down the side of her face. Over her full lips and down where her pulse drummed on faster than before, relishing in the way her breath hitched at the contact, the way her eyelids fluttered. Her chest rising and falling with increased pace with every breath she sucked in.

I should pull away now. I knew it.

I knew it but I just couldn't bring myself to care. It was an effort to keep my entire body from shaking from the restraint. There were so many things I needed, *wanted* at that moment. I needed my name on her lips. Her mouth on me. My mouth on her. I wanted her to think of nothing but me, no matter what she did or where she went. I wanted her cries, her whimpers.

I wanted fucking *everything*. I wanted her broken, and begging and to be *mine*. That was why I should have pulled away.

Instead, I leaned in so my lips were at her ear, "You're a liar, Lucky."

Her swallow was audible.

"I think I scare you, but that's okay." I kept my eyes trained on her expression, absorbing every single noise that escaped her full lips like my life depended on it.

"Would you like to know why?" I pulled back to see her face. "I *like* your fear, almost as much as I liked you being on your knees for me. Almost as much as I liked the feeling of your tight little cunt pulsing around my fingers with my name on your lips. *Almost* as much as I want to slide into you, slowly. So. Fucking. Slowly." My hand held her jaw firm in my hand, my thumb swiping across her bottom lip, "So you can feel every single part of me as I stretch you. Feel you come so hard around my cock you'll forget every single thing about yourself except for one undeniable truth."

I slowly dragged my hand down to grip her throat, my other cupping her pussy over her panties.

A whimpered moan escaped her which served as a reminder of how painfully hard I was.

"Lucky," I whispered against her skin, sounding like both a taunt and a plea. My lips traced the curve of her jaw as I began to circle her clit lazily through the dampened, lacey barrier. "Do you know what that truth is?"

I pressed my body against hers, the soft curves and dips of her moulding against me perfectly, the scent of her invading me making my balls tighten and my teeth clench against the tingling pressure at the base of my spine. It was an effort to hold onto my own groan, to keep a grip on my own desire.

"N—no," she panted, her eyes fluttered shut as I marked a path down her neck, sinking my teeth into the soft flesh between her neck and shoulder. She let out a cry, her hands flying up and around me, sinking into my hair and gripping it hard, pulling me closer.

"The only thing you will remember is that you're *mine.*"

Before I knew what I was doing I dropped to my knees before her, the rip of her lacey nothings barely registered outside of a breathy gasp.

"*God,*" I leaned in to breathe the smell of her, my fingers digging into the soft flesh of her thighs hard enough to bruise while I battled to regain control of myself. "Let me see you, Lucky."

She looked down at me, her expression unsure but only for a second before she began to lift one unsteady leg from the ground.

I guided her over my shoulder and the sight of her, glistening and swollen before me, bare beneath her skirt and hands sinking into my hair so hard I could feel the bite of her nails on my scalp, almost undid me. Almost.

"Is this for me?" I was so close I knew she could feel my breath against her, the smell of her was intoxicatingly mouth watering.

Her response was only a sob muffled by the grip of her bottom lip between her teeth, and the slight rock of her hips towards me.

"*Beg.*"

"P—*please,*" she gasped. "God, I— Cole, *plea—*"

My mouth latched onto her swollen clit, licking and sucking without restraint until her leg shook so violently I was forced to lift her so she sat just on the edge of the counter, her leg joining the other over my shoulders.

Lucky released a cry that sounded more like a world renowned symphony than any of the music she had playing around us.

I wasted no time burying my tongue inside of her, desperate to taste every single part of her. Her hands remained gripped in my hair as her hips began to move on instinct, grinding and desperate for release.

"Cole, *fuck.* I need, I—*oh my god, wait*, please. I can't—," she cried and moaned, protesting and begging in the same breath.

"Yes, darling. You can." I pulled back to look up at her, "Do you see the mess you're making, Lucky?"

Her head bobbed in something that could have been a nod but more like she was running out of the energy she needed to answer me properly.

I held her gaze as I slowly dragged a single digit through her silken folds, revelling in the way she tried to thrust her hips at the contact. I pulled my finger away with the truth of her arousal, her need, glistening on it and lifting it up to her.

"Suck."

She did. Her mouth opened immediately, tongue swirling around and collecting her own pleasure from me.

I groaned at the depravity and savoured the satisfaction of her finally doing as she was told. "Good girl."

Her entire body was shaking, like the pleasure was too much and not enough at the same time. Her eyes lit with something dark and desperate knowing that she could see the truth, *taste* the truth of exactly what I did to her and the carnal delight that she knew that *I* knew.

I thrust two fingers into her core, working them in and out from tip to the second knuckle. The sounds were wet and filthy, her arousal dripping down my hand, tangled with her mewing cries. I'd never heard anything so fucking perfect. My cock throbbed in time with the way her inner walls pulsed around my fingers, her back arching, and body cascading in violent shudders.

Her hands gripped my hair like a vice as she cried out, completely at odds with her attempts to retreat from me. From my hold of her over-sensitised clit gently between my teeth while my fingers pumped in and out slower and slower.

Lucky looked at me, her eyes bright, her expression open if not confused, as I got to my feet.

Dazed, as if I'd been dunked into a bath of iced water, my own mind barrelled into me, one half against the other.

What are you doing, Cole?

What the *fuck* was I doing?

I pushed back one step then another.

Had walking always been this fucking hard?

Lucky still gripped the bench, her chest still heaving, her breathing still ragged, cheeks flushed and legs spread slightly, the scent of her arousal permeating the space between us, coating me so completely I didn't think I'd ever be able to wash her off. Her eyes were glassy and heavy lidded with lust as she remained where she was, taking me in.

I looked at her and made myself remember every single reason I hated her. *Every single reason.*

I reached for the blazing inferno of rage, and pain, and fucking *misery*. I *willed* it to twist the picture before me into something disgraceful, into something wrong. All that came was a flicker. A dying ember of what had once consumed me. A twinge of betrayal, of anger.

I reached for it and held onto it like a lifeline as I tore my eyes from hers and did not look back, didn't say a single word.

I strode with one foot in front of the other deeper into the apartment, going absolutely anywhere else than where she was.

As I walked farther away I found myself standing utterly alone amongst the silence that pressed in. It was painfully quiet around me, not a single whisper of anything, but my mind had never been so loud.

22

Lucky

Cole had fractured my mental state.

The entire situation had backfired and all I wanted to do was go home, get into bed, and forget everything. And that's exactly what I *tried* to do.

I counted to ten about nine different times in my head every time a voice trickled up from the kitchen, promising myself that as soon as I got to ten I'd haul myself out of bed and shake off the heaviness, the *shame* of it all.

In reality, I did none of those things. Eventually rolling over, pulling the covers over my head and closing my eyes, focusing on the familiar hum of the fan and waiting for it to lull me back to sleep.

By the time I woke up again the sky was dark outside, the house was quiet and my phone was vibrating on my bedside table.

I reached over, pulling the device from the charging cord and peeked at the name. I rubbed at my eyes before picking up the call, my voice thick with sleep, "Lid, sorry I've--"

A piercing wail made me pull my phone away from my ear with the sort of reflexes I wasn't aware I even had. I looked at my phone screen and yep, it was definitely Melody on the other end. Tentatively, I put it back to my ear just in time to hear another soul crushing cry from my best friend.

"He— he, and I—"

"Melody?" My voice was quiet and I waited until she was able to collect herself and tell me what was going on. But every time she took a breath, the only sounds that continued to pour from my beautiful, sparkly friend was, well, was *this.*

It was on her fifth attempt when nothing came out that I couldn't bear it for a second longer. "That's it. I'm coming over, are you home?"

I was already up, pants in hand with my phone squished between my shoulder and my cheek as I pulled the denim over my butt and pulled a fresh plain cotton grey shirt from my closet.

"Yes." Melody's voice cracked on the single word and I swallowed the lump in my own throat. The sort that grows and thickens whenever you hear someone you love in pain and feel helpless to do a single thing about it.

"I'm right here Lid," I said to her gently, rushing down the stairs. I pulled my coat from a hook near the door along with my keys before flying outside, straight for my car. "I'm going to stay right on the line until I'm at your front door, okay?"

She only responded with a ragged, hiccuped-laced inhale. Melody cried for the next fifteen minutes as I drove through the early evening to her house.

"I'm coming, Lid, hold on. I'm coming." My own voice got tight as I fumbled with the seat belt and rushed for her front door.

Flinging the door open, she threw herself into my arms. We both sank to the frozen concrete of her porch and stayed there. All I could do was hold my best friend close as she broke apart in my arms.

It had taken a solid forty minutes before I managed to get Melody calm enough to bring her back inside and settle her on the couch. That's when she told me what happened.

"He said we weren't compatible anymore," she sniffled, wiping her red rimmed eyes with the sleeve of her sweatshirt. "Three whole years and all he said was that we *weren't compatible*. He'd already packed his backpack and said he was going to stay at his parents place for a while until he could get his stuff and move out."

I reached for her hand and gripped her frozen fingers tightly.

"And the—", a hiccup escaped her as the tears started to fall again, "—the worst part is, I kept asking him what happened, I kept asking him to *talk* to me about what had gone wrong. He said he'd woken up and, and—", her face crumpled in the most devastating way, her body shook with another sob, "—and realised he didn't love me anymore."

"Oh, Melody." I pulled her to me and held onto her tightly as her arms wrapped around me.

"He said he realised it about a month ago and waited to say because he wanted to be sure," she said into my jacket, her voice muffled a little.

I just kept rubbing circles onto her back as she cried into me knowing that there was nothing I could say in this moment to make it better.

"And you know what I said?" She snapped back into a seated position, her face red and blotchy, eyes swollen and breathing hard, "I said he should have told me *then*, that when that sort of stuff happens you're supposed to talk, to work through things together." Her hand, which had been pointing an accusatory finger at me in demonstration, dropped into her lap. "He said you shouldn't have to work for love, that it should be easy."

I scoffed as a wave of pure, undiluted anger rushed through me at the sort of man that had managed to capture my best friend's heart. The sort of man who was so completely and utterly the walking breathing definition of a douche bag that any time I tried to think about how she could've been logically happy with him I actively lost brain cells.

"What an—" I cut myself off, knowing that bagging out Brian wouldn't do anything to help her.

"You can say it."

"No, Lid, I'm sorry I—"

"Go ahead, I give you permission."

I took a deep breath, "First of all, 'you shouldn't have to work for love' are the stupidest words to ever be strung into a sentence ever. Second, Brian is an actual adult-baby who never deserved you, took advantage of your kindness and pure fucking light. And I'm sorry that you loved him so much that it's broken your heart but I will help you put it all back together, I promise. You will see that life is so much better without someone who makes you feel anything but like the goddess you are."

She looked at me, a little smile pulling up the sides of her face as she squeezed my hand that still clutched hers. "I guess there is another positive too."

"Oh?" I lifted my eyebrows at her.

"At least I don't have to have sex with someone who smells like cheese anymore."

We both broke out into cackling fits of laughter and when Melody's laughter morphed back into her tear filled sobs, I held onto her tightly and I didn't let go.

Melody didn't move once through the entire night – she was completely out cold. I, on other hand, was wide awake the whole evening thanks to my entire day of self pity spent in bed and only managing to drift off in the early hours of the morning.

By the time I woke up, it was around nine and Melody was still asleep.

When ten o'clock hit and she showed no signs of waking, I slowly made my way to her side and held my breath while I watched for the rise and fall of her chest.

She was alive, obviously, but can't blame a girl for checking.

I left her to her sleeping while I ducked out for coffee and breakfast, thinking that she'd be up by

the time I got home. I used the little outing to call my mother, just checking in on account of my rather abrupt departure from the family home last night and the eleven, *eleven*, missed calls I had from her on my phone this morning. She called Brian a few choice words that I wouldn't repeat and to let her know if she needed to drop off anything for us to eat.

Turned out Melody was in some sort of broken heart, grief-based hibernation because she was, in fact, not awake when I got back to her house, and didn't wake up for another seven hours. I ended up drinking both our coffees and eating both the breakfast rolls.

The kettle had just finished boiling as I grabbed two mugs off the little hooks that they lived on in Liddy's kitchen, making up two peppermint teas, even though she was still asleep last I checked.

"Put those teas to bed, sweet Navy girl, there's no more need for them."

I screamed, sloshing the boiling water out of one of the mugs and onto my hand which made me scream again, and rush to put my hand under cold water. "Sweet baby *pine trees*, Melody!"

"Oh crap. Crap, crap, *crap*. Are you okay?" She ran over to me, hands outstretched, her face scrunched in concern while she hopped from foot to foot.

I turned to face her, keeping my hand under the tap, "Seriously though, are *you* okay?"

"You know what? I will be." She pushed her dark ringlets off her face and took a deep breath, "I have reached the fourth stage of grief."

I looked at her, my eyebrows furrowing, "You— I think that's depression?"

"What? No! Maybe it's the third stage." She frowned at herself as well.

"So, bargaining?"

"You're actually not helping at all." She reached over and pinched me. "I'm saying that I'm choosing to move past this. I'm at the stage where you start to improve. I got all the tears out and I'm channelling all these emotions into something useful."

"Alright! I love it. That's a big yes from me! What's the

plan?"

"*We're* coping by channelling it into expanding our capacity to hold our alcohol to a whole new level."

"So, *we're* going out?" I lifted an eyebrow.

"We're going out, baby. I need control, you need control, we both need control."

"And we're going to get that control by...going out and getting plastered?"

"You bet your sweet ass we are!" She turned on her heels, headed out of the kitchen and up the stairs. "Saddle up sister, this is going to be a big one!"

* * *

The club we ended up outside of was...unique? Yeah, let's go with unique.

I honestly should have figured something was going to be a little left of centre when I followed her up to her room and she thrust a pleather mini dress at me - tag still on from one of her 'this is the style I want to rock but I just don't think I can' online shopping sprees, with a pair of strappy heels that crisscrossed halfway up my calf. My hair was styled to fall down my back in a pin straight sheet devoid of its natural, soft curls.

Melody stepped out in a pleather mini skirt and a halter top matched with the most epic platform boots I'd ever seen. Her curls were tight and bouncing around her face in the perfect frame.

The club was exclusive to those who apparently liked the

darker things in life, coupled with a little bit of fantasy (I Googled heavily on our way there).

I would say Melody's obsession began with Edward Cullen then spiralled into dark billionaire vampire CEO's who fall in love with their human secretaries. So, when this location became known to her through the many blogs and accounts she followed online, she said she'd popped it in her notes for a special occasion.

This, it would have it, was that very occasion.

The girl had specific tastes which I was obviously in full support of, but I couldn't say I ever thought I'd find myself at the entrance to *Bite Me* dressed like I was dressed.

Melody's bottom lip quivered exactly three times while we were getting ready, so if being at a themed, sexed up fantasy vampire club was what she needed, then fucking call me Buffy.

We stood in line for only ten minutes before we made it to the front (it's literally only 8:00 p.m. on a Tuesday, I was honestly surprised the place was open) and were let in with a little nod from a rather burly looking bouncer with 'Teddy' tattooed on the side of his bald head.

The place was incredibly impressive, I couldn't lie. There were multiple tiers to the club to take in as we entered. A lower level filled with sunken booths lined in what looked like dark velvet, the seating wrapped around crystal-like glass tables that glistened and flickered off the low red lighting. Almost every booth was filled with the silhouettes of people doing whatever it was that people liked to do in the dark. The second level, which was the one we entered on, was paved with black granite floors, leading around the sunken middle section towards an impressive dance floor. The space was completed with caged platforms where incredibly athletic looking dancers worked the shit out of some poles.

On the far side of the club was the bar, and what a beautiful bar it was. It expanded the entire distance of the wall that was completely mirrored. The bar itself was made of the same black granite as the floors and looked like it simply *grew* out of the floor. Above the bar were three massive crystal looking chandeliers with lights that flickered, making them look like they were lit with real flames.

The club was entirely too gothic for it's own good but sweet peanuts, it looked fucking *awesome.*

"This is *so cool!*" Melody jumped up and down, clapping her hands like we'd just gotten our very own set of ears at Disneyland. "Shall we drink?" She turned to me and asked.

"Anything but blood." I nodded, giving her my biggest and widest smile.

"Don't do that, you look insane." She rolled her eyes but quickly followed it with a dazzling smile of her own before she took my hand and walked straight to the bar.

About three hours in, five shots, two vodka lime sodas and an espresso martini each later, I came to find myself in one of those aforementioned caged platforms with the pole doing what I felt like was a pretty solid job.

I would've hazard a guess that Melody felt the same as she looked on from below, throwing a range of coins, receipts and a few stray bills at me from her wallet while asking me repeatedly '*Who's your daddy?!*'. She then followed that question with an answer of her own, going between '*I'm your daddy!*' and '*Philip Peters! That's who her father is!*'.

I completely immersed myself in the moment. I might not have been able to walk in a straight line, but everything that was happening was my choice.

I had the power, I had the control.

Now, in the grand scheme of things these instances of gaining control might not really be helping me gain any ground on my life problems, but right then I could just be Lucky and not have to worry about what that meant exactly.

Melody pulled me closer, our bodies moving together, both of us grinning madly before something shifted in Liddy's face. Her eyes widened a fraction and her body stiffened where I clutched onto her sides.

I saw a pair of hands wrap around her from behind.

She turned in a small panic to see who it was, attempting to un-tether herself from whoever had made their unwelcome appearance.

At first, the guy looked like he might back off, that he was just shooting his shot which I couldn't blame him for, she looked amazing. But alas, it seemed this man was the pin to pop our little bubble.

"No thanks!" I heard Melody shout over the music, backing up her words by holding her arms in a very easy to understand 'X' in front of her.

This guy had some nerve and exactly zero brain cells because all he did was smirk and try to kiss her neck.

I pulled Melody back with a yank that was anything but gentle, the move surprising both her and the unwelcome guest. She slid from his grip with ease and I could almost imagine the little suction sounds of this handsy pervert fumbling to keep his greasy tentacles around her.

"She said no," I yelled, knowing damn well he could hear me and putting myself between them. I held tightly onto one of Melody's arms, keeping her tucked close behind me. She did *not* need this shit.

"Get out of my way, we were in the middle of something," the guy in front of me yelled, doing his best to push me off to the side and reach for Melody again.

So, I did the only thing that came to mind - I kicked the guy right in the balls and when he doubled over I brought my knee up, slamming it into his face after.

There were a few looks from the people around us, but it seemed most were too far gone to give a damn about what was happening.

My heart pumped loud in my ears, adrenaline coursing through my body, and I leaned down putting my mouth next to his ear, "Learn to watch your fucking hands, asshole. No means *no.*"

I turned my back on the guy figuring he'd be down and out for a while and took in an open mouthed, shocked Melody, "Holy shit. What the crap, Luck?!"

I needed no help hearing her over the music that time.

"You just did that, what the fucking fuck?!" she said again.

I honestly couldn't believe it either. I'd never executed that move before, though I'd thought about it about a million times in case I was even in that sort of situation.

"I sort of don't even remember doing it at all!" I yelled back to her, sounding a little deranged, "It was like I was overcome by some higher power!" I beamed, lifting my hand up to high five the one she was holding up for me.

"Hell yeah, you were! This has all made me really need to pee though!"

"Excitement pee or terrified pee?"

"Probably a bit of both!" she called back with two thumbs up.

I gave her a salute in understanding and motioned for her to lead the way. I looked back behind me just to see if Mr. Handsy was anywhere to be seen. He wasn't where I'd left him so I was confident he'd moved on to lick his wounds.

Fucking right, that'll teach him.

We made our way to the hallway next to the stairs that lead up to the VIP area. As soon as we stepped into the secluded area, the music backed off to a dull throb at the back of my head and Liddy made a run to the end of the hall to the bathroom. It was so dull back there that as soon as she moved away from me I could barely see her, only really able to make out the doors of both restrooms once I was standing right in front of them.

It took me all of two minutes to realise that the throb in my head was not actually the music, but one hell of a headache that started to come on.

Closing my eyes, my head dropped back to rest against the wall and I took some deep breaths to try and help disperse some of the pressure behind my eyes and when the door to the bathroom swung open.

I started talking without opening my eyes, "Lid, I think I nee—"

My eyes snapped open a millisecond after a broad hand wrapped around my neck, immediately cutting off my air supply. My hands flew up to grip the wrist attached as I took in the man whose balls had been toast five minutes ago on the dance floor.

He was standing right in front of me, his face a mask of absolute rage, "Not so fucking tough now, are you bitch?" He pulled me towards him until the alcohol on his breath burned my eyes. He squeezed my neck even tighter before thrusting me back against the wall of black stone behind me, my head smacking with a painful crack. Once. Twice. *Three times.*

"Fucking worthless whore." He spat in my face, while his other hand roughly grabbed my thigh trying to force it to the side.

No. No. God, no.

I started flailing, trying to dig my nails into the hand around my throat while also trying to find purchase in the one that was trying to make its way up my dress. I could feel my eyes widen in panic, feel the pressure build behind them the longer I went without air. I fought and kicked and threw punches, all without any care as to where they landed, but only with the goal that I needed to *stop* him.

"Stay still you fucking bitch." The man squeezed tighter, smacking my head for a fourth time into the wall behind me so hard black spots started to invade my vision and I battled with myself to hold onto consciousness.

"Fucking serves you right. You think you can tell me what I can and can't do? Bet you wanted this for yourself, didn't you? Greedy whore."

None of his words were hitting a mark. All I could keep thinking was *no, no, no* as his hand gripped my inner thigh with so much force tears pricked my eyes. *No, no, no* as he pressed his body against mine, trying to keep me still and move his hand higher.

I felt the bile rise in my throat, sure that if his hand wasn't gripping it I'd have thrown up already at the thought of what was happening to me.

When he got to the line of my panties and began to hook a finger into the elastic, I willed every ounce of my draining energy into fighting him and I knew even through the roaring pain in my chest I was screaming. I knew I was and if his hand wasn't stealing my ability to breathe it would have been blood curdling.

I kept screaming even when no sound came out of my mouth, continued to grip and claw at the hand that was touching me, pushing through the throbbing at the back of my head. Even as I felt the moment I'd lose consciousness a second before it descended upon me, as I refused to come to terms with what that actually meant for me.

I was solely consumed by the moment I felt his hand roughly move across my bare sex after he'd ripped the fabric of my underwear away from me, at the way his fingers touched and groped and probed that I barely registered a shriek pierce the air around me, and then Melody was there.

In a move I'd only ever seen on television, she formed a closed fist and aimed it straight at the man's throat.

The sound of her scream got the attention of the bouncer built like a semi who was on watch at the base of the VIP stairs.

The punch threw my attacker off enough that he retracted his hand from up my dress, my stomach still rolling as the ghost of his touch *lingered.* His grip on my throat loosened enough to drop me, my legs immediately failing me.

Melody was right there and a second later the bouncer had the guy on the floor, crushing him with his immense weight and calling something into the little earpiece he was wearing. I didn't have enough sense to make out what he said, no sense beyond taking in the gulping breaths I kept sucking down and the coughing that ensued.

Melody's tear-stricken face was in front of me, her hands shaking as they held onto my face, her lips making out shapes like she was saying my name. I couldn't focus on it with the ringing in my ears. The pain in my chest.

All I could do was grip her hand while she sat in front of me until I was calm enough to take in the scene around us.

There was a fire escape door at the very end of the hallway and the security dragged the guy out there followed promptly by another man while three more guys stood around us now in a protective semi-circle.

They tried to speak to me but I couldn't hear anything past the ringing in my ears and my own frantic heartbeat. Couldn't *feel* anything apart from his body pressed against mine, his hands on my skin and the absolute terror that had gripped me.

Melody explained enough to them that an ambulance had been called as well as the police.

They assured me the marks on my throat would fade over the course of the next couple weeks. I declined an offer to be checked out further at the hospital, even as I heard the list of things they told me had happened on account of the strangulation. Aside from that, I had a minor concussion and should refrain from doing anything too strenuous for the next forty eight hours.

I could see the guilt in Melody's eyes after I stepped out of the bathroom, opting to rid myself of my ripped underwear that was barely holding on. I refused to look at myself in the mirror when I washed my hands. I knew that she thought this was on her because she'd brought us here, that she had been in the bathroom. No matter how many times I told her it wasn't her fault I knew she'd still blame herself for a part of it.

Gripping her hand in mine, we walked out of the club and

I finally turned to her with a smile that I didn't feel, that honestly hurt my face a little to carve my features into, "I didn't even know you knew how to deliver a throat punch." My voice was raspy and it hurt to talk, but I tried to keep my tone light.

She cracked a smile back, "Sort of came out of nowhere, huh?"

We stood on the sidewalk, the bitter cold of the winter evening biting at all our exposed skin.

Goosebumps immediately erupted on Melody's arms.

I pulled her in for a hug. I didn't have it in me to look at her, knowing my face would give me away. I swallowed thickly, trying to keep the tremor from my own voice, meaning every single word I whispered, "Thank you for getting there in time."

"Navy, if it—" She tried to pull back but I kept her locked in my embrace.

"No. It was an awesome night out, and this was a crappy ending but it changes nothing." I finally pulled back and looked down at our joined hands and then back up at her.

"Are you sure you're okay?" she asked again, her voice trembled and another tear escaped her.

"I'm sure," I said, swiping my thumb across her cheek knowing that even if I wasn't sure right now, I would be soon. "And no more crying, remember you're in your sixth stage of grief." I winked at her.

The smile she returned wobbled as her eyes continued to take in the damage that had been done to me.

"Depression?" She pushed out a breathy laugh.

"No, moving forward. I'm proud of you for going out tonight. You're stronger than you think."

"You are too, Luck." She held my gaze until I nodded back to her, accepting her words. Releasing a heavy sigh she asked one more time, "And you're sure you don't want to come back with me?"

"I'm sure, you go home and get some rest and I'll call you tomorrow. Let me tell my folks though, okay?" I smiled at her in the most reassuring way that I could before she gave me a final hug and a promise for my last request before getting into one of the waiting police cruisers.

I waited until she drove off, the cold hardly while I watched the car disappear. Only then did I turn and walk for the car they had waiting for me.

It wasn't my childhood home that I wanted to go to, what I *needed*.

I gave the officer the address and clicked my seat belt wondering if I'd lost my mind.

23

Lucky

I didn't think through the fact that both Jim and Abe would be sitting at the bottom of Cole's building.

And so, there I was at midnight, staring up at the building that was my jail for all intents and purposes, that *housed* my jailer for lack of a better word and turned out to be the only place I wanted to go to let myself...what? Fall apart? Crack wide open? *Feel safe?* Oh, the irony.

Shut up, shut up, *shut up.*

No, I couldn't go back to my parents' place. So, here I was.

There was a door on the side of the building that, once entered, if I hauled ass I could be well and truly in the alcove of the elevators before either of the sweetest men I'd ever had the pleasure of knowing would see me. And them seeing me was *not* an option.

I stood outside for another minute, soaking up the freezing

temperature in an effort to convince myself the trembling was from my lack of layers and not from anything else before walking around to the side of the building.

Pulling the door open I made quick work of the steps between the door and the lifts, bringing my hair around in an effort to hide myself as best I could.

"Hey guys!" I tried for a casual yell while I sped past them and pretended not to notice when my voice came out gritty and rasped. Throwing my hand up in a floppy wave I kept my face down and angled away from them.

"Lucky?" Abe called out, shock and pleasant surprise in his voice.

"Yeah, just me! Sorry, I just forgot something upstairs!" Tucked safely in the alcove and I started to tap the call button for the elevator like my life depended on it.

"Hey, where are you going in such a hurry, and at this hour too?" It was Jim this time who called out, followed by the telling squeak of his office chair as he pushed away from the security desk. The soft squeaks of his shoes were like the countdown of a bomb as he rounded it to no doubt come in my direction.

Oh, god. Come on, come on.

"Lucky?" Jim called again, his voice a little concerned as I just kept tapping the button, both not able and not willing to say anything in return.

My heart was *galloping* in my chest making the pounding at the back of my head even worse. On reflex I move my hand up to press against the pain, feeling for the first time the lump that was left by four smacks onto solid stone. My mouth parted in a barely there gasp. It was the size of a tennis ball and that fact alone made me wobble on my feet.

The elevator's ding announced its arrival and I wasn't sure if the nausea rolling in my stomach was from relief or fear that he'd still see me. That he'd see me and know.

"What's going on, kid? Are you al—"

I'd never punched in my code for Cole's penthouse so fast. "Sorry Jim! Have a nice night!" I called out, keeping my face angled down and seeing the toes of his shoes just as the elevator doors closed. I immediately sagged against the wall, closing my eyes and keeping them that way, refusing to see any reflection in the mirrors that surround me.

I used my time in the elevator to take off my shoes and pull the pins from the front of my hair that were keeping the slick hairstyle in place. My nose tingled twice on the trip up, both times I refused to let the emotion out, locking it down and knowing all I needed was just a second. A second to myself and then I'd be okay. Then I would tuck this day away, along with yesterday and I would be *fine* once the sun came up.

The sound of the elevator arriving echoed through the entry space of Cole's apartment. I didn't flinch at the noise, at its very blatant announcement of my arrival. He wouldn't be here and I'd be gone before he got home.

I discarded the heels by the elevator, along with the pins and my tiny little purse that held barely anything as it swung from my wrist all night, and squeezed the solid hand of Mr. Invisible, heading straight for the kitchen. There were no lights on and I decided to leave it that way. I didn't want to be in the light right now. I wanted to be consumed by the darkness. I didn't want to see, I didn't want to feel. Not when all I could do was see and feel and remember everything, every single second playing back in my head. Over and over and *over*. How close I had been to...to what? Losing my body?

Losing my life?

Another rolling wave of nausea consumed me while I busied myself on boiling the kettle and grabbing a mug, the pressure behind my eyes burning all the while with the need to erupt.

I held up my mug of steaming tea to my lips and felt the hot liquid move its way through my aching chest. I felt the cold stone beneath my feet, the safety and security in it. The safety in where I was and for *once* I didn't berate myself for those feelings and why they were there when they had no right to be at all. So, when the pressure behind my eyes came again I didn't fight it.

I let the tears fall. I let the ache grow until it encompassed my entire body and all I could do was grip onto the only warmth I had from the mug cradled between my hands.

The first sob rock through my body. My hand reached out, fumbling to take purchase on the cold counter top, both to steady myself and a source to pull strength from I silently willed my bones to keep. I kept my gaze on the cityscape before me, and promised myself that I could feel all of this now but as soon as the sun came up I would dry my eyes and hold my head up high. I'd look back at this moment and—

The lights snapped on, illuminating the entire kitchen and dining room in stark, cool lighting that burned my eyes.

My gasped inhale was audible.

No.

He couldn't be here. He was *never* here at this time,

"Lucky," he said softly, in a way he never had in the months that had passed. Never had in the years before.

It existed in the space around me so completely that it felt like there was no room left for anything else. The timbre of his voice filled me with a different sort of warmth and I couldn't stop myself from closing my eyes and savouring it. Savouring the way it filled me, the way it saved me in a moment when I hadn't totally known what I'd needed until I found it because even though I knew he wouldn't be here, I'd hoped. And even though he hated me, I would bear it.

I was a masochist, that much had become clear to me, but right now? I didn't have it in me to care.

24

Cole

"Lucky." Her name fell from my lips in the way it had filled the spaces in my mind during the brief moments I had forgotten myself. When my mother had screamed, and left her marks on my body, when I had wanted no one and nothing but peace. But her.

I moved in behind her, my feet still silent but the rustle of clothing indication enough of my movements. I stood so close I should've been able to feel the warmth of her body and the lack of it made me notice just how little she was wearing. Just how cold it was. How cold *she* was.

"Lucky." My voice came out stronger, deeper.

I watched as another shake wracked her small frame. I didn't think, couldn't stop myself from reaching out, dragging the pads on my finger across her shoulder and down her arm.

COLE

"Turn around." There was an edge to my voice, a very clear tell of the mixture between confusion and the lack of patience, of not knowing. Like I was missing something vital because she hadn't said a single fucking word.

"Lucky—"

"Don't." Her voice was hoarse. Like the usual tone had been dragged through glass and left out in the very cold that had seeped into her skin.

I'd heard every word that she'd thrown at me, heard every insult and foul thing she flung back at me in response. She met me blow for blow without a single slip up but never, not even when we were growing up, had I heard her sound like *that*.

I realised that it was the complete lack of warmth in her tone. That it was a brokenness. Something I had wanted so badly to cause, and now that I heard exactly what it sounded like...

My stomach rolled.

My body tensed with the need to look into her eyes, to see everything she was feeling. To read her like the open book she'd always been to me.

"Lucky," I said her name again, my hand slipping around her upper arm, ready to turn her around myself when she flinched.

She fucking *flinched*.

A quiet fury bled into every part of me as I pulled my hand back and let it fall to my side. My heart rate slowed to a lethal calm that thumped steadily in my chest, my jaw clenched so tight it ached.

"Turn. Around." I barely registered the words leaving my lips, my eyes boring into the back of her head with such intensity I knew she could feel the finely veiled violence I was keeping in check.

Her shoulders raised and lowered in a barely there inhale, like the act was painful. Setting her mug on the counter, she dropped her head and slowly, so slow it was a fucking test to my patience, she turned to face me.

My jaw clenched tighter and a faint crack resounded through my skull as I flexed my hands, pulling them into tight fists locking every single one of my muscles into place.

Lucky kept her face angled down with her eyes closed while mine took in the savage deep purple bruising around her neck. Angry red crescents that had sealed closed were at the end of each individual deep purple bruise, three on one side of her neck, one on the other.

Finger prints. They were fucking *finger prints.*

Someone had done this, someone had *touched* her.

Her chest was red, rising and falling in rapid, shallow breaths.

"Lucky, look at me." I kept my voice low, but there was no missing the venom that laced every word.

Her eyes pressed closed and she shook her head, wincing slightly.

"Please, Lucky." It was barely a whisper and I watched a single tear descend from each closed eye a moment before she opened them, settling her bright blue eyes on me.

I was going to kill whoever did this.

I wanted to rip them apart. I wanted to slice them up into little tiny pieces only to stitch them back together and do it all again. Over and over and fucking over again.

Lucky's left eye was filled almost completely with popped blood vessels, rendering a good portion of it red. She held my stare, didn't falter for even a second as I unclenched one of my fists and lifted it between us. My hand shook and I knew that she was just as aware of it as I was but she still didn't take her eyes from mine. The pads of my fingers skimmed across the marks that consumed the once unblemished skin of her neck, trembling still as they ghosted across her cheek, wiping away the path of moisture that continued to flow, stopping only under her damaged eye.

"Who." It wasn't a question and she knew it, but she still shook her head telling me that it wasn't that she was keeping it from me, but that she didn't know the name of the man that did it. The thought rocked my body with a tremor and I gently moved to sink my hand into her hair to hide the evidence of how I was losing control.

Lucky's hand shot out immediately, gripping my wrist in her hand. It seemed so much smaller than it had before, so much more delicate.

Breakable.

My eyes snapped to hers and I knew without her needing to tell me, I saw it written across every inch of her face.

Her grip loosened enough for me to move.

Lightening my touch so that I didn't hurt her, I felt for the source of her pain with gentle fingers. The lump on the back of her head was something that would only have developed from her head hitting something very fucking hard.

Her hand didn't leave my wrist, instead her grip tightened like she needed to hold onto me to steady herself.

Her face through every single age that I had adamantly hated her through seeped into my mind. I couldn't pull my eyes from her as I recalled every moment where I would slip and feel the grief of her loss, where I couldn't only make it better, made it *bearable* by filling it with something darker. Something more bitter, until hating every single thing about her gave me something to hold onto, gave me purpose.

I held her violently blue eyes and wanted to be consumed by her, even if I hated myself for it.

I wanted to be *burned* by it, this thing growing in my chest, clawing me to pieces, even if it meant sacrificing a part of who I was.

The dying, flickering ember I had tethered myself to so I could walk away from her finally gave in to the tidal wave of chaos that those ocean eyes of hers brought with them, snuffing out completely.

"Cole." My name fell from her lips in the most helpless sort of way and if I hadn't known it before, I knew it now.

I would rather burn the fucking world to the ground than ever see that look in her eyes again.

25

Lucky

I don't know what I expected, but it wasn't the barely restrained rage that coursed through the man before me while he took stock of the marks that covered my body.

This moment should've felt foreign between us, it should have felt like it didn't belong here, like it shouldn't be happening, but it didn't feel like that at all.

I felt *safe.*

Cole's hand settled at the nape of my neck, his thumb making small soothing circles that were so at odds with the tension he held in his body. I had no idea who this version of him was, so conflicting with the man I'd come to know.

I opened my mouth to try and crack a joke, to ask him what in the world he'd done with the asshole who owned this building, to try and bring any form of myself back to the surface after breaking so thoroughly in front of him. I tried to get the words out but the act hurt more than I cared to admit, my throat still raw and aching as the injuries continued to settle. I knew the pain crossed my face and any hope I had that it would go unnoticed was futile.

Cole's eyes darkened in a way I was familiar with but also like his anger was no longer directed at me, rather like his anger was *for* me.

The thought made a weight form in my stomach, an immediate ache coming to life in my core and my pulse thrumming between my thighs, but the moment the feelings flooded me all I could feel was *his* hand. All I saw was *him*.

"Stay with me," Cole said before me. He was even closer to me now, his tone much like the gentle touch of his hand. Like I might be able to trust that I could let down my guard here and that he wouldn't use this against me later.

I knew he read the thought right off my face when his hand dropped from my neck and he instead held it out between us, palm up.

"You're safe with me, Lucky."

I watched his lips form the words and felt the treble of his voice in the air between us. I shouldn't have believed him, he'd shown me *why* I shouldn't. Why the only thing I could expect from him was my downfall, the only thing that I could trust with absolute certainty was that he wanted me broken.

I knew all of that and yet I still slipped my hand into his and followed his lead into a part of his home that I'd never seen before, all while he was showing me a part of himself I hadn't known existed.

Neither of us said a single thing. I didn't think I could, but his grip on my hand stayed firm with his fingers laced through mine. The way his hand swallowed mine so completely was the only thing I could keep my eyes on as I counted my breaths to keep calm.

Cole's room sat behind a set of wide, heavy oak double doors. They stood out in such heavy contrast with the rest of his home, or at least the parts that I'd seen.

He pushed the doors open and I didn't even feel brave enough to look around. Something that, given any opportunity, I totally would have done. But right now? I didn't want to damage whatever flimsy bridge of calm had been built between us. Where he looked at me like he didn't hate me and I held onto his hand like I believed him.

Cole didn't stop until we were standing in what I assumed was his private bathroom.

This space? Oh, I soaked it the hell up. It was *huge* and very much in his style as I was coming to understand it. The tiles beneath my feet were a dark charcoal and pleasantly heated. There was a vanity that looked like it was made from the same material as the floor, tiled with two sinks that spread across one wall, completed with a massive mirror that I avoided looking directly at.

There was a shower big enough for a good ten people spanning another wall. It also had three shower heads, one at each end, as well as one right in the middle on the ceiling. There was nothing to section it off, no glass or curtain, it just led into the rest of the bathroom. The plan was completely open. The very last wall held what had to be the biggest, most beautiful claw foot bathtub I'd ever seen. It was huge, like it would fit my whole family, sort of massive.

This was nothing, and I meant *nothing* like what I would have pegged for Cole's bathroom. I mean, there was a plant in here, a very alive, very happy looking plant. And hand towels and a little ceramic soap dispenser next to one of the two basins. There was even a bath mat that said '*You look great!*' near the shower and another one that said '*This is your best angle*' near the tub.

A laugh bubbled up in my chest, but it never made it further than that. I kept my eyes on the tub and felt his eyes leave me as he walked over to it and turned on the faucet, checking the water temperature and adjusting it bit by bit until it was perfect.

It was at that exact moment that I realised Cole wore nothing except for a pair of loose fitting black sweatpants.

I let my eyes drift over him, taking in the way the muscles on his back moved with every little action he made to adjust the water, the way his skin stretched and settled when he stood up to his full height and turned to face me. I couldn't stop myself from following the contours of his stomach, the firm defined muscles and the small smattering of dark hair that covered his chest, only to make a reappearance below his navel and disappear beneath the band of his sweats.

I'd seen him like this before, but he was no less captivating the second time around.

I could feel his eyes on me, feel the violence permeate the air around him. My body shivered from the heat in his gaze, like he was remembering the way I looked kneeling before him, remembering the way he had touched me and how I'd reacted to that touch.

My eyes closed at the pang of nausea that bloomed in me for the fucking billionth time tonight. How, in my head, I reached for the memory of Cole's hands on me, his hand wrapped around my throat, the way he had squeezed. How that very action seemed to have a direct line to my core, the way I clenched around nothing but knew that it was him I needed desperately.

I reached for those memories and gripped them as tightly as I could, even as a new memory worked to pry my grip from them. Memories of my eyes watering from the burning scent of alcohol that filtered from a mouth I didn't know. My mind was caught in a brutal tug of war between savage and merciless hands that slid up my body to force apart my thighs and hands that I knew. Hands that I *wanted* and dreamt of and craved.

I gripped on to those flashes of Cole, with his mouth and tongue and lips on me like I would die if they were pulled from my grasp. I felt my body seize up as a shudder wracked through me, making me fumble with my grip on those jade green eyes. Leaving me to watch on in horror as they were replaced with a shadowed gaze where I couldn't quite make out the colour but I could *feel* the vile intent–

Cole's hands were on me, curving around the back of my neck, holding the hair at my nape firmly. He didn't so much as blink as I flinched from his touch which pulled me from the battle I was fighting, and losing, in my own head.

"Eyes on me," he gritted out as he reached for my hand and placed it on his chest. The beat of his heart was steady and grounding beneath my touch and it made me realise just how fast mine was going. How fast I was breathing.

He took a deep breath in and I copied him instinctively. He did it over and over until my heartbeat matched his, until it was only his blazing green eyes that I could see.

Cole reached around me, pulling my body close to his before his fingers found the zipper at the back of my dress and started to pull it down.

A fresh wave of panic surged through me, my hands pushing at his chest in an effort to step away.

"I—" I rasped, trying to shake my head as I felt my eyes widen.

"Just for the bath, nothing else." His voice was still soft even as I watched the colour of his eyes darken. I relaxed into him immediately, still trusting his promise that I was safe here with him. I turned my body so that my back was to him, giving him permission to finish unzipping me, letting him know in my actions that I trusted him with this. I kept my eyes downcast from the mirror in front of us, still not ready to see myself.

I knew exactly what he'd see once there was nothing between him and I. The marks had been forgotten until that moment. Until a broken sort of sound that I'd never thought I'd hear coming out of the man behind me made my eyes snap up to look at him in the mirror, his figure towering behind me.

His eyes were locked on the bruises that littered my left inner thigh. I knew he'd taken note immediately that there was no sign of anything else on my body besides the dress.

Cole's hand settled on my waist, gripping me firmly like he couldn't help himself. Like if he didn't touch me I'd disappear right before his eyes. I couldn't care for a single second that I was standing before him completely naked. I was no less vulnerable now standing with him as I'd been in the kitchen.

It was a weird, tangled sense of shame and relief. Relief that he knew, and I wasn't sure exactly why that had been so important to me but it was. And the shame that I hadn't been strong enough to fight, to stop it from happening to me.

My eyes shuttered again from the rush of emotion and I

let the final tears fall and, sunrise be damned, I swore they would be the last.

Cole's hand grazed my back, lifting one of my arms around his shoulders and sweeping me up in a single move. It made my heart flip in a stupid sort of way and I couldn't tear my eyes away from his face as he carried me to the bathtub, setting me down with a tenderness I hadn't thought him capable of, before he placed a kiss on my temple. He didn't say another word as he turned to walk away but I had to ask.

I had to understand *why*.

"Cole."

This time I saw *him* flinch, like the gravel of my voice scraped across every nerve ending in his body. "You— why?"

He didn't turn to face me, only stood there for a minute before his hand reached out to grip the door frame, knuckles white.

"I wanted to be your end, Lucky. I wanted you to know nothing but me. I wanted to break you." His confession didn't surprise me. I knew that was what he'd wanted from me. Why he hadn't let me go, even as the details for those dark desires still escaped me.

"What changed?" I whispered back to him, my lids falling heavy as the warmth of the bath softened my cold and aching muscles.

"A lot." His voice was barely a whisper too.

My eyelids closed, my body losing the battle to stay awake. Right before sleep claimed me completely I thought I heard him speak again.

"Those things haven't really changed though, have they?" he mused, and in my sleep state I could almost feel the ghost of his fingers trace the shape of my face. "I want you to know nothing but me. I want you to *think* of no one but me. I want to consume you like you've consumed me. I want you to burn in it, just like you've drowned me. Will you do that, Lucky? Will you break for me?"

Yes.

I wanted to say it, I was sure that I did.

Yes. I wanted to tell him, because it was already happening.

"Cole," I grabbed onto the strands of consciousness that dangled around me, feeling half in the real world and half not, "will you stay?"

He was quiet for so long I didn't know if I'd even said the words aloud. The deep rumble of his voice pulled me that little bit more towards consciousness when it broke the silence around us, "I'll stay."

"Promise?" The water rippled as I lifted a tired arm from the water to lean my hand on the edge of the tub. The act felt second nature to me. Would he even remember that part of our history?

I was on the precipice of sleep when I felt his pinky hook through mine, when he whispered his reply to me, voice raw and haunted, " I promise."

I fell asleep with the feeling of his lips leaving a gentle kiss to the pad of my thumb.

26

Lucky

I woke with a gasp, my body desperate for air after the memory of being so completely deprived of it fled from my mind.

With a jolt, my hands fisted the sheets at the same time my eyes snapped open. It took a whole ten seconds to realise where I was, why I was there and a further few to figure out *how* the hell I'd even gotten there.

I was naked the last time I was awake. Yes, I had been covered in bubbles but I had still been very much naked and — I lifted up the soft, plush duvet that was settled around me like I was in a freakin' cloud — yep, no longer naked. I was wearing a shirt.

A very big, very *not mine* shirt.

My head whipped around too quickly towards the movement that caught my attention.

"*Ah—*," a pained, rasped sound left me at the sharp movement. Like life couldn't help but shit on my parade while I was down and out.

This whole 'lack of luck' thing was really on a roll now.

The movement pulled my attention again, the spiralling thoughts I'd begun to travel down evaporating like smoke as I took him in.

Cole sat in one of the plush forest green chairs that he had in his room, the twin of which was facing the other direction; out at the cityscape below, lit up and sparkling with the lightening sky in the distance pulling the world into shades of oranges and reds and pinks.

The weight of Cole's gaze felt different. No less heavy and no less dissecting than it had been before, but different nonetheless. He wore the same thing I remembered from last night – black sweats and no shirt – his black hair mussed and sticking out every direction like he'd tried to pull every strand out of his head repeatedly.

His gaze was trying to pull the answers from my body before I'd said a single thing. I knew what he wanted to know and my body flooded with a panicked wave of heat. The only thing I thought to do was change the subject. To do *anything* but be any more vulnerable than I'd already been.

"Bet you never thought I'd be naked in your bed." I cracked a grin that still hurt to paste on. The croak of my voice pulled any bit of humour that could have bloomed from the words and the small cough that followed did a heck of a job of really killing it in the ass.

His jaw ticked once.

Twice.

He just looked at me, his eyes roaming over one of my eyes

in particular and then the necklace of bruises.

"Drink." He nodded towards his bedside table where a big glass of water sat with two of what I was assuming were painkillers.

My eyes flicked to him in question.

"For your head," he answered, knowing what was in my mind even if I hadn't said it aloud.

I drank the whole glass thing down slowly, taking the pills. Each swallow eliciting a painful ache. I definitely did not need to be a hero in any capacity, just the feel of the dull throb in the back of my head was enough to roil the nausea again. I don't know how long we sat there in silence, my eyes focused on my hands but every ounce of my attention was on him.

I could see him from the corner of my eye and I focused on the rise and fall of his chest. The way his pointer finger on his right hand tapped the armrest of the chair he was in.

"Who touched you, Lucky?" I'd never heard him sound like that before. Jagged and blistering and *savage*. His jaw clenched even tighter, expression darkening even further.

I'd rather he looked at me the way he did before, with hate and anger and darkness. I didn't know what to do with the way he looked at me now.

"Cole—" I wished my voice just sounded normal, if only so I could just speak without wincing.

"Who. *Touched*. You." It wasn't a question this time, his words were short and clipped and delivered without an ounce of patience.

I took a deep breath, the tightness in my chest still present but lesser than last night, and I explained. I told him about the dance floor, about the kick to the balls I'd delivered with enthusiasm. How the guy came out of nowhere and I hadn't seen him head in the direction that we'd unknowingly followed in, how *lucky* I'd been that Melody came out of the restroom when she did.

It was the second time in my life I hated my name. If anything, this just showed – no, it fucking rubbed it right in my face – just how very devoid of luck I was.

"And your thigh?" Still jagged. Still savage.

"He— well, he had his hand around my throat," instinctively my hands moved up to wrap around the tender skin, "and so I'd focused on stopping him from—from—"

"Did he rape you, Lucky?" God, his voice cracked. It *cracked.*

"No, he didn't."

"Did he touch you?"

"Yes." I wanted to sound brave, but I didn't. I sounded small, and frail and shameful.

The silence was painful. I wanted him to do anything but look at me like he was now. Like he'd tear the world apart for me, like he *hated* this for me, because I wasn't sure if I believed him. I was even more terrified that if I did believe him it would be a mistake I'd pay for in the sort of way that I wouldn't come back from.

"Cole, I'm—"

"Why did you come here? Why didn't you go home?"

"I'm sorry, I know it was stupid. God, I just— look at me." I moved to face him finally and gestured to my face, "My parents— And there are kids at my house *all the time*. I just, I needed quiet. I needed—" *Safety and strength and fucking, oh my god, I needed you and I don't know why.*

I wasn't afraid to hold his gaze even as he levelled me with a look I knew had likely sent many running for the hills. I knew that he'd see everything anyway like he always did and whether I tried to make something up or say nothing at all he'd *know*.

"You'll stay here until you heal." He got up swiftly, every movement rigid as he walked towards a room off the main one we were in and exited a second later with a black shirt pulled over his torso.

"What?" It would have been a yelp if it didn't sound like I'd eaten a porcupine. "No, *no*. I can't *stay* here, you don't even *like*—"

"You'll stay here, Navy." He turned to face me, his face providing no space for negotiation of any kind, and my body warmed at the way he used my real name. "Message your parents, tell them we'll be travelling for work for the next couple weeks, then you can go home."

And then he left and I sat there staring after him for longer than was a respectable amount of time. But he didn't come back.

I looked at my phone, realising it had been plugged into his charger after I'd dropped it by the elevator when I'd arrived. Just another thing I didn't want to think about. Not between the bath and the shirt and the *look* in his eyes. The sound of his voice. Maybe he was just decent and the way he'd been with me was just another little stroke of bad luck. That he felt bad or responsible because I was his employee as he'd once said before.

I didn't message my parents. I didn't call them, or Melody, or Jamie, or anyone. Instead, I threw off the covers and walked into his big, beautiful bathroom, and finally looked at myself in the mirror.

27

Cole

The clear lock screen of my phone shone back at me, showing me absolutely sweet fuck all, just like it had the entire day. I turned the device over in my hand while I held my office phone to my ear.

I wasn't sure when they would call or how they'd get in touch. I'd requested a phone call to either the office directly or to my private phone. I'd sent off the email this morning before the sun had risen, before Lucky had stirred, while she slept in my bed with her hair fanned on the pillows around her. I'd heard nothing back and I was losing the incredibly small amount of patience I had left.

"Yes, Mr. Landis, I can absolutely see how the shift in dates could disrupt some of your travel plans. Though I do feel obligated to mention that the company is paying for those particular flights." I rubbed at my eyes, leaning back in my office chair and wishing for the fortieth fucking time today that I was doing anything else but taking phone calls from all the executives about moving the New York holiday event from the end of this week to the end of next.

"Tell you what, Landis. How about we bump you from business to first class as an apology for the inconvenience? – Perfect, I'll have Felicity send through your updated flights. – Look forward to seeing you too."

God, I wished he wasn't such a wet noodle. Mark Landis was one of the few stuffy older men with too much money that I could actually stand.

I took a breath and typed out a quick message to Lucky, pressed send and told myself it was stupid for her not to have my number for work emergencies.

Me:
Save this number for emergencies.

I stared at my phone until the three little dots popped up and I watched them disappear and reappear twice more before her message came back.

Lucky:
Kinky, but who is this?

God why was my heart pounding so much, I wasn't fucking fourteen. Was I *smiling at my phone?*

Me:
Cole.

I locked my phone and tucked it into the inside pocket of my jacket. It was four in the afternoon and I'd never had a day drag as much as this one had. Lucky was still sitting in my bed when I'd walked away from her, something I was trying incredibly hard not to think about. Almost as hard as I was trying not to think about how I watched consciousness slip from her as she soaked in the bathtub.

My bathtub.

How I watched her chest rise and fall with every breath, how they were still quick and too shallow because even in sleep she was in pain. I was trying not to think about how I could feel the heat that she had gotten back thanks to the near scalding water in the bath, water she didn't even flinch at as I set her down into it. How I could feel that heat radiating against my fingertips as I let them hover over the lines of her face, her eyelids, her cheekbones, all the way to where my hand paused over the marks on her neck.

My hand hovered there, shaking with restraint to not murder whoever had done it. With an overwhelming need to replace every look in her eyes that was doused in shadows with memories of me; replace every mark on her skin with ones I made. I sat there and watched her as she slept, not fully trusting that if she somehow sunk deeper into the water that she would wake up. She didn't stir once, not even as I lifted her from the water. I was only barely holding it together as I sat her on the end of my bed.

"I'll ruin the bed," she'd grumbled, eyes still closed but a small furrow in her brow.

"No, you won't," I'd said softly, knowing she wasn't really awake. "Arms up, baby," I'd asked her, ignoring the word that had slipped out of my mouth and focusing only on pulling my shirt over her head and settling her into the covers.

I watched her all night, half scared to look away from the rise and fall of her chest and half because I wasn't sure that if I left I wouldn't find the guy and kill him. I needed to hear the words from her, I needed to know everything that had happened.

The coffee cup I'd picked up came down on my desk with a crack. My *glass* desk, causing a fissure to form beneath it.

Fucking *great*.

This was what my day had been like. Sitting through meetings and reading through emails. It was a day filled with focusing my efforts on keeping my temper in check.

I let out a frustrated growl at the way my whole fucking system was being flooded with *new* feelings. Feelings I didn't know what the hell to do with or how to get a grip of myself over. That's not how I had made it this far in life. I'd always had a...*darker* side that demanded an outlet.

A release. Something to *quench* it.

As I grew up I'd come to learn that I needed *more*. That there was something particularly helpful about the way my fist connected with someone's face.

That was how Fyn Bennet, Felicity's father and my then professor, had found me during my second year of college. He had a choice as to what he would do with me. He'd called me into his office and told me he'd put my name down at a boxing gym and that he'd be going with me.

I laughed so hard I cried. I had actual tears rolling down my face. When I came up for air his face was the exact opposite of mine. He'd said I had two choices; I could learn to control it or I could let it control me.

I'd honed it, I'd *leashed* it.

Until her.

But then it became easy. Lucky became the perfect release. Her warm heat around my fingers, the taste of her on my tongue. Flowers and rain and *god*, her lips wrapped around my cock. I'd been angry at her then, I had been taking it out on her and enjoying it. Every scowl, every jab she sent right back, I'd been enjoying the fight with her. And then it had all changed, she had gotten under my skin and made me *want*.

Now, it wasn't her that my anger was directed, but *for* her and my control was slipping.

The buzz from my intercom filled the room and my eyes snapped open.

I reached over to hit the button to reply, "Yes?"

"Mr Thompson?" Daisy, Facility's in-office temporary replacement said through the line, her voice hesitant.

"Yes?" My voice gave absolutely nothing away.

"Acer Malcolm is on the phone for you."

"You can patch him through." I waited for the phone to ring a couple times before picking it up, "Cole Thompson."

"Mr. Thompson." The voice on the other end belonged to a very bad man who was very good at hiding it. In the business of investing you had to know where you were putting your money. Who you were putting it into. What they had for breakfast, who their family pet was, their last fuck, their *favourite* fuck. All of it said everything about a person. That's what Acer did for me, and he did it very well.

I couldn't stop the wave of feral rage that moved through

me, rolling my neck in an involuntary manner and undoing the top button of my work shirt as he told me what I'd been waiting to hear all day.

"We have the information you've asked for."

28

Lucky

"Lucky?" My mothers frantic voice was on the other end of the phone after only a single ring. She didn't even wait for me to reply before the phone was clearly pulled from her face and she yelled out to whoever was around her, "It's Lucky! Philip, it's Lucky, quickly will you tell Oakleigh? – Lucky? Are you there?"

"Hey, yeah. I'm here," I said through a sigh.

"Where are you? Why haven't you picked up a single phone call? Your brother has been worried sick—"

"I've actually been fine, Luck!" Oakleigh called out from somewhere behind my mother, his voice distorted in a way that told me he definitely had a mouth full of food.

"You didn't need to worry and I *have* been messaging. Things have been really busy over here."

"Over where? You haven't even said where you are." She

sounded like she had her free hand on her hip and a scowl on her face.

"We're travelling around lots for Cole's work." My words were clipped. "Sorry, I—" I took a deep breath and softened my voice, "—really, I didn't mean to worry you."

"I tried calling Melody and she didn't pick up either." My mother exhaled sharply and it tugged at my chest. She was always like this, always worried that something was wrong.

"That doesn't surprise me, she's had a tough time too with Brian and all."

"Brian was an ass," my mother said in a huff on the other end of the phone.

The first real laugh since I don't know how long, bubbled up and out of my mouth, "No argument from me there, the man smelt like cheese." I smiled into the phone.

"Brian? As in Melody and Brian?" Oaks called out from wherever he still lingered. Mum's voice turned muffled as she no doubt took the opportunity to share the news. There was a strained scuffle on the other end with a few concerning grunts before my brother yelled right into the phone.

"Lucky, hey. They broke up?" He sounded out of breath like he'd had to work incredibly hard to get the phone from our mother.

"*Yes*," I said sceptically, the word dragging as I said it, "why is that such a highlight in your day? And why are you always there, don't you have a job?" My eyebrow quirked.

"I'm concerned for your friend, obviously," he said defensively, ignoring my second question entirely.

"You don't even like Melody." I frowned.

"Yeah, well, how about you explain to us where you've been, Lucky? *Where* have you been? Do you know how worried Jamie's been?" He shot the questions at me in quick succession.

"I've been messaging him all week?"

"Oh. Well, have you been messaging Addie? Or Riley?"

"Yes. I'm pretty sure I've messaged everyone at least once. Even you. Thanks for leaving me on read by the way, you jackass."

"Have a little more self awareness, we've been worried sick," he chuffed in the end before he dropped off the line.

"Lucky?" my mum said again from the other end.

"What crawled up his ass and ate his breakfast?" I grumbled, fiddling with the edge of Cole's shirt, the third one of what was the only thing I'd worn all week.

"He was just worried, Navy. You ran out in the middle of the night—"

"I called you the next day to let you know I was with Melody," I deadpanned.

"—and then disappeared off the face of the earth for three whole days," she scoffed.

"I have literally been messaging you every day. I am a grown woman, you remember that right?"

"You'll always be our little baby lucky number seven," she said, her voice wobbling.

"No, plea—"

"Here's your father!" she wailed and dropped off the line.

"There she is, my world traveller!" my dad said. The smile I could hear in his voice was infectious.

"Hey, Dad," I grinned into the phone.

"How are you, Superstar? We miss you 'round here. When are you back?"

I heard his paper crinkle in the background and pictured

him so clearly; glasses on the end of his nose, paper in front of him and a cold cup of coffee on the table.

"Miss you too, Pops. Home soon, though. I've got to jet, will you tell Mum I said bye?"

"Go get 'em. Love you, Luck." His voice was full of warmth.

"Love you, Dad."

I ended the call and dropped my phone back onto the side table in Cole's room. It still felt weird to come to the realisation that I was sitting in his room. I hadn't seen him all week, not since it all happened.

The man was so elusive I was starting to wonder if he was even real or just a really strange aspect to my imagination that had come to life. If he wasn't real, it meant I'd given one hell of a blowjob to the air in that gym.

In all honesty, I had to find some humour in it, because if I didn't then I was faced with the realisation that he knowingly left me here on my own. *By myself.* That he had seen the marks on my body, that he had pulled the words from my throat and left me on my own.

That he *knew* and he *left me alone.*

It was this weird chaotic mix of emotions. It was pain and embarrassment and hurt and anger and shame. There were so many different ugly things. I knew these feelings, like most people I'd felt them at one point or another in my life, but never like this. Like some swirling pit that threatened to swallow me up when I thought about it too much. Despite my better judgement, for some insane reason, I really didn't want to think those things in relation to Cole, so I pushed it all down. *Again.*

There hadn't been a single other person in this apartment since I'd arrived. None of the cleaners or those people that wipe the windows from the outside, or even the cleaning staff that sometimes sat in his at-home-staff-office room. They'd all vanished and I was on my own.

My head dropped into my hands and I groaned long and loud out of just pure, unfiltered frustration. God, why was this so weird to work around? I was fine one second and then I wasn't. I suppose there was a very small, super thin silver lining to Cole's complete and total lack of presence.

I'd snooped every inch of this apartment to my heart's content. I made it my personal mission to know every nook and cranny that was Cole Thompson's home. I wasn't scandalised like I thought I might be, expecting to find a room with a range of various torture devices and another filled with all those vials of children's tears I'd accused him of hoarding or maybe even one weird drawer of sex toys and flavoured lube, but what I found was more...unexpected.

The side of the apartment that was more Cole's home than any other part was a real Pandora's box. I opened every door that wasn't locked, and to my very real surprise, none were. The first door I opened was massive and filled with art. Beautiful art, such a range of period pieces decorated the walls that it made my head swim. Romanticism. Expressionism. Baroque. They were all intense and overwhelming and there was no doubt that each piece before me was authentic and real. The sculpture he had in the middle of *this* room made me pause.

It was a child lying on their side. It was clear that they were asleep clutching a teddy in one perfectly carved stone hand. I knew it was made of stone but the bear looked *soft*. It was hard to take it all in, the carved boy on the floor, sleeping and alone, completely surrounded by these paintings that were loud and dark and almost haunting, but still dignified. Like those emotions were there but they were hidden, only found if you really looked for them.

I wanted so badly for him to explain to me why this room existed.

What made him pick the pieces?

Who was the boy?

I'd wandered from that room completely, totally drained of energy. When the anger and pain and ugliness reared its head, I got up and moved to the next room. Eventually, I stumbled towards the sunken lounge space where he'd helped me – begrudgingly so – with my bleeding nose. It was just like I'd remembered, all warm colours and beautiful pieces of wooden furniture and...plants.

Had there been plants before? Who knew, but there were plants there now. Cole had plants *everywhere*. They were all alive and happy and smiling just like the one in his beautiful bathroom. Between all these green leafy happy plants and his secret art gallery, I was a pair of leather spandex away from wondering when I'd swallowed a red pill that threw me into *The Matrix*.

Cole Thompson was an enigma.

I sat on his sunken couch, completely absorbed by the comfortable cushions around me and thought on it too much and too intensely. Trying to find the comparison between the guy who I'd just discovered lived here and the guy who I *knew* lived here. The one who had saved me from the very worst moments of my life and then left me locked in his ivory tower.

They were just so different.

I'd eventually fallen asleep with the calming darkness

pushing in on me with nothing but the city lights streaming in through the windows. I'd awoken in his bed, with him nowhere to be found.

That wasn't the only time I'd fallen asleep somewhere in his apartment that wasn't his room.

On Thursday, I made my way back to the gym.

I sat there and I remembered every single moment of his hands on my skin, of my hands on his and willed myself to remember *who* it was. The bronzed colour of his skin, the rough pads of his hands, the taste of his hard length on my tongue as I took him into my mouth, the salt and soap and *smell* of him. And when the flash of wrong hands invaded my mind, the wrong eyes, I started again.

I did it over, and over and *over*.

I was there for hours before my eyes started to droop, aching from the tears I hadn't been able to stop and I curled up on my side, promising myself it would be for just a second before I made my way back to his room, where I knew he wouldn't be.

When I woke, I was back in his bed.

My heart immediately picked up along with my breathing.

This was worse than him leaving me in the first place and maybe it's why I had been falling asleep anywhere but his bed. Simply being left in his home without a single fucking trace of him was painful enough, let alone being in his sheets and his bed and his fucking shirt that all smelt like him.

I was still bruised. I was still desperately trying to fight the memories that continued to claw to the surface, and I was doing it alone.

Surrounded only by the smell of him.

29

Lucky

By the time Friday rolled around, I still had no idea whether I had taken up sleep walking to bring myself back to Cole's bed every night or if it was really him and he up and vanished after the fact. The former was preferred because the latter made me want to scream into a pillow then rapid fire punch it before swapping back to screaming, ending it all by clutching it tightly to my chest while I rocked in a corner.

But you know, apart from that, I was fine.

I knew he was coming and going, but no matter how much I battled myself on thoughts for and against, I couldn't figure out why he was avoiding me. He certainly wasn't making any efforts to be present.

Why *his* bed? Why his shirts? Why the phantom hands and touches and the heaviness of his eyes on me that I could feel when I stirred in the middle of the night.

I wasn't making that up, I *knew* I wasn't.

I knew he really was around because he had texted me a total of four times. The first being to just make sure I had his number. The second was in the same conversation confirming that it was actually him. The third was because I'd made an effort to cook something the morning of my art gallery escapades and put some in the fridge for him to eat. I was responsible for his eating habits after all.

The next day my phone pinged.

Cole Thompson:
You're not working this week. Other arrangements for food have been organised.

I'd scoffed, naturally.

Me:
That seems a little unnecessary. I am technically your employed chef.

He never graced that with a reply but instead, when I headed for the fridge yesterday it was completely empty. Like, not even milk for coffee. Not a single fucking condiment.

The man was insane.

And the last text, I didn't really know what to do with. It said it was delivered at 1:52 a.m..

Cole Thompson:
You sometimes snore when you sleep.

When I read it upon waking, I laughed so much that my eyes watered. It reminded me so much of the boy who sat with me through tea parties and used to poke fun at the way I always liked to wear two different pairs of socks but whenever I'd try and go change them he'd always tell me it took a certain type of cool to pull it off, and I *had* that certain type of cool.

It made me miss him and that was the worst part of it all. I *missed* him.

I'd resolved myself to sit and wait for him on Friday night, and what better place to do that than the kitchen table.

I was still in his shirt, which was honestly more like a dress. He'd been leaving a fresh one out for me every time I'd woken up. It would be draped across the arm of the chair that was still faced towards the bed.

That confused me even more. Then it pissed me off. It made me fucking *blind* with anger because he was coming and going like a phantom in the night, hanging around long enough to hear me snore before having the audacity to leave me his shirt like someone who fucking *cared?*

He'd promised me he'd stay and he didn't. *He left.*

I'd picked this spot at the kitchen table because I could honestly say I wouldn't have been comfortable enough to fall asleep there and if I was uncomfortable I could be angry.

It was the first time I'd woken from him moving me.

Cole's touches that roused me were soft and gentle like he didn't want to startle me but strong enough to support my noodle-like form.

"Come on, Luck," he murmured against my hair, the rough pads of his hand making a path along the exposed skin of my arms and legs, leaving a trail of goosebumps in their wake and a tight coil of heat to come alive in my belly. He pressed me against his chest, clad in a crisp white shirt and a tie loose around his neck.

All of a sudden every ounce of burning hate I'd built up for him just slipped through my fingers. I decided I wouldn't hate myself either as I pressed my cheek deeper into the crook of his neck and breathed him in.

The clean minty scent of him that was surrounding me at almost all times was nowhere near as perfect as the real thing and my fucking chest ached. It ached and *ached* and it was all I could do to just press myself closer into him.

He held me tighter and I convinced myself for a second that it was because he might have missed me too.

"Stay," I said, my voice a wisp of a thing from where he set me down on the edge of his bed. I wasn't even sure if it would make the distance between us and I didn't trust myself to say it again, to say it louder.

His features sharpened, removing my grip from his shirt with a little more force, "You don't want that, Lucky."

"Please, Cole. You promised before and you broke it. Please keep it now, I–"

The unfinished words sat between us like taut wire. I didn't think he'd listen, not when he stood there near motionless for what felt like forever.

I was close to telling him to forget it when he spoke, "Get in," jerking his chin back towards the pillows at the top of the bed. I turned to crawl towards the pillows in a way that I was hoping looked modest and casual and not like I was a newly birthed giraffe.

He pulled off his tie and unbuttoned his shirt in an achingly slow motion, like he was hoping the slower he went, the more time he had to find a reason to not stay with me.

I was consumed with every move he made, worried that if I blinked it would be too long that my eyes were not on him.

He sat on the edge of the bed to pull off his shoes and shuck off his work slacks, standing there in plain black briefs before pulling back the covers and sliding in with me.

My heart was hammering so fast I didn't think it was possible for him not to hear it. Laying on our sides we just stared at each other. I would see his eyes flicker to my left eye and down to my neck every so often and when his hand slowly slid across the bed between us and grazed my knee I think I stopped breathing completely.

I didn't drop his gaze.

I let him keep me captivated, let him read every emotion I was feeling as he traced the line of my leg all the way up until he got to the hem of my shirt and stilled. Like he was deciding which path he would take, above the fabric or under it.

My swallow was audible and a moment later his hand continued up above his shirt to the dip of my waist before changing course, tracing a line along my sternum and up between the valley of my breasts. A gasp was ripped from me as my eyes shuddered. I wasn't holding my breath anymore, but breathing so rapidly you'd think I just ran for my life from a hoard of flesh eating rabbits.

"Cole—" I was going to tell him I couldn't, that I had been trying to move past this...this *reaction*. That I'd tried in the gym and I was trying now and even though I knew it was his hand I couldn't *stop*—

"Eyes on me." His voice was strong with the command he laid out for me and I couldn't do a single thing except comply. I hadn't even realised I had closed them, that I was squeezing them shut, and that my hand gripped his where it stilled between my breasts.

We stayed like that until my breathing calmed down and then his hand started to move again.

"Where are you, Lucky?" he asked me as his hand continued to move upward, eyes tracking my every move.

"I'm with you," I breathed, feeling the rise and fall of my chest against the weight of his hand.

"Who's touching you?" His hand moved up to curl around my throat, his fingers moving to the very points where I knew the bruises lingered, still blue and purple and brutal looking. Replacing every vile touch with one of his own. Chasing away my demons with his own darkness. Darkness that soothed and caressed and kept me safe.

"You are." Neither of us missed the way my voice caught and I was so sure I was going to throw up as the weight of his hand pressed against the column of my throat.

He shifted, moving across the bed closer to me until we were practically nose to nose and I could see nothing but the green of his eyes.

"Say my name, Lucky. Who is touching you?" He sounded moments from snapping, like this was harder for him than he was letting on, like he was holding himself back.

"Cole."

His name was barely past my lips when his mouth crashed to mine. If it had been any other time I might have been embarrassed at the whimper that he pulled from me, that he swallowed with his own mouth. Each swipe of his tongue against the seam of my lips, the way he coaxed me to soften under his touch, his mouth commanding and taking and taking and *taking*.

I wanted to give him everything.

We broke apart for a second, his chest rising and falling in an equally ragged tempo as mine and I couldn't help myself, reaching out and winding my arms around him. Weaving my fingers into his hair, pressing my entire body against his like he was a lighthouse I'd finally made it to in the midst of a storm that was drowning me, the hand against my throat all but forgotten.

"You've been gone," I whispered against his lips, my voice shaking ever so slightly as I felt his other hand move from its place pinned between us. "Why?"

His mouth, parted and swollen, pulled at the side, turning his face into something devastatingly beautiful. "You weren't ready. You needed space. Time. But I never broke my promise, I never left."

"I'm not sure—" I started to say, my body locking up and pulling away from him.

When his hand skimmed my inner thigh, I jolted back which only made Cole release my neck and wind his arm around my waist, pulling me closer.

"Eyes on me," he repeated as his hand glided up my inner thigh, across the bruises I knew lingered there.

When I said all I had to wear were Cole's shirts, I meant that in the quite literal sense. So, when his hand made it to the apex of my thighs, cupping my bare pussy, I shuddered at the contact.

"Your eyes, Lucky."

My lids opened once again and locked on his unrelenting gaze.

"Who's touching you?"

"You are," I gasped.

Cole's hand moved, his fingers gliding against my wet folds, my stomach tightening and my lips parting as he continued his exploration, "You're so fucking wet." The breath of his words fanning across my face, all mint and clean and *him*. "Is this for me, Navy?"

"Mhm." God, I couldn't even speak.

He stopped his movement and my spine straightened in protest.

"Is this for me, Navy?" he asked again, a glint to his eyes that elicited a full body shiver, the movement shifted his fingers to the start of my entrance.

"*Yes,*" I panted, all but salivating at the sight of him, trying to wiggle my hips to get him to *move*.

"Who's touching you?" he asked again.

"You are."

And then he thrust two fingers into me hard and fast and didn't stop. Forming a steady, unrelenting pace, the palm of his hand grinding against my clit. "Every time you think of hands on your body, I want you to remember *this*," he gritted out between clenched teeth, "and only *me*."

His eyes tracked my face in a frenzy, like he needed to see every single thing that crossed my features and he couldn't take it all in fast enough.

"I want you to remember how it feels to have my fingers buried deep inside you," he panted, his eyes hooding and hips rocking his erection against my leg, "and the way your perfect cunt clenches around me."

I wanted to touch him, to *feel* the length of him in my hand but my arms were still wrapped around his neck, my hands in his hair holding onto it like my life depended on it.

"Cole, I'm going to—"

"Not yet." He bit out and then his hand just stopped moving. Just *stopped.*

A growl ripped from my throat and I knew for certain all the things he was seeing flash across my face. When his face split into a full blown grin full of a sinful sort of pleasure, I felt my features slacken.

"Fuck my hand, Navy." He didn't even blink.

"Wh-what?" It was hard to process. *Those* words coming out of *his* face.

"I want you to fuck my hand until you come."

He didn't need to tell me twice. I knew he was saying it to challenge me, but also because he wanted me to take it for myself, that he wanted *me* to control this.

Control.

That's what it was always about. Control is what he coveted, what he demanded from me time and time again. I knew what it meant for him to give it up now.

I started to move my hips against his hand, feeling his fingers drag against my walls, feel the palm of his hand push against my clit.

He added a third finger and my eyes rolled back into my head. I picked up the pace, his breaths increasing the faster I moved, and holy *fuck* was I moving.

It was almost too much just watching him react to me. Seeing the want, the *need.*

"That's it," he said, his gaze hooded with lust, the hard thick length of him still pressed against me, his hips moving in sync with mine. "You look so perfect right now, you have no fucking idea." He placed a kiss on my jaw before running his tongue up the length of my throat.

I felt my orgasm start to build, felt my back arch and wished he was touching me *everywhere*. I wanted him *everywhere*.

With his mouth at my ear, his tongue darted out, sending a zap of electricity through me, right to where I continued to use his hand for my own pleasure.

"Come for me, Lucky."

That was it.

Cole's name was ripped from me before he swallowed it greedily, his tongue lashing out and completely dominating every inch of my mouth.

My body softened, going limp in his hands as he took over, plunging in and out of me while I rode out the rest of my high.

"Holy shit," I mumbled, my eyes heavy and my body so relaxed my bones may have actually turned to jello.

Cole didn't move away from me even as his hand left me feeling somehow emptier than I had before.

"I want more."

Cole's eyes lightened a fraction as he let out a breathy sort of laugh. His voice held all the darkness I was so familiar with, the sound of his voice was wrapped in a promise that he emphasised with a slow grind of his body against mine.

I knew why he was doing this. I knew why he let me use his body, why he helped me take control. I knew that he was watching me to see how I'd react to the way his body wanted me, but I wasn't frightened of him or his intentions, just the opposite in fact. I *yearned* for him, to the point where I could feel it in my chest, in my lungs, in the marrow of my bones. For the feel of his body against mine, for the darkness that swelled in and settled over me, putting distance between my mind and the things of my nightmares.

Cole's body softened as he saw the truth of that flash across my face, as held me closer and placed a lingering kiss to my lips.

"When I fuck you, Lucky," he said, his fingers tracing the shape of my lips, like I'd thought I felt him do in the nights since I'd been here, "you will never remember what it was like to be touched by anyone else." His lips pressed against mine again. "When I fuck you, you will feel it in every single part of your body. You'll never find where I begin and where you end."

He was gone when I woke up.

30

Lucky

"Shut the fucking front door!" Melody bolted from the elevator, ripping her sunglasses from her face in such a fluid motion you had to wonder if she'd made this sort of entrance before.

My mood lifted immediately just seeing her.

"*Shut the big fucking elevator doors!* Are you kidding me with this place?" She twirled, only missing Mr. Invisible because I yanked her out of the way and into a crushing hug.

She hugged me back instantly, a big squeezing sort that emptied your body of air immediately. As soon as we pulled away, she took one look at my fading marks and burst into tears.

That was two hours ago.

I'd managed to lead her to my favourite place to sit, the sunken lounge with all the happy plants, and finally put on some pants from the plethora of clothes I'd requested she bring.

Melody updated me on how she was still in her fifth stage of grief but she was feeling more herself all the time. She'd put aside a few things that she wanted to burn in a 'end of relationship ritual' she read online.

"Did this website belong to a cult, perhaps?"

"You're so dramatic."

"Says the woman wanting to burn her ex-boyfriends old pillow cases." I lifted an eyebrow at her, entirely unconvinced we wouldn't be unknowingly cursing the guy. I didn't like him but I didn't want to ruin his life.

Her eyes kept flicking back and forth from my eye to my neck, "Do they hurt?"

"Not so much anymore," I smiled, squeezing her free hand with mine while we both held cups of tea.

"Lucky, I—"

"You nothing, and I'm actually okay. Being here has been...good for me." I scrunch my nose up at the same time Melody's eyes widened in shock. "And my parents think I'm travelling for work."

"I've been diligently avoiding all of Meredith's calls." She nodded to herself firmly.

"I finally picked up yesterday and—"

"She ripped you a new one?"

"More or less." Grinning at the way she just *knew*.

"And Cole?" she hedged. Finally having the guts to ask. She'd been beating around the bush since she'd stopped crying.

The moment I saw her, I wanted to pour every single feeling I had about Cole out at her feet. I wanted to tell her what he'd done, what he *didn't* do. I wanted to tell her how he'd left me here on my own and only showed up when it was convenient for him. How every single time he was close, I forgot everything I had wanted to scream at him about because being surrounded by him had somehow become my safe haven which confused me even more and made me even angrier.

Instead I took a sip from my tea and said, "Things have changed, he's..." *Intense? Confusing? Fucking oblique?* "...I don't know." I sipped my tea again, for the first time not being entirely sure how much to share. It was this weird feeling of needing help and guidance and for someone to just fucking *hear* me, but the person who I wanted was, for the first time since I was twelve, not Melody.

"That's...broad?" She looked at me, head tilted to the side as if trying to read through the lines, knowing me enough to see that there was more even if I wasn't ready to divulge it.

Melody sat up a little straighter, her expression morphing into one that was prepared to fight for the answers she was wanting. "Okay, subject change."

"Oh, no." I all but hid behind my mug.

"Oh, *yes.* It's been a year."

"I'm so happy for you?"

Melody reached out to stick one of her fingers into my ribs. "I mean it's been a year since *Seven* closed."

"Yes, that's factual," I mumbled, picking the invisible flint of the couch. It took a minute, but Melody slowly lowered herself into my line of sight.

"Navy."

"Alright. *Alright.* I have plans, they're just still in their foundation stage."

"What does that even mean? What's the foundation stage?"

"Like at the start."

"The start of what?"

"You know," I frowned at my best friend, "I don't remember you ever being this nosy."

"You're hiding something." She frowned at me, not backing down. Boy was she on the nose. It became very clear to me right then that I could either crack over this, or over Cole.

The decision had been a no-brainer.

"I have nothing," I blurted out, my hand flying up to cover my mouth and my eyes widening at the realisation that I'd said it out loud. "I have nothing. Okay? I have ideas, sure, but plans? Like, emails and phone calls and discussions and actionable items in a list? I have none of that."

"But you said—"

"I know what I said, Lid." I stared intently at the rim of my mug, "But I also remember what I had to say to the people who had relied on me to support their families. Who trusted me to keep their jobs safe, and I couldn't do it."

"That wasn't your fault and you know it." She said the words with such surety that I was tempted to believe her, and I loved her for even believing them herself.

"It was my job, and I had bad judgement. I trusted the wrong person."

"You're an incredible chef, Luck. And people are waiting for you to step back out into that light. And you *need* it. God, you're so *good*. This is what you do, it's who you are."

She was right. It was. I loved everything about it and I couldn't pinpoint a time I felt more at home than in the kitchens of *Seven*.

"I'm terrified, Melody," I whispered the words between us, like if I could say them soft enough they'd still remain a secret.

"I know. Sometimes you just have to feel the fear and do it anyway." She reached for my hand and waited for my eyes to meet hers.

"Tell me you'll think about it."

"I'll think about it."

She took a deep breath and released it in a whoosh like a weight had been lifted.

"You know," she mused, looking around. "I never would have pegged him as a plant man."

"*Right?!*"

We'd moved to the movie room and put on our favourite childhood movie: *The Jungle Book*.

I fell asleep with my hand gripped in Melody's, feeling lighter than I had this entire week. I hadn't realised how much I needed her until she'd walked out of the elevator and almost took out Cole's glass statue.

My hand was empty when I woke up in the dark, and standing right in front of me was a figure barely able to be made out, draped in shadows.

Cole.

31

Cole

It had taken little to no effort to shut down *Bite Me.*

It had taken even less effort to walk into the establishment find whoever the fuck was in charge and get the information I needed about the man who'd attacked Lucky.

It was information I already had thanks to my own contact but there was a certain satisfaction that you got from holding the worth of a man in the palm of your hand and seeing him beg for you not to crush it.

All the business could offer me was a few grainy video snippets and a scan of his licence.

My knee bounced so badly I could almost feel the little tremors pulsing through the idling car beneath me. The privacy window between was up and sealed and John knew me well enough not to try and speak to me. Not right now.

My eyes kept snapping between the manilla folder on the

seat next to me and the warehouse outside.

It was run down, in a shitty neighbourhood and not the sort of place you'd want to idle in a hundred thousand dollar car. That was certainly the vibe that the people who frequented this place wanted to keep, because inside was a fucking paradise. A place that attracted all the most skilled and serious fighters. The very same gym I'd first gone to with Benny and then really never stopped.

It was where I'd had my ass beaten more times than I could count, but also where I'd learned to hone the raw and explosive energy that coursed through me when my regular outlets weren't enough.

I hadn't been here in months, since the day before Lucky had ended up in my kitchen.

So much so that Benny had messaged me more in the last five months than he usually did in an entire year. They weren't particularly heartwarming or special, at least not looking in from the outside, but I knew that he'd have to have been pushed to the edge to pick up his phone to do it.

Benny Boy:
Are you even fucking alive?

What can I say? A real teddy bear.

Me:
Professor Bennett? Texting again?
This makes for number seven.

COLE

Are you feeling okay?

Fyn Bennett was probably one of the scariest looking men I'd even encountered in my life. He was also my Physics professor.

When he'd first stumbled upon me, I'd overlooked the keys hanging around his neck and the folder clutched in his hand and more so zeroed in on the tattoos that encompassed every part of his body, including his bald and shiny head.

I'd gotten him into a headlock once, *once*, and decided to breathe on him and shine it with my forearm. Needless to say that the was the last time he'd ever let me do that and sent me off with two broken ribs.

"I don't fucking care if you don't want to go," Benny had said, looking ridiculous behind his tiny desk. "I will drag you there myself every day if I have to. Get out of my office and don't be late. I've emailed you the information."

I picked up my bag, slinging it over my shoulder and stalking for the door of the office he'd summoned me to. "Why do you even fucking care?" I'd gotten out between gritted teeth, aware that I was toeing a fine line and that one wrong move would see me removed from my degree. A degree I needed desperately.

He looked up and held my stare for a long while. Most people couldn't do that, not when I was...unrestrained. They shied away or dropped their gaze or just straight up left, not entirely sure what it was they were seeing in my eyes, only knowing it was dark and wrong and festering.

"Someone should," he mumbled, and then he flipped me off.

I owed a lot to Benny, hence why his daughter was now in my employ.

Benny Boy:
Fuck you

I'd laughed reading the message when it came through this morning, sitting in bed with Lucky nestled in beside me.

He knew I was alive because his kid still had a job, but I knew he was asking more than that.

It was only after getting an email that the information I wanted was ready to be picked up did I reply.

Me:
You're not my type, I'd kick your ass for free though...

Benny Boy:
9 AM

It was five past nine and I still hadn't gotten out of the car.

My hand had twitched towards the button that would lower the barrier between me and John four times, each time I had to pull myself back from doing it. Knowing if I got that far I'd make him drive to the guy's house whose life I now knew everything about. Whose secrets I now knew as my own.

My lip curled back in disgust at the photo of him I'd glanced at briefly before throwing the file down. I was *willing* myself to go into the gym and work with Fyn instead of going face to face with the man who put his fucking *hands* on what was *mine*. To feel his skin split beneath my knuckles, to hear his bones crack and his cries stain the air around me as I—

Three knocks on my window pulled me back into the present and I shifted my finger from where it hovered so close over the button for the visor to the button for the window.

"Benny," I said, my voice cold.

"Get your ass inside, Thompson," was all he grumbled before turning around and stalking back towards the gym.

So much sweat poured from every part of my body that it was pooling beneath me. I knew Benny was also waiting for me to slip on the moisture as we watched one another, him with his padded hands up before him waiting for my next hit and me still bouncing with my own padded hands up in front of me.

We'd been here for hours. Well past the point of when my screaming muscles demanded rest, long past running out of all the water we'd brought in. From the moment my fists made contact I couldn't stop. I could see the exhaustion in Benny's eyes, his clothes soaked with his own perspiration. I'd ditched my shirt within the first hour, unable to move the way I wanted with the damn fabric clinging to me.

I flicked my hair out of my face, the action causing a drop of sweat to roll directly into the split on my lip, the sting immediate. The zap of pain highlighted the ache in my jaw too, and I knew a lovely little bruise had already bloomed. Both of those things were uncommon occurrences.

Benny was a big guy, and yes he'd managed to evade almost every manoeuvre I sent his way, but it had been a very, *very* long time since he'd managed to get a hit on me. Not to say he looked any better. My eyes tracked the small trickle of blood that dribbled from his eyebrow, mixing with his sweat and making it look a lot worse than I knew it was.

With a final bounce between each foot I finally stopped, lowering my hands.

"Thank fuck, you little psycho, you were going to kill me," he grumbled, throwing the pads to the canvas and falling down to join them shortly after.

"Come on now, old man. You're like a cockroach, nothing can kill you." I sat down next to his sprawled figure and let my body give in to the desperate need to just *stop*.

"Fuck you, Thompson."

"You keep saying that but I keep telling you, you're just not my type."

Benny lifted his hand up to flip me off, earning a breathy chuckle. It was honestly the only thing I could muster up at this point. I let my eyes start to flutter shut at the sheer relief from the swarm of emotion that had been raging in my head finally having quietened to a dull murmur.

"So," Benny broke the silence first, "you going to fill me in on where you've been for the better part of the ass end of the year, and also what's got your panties in a twist?"

My inhale was deep and long, just like the exhale.

"I told you about Lucky once," I started, my voice sounding as tired as I felt.

COLE

He didn't say anything, just waited.

"She was dropped in my lap like some fucking gift and I had her Fyn. I *had her* right where I wanted her. I had *everything*. And then..."

"It changed," he finished for me, his voice ringing clear with the knowledge of what it felt like.

"She crawled under my skin and it's too much and not enough at the same time." The confession was pulled from me without much of a fight. "Someone hurt her."

"*Fuck.*"

"I want to kill him."

"You know who it is?" His voice was stronger now and laced with concern like he was seeing a whole new future paved out before me. We both knew I'd have no problems ending a life. It was the entire reason we were where we were, why this gym had become a haven to me.

"Someone *touched* her," I seethed, ignoring his question.

"I have two things to say," he started, "Lucky can be something else to you now than what she was to you then. You're the only one who's standing in the way of that being fine."

"Mmm," I mused, already knowing that to be true. "And the other thing?"

"There is more than one way to end a man's life."

The words stayed in my mind when we finally parted ways. It lingered as I quickly rinsed off in the showers at the gym and collected my things to head back out to the parking lot.

John was up and out of the car the moment he saw me, hustling to my door to open it for me. "Sir."

"You're still too old to be calling me 'Sir'," I mumbled before sliding into the car.

"Appreciate the reminder as always, Sir," he chimed before closing the door and running back around to the driver's side door. I must have looked much better than I did heading into the warehouse for him to be happy enough to speak to me.

As soon as the car was moving, I dialled the number for the lawyers I paid a substantial amount of money to, to be on call every second of every hour of every day. They picked up on the second ring.

"Alister Jacob Rainer." The words were foul as they filled my mouth. "I want him left with nothing but his fucking name and charges that will put him away from the rest of his miserable life. Make it happen or I will find someone who can."

I walked around the entire apartment when I got home, knowing that the likelihood Lucky would actually be asleep in the bed for once was little to none. It seemed she slept where she dropped. I scowled at the thought but only to stop the grin that wanted to split across my face. It felt wrong that I *knew* it was such a Lucky thing to do. I shouldn't know, not after everything that had happened between us, even as there was a little flutter at the back of my mind that was satisfied with the knowledge.

She was nowhere. Not in any of the usual places that I'd found her before, and not in my bed, where I'd checked last with a swarm of hopeful fucking bees churning in my gut.

She's gone.

That thought sent a pang of dread through my entire body and I was two seconds away from giving up on my silent approach and yelling her name into the apartment when I noticed the door to the theatre room cracked. My heart was still hammering in my chest as I slipped into the darkness.

Lucky was asleep, curled on her side and breathing evenly with her hand wrapped tightly around another that belonged to an equally as curled up sleeping woman.

Melody looked the same, sort of. I hadn't seen her in person since high school and even though her features had sharpened, it wasn't hard to recognise the girl that was stuck to Lucky every second of every day.

I leaned down and tapped Melody's shoulder, gentle enough not to startle, but firm enough to rouse her.

Her eyes opened in a way that told me she hadn't really been asleep. She held my gaze for a long while, her eyes assessing and her mouth pursed in an uncertain pinch before she delicately pulled her hand from Lucky's and followed me out of the theatre room.

"What a pleasure, Melody Amelia Harper." I smirked at her where she stood in front of me.

Melody's eyes narrowed in annoyance. She was always one of those kids that introduced herself with her full name up until she was thirteen or so, and I knew she was remembering that. I had, after all, been the one to give her shit about it.

"You're a real asshole, you know that?" Her eyebrows hiked up halfway to her hairline as she folded her arms over her chest.

"Well aware," I replied smoothly, hands in the pockets of my sweats.

Melody's head tilted to the side slightly, like if she looked at me in a different way she might learn more. "What's your angle, Cole?"

"You're welcome to pick one, they're all sublime." I gave her a grin that I knew pulled heart eyes out of anyone who saw it, and followed up with a wink.

I didn't think it was possible but her eyes narrowed even further and danced with a suspicious sort of humour. Her gaze flicked to the cut on my lip and then to the bruise on my jaw.

"Still fighting?" She scoffed like she'd found the answers she was looking for to all her unspoken questions. "You haven't changed at all."

I couldn't say I blamed her. Melody didn't know that most of the marks that littered my body growing up had nothing to do with my less palatable tendencies.

Of course, she was still wrong.

I had changed. I'd gotten much, *much*, better.

I didn't say a single thing, just let my expression darken bit by bit while she held it. She didn't look scared, interestingly enough, just pissed off.

"I swear to god, Cole." She jabbed a finger into my chest, resembling what I thought it might feel to be charged at by a squirrel, "If you harm a hair on her little blonde head, I'll break every part of your face and rearrange your junk to look like a baby hippo."

"That's...oddly specific and weirdly visual. Have you ever threatened someone before?" I wanted to hold in the amusement, knowing if she thought her threats stung, she'd be up and out of my house faster, but I couldn't help myself. Pushing her buttons had always been so much fun.

"I—" She dropped her hand back to its favourite spot on

her hip and scowled. "Well, that's not the point here, plant man."

I placed a hand over my heart, letting my face fall with mock hurt, "You wound me."

"Not as badly as your plants will be wounded if you so much as *hurt* a ha–"

"Hair on her head, I know. And leave my plants out of this." I gave her a scowl of my own. What was with these two and their beef with my fucking plants?

"Ah," she mused, taking a step back from where she'd completely invaded my personal space, "good to know your weaknesses lie in the green leafy things variety."

I surprised myself with the eye roll that took over my eyeballs without permission and I saw the little quirk to her lips as she tried to fight her smirk.

Melody had always been on Lucky's side of things, which was always very much *not* my side. But before that? We had been friends too. Sort of.

"I won't hurt her, Melody," I said, hoping the words were true. Sometimes I felt their certainty so clearly it was like they'd always been the mantra that ran through my mind.

"Mmm," she mused, her expression turned contemplative, "there is more than one way to hurt a person."

You're preaching to the fucking choir here.

I walked past her, knowing she would see it for what it was; an end to the conversation I had humoured her with and a less than subtle request to leave. Her footsteps were short and silent as she strode behind me, so different from Lucky's loud, unadulterated squeaks.

"I know what you've been doing," she murmured, so low that I knew she'd worked hard to build the nerve to say the words.

"Oh?" My voice was utterly bored. That wasn't an act though, I'd had just about enough of being put in my place. "And what would that be?"

It wasn't hard to know how Melody looked behind me. It was the same look everyone got when I removed all the emotion I always forced into my voice. It was unsettling. The only person who had never run from it was Lucky.

"How you've been keeping her here," she replied with more steel than I would have anticipated. Looks like little Melody Amelia grew a backbone.

I didn't dignify her accusation with a reply. I didn't need to. I knew exactly how I'd stopped Lucky from running away as well.

I tapped the button for the elevator and waited silently for the ding that signalled its arrival, stepping to the side and swooping my arm across in a mocking gesture of gentleman-liness.

Melody stepped in, her grip on her bag white knuckled. "She needs to rebuild," she started, lifting her eyes from where they'd been trained on the floor, and I didn't miss the extra shine to them. "She lost everything, and then we nearly lost her. If you won't help her rebuild then you need to let her do it for herself."

The doors shut between us and I decided I'd tuck away her words to decipher later.

For now, I turned around and walked back to the room where I knew she slept. My unhurried steps were an utter contrast to the way my heart thudded louder as the distance between us lessened.

My body zapped with the knowledge that I was finally here

with her.

Alone.

Walking back to the front of the room, I took my position in front of her, and I watched. I let my eyes track the lines of her face, how her lips were parted just lightly. The way her eyes fluttered under her closed lids as she navigated through whatever dream was playing in her mind. The way her fingers twitched around nothing, making me wonder if she was dreaming of me.

Like it was divinely intended, Lucky's eyes fluttered open. Could she feel the burn of my eyes along her skin?

Did she ache for me?

I was far enough away that it would have been difficult to make out my form immediately. The shadows had always been my favourite place to exist.

Her gaze moved over me before snapping back immediately, her breathing hitched as she locked her eyes with mine and there was nothing I could do to stop the grin from spreading across my face. Nothing I could do to hide the darkness that existed within it.

A predator, finally finding its prey.

32

Lucky

I felt his eyes on me before I'd even started to rise from sleep.

The dreams that had been so real and vivid immediately started to slip through my fingers no matter how hard I tried to grab onto them, every part of them but one.

The eyes. *His* eyes. In every shade. They shifted from bright jade, how the colour seemed to swim and glitter, how it looked so alive. To the hardened, stoney, muted version that still glittered but with the roughness of uncut gems and sharp edges. With the promise of something brutal and sinister and dark.

I had wanted both sets. Both versions.

It was with that realisation that I was pulled from the dream with the undeniable knowledge that I was being watched.

It took me a second to find him, and when I did, his features were carved from the sorts of things that didn't live in the light. *This* was the part of him I knew he kept locked down and hidden away. It was why Abe and Jim sung his praises. It was why he was so successful, so *liked.* Because no one ever saw *this* side of him, when he wore no mask at all.

He stalked towards me, his face changing as soon as he stepped from the darkest part of the shadows he'd watched me from. His expression morphing so fast it made my heart rate spike.

The sharp blade of fear dragged down the length of my spine and a shiver wracked my body so violently my teeth rattled.

I wanted to know what he was thinking, wondered if this was the moment I was waiting for, when I'd regret my decision to come here.

His face was blank when he walked right before me. The pad of his thumb reached down to run along my bottom lip, pulling it down and letting his touch hover over the marks on my neck that were slowly starting to turn shades of yellow and green.

He'd left me again.

The numbness of this morning had begun to disintegrate through the day, with the comfort of Melody's company and the reminder of how people acted and showed up for you when they cared. It had allowed the emotions I kept pushing down to swirl up and up and up until they sat at the base of my throat and I was ready to scream.

My chest began to rise and fall with the overwhelming feeling of it all, my eyes burning and heart aching and gut churning, but as he came closer my eyes immediately snapped to the bruising on his face. The swollen side of his lip and it disappeared in an instant.

"Are you okay?" I frowned, knowing he could see the concern on my face, the panic.

He didn't say anything as he took my hand in his, warm and rough, the size completely swallowing my own. I didn't hesitate, though maybe I should have, when he tugged me to stand and wordlessly led us out of the room.

When the doors of his bedroom closed behind us, he left me standing in front of his bed and made his way straight to the bathroom, all without a word. He was dressed in nothing but a plain black shirt and sweats but he smelt like clean, fresh clothes and that minty, woodsy scent that followed him everywhere he went.

I had no idea what he'd done the entire day and I doubted he would tell me. I may not have been entirely sure what the hell was happening here but I did know that Cole wasn't about to stroke my hair and sing me a song about the adventures of his day.

I heard the shower turn on and resolved myself to sit on the edge of his bed until he finished. I'd changed out of his shirt I'd been in, wearing a pair of cotton shorts and a worn band tee from the collection of things Melody had arrived with and if he'd noticed, he didn't say anything.

Releasing a sigh, I flopped back onto the covers that puffed around me, sinking into them in an immersion of complete luxury and closed my eyes, still feeling the lazy tugs of sleep in the corners of my mind. When fingertips skittered across my inner thigh, I let loose a scream that I was sure would have shattered the windows if they hadn't been reinforced.

"*Holy sh–*," shrieking the words, I bolted up and gripped a fistful of my shirt above my heart.

"Frightened?" he murmured, his head tilted to the side in

that predatory way of his.

"No." My reply came too quickly for it to be completely true.

He just observed me like that for a second.

It both unsettled me and made me become frighteningly aware of the dampness between my legs. The way I lifted my arms when he reached for the hem of my shirt and tugged it over my head could have been blamed on being caught so off guard by him that my body went into autopilot. But that wouldn't have been completely true either. It was a familiarity of the movement that made me raise my arms, it was another surge of the blinding *need* I had for this man.

'I'll ruin the bed.'

'No you won't. Arms up, baby.'

I know I didn't imagine it. He'd been soft with me that night. *Gentle.* It still did nothing to erase the way he looked in the shadows as he watched me. In the way he'd taunted me in the months that passed. The way his hand curled around my throat, the way he'd fucked me with his fingers against the wall, roughly and without restraint. The way he had kept me here. The way he'd left me *alone.*

As every memory moved through me, I found myself still wanting the same thing I'd wanted in my dream.

I wanted *both*. I wanted the soft, barely there touches as he traced the line of my nose and the shape of my jaw, and I wanted the dark, brutal edges. The unbridled violence that I could feel beneath his grip as he held my life in his hands, as he made me clench around him.

If I wasn't on autopilot before, I certainly was now. So deep in my own head that he'd guided me to standing and stripped me of the shorts and panties I'd been in, leaving it all in a pile on the floor of his room before taking my hand again and leading me into his bathroom, straight into the spray of hot water.

I let it soak me through, tipping my head back and immediately feeling some of the tension leave my body as the water, just this side of scalding, pelted the taut muscles of my neck and shoulders.

I felt him behind me almost immediately. Felt the way the water glided off him and dripped onto me. Felt the way his breath caressed the back of my neck.

I was so sick and fucking tired of *waiting* for this man. For holding myself back because of what I was afraid would happen after. Of not knowing which version of him I'd get, but I couldn't bring myself to care anymore.

I turned so fast I caught the briefest hitch in his inhale. The closest thing to surprise I knew I'd get from him. Our eyes locked for the barest hint of a second before I surged up onto my toes, wrapped my arms around his neck and brought his lips to mine.

His response was instant. Cole's hands gripped my waist so hard I was aware of every expansion and contraction of my rib cage. His mouth was brutal and unrelenting as his tongue swept into my mouth, taking and taking, absorbing every moan that he pulled from my throat. His arms wrapped around me just enough to lift me off the ground and move us, our kiss never breaking its frantic pace until he pressed me against the cold tiles of the shower wall.

"Do you know what you're asking for, Lucky?" His voice was guttural and I knew that whatever way he'd managed to keep himself in line before would be completely and utterly obliterated upon my reply.

Finally.

"Yes." The word was just a whisper against his mouth where it hovered in front of mine.

His chest rising and falling with heavy inhales as he pulled my bottom lip between his teeth, tugging it with enough of a bite for a whimper to rise out of me, before soothing the sting with his tongue and placing a gentle kiss on my lips in total opposition to the kiss we'd just had. His slick body was against mine, the thick hard length of him pressed against my stomach.

I couldn't stop myself even if I wanted to, which I definitely did not, from looking down and taking in his swollen tip, a bead of pre-cum already coating the head of his cock.

My hand reached for him, wrapping around the base and gently stroking, unable to move my eyes, to look away from the way my hand gilded effortlessly up and down his shaft, the way he felt under my touch. A heaviness had settled in my stomach, moving through my body in waves. My nipples pebbled at the sensation causing slickness to pool between my thighs.

Cole's hand trailed up the side of my body pulling every ounce of my focus to the way his fingertips lit a searing path across my skin until his hand reached my breast, cupping the full and heavy weight of me. I watched completely enraptured as his thumb moved across my nipple, my back arching into him in response.

"You don't," he said, his mouth lowering towards my chest, "but you will soon enough." Cole's tongue closed over the taut peak.

My head fell back against the wall while my hands moved up, sinking into the dark strands of his hair. I couldn't stop the gasp that fell from my lips. His mouth was hot against my flushed skin and his tongue moved in lazy circles, soothing and teasing before his teeth grazed and clamped down, only to soothe away the ache again. He did it again and again, sharing his attention equally between each of my breasts. Whichever held the undivided attention of his mouth, the other was being cupped and pinched with his hand and fingers.

His movements were unabated and didn't stop until my chest felt raw and aching, until I was rubbing my thighs together in a feeble attempt to ease the pressure growing between them.

With my hands still gripped in his hair, I felt the moment he started to descend, my eyes opening to look down and watch as he knelt before me. My grip on his hair had pushed the sopping tendrils from his forehead and when I lowered my gaze to meet his, there was nothing to obstruct the view before me.

Cole didn't shift his eyes from mine as he guided one of my legs and moved it over his shoulder, exposing me completely to him.

"Eyes on me, Lucky," he murmured before swiping his tongue up the centre of me in one fluid and agonising stroke. It was me who finally broke the trance he had pulled me into as he sucked and licked in wicked, practised movements.

"I—" My eyes fluttered close involuntarily. I *nothing.* I had no idea what I was going to say, especially when he sank his tongue deep into my pussy. He didn't give me a second of reprieve, moving his attention back to my clit, sucking and nipping at the sensitive, swollen bud.

"Fucking incredible," he purred against me.

The vibration of his words was all it took for my orgasm to build. My hands shifted in his hair, one still gripping the strands in a punishing hold while the other curved around to the back of his head. I moved onto my toes, my leg shaking with the effort of keeping myself upright and started to work my hips against his mouth.

A growl ripped from his chest just as he sunk two fingers deep into me.

I came absolutely undone.

His name tumbled from my mouth in a fumbled slur of sounds, the pulses of pleasure hitting me so intensely I couldn't hold myself up through them.

Cole rose to his full height before me, mouth glistening with my arousal and eyes hooded with dark, possessive need. He picked me up by the back of my thighs on his ascent, the act not winding him in the slightest, and crashed his lips to mine.

I could feel the thick, swollen length of him between our bodies again, and felt no shame as I ground myself along him.

Dripping and sensitive and ravenous.

"Fucking hell, Lucky," he hissed against my lips, his grip on my thighs turned bruising. "This will be over much faster than you think if you don't—"

His words were cut off when he set me down on the edge of his bed and I instantly leaned forward, taking him into my mouth in one, seamless stroke.

"*Fuck.*" The word was nothing but a husky breath, like every sensation was as overwhelming for him as it was for me.

I took him as far back as I could, relaxing my tongue and opening my throat. The feeling of him swelling further against my tongue was enough to drive me insane, like my body was overcome with a maddening need to have him deep inside me and if I didn't I would actually, *actually,* die.

The moan that hummed through my body was completely involuntary and clearly all it took for Cole to take back control. Control he'd afforded me so much of in the last week and control I found that I had absolutely no problem giving back to him.

His grip on my upper arms was firm but not painful as he wretched me off him. "Move up the bed."

I followed his demand and lay on my back, completely exposed and at the mercy of his roaming eyes.

"I want to see you, Lucky," he said as he gripped his cock, giving it slow, shallow strokes.

I couldn't stop watching him.

"Let me see you." His second command was harsher and I only hesitated a second before I let my knees fall apart, baring myself to him completely.

It was almost too much, being like this before him, knowing everything that had happened between us since the moment I showed up here, knowing how I'd found myself here after one of the most traumatic experiences of my life. It all built up in that moment and all of a sudden the weight seemed too heavy for me to bear.

I shifted my gaze from him, unable to witness it, witness *him.*

"Eyes on me." His voice cracked through the air between us, swift and final. He didn't move an inch except for the languorous strokes he continued to deliver up and down the proud length of his cock, his thumb swiping over the tip smearing another bead of pre-cum before stroking again.

Watching him touch himself like that, with his eyes on me, might just be the most erotic thing I'd ever seen. The force of his gaze so intense I couldn't stop the squirm, from fisting the sheets in my hands that were now completely and totally ruined from my soaked hair.

God, it was *torture.* All I wanted was for him to just *touch* me.

"Do you know how you look, Lucky?" he rasped, his eyes still locked on my pussy and another wave of pulsing, aching need washed through me. "I can see how wet you are for me from here. And it *is* for me, isn't it?" he asked.

"Yes." It came out as a sob, my hands aching from how tight I was gripping the sheets. I could feel the pressure of tears in my eyes, purely from how much I wanted to pull my legs back together if only to find some friction, to alleviate the throb that mimicked my rapid heart rate, that was driving me mad.

"Perfect." The word dropped from his mouth like a prayer as he stepped towards the bed, moving his body over mine.

The shudder I felt when his chest pressed against mine was like shedding unwanted skin, like the promise of something *more.* But it was absolutely nothing, and I meant *nothing,* compared to the relief that flooded me when he grabbed one of my knees to hike over his hip.

He ran the head of his cock up the slick folds of my pussy once, twice, before lining himself up with my entrance. He didn't move, even as my hips bucked between us, limited as the movement was because of his weight above me, even as his body physically shook with his own restraint.

"Eyes on me, Lucky," he gritted between clenched teeth and he sunk into me inch by inch, my mouth slack and unable to produce any sound at the feeling of being filled by him until I was sure I was going to burst. Cole's chest vibrated against me with the sound of his groan as he finally found himself fully seated inside me.

I was going to die like this.

I knew he was big, but I hadn't been totally prepared for the aching stretch of him, for the feeling of being so full I might split in two.

He waited, his body still shaking. His eyes never leaving mine, not until I gave him a small nod of my head and I knew that it would be the last kindness he'd show me in this.

Cole pulled out to the tip, all before slamming into me so hard a scream tore from my throat and I felt him in my chest. His pace was punishing and I felt every inch of him glide against my inner walls, felt every part of him so completely as he filled me over and over again.

"Fucking. Perfect," he bit out in time with his thrusts, "Feels. Fucking. *Perfect.*" He reached for my other leg and moved both so they were up and over his shoulders, his arm a band over my thighs keeping me in place making everything a tighter fit, a *deeper* thrust.

My eyes rolled back into my hand as he hit a different spot so deep inside me I didn't even know it existed. My hands dug into his biceps, nails digging in for purchase as he drove into me. The sounds leaving my mouth were so incoherent I wasn't totally sure it was even english, needing to concentrate on simply *holding on* while I was quite literally fucked within an inch of my life.

I could feel his hands on me everywhere. Feel the way the tips of his fingers dug into the softer parts of my body, my breasts, pinching my nipples just hard enough to make me clench around him. The way he planted chaste, tender kisses on the insides of my knees, followed by the swipe of his tongue or the sting of his bite.

"*Cole—*" His name came out distorted from the way he continued to meet his hips with mine.

"I know," he breathed, his open mouth grazing my calf one last time before pulling out of me abruptly.

The loss of him so sudden, I cried out, the sound incredulous and pulling the cockiest grin from his devastatingly handsome face. It was the only reaction he gave me as he slid off the end of his bed, grabbing my ankles and twisting me onto my stomach. He grabbed my hips, lifting my ass into the air and for one, terrifying second I thought he was going to explore...*other* entrances.

"Wait, Cole. Wait I—" My attempts at trying to reach him in the lust filled haze he had descended into were feeble, and thank everything that was sacred we'd been in two very different places on what he was doing with the sudden change of position.

Cole slammed so hard into me that if he hadn't had a firm grip on my hips I likely would have gone flying. The invasion was so deep another scream was ripped from me, but there was no waiting for me to adjust this time.

My arms gave out at the pleasure that coursed through me from the new angle, the budding swell of another orgasm coming to life at the base of my spine.

Cole's hand reached down to wrap around my throat, pulling me up and holding me close against his body as he continued to move inside me.

"You're so fucking tight, baby." His voice was rough and strained.

All I could do was moan and try to keep my eyes from staring permanently at my frontal lobes.

I could die from this. I thought it, and I knew it could be true, and I didn't care.

My hand shot up, circling the wrist of the hand gripping my throat, feeling the muscles in his forearms shifted to grip me tighter. I knew in my bones how very different this grip was from the one that left the marks.

Every thrust he delivered brought me closer to my release, and I could tell by the frantic jutting of his hips that he was close too.

With his other hand he reached for my free one, opening my palm and splaying it across my lower belly.

"Oh god. *Oh god*," I choked around the reduced air moving in and out of my lungs just as he put his hand over mine and pushed down.

"Do you feel that, Lucky girl?" he taunted me, his mouth against my ear again, pushing even harder so that I could feel every single thrust, every single surge of him moving inside me.

"*You— your—*" I sobbed, the build of pressure getting even more intense.

"Do you *feel* that?" he asked again, voice louder.

"Yes," I said as his teeth scraped up the side of my neck. "*Yes,*" I all but shouted again.

"Do you know what it means?" He didn't wait for me to reply this time. "It means you're *mine.*" He took my earlobe into his mouth, sucking on it before biting down just as he moved his hand from where it had been pressed over mine and slid it between my legs. "*Mine.*"

His fingers moved in fast circles over my clit and I shattered.

My cry was hoarse and strained, my head flying back onto his shoulder and back arching so completely I was so sure I'd need some sort of chiropractic realignment after this.

Cole's arms bound around me like bands of steel, keeping me against him and holding me through the most earth splintering orgasm I'd ever had in my life.

I felt his roar of release more than I heard it, my ears ringing as I tried to suck in more air only finally getting the full gulps of fresh, sweet oxygen when he let go of my throat. Continuing to slowly pump himself in and out of me a few more times then collapsing on the bed.

He landed both of us on our sides, his arms not moving an inch as he kept me pressed against him.

For a long time it was just the frantic beat of his heart pounding relentlessly against my back, mine pounding under his palm and our deep, laboured breathing. Trying to come down from what had been the closest thing to a religious experience I might ever have.

My eyes had begun to droop, my body exhausted, spent and completely satisfied when he pulled his cock from inside me, the move making my eyes fly back open and my face twist with a grimace, both at the loss of him and the already growing ache of what we'd done.

I was, without a doubt, not going to be able to walk.

Cole shifted us further up the bed, turning me to face him so we were now lying nose to nose, his arm under my head and my body tucked once again against the solid expanse of his.

"Tell me something no one else knows." He spoke the words against my still wet hair, the realisation that his entire bed was soaked through only then coming to my attention.

I stared at him, watching as he watched me, seeing the way his features were also altered with the satisfaction of what we'd just done. The way his damp hair clung to his forehead.

My eyes widened at the realisation of what just happened, "Cole, we didn't use–"

"I'm clean, you're clean and you're on birth control," he said it so casually it took me a second to realise there was no way on god's green earth that he should actually know that. "And you're on the bar," he added.

"There is no way you should know that."

"I know everything about you, Navy Grace."

"I could have crabs."

"You–"

"Or, like, a really hospitable environment."

"I'd know."

"Are you aware of how weird it is for those words to come out of your mouth? We need to talk about your lack of respect for boundaries. You–"

I struggled to pull a viable sentence together between the feel of his bare chest, warm and steady pressed against mine, and the small circles his thumb was making against the skin of my back.

"Please," he added on like an afterthought, maybe confusing my hesitation for something other than what it was; annoyance, maybe, at how exactly he knew everything about me. It was a conversation we would absolutely be having later, one I needed more energy for than I had now and Cole had been many things, but a liar had never been one of them.

The first thing that came to mind were the plans I had for the life I wanted to rebuild. The small details, down to the paper on the walls, to the plates that people would eat off of, the size of the ice cubes in their tumblers.

I wanted to tell him that I was trying to look at everything that happened as a chance to do it all again. A fresh, clean start. I wanted simple and beautiful and calm. Everything that *Seven* hadn't been.

Now I wanted reliable, and gentle and *quiet.* And I knew how I'd do it too. The plans in my head, how I saw everything coming together. It was so, *so,* beautiful that I felt a pang in my chest just at its mere possibility, that I knew the moment I sat down with any investor, any board of willing listeners, that they wouldn't be able to say no. That it would be exactly what I'd dreamed of every single day since I closed the doors of *Seven* and walked away, leaving a part of myself behind in the places I'd poured so much of my soul into.

That's what I *wanted* to tell him. But I couldn't.

I couldn't give that part of myself over to him, or to anyone. It was mine, and by being mine it remained safe.

"Alright," I said as he waited patiently, his thumb still rubbing soothing circles on my back. "When I was fifteen, I was trying to remove the hair between my eyebrows because Oakleigh had told me it looked like a caterpillar was sleeping over my eyes. It was the first day of summer and he told me a bird would mistake it for food and try to eat my face."

Cole's eyes were alight with the picture of the scene he was no doubt visualising in his mind.

"So, I decided to do something about it."

"Oh, no," he said softly, his mouth starting to curve.

"Oh, *yes*," I replied, cringing at the memory. "I'd picked up my razor and just as I was going for the landing swipe, I sneezed."

"That adds up." His grin was growing and it was impossible

for mine not to grow either.

"I ended up shaving off half of my left eyebrow and I had to spend every single day of the entire summer break inside until it grew back. I had a little side fringe at the time, you probably don't remember, and—"

"I remember." He said it so quietly I knew I could pretend he hadn't said it at all. But I heard him. I *knew* I heard him.

I swallowed before continuing, "—and so I kept it over my eye the entire time. My parents thought I was going through an emotional, mid-teen depression and my entire family gave me an intervention on how my hairstyle was bad for my eyesight. They still have no idea."

Cole's face finally split into the most captivating smile I'd ever seen. His hand came up, fingers sinking into the damp strands of my hair, holding my head gently against him. "Why does that not surprise me at all?" he chuckled.

I pulled back, his hand falling from my head easily. I looked back up at him, my fingers reaching up to trace the lines of his fading smile, utterly in awe. "You should always do that."

"Do what?" He kissed the tips of my fingers as they passed over his lips for the fifth time since my exploration started.

"Smile."

33

Cole

The warmth of Lucky's body tucked into mine soothed whatever it was inside of me that woke constantly through the night.

Sleep would pull me under for me only to claw my way back out of it. Until I could feel the expanse of her stomach beneath my palm, feel her legs entwined with mine. The moment I remembered she was there it was an onslaught of memories that cascaded through my mind.

I played back what it was like to have her beneath me. To hear my name on her lips as I drove into her tight, wet heat. To finally know what it was like to be consumed by the softest parts of her and watch as she came undone in violent shakes around me.

Once hadn't been enough. I didn't know how I could have ever thought one taste of her would be enough in any capacity.

The bed had been soaked through after I'd walked us both from the shower and laid her down on the sheets. I watched the gentle rise and fall of her frame, still buried deep inside of her, and felt her body soften, losing all its tension.

I was struck in that moment with this panic that there were too many people that knew her more. Knew her *better.* That there were things she shared with her friends, her family, that painted a picture of who she was no matter what angle you stood to observe her. My heart rate picked up with a wave of bitterness that I had once been one of those people until it became easier for me not to have anyone at all.

Until it became necessary.

It was like being ripped apart right down the middle, seeing Lucky's twelve year old tear streaked face as she stood in front of me, taking every word I aimed at her with deadly precision. With the intention to wound her so thoroughly she'd never be able to come back from it. I wanted to hit her with blow after blow until she felt the way I did. That hot anger built until it was overflowing, singeing me from the inside out, until I wouldn't be able to come back from it either.

Then there was the other part, that wanted to run after her, to explain *why* and take it all back. It was the latter of those two versions of myself that I had succumbed to more and more since she'd come back into my life and all of sudden I was greedy. I wanted to know more, I wanted to know *everything.*

I wanted bits of her that no one had ever had before, that would just be mine. I was transfixed, while she spoke. When she gave her secret freely. It was a whole new sort of thrill, one I'd never experienced before. One that I had become addicted to with only a single taste.

COLE

Lucky's body had begun to relax in my hold again when little shivers started to rake through her. I felt her eyes on me, watching and probing and dissecting while I changed the bedding, laying her down on the dry sheets where she let her legs fall apart and pulled me close to her. Where I drove into her in one punishing thrust right to the hilt over and over again until I couldn't remember my own fucking name, only hers.

I woke with a jolt, being ripped from the dream with the immediate realisation that she was gone.

My hand reached out blindly, my eyes not yet following my brain that was trying to figure out what had happened between the last time I'd felt her pressed against me and now.

My body was moving before I knew it, with no idea where she might have gone. I wiped a hand down my face and headed for the en suite, determined only to find her and bring her back with me.

Lucky stood in front of the vanity mirror, her eyes closed with a hint of a smile on her lips, still swollen from last night.

I took her in, letting my eyes roam across every inch of her exposed skin, across the marks around her throat that sent a spike of molten rage through me, and at the ones that her own fingertips glided over as if in reverence. The finger prints I'd left on her hips, the light outline of my bite between her neck and shoulder. It was a completely different feeling that pulsed through me, so brutal and jarring that I almost took a step back.

It wasn't just that I wanted Lucky, and I *did* want her. I wanted every single piece of her. I wanted her mind, I wanted her body. Her soul. I wanted it to be tethered to mine in every possible way.

Yes, I wanted all of that.

But it was also this suffocating *need* for all of those things too. Like I might never be able to breathe right again without her.

I walked towards her, her eyes remained closed but I knew she'd heard me, felt me. The tips of my fingers reached out, skirting over the shape of her, committing it to memory all over again. My lips found her jaw, pressing a kiss to the spot just behind her ear. One hand lifted to settle on her breast, the weight of it heavy and warm in my palm as my thumb ghosted across her nipple. I moved the other to splay across her stomach, pulling her close to me.

Lucky released a sigh that seemed to pull every last morsel of air from her lungs while she melted into my hold for a moment before turning to face me.

"Lucky," I breathed against the skin of her neck while continuing to trace a path with my mouth. "You left," my voice was still thick with sleep.

"I won't leave," she whispered back, her arms wrapping around my waist tightly, her chin lifting and seeking out my lips for a slow, lazy kiss that pulled me closer into her.

I pulled her into the shower and she let me wash every part of her body, her eyes tracking my every movement.

She watched me until I'd finished, standing back up to my full height and when I was done she did the same for me. It was impossible to look away from her. To not experience the way she touched me like she never wanted to stop.

Making a point to dry us both off thoroughly, I led her back to the bed where she settled into the covers and I settled into the valley of her hips.

"Don't say things you don't mean, Navy," I said the words

between kisses I peppered against her skin, unable to help the movement of my hips as she melted further beneath me, her skin soft and her body pliable. "You've wanted to leave from the moment you got here."

Her hips began to meet mine, hands gliding up my arms and settling on my shoulders. I reached between, finding the swollen bud of her clit already so sensitive and began to make slow and lazy movements there too, earning a breathy moan from her.

"That was different. You were different," she panted, her hands sinking into my hair and pulling taut.

I pulled back to look down at her, *really* look at her. "You were different too," I said, wanting her to see everything I felt, wanting her to know exactly what she'd done to me. "You're still a pain in my ass," I grinned down at her, "but it's different, isn't it?"

"You drive me insane," she said with a small grin of her own, her hands moving from my hair and pressing into my back, a shiver wracking through my body when she dragged them down, digging them into the hard muscle of my ass. "But yes, it's different. Why? Why's it different?" she asked, like she needed to know the answer but wasn't sure where she'd be able to find it.

I leaned down to place another lingering kiss at the corner of her mouth, lining myself up at her entrance already slick with her arousal, and started to pushed in.

"I couldn't stay away." The words were soft as they tumbled from my mouth, but they might have been the most bluntly honest ones I'd ever let past my tongue. "Because you have always consumed me. Every single part of me and I couldn't stay away anymore." I sank into her fully. "God you're so *tight*. Fuck I have to— I need to—"

The words wouldn't come. I found I didn't need them to, in the end. I saw everything right there on Lucky's face, how she needed me too, just like this.

I moved in slow, deep strokes. In complete contrast to the greedy, roaming hands of last night. I took my time this morning, my pace never changing, making sure she felt every inch of me. When I felt the walls of her pussy tighten, when her breathing became rapid and her hands became frantic in their movement across my back, my shoulders, my arms, I sat back and lifted her hips from the bed, getting impossibly deeper, groaning at the new angle, of how it felt to be consumed by her.

"Come for me, baby," I breathed against my ear, "you're taking me so fucking well."

She was *everything.*

The way Lucky responded to the words I spoke was mesmerising. Like she was both enraptured and confused by her response to them.

"You're perfect," I breathed against her lips, "*fuck.*" I swallowed every single mewling cry that she released, completely lost in the feel of where we were joined.

My pace had become frantic until my grip on her ass would no doubt leave marks, as I tried to get deeper still. My orgasm washed through me without warning, delivered in a final, brutal thrust.

Lucky devoured every grunt and curse, every last drop of praise I gave her with every swipe of her tongue, every nip she gave my bottom lip between her teeth, keeping every last bit of me for herself.

And I found I didn't mind that at all, that I belonged to

Lucky Peters just as much as she now belonged to me.

Lucky asked about the bruise on my jaw, and the cut on my lip, her face so full of concern it twisted something deep inside of me. I explained them away before pulling her back into me and showing her how many other things there were that were more exciting to focus on.

We had done very little over the weekend, eating only when we had to, every other moment was spent with Lucky above me, beneath me, in front of me.

She overwhelmed me, devouring me from the inside out and the very thought that it would ever stop tested the stability of my sanity.

I picked up a golden strand, rolling it between my forefinger and thumb, wholly and utterly entranced by it.

"Tell me something no one else knows," she whispered to me in the darkened, quiet room.

"Hmm," I mused thoughtfully, still unwilling to shift my focus from the way her hair reflected the moonlight that cut into the room, luminescent behind her, giving a soft glow to the silhouette of her body. "I hate grapes."

"Really?" Her voice was lit with a smile I couldn't see.

"Scouts honour." I dropped her hair and lifted three fingers up between us, my eyes finally meeting her, unable to keep the amusement from my gaze or the twist of my lips.

Lucky reached out a hand, resting it on my jaw and it was instinct to lean into it. She did that more and more. Touching me however she could, even in the lightest of ways.

I craved it, the feel of her hands on me.

"Everybody likes grapes." She grinned at me, my eyes latching onto her, eyes roaming over and over again, needing to remember how it felt to have her look at me, just like that.

"It's the skin," I murmured, still staring at her, "I hate the way it feels when I chew."

This exchanging of secrets, no matter how small and inconsequential, was something Lucky clung to as fervently as I did. The new and completely untouched truths we shared had become more precious than everything that littered the path that stretched behind us of our intertwined lives.

"No grapes then," she said, her hand coming up to trace the smile that still curved up the side of my mouth before I pulled her close, placing a tender kiss on her temple.

"No grapes."

Lucky fell asleep with her body tucked into mine, the rise and fall of her frame and the steady beat of her heart the sole focus on my attention.

Every time I drifted off, my mind warred, ripping and clawing at itself, at how it felt to have her next to me, moving around me. To see her face break into a smile that existed simply because I'd put it there. Those images thrashed and struggled against the hold of memories that had plagued me my whole life; my mothers palm across my face, Lucky's seeking eyes finding me at my lowest.

I pried myself away from her in the middle of the night, moving to the chair that still faced the bed and watched as every so often her hand would reach out in her sleep, searching for me, seeking me out. I stared at her until my eyes hurt, until my body shook, until it wasn't her who I hated anymore, but myself.

34

Lucky

I started to cook again which was both weird and not.

Cole hadn't put up much of a fight, though I half expected the fridge to be completely empty again when I opened it Monday morning marking almost a whole week of me staying with him.

The bruises around my neck continued to fade every day, giving me a very visual and very real countdown to my departure from his apartment. My eye was improving too, and I was sure by the end of the week I'd be able to claim it came from holding in too many sneezes in a row.

It felt good to get back into routine, and even better to have some pants of my own to put on, to take off Cole's shirt, which he'd still thrust in my direction every time putting anything on was absolutely necessary on our trips from his room to the kitchen and back. It told me enough of what he thought about my little bag of things I'd tucked inside the door of his closet. Namely that he wasn't all that fond of the fact I now had some underwear at my disposal and some hair care products that didn't smell like him.

Things had changed, but they also hadn't. He was there, but not.

I wasn't alone, but I was.

It didn't matter right now though. Not today.

I'd made myself breakfast and then continued to prepare for the rest of the day, not knowing whether he'd be back for lunch or even dinner (he never came back for either).

After I'd cleaned the kitchen more thoroughly than was needed, I stood there for a while, trying to build up the courage to do what I'd been planning.

Procrastination was in full unyielding force, so I headed straight for the shower as if it had become a do or die situation. I'd stood under the spray for a long time, committing to making an exit upon the first hint of running out of hot water. Instead, I'd stayed where I was for an incredibly unreasonable amount of time and marvelled at the discovery that Cole's building didn't seem to have an expiry on the hot water, at least not within a forty minute period. That wasn't something I had ever experienced growing up with six older siblings, consistently getting the short straw on the shower schedule. I didn't think I even knew hot water was a thing until I was thirteen.

I was stalling. Why? Because I was a big scaredy cat.

I took my time brushing my hair, pulling on a pair of jeans and a black sweater and finally leaving the comfort of Cole's room. I made my trek with purposeful strides to the other side of the apartment and began to perspire immediately.

It wasn't just me who was getting back into routine, because unlike the entirety of the last week, there were other members of Cole's staff that were now milling about.

I passed by Arnold - still not sure that was his actual name - from where he was in the kitchen I'd just cleaned, cleaning it again.

I stood in front of the little computer lab for an extra five minutes before I stepped inside. It was empty, of course, because the entire space was over-kill.

Besides me and Felicity who had access to Cole's private residence, there was Arnold and Sonya who worked to keep his apartment clean, fully stocked with food and in complete working order. There was no need for a computer lab fit with six different desks and six different computers.

That was another thing I'd learned about Cole; if he was going to do something he was going to do it without holding back, he'd go above and beyond. This apartment? Case in point. His business empire? Case. In. Point. The way I still felt him between my legs every time I took a step? Case in fucking point.

I left the light off in the room, walking to the back corner and sitting down at the same one that I used every week to type up and print out the notes for his food instructions. Leaving the lights off made this all feel less like it was happening, like it was still just a secret between me and myself.

I didn't feel any shame as my hands shook when reaching out towards the keyboard and mouse, not when it took me three times to hold the mouse in my hand well enough to open a Word document and not when it took me twice as long as it should have because I kept hitting the wrong letters on the keyboard as I began to put my plans into action.

I started to flesh out the concepts for the new restaurant I'd been dreaming of, taking the first of many steps in the direction of rebuilding my life.

"We're going *where?*" My voice cracked on the last word and pitched up to an octave that would probably screw with the satellites. Honestly, if I wasn't so absolutely gobsmacked it would've sounded comical.

"New York," he said for the third time as he walked in front of me, hands in his slacks, the picture of complete and total indifference.

"I'm not going to New York, Cole. I'm going home. As in, back to my parents place." It was officially Friday night which meant I'd been sleeping in Cole's bed for almost two weeks.

Well, that got his attention.

He looked at me with his face set in that unreadable mask that told me one thing for certain; whatever was happening behind his eyes was the complete total and opposite of calm.

"I mean," I tried again, feeling all sorts of awkward and unsure like he didn't just have his dick all in and around my lady garden a handful of hours ago, "the bruises are mostly gone now and the eye is...manageable." I even cringed at that.

I'd put together a mostly foolproof and solid story for when my mother no doubt made me remove the sunglasses I had fully intended on wearing inside at all times.

"I know I've been in your space for a long time. I'm not actually completely sure why I'm still here. I'd planned on leaving this morning but I just had a couple more things to do and my computer at home is actually kind of shit and—"

Oh, put a sock in it, Lucky.

"I don't care that you've been staying here." Even his voice held no emotion.

"Well that just made me feel all the warmest and gooiest emotions. Way to make a girl feel special." I gave him a forced tight lipped smile before storming past him and heading straight for his room to grab my bag.

"Lucky," he said from close enough behind me.

"Save it, Cole. I am totally picking up what you're putting down and like I said, I'm going home. I'll ask Felicity to let me know when you're—"

"No." He didn't even need to raise his voice for it to be menacing. It made my blood boil, like the pilot light on the simmering, festering build up of *everything* I'd been feeling since I showed up here had been ignited.

I turned on my heels to face him slowly (for added dramatic effect and also to collect myself before I accidentally turned him into a eunuch).

"*No?*" I repeated back to him.

"You're not going anywhere."

"Oh, I'm sorry, *Dad*, did I forget to have you sign my *permission* slip?" It was happening. My hands were sweating and I could feel my pulse in my eyelids. I wanted to cry and scream and throw up and I was fucking *furious*.

It hit me all at once, every single thing I'd felt, every morning I'd woken up alone, every time I wanted to *say* something but didn't.

His eyes closed fractionally before taking a big, deep breath, "You're coming to New York."

"And *you're* certifiably insane. What is wrong with you? I don't need to spend hours in a plane only to wake up in a different bed *by myself* just because I replace your need for an electric blanket and your right hand," I snapped at him before I continued in the direction of his room. "Actually," I turned back to him because I was on a roll. He was closer even though I hadn't heard him take a single step. "I quit."

"What?" He had the audacity to sound marginally shocked. It just made me even angrier.

"I quit. This is me submitting my big, huge, whale of a resignation." I held my hands out in front of me and thrust them towards him. A physical, if not completely ridiculous, show of said resignation.

"Nope." He popped the 'p'. He *popped* it.

"You cannot be serious."

"You're coming to New York, it's in your contract."

"My *contract?*"

"You're reminding me a lot of a parrot. You repeat things a lot when you're…emotional."

"When I'm *emotional?!*" I yelled right at him, no holding back and all he did was cut a grin. God, I wanted to claw it off his stupid, pretty face.

"You're coming to New York." His jaw ticked in a way that told me he was losing his patience.

Yeah, well that made two of us, bucko.

"Why? *Why?* It's not like you're even eating any of the food I cook anymore. Why is it so important for me to go to New York with you?"

"Because." He delivered the word short and clipped.

"*Because?* Are you twelve? Because *why*? What...what even *is* this?" I gestured between the two of us, "What are we even doing here, Cole?"

My chest was heaving. I'd been simultaneously waiting for this to happen and scared that it would, that I would snap and everything ugly would come pouring out. Because anger meant tears and tears meant crying and snot and it wasn't exactly the visual I was hoping for while attempting to deliver the verbal ass kicking of a lifetime.

The worst part might have been how he just stood there, expression still blank and unchanging, breathing calm and steady with his stupid hands in the pockets of his stupid slacks all while I was hyperventilating and in serious need of a paper bag.

"What is this?" I threw my arms out either side of me, taking a step towards him, trying to pull all the little pieces of myself he had taken for keeps back over to me. I didn't want him to have any shards of me, even if it meant he might cut himself on them and hurt too. "I need you to tell me, because I have no idea. One minute I see you, and not just see you but *see* you. And the next? It's like you're trying to keep me a secret—"

"Who would I be keeping you a secret from, Lucky?" He sounded...put off. It was a step up from nothing.

"From yourself. Like if you only see me in the dead of night, when the lights are off and the house is empty that it make you feel...*fuck*, I have no fucking idea." I threw my hands up and then pushed them into my hair.

"Oh, but you were doing so well," he cooed.

"Is this a joke to you, Cole?" I hated how my voice cracked, how my eyes welled with more tears, how my hand shook when they ghosted over my lips remembering every time he'd touched me. I remembered it all while he stood there, not showing a single ounce of the storm I knew was raging behind his eyes.

I felt my face go slack, "Oh my god. Was this what you meant? Was this what you were— Is this what you planned this entire time? To fuck me, to worm your way under my skin, into my heart, to obliterate whatever was left that you could find?"

"No." There was a flash of something quick and sharp in his eyes, not long enough for me to see exactly what it was but enough for me to know he was losing whatever war he was battling. It was like that single word had slipped through his defences as his jaw continued to tick, as he fought to hold himself in check.

"Tell me," I whispered, not caring that the tears kept spilling over, that they were tracking down my face, that he'd see how stupidly deep I was getting all while he was pulling back.

He was pulling back and I had stayed, feeling safe despite all the signs, despite all the mornings without him. Safe enough that I'd started to do something about my life, started to see my plans come together in some sort of coherent way.

It didn't seem to matter much that my lack of luck had tried to break me in the worst of ways, that I'd lost control of my body for just one terrifying moment. It didn't matter that I'd ended up here, with the man who had once been the boy I had loved, who turned into a man that hated me, who I'd hated back because what the fuck else are you supposed to do in that situation? It didn't matter that he might hate me still, even amongst the moments where it felt so impossible for that to be possible, even if I still didn't know *why*. That unanswered question felt as if it was about to douse all the progress I had made in gasoline and the curtains would lift just in time for me to see him smile as it went up in flames.

It had been so easy to let myself fall into him.

I'd realised in that moment that I was dangerously close to handing something over to Cole that I wouldn't be able to get back, at least not in the shape that he'd received it. I had no interest in figuring out what it was like to live without another piece of myself because I'd been too blind to see what was happening.

Felt too safe to care.

It was like gaining an inch in life only to have fate wag its finger in my face and tut in disapproval, as if to say '*don't you get it, Lucky? You're never going to win.*'

"Tell me," I said, louder this time. "Tell me, tell me, *tell me, fucking tell me what you want!*" I screamed at him so loud it was like every word tore at me as I unleashed them like blades meant to slice into his composed form.

To see a glimpse at what lay beneath, because I'd seen it. I had *seen* who he was beneath it and I still wanted him, even as I waited for him to confirm the worst of my thoughts, I still wanted him.

He didn't speak. He only stood there, staring at me.

I had my answer.

"Congratulations, Cole." I palmed away the tears on my face giving him my best smile, "You did it. You won."

All I had to do was get out of this apartment. This moment was made about fifty times worse by the fact I'd only just remembered that Bessy was at Melody's house and I'd be catching the bus.

I turned on my heels and stalked over to his room. My whole body jolted in shock when a hand wrapped around my forearm and turned me with a jerk. I swear Cole floated when he walked because he never made a sound.

"Get off me, Cole." I tried to yank my arm from his grip but all he did was tighten his hold. "Get your hands *off--*"

"What do I want?" His voice was so low I almost missed it. "*What do I want?*" Louder now, his face started to split into a smile that honestly scared the living shit out of me. Like there was a reason he'd always kept himself so in check and I was about to see exactly what happened when he slipped.

"What do I *want?*" He dropped my arm and held his arms out either side of him. He released a maniacal laugh before it stopped abruptly, like the answer to that question should be obvious to me. "I don't *know*, Lucky." He pushed his hands into his hair and started to tug at it. "I don't know. How the fuck am I supposed to know?" His voice continued to rise in volume, and with each rising octave I could see the edges of his composure fraying until finally they just snapped. "Huh? How am I supposed to know? I'm trying here, fuck me, am I trying but you...*you.*" He lifted a hand to point an accusing finger right at me but he didn't move any closer. His eyes...they were no longer empty and bored but suddenly they were wild and chaotic and unhinged. "You don't understand." He spun away from me, hands still pulling his hair.

"I don't understand because you haven't told me anything." I gritted out.

"Fucking hell, Lucky, what is it exactly—"

"Why do you hate me?"

Cole didn't turn around to face me, he stood farther out of my reach than he'd been before. As if that wasn't achingly poetic.

"You're wasting both our times, Cole. I already told you, if this was what you wanted from your fucked up need to tear me dow—"

"I don't hate you."

"Oh? Because I'm having a super *duper* easy time believing that you like me." I didn't wait for him to say anything, because this was stupid. We were going back and forth and someone needed to end it.

It took me less than a minute to practically jog back to his room and grab my bag. I didn't think about anything but my need to leave as I headed for the elevator.

"Stop," he said from where he stood right outside his bedroom doors.

I walked right past him, focusing on putting one foot in front of the other.

"Fucking *stop*." He hadn't raised his voice yet, not really, but that was the closest thing to it. The command in his tone was clear, and a part of me rebelled at not staying and listening but I couldn't. I needed to go.

"I said—"

"I heard what you said." I whirled on him, making him stop short so close to me I had to crane my head all the way back just to look at him. "*You* stop, because I'm not built for this, Cole. This," I motion between us, ignoring the way my voice shook, "I'm not doing this. Do what you want, tell whoever you want about whatever it is you'd planned to say, I don't care anymore. I can't do this with you."

His grip on my arms was there before I even began to turn, "You're not going anywhere, Navy."

"*Fuck. You*," I seethed at him between gritted teeth trying to wriggle out of his hold. And then I just started shoving at him.

His broad, immovable frame took every one of my shoves but he didn't move. Not an inch.

"Fine," he said, but he didn't release me and now that I'd started I couldn't stop.

I kept pushing at him, trying to get him to move, to let me *go*. I needed him to just let me go.

"*Let. Me. Go.*" It was a desperate plea now, asking for more than one thing I didn't think he'd ever really be able to give me. He'd always have his claws in me no matter what and something about that comforted me in a sick way.

"Fine. *Fine.* FUCKING *FINE!*" His voice cracked between us and the power of it just made me stop.

My arms falling limp at my sides, my eyes moving up to meet his. They were wild and angry and confused and I'd never seen so much so clearly on his face.

"What? What do you want to know, Lucky? You want me to tell you that looking at your face every single day growing up was like salt in the wound of just how much I wasn't marking up? How every fucking day it was '*Why can't you be more like Lucky, Cole?*'. Why couldn't I *do more* like Lucky?" He released me abruptly and stepped back, head dropping as a bitter, broken laugh left him. "That every fucking time she hit me with whatever she could find – her hand, her shoes, the fucking kitchen *chair* – it was always because someone else was doing more than me, being more than I was? Because I wasn't finishing school as fast as Brooks? Because I wasn't better than everyone else? Better than *you*?"

He'd stopped yelling now and everything around us just felt so quiet. So heavy. I wanted to move but I couldn't, every ounce of my energy was being used trying to understand what he was saying.

"I couldn't look at you without hating you and I hated myself for it because, damn it, I didn't want to hate you. But how could I not? At that moment, for all those years, to me, you were the reason for the marks on my body, for the broken bones and bruises. And you *smiled*. The entire time you did it, like you *knew* and you *revelled* in it. You sought me out and went out of your way to fuck me over time and time again."

I finally got my body to move, finally took a step towards him. But what he was saying didn't make sense to me. How was any of that true? How did anyone not know?

How did *I* not know?

At my movement he lifted his eyes to finally meet mine, my breath catching at the way they shined, the way he finally let me see *everything*.

"Cole, I—" What could I even possibly say to that?

"It was easier to hate you. I needed to. It gave me something to hold on to, something to drive me, to bear it until I could leave. Every single day you always looked at me like I wasn't enough. You weren't the only one, but yours hurt the most. So, I became more than enough. And then you were in my house. My *house*. The person I wanted and hated and despised. So, I tried. I really honestly tried to end you and I wanted to, so badly. I wanted to ruin you. I wanted to, until—" He cut himself off abruptly, looking anywhere but at me.

"Until what?" My voice was a whisper and still it was too loud for the space between us.

"Until I didn't. Until I couldn't get through the day without thinking about you or wanting you or *needing* you. And I hated myself for caving on the only thing that I'd promised myself. That I would be your end, that I would break you like you'd broken me."

"Cole." I watched as a single tear tracked down his face. I reached out to try and wipe it but his hand gripped my wrist stopping me from touching him.

"No, because you don't get it, Lucky. I still want that. I want to break you until there is nothing left. I want to bend you until it's only my name on your tongue and you know nothing else but me, want nothing else but me. I want— I *need*—"

It was fascinating to watch as the darkness in him shifted. Changing him so quickly and moulding his features into something so *other* it was like looking at two different people.

"I didn't know, Cole. I— I swear to god." I didn't care how my voice hitched or how I fumbled with the words, desperate to get them out, "I didn't know. I would have— I would have done anything." Tears fell down my own face as I tracked the descent of the single tear he'd let escape.

His eyes shuddered as the grip on my wrist loosened a fraction, turning into a caress. His chest expanded like he was testing out this new version of himself, someone who wasn't shouldering the heaviest secrets of his life alone.

Cole took the last, tiny step between us, our chests touching and lifted his other hand up to thread through my hair.

"Say it." His eyes opened and I knew I was looking at a much more composed version of who he'd been just moments before. "But know that you won't escape me once you do," he added. "I'm not a patient man, Navy. I won't give you another chance to leave."

"I don't want to leave." And I meant every word, no matter

how terrified I was. I sealed the deal with the last two words that I knew would bind me to him without a reasonable doubt. "I'm yours."

Cole leaned down, pressing his forehead to mine, his hands coming up to cradle my face, "Come to New York."

My pointer fingers traced the path of the single tear he'd let escape, heartbroken that it ever needed to exist in the first place. "You'll be there when I wake up?"

"Yes." He said the word with such finality, like it was the easiest promise he'd ever made.

"Okay," I lifted my chin, my lips ghosting over his, "I'll come to New York."

35

Lucky

Turned out that when Cole said we were going to New York he meant we were going right then and there, and we were going in his private jet.

Sorry, not sure you got that. *Private jet.*

I did the only thing anyone would do in my situation. I messaged my best friend.

Me:
You'll never believe where my butt is sitting right now at this moment.

Liddy-Cakes:
I feel like this is a trick question.

Me:
I'm about to experience something I never thought I would.

Liddy-Cakes:
Anal?

Me:
Something you have also never thought you'd experience.

Liddy-Cakes:
...so, anal?

Me:
This has absolutely nothing to do with either your butthole or mine.

Liddy-Cakes:
OMG, you're on a game show?

Me:
I'd be fascinated to know how you got from anal to game show in that short amount of time.

Liddy-Cakes:
I have been told my mind is a beautiful, complex thing.

Me:

> Never lose your sparkle, pony boy.

Liddy-Cakes:
I give up, enlighten me.

> **Me:**
> I'm on a private plane. A jet, no less.

Liddy-Cakes:
You're absolutely about to join the mile high club.

Liddy-Cakes:
Do they give you warm little towels?

Liddy-Cakes:
I always imagined they'd smell like the inside of a new car. Can you confirm?

Liddy-Cakes:
I can't believe your boyfriend owns a jet.

> **Me:**
> Not my boyfriend.

Liddy-Cakes:
Right, sorry, just your boss who you do the no pants dance with. My bad.

> **Me:**
> Why are we friends again?

Liddy-Cakes:
Because I'm the straw to your berry?

"I've never seen anyone grin at their phone like that," Cole spoke up, shocking me with his presence even though I was on *his* plane, my phone flying straight out of my hand and landing right at his shoes.

The sound of his voice snapped me from my immersive conversation with Melody. I hadn't even realised he'd taken the seat across from me.

Perfect.

The screen lit up just as he grabbed it and I'd never wanted to die quite as much as I did at that moment. I could see the messages from where the phone was extended between us still gripped in his hand.

Liddy-Cakes:
I bet he has a huge dong.

Ding.

Liddy-Cakes:
He's so big and you're so small, aren't you concerned about internal haemorrhaging?

Ding.

Liddy-Cakes:
Do you have to turn your phone onto flight

mode if it's a private jet?

Cole and I both saw the messages come in, one after the other. It felt sort of like what I'd imagined waking up from a dream where you thought you were naked in front of a group of important people to then wake up and find that wow, you're indeed naked in front of a group of important people.

I snatched the phone from his hand, feeling my face turn into a living, breathing tomato.

Cole lifted a glass of what looked like whisky over ice to take a sip from, covering his smile. He couldn't hide the little glint in his eye that told me he'd read every single message.

Ding.

Liddy-Cakes:
  Nothing says 'hello, New York!' like a good
  airborne dicking. Fly safe, love you, lube up!

Jesus, just take me now.

I was being punished for something I did in a past life, that was the only reasonable explanation.

"Drink?" he asked, eyebrows raised. He was clearly trying, and failing, to restrain a smile.

"A very strong one, thank you," I grumbled, mentally noting to give Melody the biggest nipple cripple of her life the next time I saw her.

JUST MY LUCK

"Lucky." Cole's soft murmur roused me from sleep.

I opened my eyes and found his on me in the same way they always were; dark, intense and full of wanting. For me to see the heat in his eyes and not remember the hell we'd walked through to get to where we were, it was going to continue to take time for that to not feel weird. I wasn't sure I wanted to forget it though, knowing what had happened between us and seeing where we were, it made me hold him tighter. It made me want to love him *more.*

"Oh no, I was drooling wasn't I?" I croaked, wiping the back of my hand over my mouth.

I righted myself in the seat as Cole leant back in his, casually settling his ankle on his knee. Leaning his elbow on his arm rest, he brought a finger to his lips, eyes alight with mischief. The mischief? That didn't take any getting used to. I was as familiar with that look as I was with my own name.

"I already have some photos for later," he murmured.

"Oh, perfect. I'm so gla–*aah.*" I clutched the arm rests of my seat with the sort of strength I didn't even know I possessed. My eyes clamping tight on reflex when the plane continued to shake with turbulence. "*Not gonna die, not gonna die,*" I chanted through heavy breathing until it subsided.

My eyes were closed but I could feel Cole looking at me, inspecting. I dared to open one eye to find his eyes exactly where I knew they'd be, rapidly taking in my face. His own features were dark and mostly unreadable except one emotion: surprise. He hadn't picked this.

If I wasn't about to pee myself in fear I'd probably have

rejoiced in finally getting one by him.

He offered a hand that I took without hesitation, a small squeak of surprise escaped me when he tugged me from my seat onto his lap, arranging my legs on either side of him just as the light for the seat belt sign turned on.

"Cole, I'm thinking I should be buckled in," I said, voice shaking, and settling my hands onto his shoulders while his found their home low on my hips.

He just hummed into the crook of my neck and planted slow, teasing kisses.

I reached up to put a hand on his face to push him away. "Your turn-ons are so bizarre, did you know that? I'm in *peril*."

Cole removed my hand from where it hardly covered his face and placed it back on his shoulder, a barely there smile gracing the curve of his lips. "Are you scared, Lucky?" he asked between kisses, sliding his hands down to the hem of my dress and fiddling with fabric.

"Scared? *No*," I scoffed, half-heartedly attempting to slap away his wandering hands. I rolled my eyes in an attempt to cover the tremor in my voice. It wasn't that I was *scared* of flying. It just wasn't really my favourite thing to do.

The plane shook again with vigour and my fingers clung to the thick material of his suit jacket. "Oh shit-sticks, Cole. We're going to die, *I'm gonna die.*"

"We're not going to die," He said, tone far too calm for the situation as his thumbs made small soothing circles just beneath the fabric of my dress. "You didn't tell me you were scared of flying."

"I didn't know it was important," I bit out, mentally chanting *'goosfraba, goosfraba, goosfraba'.*

"Everything about you is important," he said without a morsel of humour.

"Bet you didn't realise all you needed to do was throw me in on a plane to torment me and I'd crack faster than green grass through a goose." I gave a strained laugh as my hands still clung to his shoulders in a grip that surely had to be painful, but I couldn't unfurl my hands.

He gave me a deadpanned look that said he wasn't all too impressed with my attempt at light humour.

"Sorry," I closed my eyes, drawing in a deep breath. "Southern sayings are my safe zone."

"Are you done?"

"Yep. Super done. Done like a dinner. Done, done, d–*oh sweet tangy lemons, Cole--*"

The plane continued to shake and my body started to tremble.

"Lucky." Cole's voice was still so calm it made me want to hit him.

"I n-need to put on my s-seat belt." My teeth started to chatter with panic.

"Lucky," he said my name again, leaning in to place small kisses up the column of my throat.

"This is so not how I planned to go out. I haven't even gotten a dog yet. I wanted a dog, did I mention that? I wanted a dog and I wanted to name him Lewis. Like maybe a Sausage Dog or a Great Dane. Holy hell, I'm twenty-eight and I still live with my parents. I wanted to do things, like buy a weekly subscription of fresh flowers and have a family. And now? Well, now my line is going to end with me." There wasn't enough oxygen on this plane. I started to wheeze, "Okay, *okay,*" I relented to the universe. "If I survive, I'll stop ordering the same thing on the menu every time I eat out I swear I'll--"

Cole's hand wrapped around my throat effectively cutting me off, his other hand moved all the way up my dress and splayed across my back, pressing my body into his.

"You're babbling," he spoke into my skin, dragging his mouth across my jaw, my body erupting in goosebumps. "I didn't know you babbled."

"This is not the time to point out my faults," I breathed, my body in two very different states between fearing for my life and needing more of his lips on my skin.

"This feels like an appropriate time." I could feel his smile pressed to the corner of my mouth as he moved the hand splayed on my back to my stomach, slowly dragging it down to cup my sex. "*This*, on the other hand," he began running a finger up the length of me over the barely there lace of my panties. His pressure was just light enough to send heat coursing through my body. It took everything in me not to lift my hips up to increase his pressure, "This feels entirely inappropriate." His breath caressed me in a mixture of mint and whisky.

Cole's pressure stayed borderline non-existent as he devoured my mouth. He kissed me in so many different ways with every side of him he'd started to let me see, but this way was one of my favourites. Like he needed me to breathe.

My hands abandoned their perch on his shoulders to sink into his hair. It was still hard to wrap my head around the fact that I could feel the soft strands of his hair move between my fingers. I pulled myself harder into his body, giving in to the need to move against him, to deepen the pressure, to feel him.

I broke away from him gasping for breath, continuing to grind my throbbing core against the bulge in his slacks, "Tell me something," I panted, my eyes fluttering shut at the feeling of the hardest parts of him against the softest parts of me.

With his grip still around my throat he moved me back, holding me still until my eyes snapped open to lock with his. "You overwhelm me," he rasped out and all the air left my lungs.

I knew exactly what he meant.

Would it always be like this? My want for him so crazed and unquenchable?

My hands fell from his hair, shoving his hand aside in favour of undoing his belt and zipper, releasing his swollen cock from the confines of his clothing. The hard length of him sprang free and a shuddered breath left him. Holding the heavy, silken weight of him in my palm, I ran my hand up and down his shaft before moving up on my knees. The fact that I had done that, that I was the reason for the searing heat in his eyes filled me with a heady sense of power that I was quickly becoming addicted to.

Cole reached for my panties, pulling them to the side. I positioned him at my entrance and, unable to wait for another moment, I sank down. My mouth went slack at the feeling of being stretched by him, of feeling the entirety of his hard length fill me until I was sure I couldn't take anymore, until he was the only thought in my head, the only feeling in my body.

"I don't—"

"You can," he gasped.

He'd hiked my dress up to give himself an unencumbered

view of where we were joined, stretching me. His hands gripped onto my hips before thrusting up in the same moment that he pulled me down, sinking in the final inch.

I cried out, my back arching, pushing my chest into him.

"You're so beautiful," he whispered, eyes of emerald darting between where we were joined and my face.

I'd been so entirely naked in front of him but I still felt the blush move up my neck and take over my entire face at his words. It was all of a sudden very hard to keep his stare.

I dropped my eyes before murmuring quiet words that were so at odds with the roaring emotions thundering with each frantic beat of my heart, "Thank you."

Cole leaned close to me, lips finding mine and owning every single part of me in a slow, sensual kiss. Every searching and exploring swipe of his tongue against mine sent jolts of pleasure that tightened my nipples to painful points. This kiss was so slow and made my chest ache with too many feelings.

"You're welcome," he said, signalling the end of the softness between us. His grip on my hips tightened to bruising points before he pulled out only to slam into me again and again, taking up a punishing rhythm that drew out sounds I didn't know I could make along with all the breath from my lungs. It was animalistic, raw, *feral.*

"Fuck, you look so sexy taking my cock," he said between clenched teeth, hips pushing harder against me, getting so much deeper than I thought possible, my clit grinding against him with every moment of contact. His hands clenched and unclenched where they gripped me. "So fucking wet for me."

I reached a hand out to grip the back of the seat we were on to keep myself steady against his ravenous pace, grateful with a passing thought that the flight attendant was buckled up at the back of the plane even though I was positive she could hear us and so could the pilot.

The idea of being overheard sent another wave of pulsing pleasure through me. A whimper fell from my lips as I desperately moved above him, as much as I could within his iron hold, meeting my hips with his, needing *more.*

"Touch yourself," he ordered, eyes still watching us where we joined. "I want to see," he growled, eyes darting up to meet mine. "Come on my cock, Lucky girl."

I moved a hand to my clit, gasping at the way my orgasm roiled inside me immediately, the nub swollen and sensitive. Cole's eyes were locked onto where my hand moved, releasing a small pained, "*Fuck.*" He started thrusting in wild movements that told me just how frayed his control was. The cabin was filled with the heavy breathing and the wet sounds of our bodies meeting over and over.

"Tell me to come inside you," he gritted out, a fine sheen of sweat now coating both of us. "Tell me you want it."

"I want it," I gasped.

Cole had a filthy mouth. It had surprised me at the start, only because no one had ever spoken to me like that before. I fucking loved it.

My orgasm barrelled through me out of nowhere, my inner muscles clenching around his cock. His grip turned perfectly painful before a sound close to a snarl rumbled out of his throat and I drew his release from him, feeling my pussy flutter around him and the unmistakable heat of his seed filling me. His teeth clamped on the soft flesh of my shoulder, earning a whimper as I collapsed onto his chest, trying to catch my breath just as the plane jostled. My body immediately locked up.

"You're fine," he soothed.

I looked out the window noticing with a small amount of surprise that we'd landed.

"Welcome to New York," Cole grinned, head lolling back on the seat, his expression the picture of complete and total post orgasmic bliss. His smile stayed in place, arms curling around my back, holding me close. He looked delicious.

"That was—"

He'd completely taken my mind off the piercing fear I'd been feeling.

"A good airborne dicking?" He lifted a quizzical brow at me, capturing my wrist when I tried to pinch his nipple.

"You're about as subtle as a missile." I scowled with no heat behind the gesture. "Thank you," I murmured quietly, my smile fading slowly. The buttons of his shirt had suddenly become very interesting.

"You're welcome," he said just as softly.

I could feel eyes on my face again, reading everything there written clear as day. I wondered how much he saw, and if he knew just how much he overwhelmed me too.

"This is a new level of rich." I gaped at him while we sat in the back of the private car that was so big we were facing each other. It had been waiting for us on the *private* runway we'd just arrived on with his *private* jet. "Cole, you're very rich."

"I'm comfortable" was all he said, focused on the phone in

his hand, his fingers tapping away.

"You're *comfortable?* That, my friend, is what rich people say," I gawked at him.

His eyes flicked up to mine with a little smirk.

"I mean I knew you had money considering the concrete palace you live in."

"It's a penthouse."

"You have two living rooms and a fully fitted gym."

"Two."

"Two?"

"I have two gyms."

"You have *two gyms*? How did I snoop until I was teeter-tottering on the edge of morality and not find your second gym?"

"That's incredibly dramatic, Lucky," he commented. "It's for yoga and reformer Pilates." He shrugged like it was no big deal, "There's a door that leads into it from the main gym. I know you know where that one is." He winked at me. His mouth tipped up at the corner a little before dropping again. He just kept studying me for a second before speaking again. "Thank you for coming to New York with me," he said so quietly in a sudden drastic change in conversation it took me a second to catch up.

I knew that the words 'thank you' were not often ones you heard from Cole Thompson, at least not directed at me. I looked at him, knowing I didn't need to give him words of my own to let him know that I was happy I'd come too, he was already seeing it all over my face.

"Will I be cooking for you?" My voice sounded thicker with emotion than usual. Neither of us commented on it.

"If you'd like."

I frowned at him, "Is that not what I came for?"

"To cook for me? No."

"Oh? Well, I'm waiting with bated breath." I tried not to be concerned or disappointed at his vague responses.

"This is the annual *Thompson & Co.* Christmas dinner for our most prominent investors, board members and company heads." He spoke so casually like the words coming out of his mouth weren't anywhere near as important as they really were.

Oh, sweet chimichangas.

"Cole, don't do that." My heart rate spiked to what I was sure was a dangerous pace.

"I was bringing prominent chef Lucky Peters to cook for that dinner."

"Why would you do that?" I was going to have a heart attack.

"Because you're the chef in my employ?" He sounded genuinely baffled.

"You know what I mean, Cole. It's one thing that we're doing...whatever we're doing. But this isn't funny if you're lying I—" I swallowed, trying to control my emotions. "I don't understand *why.*"

"Did you hear me this evening?" His voice dropped to that place where it was dark and dangerous and made my body draw to him like a moth to a flame.

"Yes, I heard you," I kept my voice steady, trying not to freak out any more than I already was at what he was saying.

"Then there shouldn't be anything for you *not* to understand." He sounded frustrated. "Tell me something," he said to me, his index finger tapping on his thigh while he watched me.

I thought about saying something half true or marginally funny, but in the end I opted for something as easy as it was hard to say.

"I'm scared it's not real." I let the words hang between us, my eyes falling closed at the admittance and wishing I could take it all back at the same time that I was relieved to have them out in the open. I kept my eyes closed and waited for him to respond. I didn't open them even when I felt the air shift, knowing he was kneeling before me. I felt the heat radiating off his body, my body shivering, automatically leaning closer in response to his own nearness.

Every time I felt Cole trace the outline of my features; my eyebrows, my jaw, the length of my nose, it felt like a moment I had no right intruding on. Like he was doing it in reverence, in wonder, in fascination.

What I hadn't expected was the palm he laid over my heart, frantically beating as it was, confessing every little ember of blazing truth in the words that hung between us.

Cole lifted up my hand and placed it on his chest. That's what made my eyes fly open because his heart wasn't beating frantically, it wasn't galloping in his chest.

It was steady. Sure.

There was no panic or uncertainty in the rhythmic *thump thump* that I felt reverberated under my touch, only absolute conviction and I knew what he was saying, what he meant.

He leaned forward to press his forehead to mine, breathing heavy.

My heart did a little flip flop.

After a minute he spoke, his voice quiet but commanding, "You're mine, Lucky. Don't question this again." Cole returned to his seat across from me and I took the opportunity to stare at him, finding no discomfort at all in the way he stared back.

"Are you mine?" I asked, looking for the map of who he was that would never exist on the hard to read, beautiful planes of his face like they did on mine. I didn't need to look for the hidden answer this time though, because he gave it to me freely, voice assured and unwavering.

"I have always been yours, Lucky." His eyes blazed with everything I felt; this was not enough and too much all at once and I wanted to be consumed by it. More than I was already, more than I should *want* to be. There was no way to get away from it now, I knew for certain.

I was burning with it, bending with it.

Breaking with it.

I was in love with Cole Thompson.

36

Lucky

I think Cole had a hard on for big windows and fabulous views.

The penthouse we were in currently, and you may need to sit down because I'm sure this will be a shock to you, also belonged to Cole. Though significantly smaller than the one back home, it was still massive - overlooking Central Park from where it was nestled on the Upper East Side of Manhattan.

When the car had pulled up out the front of his building last night I was completely oblivious to where we were in the city, mostly because I'd never been there before, and waking up this morning I shrieked like a banshee sending Cole into a minor cardiac arrest before grabbing my phone and video calling Melody.

It was quiet when she first picked up before she realised what she was looking at, her voice steadily climbing with each syllable that left her mouth, "*XOXO GOSSIP GIRL?!*"

"*HELLO FOLLOWERS!*" I yelled right into my phone a second before a pillow was thrown at my head and Cole groaned something about grapes and loafers. Actively choosing not to dissect whatever he'd been dreaming about, I tiptoed out of the room.

The layout of this apartment was new to me, and it was a serious stroke of luck that when I bumped into a side table holding what could only be described as a priceless artefact. I managed to juggle it between my hands and feet without dropping it *or* my phone with Melody still on the call, laughing herself silly.

"The sixth stage of grief is going well," she said as she padded to her kitchen while I settled into a chair in the living area, the drag of her feet echoing through the phone.

"Have you started admitting access to your Carnival De La Puss—"

"*Lucky!*" she groaned and then yawned, "It's too early for you."

I'd proceeded to stick my tongue out to her, chatting a bit more about the dinner I'd be cooking for before she'd told me she was late for a breakfast date.

"A breakfast *date?*" I'd gawked at her.

"It's uncertain territory, I promise if there is more to tell I will."

I blew her a kiss goodbye as we ended the call and I got up to grab myself a coffee. My eyes were trained on my phone so, naturally - because why *wouldn't* it happen twice in my lifetime - I ran face first into an amused, well dressed and incredibly nice smelling Cole. My hands shot up to hold my face.

"*Why?*" I howled through the sting, "You need to start making more noise. Ow, *ow, ow.*" I hopped from one foot to the next, my eyes watering instantly.

Cole pulled my hands away, fingers gently prodding at my face, a look of concern on his own. "You're not very self aware," he mumbled, a frown drawing down his brows while his eyes were focused on assessing the damage.

I couldn't help but remember the last time his body was the wall to which I collided and the very different way he'd been with me then.

"That wasn't my fault," I grumbled, a wayward tear escaping that he swiped away with the pad of his thumb.

"You'll be just fine." He wrapped his arms around my waist pulling me flush against him, my feet barely touching the ground.

"You're very hard, you know," I grumbled, resting my cheek on his chest.

"That's incredibly forward of you." I could hear the grin in his voice. I melted into his hold, taking a deep breath of his woodsy scent.

"Well most people are softer on a day-to-day basis." I clamped my mouth closed against grin trying to pull at it.

"I guess I'm just a rich man with a big appendage." He shrugged as if that wasn't the weirdest sentence he'd ever said in his life.

"I thought you said you were comfortable," I challenged, pulling back and lifting a quizzical brow.

Cole only leaned down to steal a kiss before he turned around and headed for the kitchen. "That's just a thing rich people say," he said over his shoulder, earning a honking laugh from me before I followed after him.

I made us a quick breakfast before he headed out to the New York office for the day, leaving me to spend the morning putting together the menu for the Christmas party. My second mug of hot coffee sat before me right next to a notepad embossed with Cole's initials (another total rich man thing to have that he'd said he owned purely to highlight his big appendage) and perched on the same chair I'd spoken to Liddy in, facing the city below me.

I settled on the entrée centering around seafood, probably scallops, in an onion broth with a leek purée. It was as cold as Santa's nipples outside so it would be the perfect warm introduction to the meal. I noted down everything I needed on a grocery list that Cole had assured me someone would be around soon to help me with.

Just as I finished finalising the menu after going back and forth on the main, probably close to forty different times, my phone buzzed and my coffee shot out my nose at my shocked laugh.

Big Appendage Thompson:
   I hear you can learn a lot about someone
   by what you name them in your contacts.

                                                           Me:
                              You think an awful lot of yourself.

Big Appendage Thompson:
   The truth can take some adjusting to.

                                                           Me:

VERY highly of yourself.

Big Appendage Thompson:
What are you wearing?

Me:
This doesn't feel workplace appropriate.

Big Appendage Thompson:
Show me.

I grinned to myself like a madwoman as I turned around to have the city view behind me and lifted up the front of Cole's shirt. I stuck my tongue out, sending him through a lovely little visual of me topless, just in my favourite pair of dark green lace panties.

Big Appendage Thompson:
Lucky.

Me:
Goodbye, I have a meal to make.

I didn't stop to think anymore about it. I used the fancy wall screen thing that Cole seemed to have in all of his luxurious kitchens and put on the newest album from my favourite band, *Lady Luck* (a tradition I had for any big cooking moments), and pulled on the strength I'd started to rely on from the beautifully broken man who consumed so much of me. Pulled from the hope that had sprung to life inside of me at the reality of taking the first steps to move forward and started to cook.

37

Lucky

My phone buzzed with a message from Cole just as I'd finished wiping down.

Everything was done. Everything was cooked, prepared and ready to go, all I needed now was mouths to feed and people to impress.

I was telling myself I was calm, but in reality I was sweating through my uniform.

Big Appendage Thompson:
How are you?

Me:
I can't cope with this name change
of yours on my phone.

Me:
Have we moved past the art of speaking in person?

Big Appendage Thompson:
I'm keeping away for reasons that are three fold.

Me:
I'm on the edge of my seat.

Big Appendage Thompson:
Reason one. Your little show from this morning caused a great deal of discomfort for me today and if I see you, I will bend you over and fuck you on the first surface I see. Regardless of who is in this house.

My swallow was audible.

Me:
That was a lengthy text for someone hosting a dinner party.

Big Appendage Thompson:
Reason two. If I'm caught canoodling with the chef, the guests might think it's part of the service, and then I'd have to kill someone.

This shouldn't be turning me on. Why was this turning me on?

Me:
I don't think you're legally allowed to say 'canoodling' anymore.

Big Appendage Thompson:
Reason three. I know this is a big deal.
I want you to stand on your own.

Me:
I'm nervous.

Big Appendage Thompson:
I know.

Me:
The answer I've been looking for my entire life.

Big Appendage Thompson:
Looking forward to my meal.

Me:
Hopefully it tastes as good as it smells.

Big Appendage Thompson:
You do.

LUCKY

Things were going well.

No, things were going *very* well. I'd turned off my phone, not able to fully concentrate with Cole's incredibly distracting messaging coming through about the sounds I would be making later and how the head of the Milan office looked more and more like Channing Tatum every time he saw him. Both very different tones of message, both equally as distracting.

Briany, one of the server girls, had done me a solid and reported back with extreme detail how everyone had reacted to the scallop entree and then the pork belly main. Every single plate came back scraped clean. We were on the home stretch. I was pretty certain I'd sweated through every article of clothing I'd adorned but I'd made it through to pretty much the end of the night and nothing had gone wrong.

I'd fucking done it.

"Hey, Luck?" Briany's voice was like yanking a string connected from the top of my head to the ceiling for how it snapped me to attention, "They're ready for you."

Crap. *Crap.*

It wasn't uncommon, in fact it was usually expected, for the chef to make an appearance at the end of the meal but I'd hoped that it wouldn't apply to this particular dinner for no other reason than Cole's first reason of his threefold list. It seemed my luck had evaded me yet again.

I smoothed my hands down my whites and reached up to fiddle with my hat.

"Come on, Navy," I grumbled to myself. "A new broom

sweeps clean, but an old one knows where the dirt is."

I walked with all the confidence I had in my body, trying to stop my sneakers from squeaking as I rounded the corner to face all eleven attendees at an impressively long table with Cole at the head.

His eyes found mine straight away and it was all I could do not to trip over my feet to get to him as fast as I could. It didn't matter how many hours it had been, the force of his gaze made a weight settle in my lower belly and an ache develop between my thighs. Immediate and shamelessly wanton.

You will not jump him. You will not jump him.

Standing a respectable distance from the table I placed myself at the corner near Cole, so that I could see everyone in attendance without making them turn around.

"Ladies and gentleman," Cole's voice rang out into the room and my body swayed towards him unconsciously. "Our chef for this evening, Lucky Peters."

My chest tightened because without knowing him you might not have noticed it, but I did. I heard the way his voice changed based on the smallest things, like the time of day, his mood, whatever emotion was coursing through him, and this man was proud. He was *proud* of me.

I swallowed the lump that formed in my throat. "Hello everyone." My voice was both soft and strong as I set my eyes briefly upon everyone in attendance, "It was a pleasure to cook for you all this evening." My heart was pounding like it was beating for every single person on planet Earth while simultaneously being lodged in my throat and falling out my ass.

A soft applause resounded from all of them followed by a quiet chorus of thank you's and praise for the meal they'd eaten.

"Lucky Peters, I haven't seen your name floating around for a while now," a woman with a strong, french accent said from the other end of the table. Her hair draped around her in a waterfall of fine braids that highlighted the angular features of her face and her large, bright brown eyes. The dark chocolate of her skin looked almost iridescent against the deep, royal blue of the dress she wore. Her face was kind and the tone of her voice immediately made me feel at ease.

"Yes, Ma'am—"

"Juliette Soleil." She offered me another warm smile.

"Mrs. Soleil. I've been taking some time with my family."

"Ah, down time. Hard to come by, oui?"

"Oui, très vrai."

"Ah! Tu parles français?"

"A small amount." I couldn't help but smile wider at the clear pleasure on her face. "Not overly well though, I'm afraid."

"Lucky Peters?" A shorter, heavier set man with quite possibly the largest and most orange beard I'd ever seen in my life cut through our conversation. His voice was nasally and gritty and made me want to grind my back teeth.

"Yes, Sir." I nodded my head in the standard pleasantry I'd always used when speaking with a patron who'd just eaten my food.

"You're the owner of *Seven*. You made quite a splash in the culinary world, I remember."

Clearing my throat I kept my face relaxed and at ease, "Yes, I was. Thank you."

"I wonder," he went on, a glimmer of something entering his eyes that told me all I needed to know about how this sad little man made himself feel big. "How does one recover from such a cataclysmic downfall?"

"I'm sorry?" The words got physically stuck in my throat and I was left horrified at what he'd asked and proud that I hadn't told him to go sit on a sharp object and rotate.

"I'd heard some rumours, a couple of my associates knew one of your previous investors. Timothy Monteith?" His face held this forced innocence like he wasn't aware that what he was saying hadn't made it out into the press in the entire year I'd been without *Seven*.

Mr. Monteith had been on the board of directors for *August Eclair School of Culinary Arts*. He'd been my mentor and when I'd come to him with plans for *Seven* after I graduated he offered to share a third of the investment if I could find another two candidates. When everything had gone to shit I'd reached out but he'd never replied. And no, it wasn't a single reach out, I had called, emailed and texted the man a total of thirty two times before I got the hint that he was actively avoiding me. It didn't surprise me now to learn he'd spoken to people in the industry about the truth of what happened. I regretted those emails every single day.

"Mr. Monteith was—"

"This must be a big deal for you now, no? Cooking for T&C?"

"Well, I—"

"I can imagine it would be hard to find investors after—"

"Greigory." Cole's voice demanded all eyes to his attention, "I would suggest you tread very carefully on what it is exactly you choose to say next." His voice was that lethal calm I'd had the displeasure of being subjected to. It sent a shiver through my entire body at the insinuation of what might happen should Greigory be as stupid as I was assuming he would be.

I tried to breathe through the dread swelling in my chest, at the reality of what that would mean.

Greigory's eyes widened a fraction before he dragged his gaze back to mine and narrowed them in disgust, "Well, that makes perfect sense to me now." He pulled the napkin from his front where he'd tucked it into his shirt like an overgrown toddler and threw it on the empty plate before him. "You're resorting to other methods of climbing the ladder of success."

It felt like I'd just been punched in the sternum, "Did you just call me a whore?"

"I can't say I'm surprised by you, Miss Peters." He said my name like he couldn't wait to get the words out of his mouth. The legs of his chair scraped on the marble floor as he stood.

I was too dumb struck to even consider moving when he walked so far into my personal space bubble it should have been illegal and gripped my arm.

"Ah–" The sound was involuntary, a mere reflex of the pinching pain that shot down my arm from where he gripped it roughly. "You're—"

"You're not the first and I doubt you will be the last to attempt to find value in your life by spreading your legs for the likes of Mr. Thompson." The words were sneered into my face like tiny little daggers.

I stood there, my mouth opening and closing like a fucking fish at the reality of what was unfolding around me. The man just called me a career whore in front of the biggest, most influential investors in the country and I wanted to immediately turn into a liquid substance and seep through the floor. The real issue was that he was claiming I was only where I was because I'd fucked my way to the position, discrediting all of my actual talent and ability. There was a very big chance that he'd just ruined everything for me and the bastard knew exactly what he was doing.

His face changed as he looked back to Cole, his expression all sorts of unfiltered regretfulness at having to be the one to tell him whatever bull crap was about to fall out of his mouth.

"Sir," Greigory's face jiggled as he snapped his attention to Cole, "perhaps you'd like to step away with me and we can discuss this further."

My head whipped to where Cole sat, not entirely sure how he was going to react.

Greigory's grip still on my arm got more painful the longer he held on, his fingers digging into the soft flesh of my upper arm with the clear intent to hurt.

Cole was already looking at us though, his eye trained on the exact spot that Greigory was touching me.

It was a single moment that I saw the way his eyes had looked, dark and bottomless, a window into the sort of endless horrors that he could inflict if he wanted to. A moment when the muscle in his jaw jumped and the hand clutching the armrest of his chair was strained white from his grip.

And then it was gone.

Poof.

Gone.

"Oh, Greig." Cole heaved a sigh, draining the remnants of his wine before standing up. He walked by me with his hands in his slacks, briefly enveloping me in his clean, minty scent.

The very act of him walking by me made Greigory step back, my arm flooding with blood painfully. I stepped back just as

Greig did and Cole stepped casually between us.

I hadn't told Cole what happened with *Seven*. The only people that knew every single detail was Jamie, Melody, stupidly Mr. Monteith, and now apparently this fart stain of a human. My stomach dropped at the thought of him hearing about it from anyone but me, at what he'd think.

Oblivious to my internal meltdown, Cole made slow and lazy strides towards Greigory. "The first mistake you made was allowing her name," his head inclined towards me, "to leave your mouth." His head then inclined towards the man himself "The second mistake," Cole stopped right in front of him, his dark, broad figure so completely at odds with the small wrinkled appearance of Greigory's, "was assuming that you had any semblance of power to be able to not only humiliate a member of my employ, but one of the best culinary masterminds of present day because your little friend had a tantrum at the loss of one of his many investments."

"Your third and final mistake...well, I would wager you don't need me to tell you what that was." The picture of Cole looming over Greigory while he all but broke his neck to maintain eye contact would have been comical if it wasn't for the fact I was watching my dreams shatter before me.

"You don—"

"I suspect that Monteith failed to let you know that the money he chose to invest was not, in fact, his money at all, but that which he had promised to a separate investment. Miss Peters' close of business only served to reveal to a lot of very important people just how much of a spineless toad your beloved little Timmy is." Cole's voice flowed from him in the sort of monotone way that highlighted just how very much he *was* feeling, and how finely the ice was that this man had stepped onto. The beasts circled him beneath, waiting for the inevitable crack that was coming.

"I beg your--"

"Shall I begin on you?" His head cocked to the side, like a predator taunting its prey. "Greigory, spelt with an 'i', Ashford, born December of seventy-nine. You have at least three illegitimate children born of three unwilling women, all of which filed reports against you only to be paid off generously by your mother, Leanora. And," he looked to the rest of the dinner party who stared at him with mouths agape, "we are speaking of *the* Leanora, of the Ashford Alpine Lodges nestled in the luxury locations of Aspen, Vail, Park City, Whistler, Banff and Fernie." He looped back to Greigory who had slowly begun to turn a shade of greyish white. "You have three different uncompleted college degrees, all of which you neglected to finish because of a rather unimpressive drinking problem. You moved through the entirety of your sizeable trust fund in the first year it became available to you at the ripe and eager age of twenty-one before asking your mummy for more. I believe that was the same year that you contracted chlamydia twice, totalled four different cars due to said unimpressive drinking problem and spent a week in France with your third cousin doing less than savoury things in yet another of your mothers properties in the French Riviera."

You could hear a fucking *pin* drop.

It was the biggest slap down I'd ever witnessed. I was loving every minute of it and mentally recording it all to tell Melody about later.

"So, tell me, *Greig*. Do you think that if I know all that about you, that there is a single thing I would not be uncompromisingly aware of that relates to the past of Miss Peters?"

Guess that explained the whole knowing about my birth control thing.

Greig had finally gotten some colour back into his face, but he was an alarming shade of reddish-purple as he stared at Cole with the fire of a thousand incredibly unhappy suns.

"No." He looked like he would have likely preferred to have all his molars removed than to have said that word.

"Mmm." Cole nodded, walking around the man where he stood so that he was at his back. I knew from experience that this was one of his favourite ways to taunt, knowing whoever was at his mercy couldn't see him, but could *feel* him.

Cole leaned down, placing his mouth at Greig's ear passing on some words that were inaudible to everyone else.

By the time he was done, Greig had begun to favour his previous whitish-grey shade before his eyes snapped to me, his jowls shaking with the tremors that started to wrack his frame.

"My apologies, Miss Peters," he mumbled quickly, turning to make angry strides towards the exit of the penthouse.

Cole still stood with his hands in his slacks, face completely relaxed as he addressed the rest of his guests like he hadn't just ripped that man a brand new asshole for insulting me.

"Anyone else?" His words were easy and light, completely contradicting the repercussions that would be faced should anyone follow in Greig's unfortunate legacy.

"Wonderful," he said at the deafening silence. "Thank you for your time, ladies and gentleman. Alyssa and Briany will fetch your coats and escort you out. Merry Christmas and Juliette, congratulations on the arrival of your granddaughter,

Belle. Please pass on my best wishes to Louis and Sara." The smile Cole gave Juliette was kind and real and reached all the way up to his eyes.

"Merci, Cole," she murmured quietly, offering him a small smile in return, like he hadn't just massacred a man's dignity.

"Lucky." He held a hand out to me.

My feet moved on their own accord, the insufferable squeaking of my shoes followed me as I slipped my hand into his, a part of me immediately relaxing at the comforting feel of his skin on mine. The relief lasted for a second only, it faded fast with each step I practically *jogged* to keep up with him as he led us deeper into his penthouse, the eyes of everyone behind us boring into the back of my head.

So much for his threefold reasons.

38

Lucky

We didn't speak as he closed the doors to the room behind us. I wasn't even brave enough to meet his stare but I could feel it burning holes in my face as he led us into the bathroom – this one without his happy plant and flattering bath mats – and stripped me of the uniform I'd been in.

This conversation between us was always going to come around, I knew it needed to happen but I clung to the silence for another moment not wanting to think about, or how he'd just done what he'd done in front of all those people. By the time he pulled me under the spray of water it was borderline scalding and I closed my eyes at the relief of the heat hitting my muscles. I hadn't realised how tightly I'd been wound until that moment. The smell of mint filled the space around us and then his hands were on me.

Gently washing every part of my body. His attention honed

in on the top of my arm where small, purple shadows had already begun to form where Greigory had touched me.

I didn't imagine the way his hands shook as they lifted to tentatively touch the area.

"Cole, it's fi–" The words got stuck in my throat when he lifted his gaze from my arm to my face.

It was then that I realised it wasn't just his hands that were shaking, but his entire body. He was *pulsing* with violence, so much of it that I didn't know what to do, how to help him. "I'll kill him." The words were spoken like a promise, one that I couldn't wrap my head around, that I didn't let sink past the very top layers of my skin.

I just lifted my hand up to his face and revelled in the way he turned to kiss my palm, the act so at odds with the words he'd spoken. Cole kissed my palm again wordlessly before he continued on with cleaning my body. From my shoulders, over the mounds of my breasts, his touch caused my nipples to tighten before his palms drifted over the flat plane of my stomach, drifting between my thighs and lingering there for long enough to make me squirm before his attention moved to my legs.

I closed my eyes and focused on the closeness of him, and basked in it for a final moment before I started to speak.

"A lot of people lost their jobs because of me," I started, hating the way my voice trembled as I started to unpack everything I'd sealed away. "I trusted someone I shouldn't have. I tried to maintain control by keeping finances and accounting in-house and when I saw things starting to decline I looked everywhere but under my nose."

I opened my eyes but didn't move them up from where they landed on his chest. I latched onto the steady rise and fall of his breathing to power through the rest of the story.

"I had to tell a total of eighty employees across both restaurants that I could no longer employ them, that I was the reason they could no longer support their families. I sold my apartment downtown and used the money along with the rest of my savings, investments in stock and property to provide a barely respectable severance for all eighty employees and pay off the extra accumulated debt Chelsea had wracked up in my name. The business had been funded privately so there was no bank involvement outside of that."

He was silent for only a moment before he spoke. "Thank you for telling me."

"You— what?" My eyes flicked up to his.

"What?"

"I just told you about my demise. About how the restaurants closed. My incompetence. My ignorant naivety. The truth of how incredibly fucking stupid I was. How I'd tried to maintain control of a multi-million dollar company in-house without any support from external businesses, took the livelihoods of all those people into my own hands and fucked it up. You have…you don't want to…there is nothing you want to say to that?"

"I already knew."

"That's not possible." I shook my head.

"I knew the second day you came into work." He reached up to pinch a section of soaked, golden stranded hair between his forefinger and thumb.

"You hated me then," I murmured.

"Mmm." He dropped the hair and trailed his fingers over my collar bones and up to settle around my neck. "Desperately."

"And you didn't say anything."

"Call it delayed gratification." The side of his mouth tipped up, his long dark hair falling onto his forehead making the green of his eyes stand out more than usual.

I gripped the wrist that he'd settled around my neck, trying to move him away but he only gripped onto me tighter.

"I don't need you to defend my honour like some delicate maiden of ye olde times. And what? Do you have some sort of weird stalker file on me? I haven't forgotten that little tidbit you let slip on knowing my stance on birth control you know." I scowled at him, feeling frustrated and confused at his confession. Thrown completely off balance by his unexpected reaction to what was my biggest secret and also the fact that he apparently knew everything, *everything*, about me.

I'd been built up to be this incredible, idolised young and successful leader and I hadn't been. I was a fraud.

Cole's grip on my neck tightened further, walking us backwards until my back was pressed to the wall and his chest was pressed against mine.

A less than intimidating squeak left me at the shock of cold tiles against my skin. "What happened to standing on my own?" I tried again, digging my barely there nails into his wrist hard enough for their measly length to draw blood.

He didn't even blink.

I was feeling too many things, not the least of which was some sort of twisted relief at the realisation that *he knew everything*. I was still wrapping my head around it, and even though it was still an absolute violation of every single one of my rights to privacy, he'd known and he was still here.

"I changed my mind." The words were pure, seductive

velvet as they slipped off his tongue and wrapped around me. His head tilted to the side in that same predatory way when he was assessing someone to absolutely obliterate.

"You're not allowed to do that," I breathed, my chest heaving and the action only serving to highlight exactly how naked we were and how exquisite the friction of my nipples against the hard, hot plains of his chest felt.

"Actually," he leaned down to press hot, open mouthed kisses along my jaw, speaking between each touch, "Yes." *Kiss.* "I." *Kiss.* "Can." His tongue burned a trail up the length of my throat until his lips were at my ear. "The only person who gets to bend you, to break you, is me. I thought we established that. Isn't that right, Lucky girl?"

"I guess," I whispered around the constriction of my airway.

"You *guess?*" He taunted and in a single move his hand slipped behind my thighs, my back was against the wall with the hard length of his cock was lined up with my entrance. He pushed in, inch by inch, so slowly I felt my soul actively leave my body before reattaching.

"Already so ready for me, you dirty girl." Cole's teeth clamped on the tender part of my neck and shoulder that he favoured, pounding into me with a punishing, relentless pace. His hand had returned to its home around my neck while the other made its way to a place we'd not ventured.

"*Woah hey—*" My life all but flashed before my eyes as his finger made taunting circles around my back hole. "That is a one way stre*e*—" My voice hiked a couple octaves as he prodded me.

The cockiest, most mischievous grin split across his face. He lifted that hand up, spitting on his fingers and moving them back to their previous position.

"Wait, *wait--*" I gripped his wrist that held me flush to the wall and tried to think clearly around the feel of him moving deep and unrelenting inside of me.

Cole moved me up the wall a fraction in the same moment that his finger breached the tight ring of muscle. My body was inundated with a completely new sensation, the feeling setting my orgasm into motion. The shallow movement of his finger and the new angle he was thrusting into me creating a pressure so intense every roll of it through my limbs was paralysing.

"Nothing to say with that smart mouth of yours now?" he teased, sounding breathless.

I opened my eyes to see nothing but maddening need and crazed lust directed entirely at me. The feeling of being able to do that to him, to make him feel that way was almost enough to push me over the edge.

"There is never going to be a time where I will not stand between you and harm," he said, choosing this moment now to say something important while I was struggling to hold onto my sanity at the feeling of him in me fully. "I will fucking end anyone who is stupid enough to assume I do not know who you are. *Exactly* who you are."

His thrusts picked up pace, turning sloppy at points as he chased his own release. "That includes you, Navy. I know every single fucking thing about you. I tried running from you, I tried hating you, neither of those things worked. So, now you will bear the burden of my love. It is sharp, and dark and ugly but it's yours and you're mine and no one fucking tries to break what's mine."

His finger moved faster and deeper as my muscles relaxed

at the intrusion, the sensation so consuming I wanted more.

"I– Cole, it's—I'm going to—"

His lips crashed to mine in time to capture the sobbing cries of my release, my back bowing with vicious intensity.

We stayed locked together like that, him right there with me, allowing me to absorb his own guttural, roaring climax. The come down was slow. Blissful. The feeling taking its sweet time returning back into my legs and arms, and even more time for my neck to have the strength to hold my head up. We stayed there, pressed against the shower wall as our breathing slowed.

"I'm not a forgiving man. He got off easy—"

"Easy? The man probably tinkled himself in the elevator."

Cole's nose scrunched up, "Greigory pissing himself is not an image I needed while still inside your pussy."

"*Cole.*"

"What?" His eyes alight with the mischief he carried so well, giving a slow thrust as if to highlight how very much still inside of me he was.

I shook my head at him, still not fully able to wrap my head around the mouth on this guy. He helped me to my feet and washed us both a second time before we settled into his bed facing one another, his hand finding its home on my back, his thumb moving in small soothing circles.

"You said you loved me."

"Mmm," he hummed, eyes never leaving mine.

It was something I'd always known about Cole, he wasn't afraid to just look at me. To stare at me openly. He'd always done it and I'd always looked back.

"I love you too." I let the words pass from me to him in a silent prayer that it wasn't something he'd said on the back of the high of an impending orgasm. What I wasn't expecting was the look on his face. He looked...vulnerable.

"Say it again," his voice broke as he pulled me closer to him, his hold so tight I couldn't take a deep breath. I didn't care.

"I love you." I didn't let my gaze falter as I said the words to him. Let him see every single ounce of truth in them.

His grip only loosened a fraction as he closed his eyes, breathing deep like he could inhale the words into the very soul of him. I thought he'd fallen asleep when he spoke again, eyes still closed.

"Just because you can fight your own battles doesn't mean you should. Let me fight for you. With you."

The words were so *not* like Cole. At least, not like the man I'd come to know. These words came from a part of him maybe he'd forgotten existed.

I wanted to fight him on it, not just because it seemed that my opposition seemed to translate into 'butt stuff', but it almost felt *wrong* to accept it. Like I didn't deserve it.

But I wanted to. So, I said, "Okay."

"Okay?"

"I'll happily allow you to put those who don't know the difference between their ass and their elbow in their place, yes."

"That smart mouth of yours, Navy Grace. I'll need to do something about it soon."

"Promise?" I asked with a wicked grin.

Cole cracked open an eye and moved a hand between us, looping his pinky with mine and bringing our hands up between us, pressing a kiss to the pad of my thumb.

"Promise."

39

Cole

We'd woken slowly with the sun and took full advantage of the fact that the plane would depart at whatever time I confirmed, within reason. The world around you didn't stop, even when everything within your own was shifting and changing so fast it gave you whiplash.

The three words she'd whispered to me had made an ache in my chest both expand and disperse, and when she'd said it again I'd needed a second to collect myself. To think for a second how I would ever be able to trust the world with her. How anything would ever be safe enough. *Good* enough.

I'd lost my control with Greigory last night. A slight bummer. It would prove to be a small inconvenience considering that every single person at that table had never once seen me as anyone other than the kind, generous and charming version of myself that I reserved for the workplace. It was exhausting but it had ensured I gained the trust of the people around me, the people who worked for me.

Lucky talked enough for the both of us at breakfast which suited me fine as I simmered in my own thoughts. We stopped in at my favourite cafe and continued on route to Central Park for a stroll before we needed to make our way back to the plane. I made a mental note to bring her back here when we had time and space to enjoy the city. It didn't matter if we walked by a street name she'd seen in a movie or one of the many different locations featured on *Gossip Girl* or *Friends*, her eyes lit up every time without fail and it was quickly becoming my personal mission to bring that look back as often as possible.

My personal favourite might have been the look on her face when we passed by the three vendors on the route from the cafe to the park that I greeted all by name.

"I didn't expect that," she said, a small smile playing on her lips.

"Mm?" I questioned her, unable to pull my eyes from the way she pulled her full bottom lip between her teeth.

"You're a regular onion you are, Cole Thompson."

"Thank you?"

I was finding there were a great many things that came out of Lucky's mouth that I wouldn't dignify with an answer. *That* was yet another to add to the list.

"Cole, you're kidding me. Have you not seen Shrek?"

"The cartoon?"

"Good *grief*, man, it is far more than a cartoon? Next thing you'll say is you haven't watched The Little Mermaid?"

When I didn't reply her face dropped all its humour.

"Tangled?"

"Tangled what?"

"Beauty and the Beast? Aladdin? The Lion King?"

"We watched all three of those together," I said, lifting a brow. "Many times."

"And you're saying that's the last time you watched them?" She looked horrified.

Before I succumbed to the laughter that was building in my chest I reached up to pinch her bottom lip between my fingers, angling her face towards me with her chin and capturing her mouth in a kiss. "You're going to kill me with this mouth."

She pulled away with a little push on my chest. I must have looked as unimpressed as I felt because her hand came up to cover her mouth, her face perfectly flushed. "We are going to need to speak about this later. In detail," she said.

I kissed her again, this time swiping at her bottom lip and delving into her mouth. She tasted like coffee and pastries and I wanted to devour her.

"You can't do that in public." Lucky pulled my hand from where I'd intertwined it with the hair at her nape and tried to drag me onwards towards the park without success. Lucky's eye roll was one for the ages. It also made me want to turn the smooth, tan skin of her ass red.

"You'll make me combust. What would you do if I just spontaneously orgasmed in public?" Her hands landed on her hips. She looked at me like she'd achieved a check mate.

"I'd do it again." I slid my hands into the pockets of my thick pea coat, and let my eyes travel down the length of her.

She was so bundled up she looked like a marshmallow, her head absolutely dwarfed by the oversized knitted beanie she wore, complete with a massively useless pom pom on the top.

"You look like a cupcake," I commented, noting the way

the end of her nose was a light pink and her eyes were the brightest, most brilliant shade of blue against the muted winter colours around us.

Her expression of pure mortification was enough to earn a real honest smile from me, the dam of my laughter cracking between us making her entire face light up. This time when she tugged my hand I moved, draping an arm around her shoulder and heading for the path I always took.

We walked right past the Alice in Wonderland statues where Lucky spent about twenty minutes making me take photos of her doing a range of different poses that she assured me would make sense if I had watched the movie.

She proceeded to add it to the notes on her phone along with all the other movies I was personally offending her by not having watched.

I led her through more of the park, completely content to be her cameraman and reassure her that even though we couldn't see any at present, I was sure a lot of people hugged the trees like she was doing before ending up at Belvedere Castle.

"One photo." Lucky held up a single finger to me before running off to an older couple standing a few feet from us. She nestled into me as I draped my arm over her shoulders, totally enraptured with the beaming smile on her face and determined to make sure she was always as blissfully happy as she was right now.

We walked around for another hour, Lucky tucked into my side and I finally started to tell her about my life. She hadn't asked outright, but I knew she'd been waiting, especially after last night and the very real fact I knew everything about her and the knowledge it hadn't all been divulged at her will.

I told her about heading to college, about starting *Thompson & Co.* not long after. How I worked on it through the years of school. I told her about my mother's passing, which I knew she'd already known. I'd told her that I spoke to Brooks once in a while but hated that I had to, that I did it more for him than for me.

"You don't spend Christmas with him?" she asked, her mouth turning down at the thought.

"No. He thinks he needs to keep close because it's only him and I," I told her plainly. "I answer the phone because I don't want him at my door."

Her grip around me tightened in a way that told me she had a lot to say about it but that she wouldn't. The moment settled between us before I took a deep breath and continued on. I told her about his wife and the couple of kids he had. Then I told her about Benny, the boxing, how he had become more to me than anyone had been before, until her.

"I'd like to meet him," she said, her tone giving no way for any sort of argument.

"Okay," I agreed, because I wanted her to meet him too.

The walk back to the penthouse was filled with the same comfortable silence that filled the different pockets of our morning and followed us until we were seated in the jet.

Lucky buckled herself into her own seat with a smile on her face even though her hands were white knuckling the armrests. When the seat belt signs turned off, I offered her my hand which she took without a second of hesitation.

I'd never been safe for someone else before, never thought I could be.

"I think if you put your log of steel anywhere near my lady garden you will cause some serious damage, so this will have to be the most platonic embrace we've ever had."

"Your *lady garden?*" I turned my head to try and look at her where she'd nestled her nose into the crook of my neck, trying not to laugh.

"Yes." I felt her nod.

"Don't call it a log of steel."

"Why not?"

I wasn't going to dignify her outrage with a response.

"Pole of pleasure?"

"*Lucky.*"

"Length of lust?"

"You're—"

"Your mighty mast?"

My hands clamped around her waist, fingers poking and prodding at her ribs while she wiggled and squirmed against me, laughing until she wheezed.

"You could have just said you didn't like them," she spoke with laughter still in her voice, trying to find her previous comfortable position all while her movements did a perfect job of sending all the blood in my body rushing south.

"If you don't want my pole of pleasure in your *lady garden*, you need to stop moving," I gripped her hips firmly, grinding the hard length of me against her core. "Right now."

"Oh, sorry. *Sorry,*" she said sheepishly before completely stilling.

That was where she stayed for most of the flight, only waking to use the bathroom and to eat. There was no turbulence on this flight like the last, but still she moved back into her position on my lap, sighing contentedly when I settled my arms around her. I'd realised then what the feeling was that had grown bit by bit over the last few weeks.

Months. What I'd wished for as a kid, what I'd given up on as a teenager, what I had been searching for in the beating of my fists as a man.

I'd finally found it in her.

The last place I would have ever looked.

Peace.

40

Lucky

I stood in the elevator with Cole at my back watching the numbers count upwards towards his penthouse.

Home.

That was the word that kept running through my mind while I pushed down the twinge of pain it caused my heart to know I'd be heading to my parents house tonight. That somewhere in the last two weeks the very place I'd accused of being my jail had become my sanctuary and the person accused of being my jailer had become my buoy in stormy seas. I let my body fall back into his even more, feeling the strength of the corded forearm he had resting over my chest, relishing in how it felt for him to pull me tighter into him followed by the feather light touch of a kiss on the top of my head that made my heart switch places with my stomach.

The elevator sounded our arrival and a small smile began to

grow at the expectation of being greeted by the quiet serenity of Mr. Invisible. Instead, the sounds of screaming children and chaotic adults talking over one another assaulted my ears. My eyes didn't catch up until they'd all gone silent.

The scene before me turned sluggish, everything moving in slow motion with every detail being catalogued. Every single member of my family cast their eyes upon my face, down to the arm that banded me to the body that stood behind mine and then, finally, on the face that belonged to said body.

I acted out of pure, unfiltered instinct as I slammed my elbow into Cole's stomach. I honestly think it was his complete lack of anticipation at the move that allowed me to inflict any sort of impact. His breath rushed out of him in shock and unfortunately for both of us, my mind had already descended into 'unhinged' territory.

My sneaker-clad foot came down hard on his own and, with the poor man in an understandable state of disarray, he didn't stop me when I ducked under the arm he still had banded across me. I gave him one final shove for good measure, really driving the point home that whatever my family thought they were seeing was in fact *not* what they were seeing at all. I put all my effort into that push and Cole didn't move an inch.

Wonderful.

Both Cole and my entire family unit stared at me in a mixture of horror and entertainment. My family being the 'horror' part, and Cole being the 'entertainment' part. Actually, maybe Oakleigh too, he looked delighted at the entire scene and I pledged to shave off at least one of his eyebrows next time he fell asleep in my company.

"I'll—" I cringed as my voice echoed around us. I hadn't meant to but I'd shouted the word like a yodeller serenading their beloved alps. I cleared my throat. "I'll put your things away, Mr. Thompson." That wasn't even my job, but the words came out of my mouth anyway.

My mother looked at me like I'd announced I was now a Flat Earther and my dad peered at me with varying degrees of concern, paper tucked under his arm.

I strode away from all of them without a single bag in tow and headed literally anywhere but where they'd all congregated like carollers.

Now, upon reflection, leaving Cole in the same vicinity as fourteen members of my family (children and significant others included, minus Riley who was somewhere gallivanting with Arthur) might not have been my sparkliest idea. I seemed to have lured myself into a false sense of security when the sounds of their presence faded with every step I took until I was sitting on Cole's bed. I tried to convince myself I was in my safe place; a peaceful field by a trickling stream where all my troubles floated away.

Needless to say, that didn't work.

The smile that dropped away when the elevator doors opened returned when I walked into Cole's bathroom and let my eyes settle on the big, leafy beauty in the corner who I'd decided to name Felix. The perfect name for the happiest plant I'd ever seen.

I looked at myself in the mirror and took a deep breath.

You couldn't see the marks on my throat anymore. Not beyond a little pigmentation change where the bruising had been particularly brutal. My eye had healed too. I looked like myself again which both made me happy and not.

I felt *different*.

I was sure they all heard me before they saw me, the squeak

of my shoes like an audible neon sign that said 'hear ye, hear ye, make it known Lucky arrives'. Cole sat at the kitchen table with my parents, Oaks, Jamie and Sophie. The triplets were standing on one side of the kitchen counter fixing plates of food while all four kids sat on the other, legs swinging on stools that stood too high for their little bodies. One thing was for sure, wherever the Peters clan went they surely made themselves at home.

"Mother. Father," I greeted them both with clear confusion in my voice.

My mum just waved her hand in my direction like I was a fly looking to make its home on her cheese platter. "Stop being so rigid, Lucky," she tutted. "You worried us sick. I was just telling Cole how we haven't heard from you in *weeks.*"

"*Weeks?*" My voice raised at least five octaves over the single word. "I spoke to you this morning!"

"You didn't." She sounded the same as she did when I was still single digits and pleaded my case on how it wasn't me that broke into the Christmas cookie stash she spent all year building up after it was found demolished.

"I quite literally messaged you last night and said 'I'm in New York'."

"It could have been anyone with your phone, Navy. A hacker or a thief." She only whipped out the given-name-card when I was testing her patience.

My eyes narrowed in suspicion. "Of course, because that makes so much sense. Why are you here?" I kept my eyes on her and she looked anywhere but at me, refusing to reply. "Dad?" I turned to him expectantly.

He opened his mouth to reply.

"Not a single word, Phillip," she snapped, finger raised

in warning. He shot me an apologetic glance and it was all I needed to know about what this was.

"Oh my god, Liddy cracked," I gasped.

"Like a little acorn." Oakleigh grinned like the Cheshire Cat where he sprawled like a gangly teen in a chair at the opposite end of the table. Jamie was quick to act as he swatted him on the back of the head from his place beside him

"That's not what happened and you know it." He looked back at me, eyes apologetic which did little to comfort me considering he too was here with the 'rescue party'. "She didn't crack, Mum pretended she knew."

"You *sneaky—,*" I gasped. "Do none of you have lives? *Why* are you all here? How do you coordinate yourself like this when you guys spent actual *years* consistently forgetting to pick someone up from an extracurricular activity at least once a week."

"I was fearing for your *life*. We hadn't heard from you in days. And there were seven of you. The system had flaws." She threw her hands up before clutching her purse tightly and looking away from me.

"You never forgot us," Addie chimed in from the kitchen.

"There are three of you," Oaks scowled. "No one could have forgotten you."

"I'd have forgotten you too," I said to Oaks, giving him my best, toothiest smile to which he responded by blowing on his thumb and slowly raising his middle finger.

"This is veering off topic," Jamie pipped in, rubbing a hand on the back of his neck.

"I have spoken to every single one of you almost every day." I folded my arms across my chest. "You never wanted me to call before. In fact, May and Addie tell me never to call in case it disturbs nap time," I gesture in the direction of my sisters.

"The kids don't nap anymore," my mum scoffed.

"Not their naps," May said, still removing the crusts from sandwiches she had clearly made with Cole's bread.

"*Our* naps," Addie finished the sentence with a nod of support from Kate who was portioning out yoghurt straight from Cole's stupidly expensive 'high protein' brand into little rubber bowls they'd brought with them.

"The cat's out of the bag now, Luck," Oakleigh taunted as he sat back down with a plate of crustless sandwiches in front of him.

"Oh good, Arthur's arrived to urinate on your shoes again?"

The smile dropped from his face. "That cat has a premature death written in its future," he grumbled into his food.

I just stood there in unabashed glee watching as Jamie smacked him upside the head in the same moment that our dad leant across the table to swat him with the paper and the triplets all yelled something along the lines of that cat being a national treasure and to shut his pie hole.

"Your mum was just inviting us over for family dinner next week," Cole spoke up for the first time since I'd arrived, smoothly changing the direction of the conversation.

"Inviting us over?" I frowned at him, sort of wanting my dad to swat him with the paper too if only to wipe the devious expression from his face. I felt like everyone was in on a joke that I was the butt of. "I live there."

"Cue the cat," Oaks said with a mouth full of a ham and cheese sandwich.

"We kept it under wraps for a few months but it's nice that everyone knows now," Cole said, leaning back in his seat, mouth lifting at the corner just a little.

"What does everyone know?" I dropped my arms to my sides, wanting to run but rooted in place with my heart doing a Zoomba dance in my chest.

"That you're bangin' your boss between courses," Oaks said as he ducked down to miss Jamie's inevitable smack.

My eldest brother just dropped his head in his hands while his wife rubbed soothing circles on his back, trying her best not to burst out laughing. Dad's newspaper was now so close to his face I would bet any reasonable sum of money he wasn't able to read a single thing.

Soph and Oaks had the sort of relationship that Melody and I did. They were twin flames of mischief, jokes and chaos though you'd never guess it by looking at the dainty brunette carrying the fifth Peters' grandbaby. Her doe-eyes wide with sweetness so thick you could feel it running down the back of your throat. Her other hand rubbed circles across her belly as if to soothe her half-baked bun in the same manner.

"Oh my *god*. Kill me now," I groaned. Needing to move, I started to walk in circles around the dining room table where half of my family sat, ignoring the knowing looks from my sisters where they now loitered behind Jamie and his wife, all three with cups of tea in their hands. How they knew where everything was, I didn't know. It had taken me weeks to map out this kitchen.

"Oakleigh, you're on your last warning," my mother chided from her seat while my dad just hid behind his paper.

On my third lap around the table, which Jamie and my mother tracked with concerned expressions, Cole grabbed my wrist and pulled me into his lap. I sat there stiff as a board slapping his hand away three times as he attempted to circle them around my waist before giving up. I blew out a breath and gave in to the draw of him, pretending I didn't see the little knowing grin on my mothers face.

"We'll probably be in through the week to grab some of Lucky's things," Cole said, like he was picking up a conversation they'd started before I arrived.

"Through the week?" I repeated, my voice coming out squeaky and completely undignified. The stinging pain of my ear being flicked caused me to jolt.

Kate stood closest to me, hand raised to deliver another flick if needed. "Stop repeating everything he says. Are you broken?"

"No," I grumbled, rubbing my ear and sinking deeper into Cole's hold. If I didn't know any better I'd say the tiny little shakes of his body were the result of laughter.

"Katie, no flicking." My mother sent my sister a disapproving look. I could feel Kate's eye roll in the air around us without needing to look at her face.

"She was glitching," Kate said in a less than sturdy defence. "She needed resetting."

"I'll reset you," I mumbled, flipping her the bird from in front of me where she couldn't see. At least I thought she couldn't until another flick landed on my ear.

"God damn," I rubbed my ear, officially fed up with whatever was going on here. "Okay, I need you all to leave." I stood up and walked around the table to remove the four smallest of my relatives off their stools, placing a kiss on each of their heads.

"I thought you didn't live here. How can you make someone leave a house that isn't yours?" Oaks asked in feigned innocence as I delivered a flick of my own right between his eyes and grabbed his empty plate.

"Hey!" he gestured to me while looking at our mother with pleading eyes, "She flicked me."

I flicked him again for being a tattle-tale. "You're leaving."

It was five minutes later when they were all squished into the elevator and the space around us was once again blissfully quiet that I turned to the man I felt lingering behind me.

"How, pray tell, did they make their way up here when I know for a fact none of them know the code to your penthouse?" I put my hands on my hips and stuck my foot out to the side, eyebrows raised in accusation.

"Jim messaged that they were in the lobby, I told him to let them up." Cole's head tilted to the side in amusement.

"You *knew*?" I gawked, "They brought the *children*." I covered my face with my hands. "It was a trial by fire. They knew what they were doing," My voice was muffled from behind my palms.

"At least some things never change." I heard the stupid grin in his voice as he bent down, encircling my waist in his arms and pulling me into a hug, my feet completely off the floor.

"Oh?" I peeked through my fingers seeing said grin coupled with the bright, clear green of his eyes, alight with a happiness I had started to see more and more.

"They still love me." He winked at me. *Winked.*

"There's that big appendage of yours talking." I wriggled out of his hold and made my way back to the kitchen, all the while being followed by the soft sounds of his laughter. I stood at the counter making a start on cleaning the mess they left.

"So," I started. Feeling his eyes on me and keeping mine on the dishes. "I live here now?"

"You do."

"You didn't want to ask me first?"

"Nope."

"I might suck at being your roomie," I started. "I have stuff that would be mixed in with your stuff."

"Is that how moving in works?"

"I can be super annoying."

"You are particularly aggravating around meal times."

"This violates our contract."

"I'll change the contract."

"You can't do that."

"Watch me."

I felt his breath on the back of my neck, my own hitching at his proximity.

"I snore in my sleep," I whispered, the dishes forgotten in the sink.

"I know," he murmured. "I have videos. I thought I'd upload them online."

"Monetisation is a given, I hope?" We were still whispering. It felt like if we spoke too loudly something might go wrong and I really, *really* didn't want anything to go wrong.

"The tone is like the first note of that *My Chemical Romance* song."

"Welcome to the Black Parade?"

"That's the one."

I huffed a laugh and turned around to face him. "Are you sure?"

"The similarities are uncanny. Exactly the same pitch."

"*Cole,*" I whined, only lifting my eyes when his finger hooked under my chin.

"You make this 'concrete palace of comfortable means'

a home, Navy Grace." His mouth quirked at the side, eyes darting to my lips before meeting my stare with his own.

His voice was barely a whisper as the words fell from his lips, but I felt each single syllable pierce the very centre of me, felt them change me right where I stood.

"Stay with me." He leaned down towards me. Reaching up to close the distance between us was the easiest thing I'd ever done.

"Always," I said, pressing my lips to his.

41

Lucky

Watching snow fall from the stop of a very tall building was a different experience than being the thing it lands on way down on the ground.

It was beautiful. The way the flakes caught in the wind, dancing with one another as they continued to make their peaceful descent was mesmerising. Watching the snow always reminded me of The Grinch, a movie Cole had also not watched since we were kids. I found that particularly amusing considering he and the main character had so much in common. When I told him that, he had aggressively tickled me until I cried and my laughs turned into this hysteric blend of pleading and wailing. When I came down from the high, his phone was out and his face was cracked with the widest grin I'd ever seen. It had stayed put even when I launched pillow after pillow at his head, his phone safely lifted above the chaos and still pointed at me.

We were officially in the third week of December, and though the outside world had descended into festive madness, we had slipped into a comfortable domestic balance that equal parts terrified me and made me feel like I was walking on sunshine. I continued to cook, which I still thought was weird considering that I now lived at my place of work. Cole had stopped coming home so late and in turn I started to serve him hot meals instead of cooking things and putting them in the fridge.

My favourite part, well one of them, had to be the one-eighty on how I greeted a new day. My wake-up calls had drastically improved from that of the jarring jingle of my phone that I was pretty sure had given me PTSD. It was the same sound some people used for their ringtone and anytime I heard it my body immediately flooded with adrenaline and I felt a desperate need to run away incredibly fast.

Now, my days began with Cole between my legs. Sometimes it was his fingers, sometimes it was his mouth, and sometimes I woke to the feel of him stretching me so full I needed moments to settle back into my own body. That was how he left me; sated and completely adrift in the sea of my own emotions. There had been the rare occasion that I'd tempted him back to bed, but mostly he cast me dark, dirty looks that conveyed everything he didn't say and I eventually found myself in the computer room, continuing to work and rework my proposal.

I was in the middle of revision number six when my phone went off.

Good with his hands Thompson:
Tell me what you're wearing?

Me:
I am genuinely curious when you have time to change your name in my phone.

Good with his hands Thompson:
They were your words.

They were my words, and the memory came flashing back to me so fast I was glad I was sitting down.

Cole's hands gripped my hip in a bruising hold in one hand, his other hand was clamped around the back of my neck. He impaled me with deep and punishing thrusts, I'd already had two orgasms and every single part of my body was so over sensitised I no longer had coherent thoughts, only that I'd never believed Liddy when she talked about her books and the characters experiencing so much pleasure they could die.

My thoughts then were that I'd have paid good money for a guy to prioritise my happy ending before his.

I was eating my words. No, I was so *past* eating my words I was writing my own eulogy.

Here lay Navy Grace Peters, the dearly departed seventh child of the Peters Clan. She, who was born into luck, lost it so gruesomely only to then find her demise as a result of an overstimulated earth bound dicking.

"This. *Fucking. Pussy.*" Cole was mad in his lust. His body continued to move inside of mine when he pulled me up so that my back was flush with his chest, his hands exploring everywhere he could reach. My breasts, my stomach, my neck, my clit. He didn't stop, not until my body was convulsing with the shock waves of a third orgasm, small pathetic whimpers the only sounds I could make and he finally surged into me, stilling as he filled me with his release, my name tumbling off his tongue like a prayer.

My body was, for fear of not painting a particularly pretty picture, limp, sticky and covered in sweat. The man had the stamina of a stallion and boy did I know it.

"You're so good with your hands," I had mumbled into the crook of his neck when he pulled me into him. His chest rumbled where it pressed against mine. "My heart won't take it one day. I'll have a heart attack mid coitus."

"Oh, you can certainly take it, Lucky Girl." His voice had dropped an octave and I tried to swat his chest in reprimand but instead my fingers behaved like over cooked spaghetti where they landed between us.

I'd fallen asleep shortly after that little escapade, only to be woken in a similar fashion to that which made me borderline comatose the entire night. I felt every single inch of his cock slide into me, my wrists held in only one of his hands where he kept them above my head, the other holding my leg up on his hip. My eyes peeled open slowly and I watched his face, the slackness of his jaw, his hooded gaze and hair mused from sleep, as he watched himself enter me.

"Cole," I rasped, my body automatically wriggling at the intrusion. Still, even after I had become as familiar with his body as I was with mine, I needed to adjust to the feel of him.

"Do you have any fucking idea," he spoke, eyes never leaving the place where we joined, "how perfectly you take my cock?"

This man's mouth was going to send me straight to hell just by association.

"I'm sore," I panted, even as my eyes began to close at the swell of pleasure at his slow and languid strokes.

He stopped immediately and didn't move for so long that I opened my eyes just to see what had been so important it was able to capture his attention away from *this.*

"Are you okay, baby?" His grip on my wrists softened slowly before he pulled away completely, moving closer so our chests were now touching and his hand pushed my unruly hair from my face. "I'm sorry, I didn't—"

"Cole," I cut him off, reaching up with my new found freedom to run a hand through his hair. "I'm okay, just a little...tender." I smirked up at him but the concern on his face didn't let up.

He started to pull back and I reached around to sink my fingers into the firm, delicious muscles of his ass.

"If you don't finish what you've started here, Cole Thompson, I will make your life a living hell." I dug the heels of my feet into him, forcing him back into me the tiniest bit.

"You're sore," he said, frowning to himself a bit like he should have figured.

I leaned up, ghosting my lips against his. "So fuck me slowly," I whispered, nipping at his bottom lip before settling back against the pillow.

He looked at me for a while longer, his eyes scanning my face, reading me in that way he knew how to and then finally, *finally,* he moved.

"Slowly," he said, voice scratching against every tender part of my soul.

"Slowly," I said.

***

I finished making dinner with a stupid grin on my face, so much so that I didn't care all that much when Cole ended up being an hour late home for dinner. Melody and I sat at the kitchen table, empty plates in front of us and talking animatedly around the latest *Acquired Taste* article.

"They absolutely ripped them to shreds." Melody was having a hard time containing her wild enthusiasm about the rather brutal review. "Took them to the bank and demanded every single dollar."

"That's not a common analogy," I mused, sipping from my glass of wine.

"That restaurant doesn't stand a chance now."

"What restaurant?" Cole's voice rumbled from the hallway behind me.

I twisted in my chair to watch as he entered the room, hair dishevelled and top two buttons of his crisp white work shirt undone. I wanted to take pictures of him. Commission paintings and statues and gardens in his honour.

"Hello, darling." He bent down to place a tender kiss on my lips. "I look forward to ravishing you too," he murmured before kissing me again and gracefully flopping into the seat beside me.

"That was weird to watch," Melody mused.

"Melody Amelia," Cole said, a hint of laughter in his voice as he delivered a two finger salute. "A pleasure as always."

"You immediately nauseate me," she deadpanned.

"I encourage you to wear a paper bag over your head the next time you visit."

"Are you sure I can't just borrow yours?"

"You've got some bite. All those years with braces?"

"Yeah, well—" Lid's mouth opened and closed another couple of times before she slumped back in her chair and crossed her arms. "Fine, you win," she grumbled.

Cole did that closed fist celebration move that tennis players do and I did feel like I'd sort of just experienced a rally of sorts.

"That was bizarre," I commented, taking another sip of wine. "When did that start?"

"When we fell asleep in the theatre," Melody said, raising an eyebrow at Cole in challenge. "He kicked me out after I threatened his manhood."

"You kicked her out?" I gasped in feigned outrage.

"She explained to me in great detail how she'd turn my balls into a hippo if I hurt you." Cole levelled me with a look that said 'can you blame me'.

I gasped again, turning to Melody and reaching a hand out to grasp her. "You did that?" I set my wine glass down to wipe away non existent tears. "For me?"

"I'd turn anyone's balls into a hippo for you," she said, squeezing my hand.

"And I for you," I said, blowing her a kiss.

"I forgot," Cole said, standing and heading to the kitchen to warm up his dinner, "there's two of you."

I shared a look with my best friend before we broke out in laughter. I wasn't blind to the small lift to Cole's lips that I saw from the corner of my eye.

"So," he went on, sitting down with his plate of carbonara, "who ripped who to shreds?"

"*Acquired Taste*," Melody said, sipping from her own wine

glass.

Cole's eyes flicked from Melody to me then back to Melody, his fork half lifted to his mouth.

I waved a hand in his direction.

"I have to show you some of their reviews. If *Acquired Taste* writes about you it's a make or break moment. They're infamous. Incredible. Their palate is formidable."

"In short," Melody chimed in, "they're a God."

"Oh?" Cole's eyebrows shot up as he chewed slowly. "And you don't know who it is?"

"No one does." I heaved a defeated sigh.

"There were blogs dedicated to their unmasking for a while," Melody shrugged, "but no one was ever found out. They're this elusive presence. Like a fairy godmother."

"I didn't know you guys liked...them." Cole reached for my glass of wine for a sip and I handed it to him.

"Like?" I frowned at him, making grabby hands for my glass back. "*Love*, Thompson. *Love.*"

Cole rolled his eyes at our dramatics and that was pretty much how the rest of the meal went and it was perfect.

Melody ended up getting one up on him, making some call about him harshing her vibe as she strode into the waiting elevator with the confidence of a woman on top of the world. Cole hadn't been able to formulate a reply out of pure bewilderment.

We cleaned the kitchen in perfect sync. I washed, he dried, and then he took my hand and led me back to our bedroom where I peeled every single article of clothing off his body and wasted no time on showing him exactly how much I'd missed him. Cole drained almost every ounce of my energy, my eyes fighting to stay open while I traced the lines of his face. His thumb tracing circles against my spine.

"Tell me something," I whispered into the space between us, "about your art room."

His body went a little taut though his thumb didn't stop making lazy circles. I didn't think he was going to answer me but then he opened his eyes, and I absorbed every emotion laid out before me.

"It's everything I feel." His words were quiet but I heard them for what they were. The art in that room was dark. It was explosive and violent and sad. It was unrestrained and confusing and broken. There were pieces that made me feel lost and lonely and full of potent bitter rage. It was as close to a confession of what lay beneath the surface of the man beside me as I was ever going to get. The very reality of that made my heart beat faster and my breathing quicken.

"Does that scare you?" he asked in equal gentleness, so completely at odds with the meaning of his words.

"Yes," I said, knowing he'd see the lie if I delivered one. "Why?"

Why was that important? Why the art room? Why the paintings? Why the physical embodiment of his soul hung up on the walls of an ordinary room?

"It made me feel seen," he said, eyes closing again. "The paintings. They depicted something that made me feel *seen*. I used to sit in there for hours at a time."

"I've never seen you go in there," I said, my fingers continuing to trace the shape of his lips.

He pulled me closer, running his nose along the side of my head and breathing in. "I don't need it anymore."

"I see you," I said and meant it desperately. This man with the soft eyes that offered me tender touches and witty replies.

Who also had the dark and dangerous stare that served as a constant reminder of how sharp the knife's edge was on which his control balanced.

"I know," he said, bringing his lips to mine.

42

Cole

I was in the gym, finishing off my workout and thinking of the bag that Lucky had packed for us that was sitting in the closet.

If there was one thing I'd never pictured myself having, it was my girlfriend packing a couples bag for us to spend Christmas with her family.

"I'll let them know we're arriving around lunch time," Lucky said over a mouthful of toast.

"What do you mean?" I frowned at her over my paper.

"It's Christmas Eve?" she questioned back, equally as confused. "You mentioned you didn't spend it with your brother. Sorry, I should have—"

"I don't spend it with Brooks. I spend it here."

"Alone?" The look on her face told me everything I needed to know about how that sat with her.

I had always spent Christmas on my own, ever since Brooks had left for college, even when I still lived with my mother, I'd always spent this holiday alone. I had a tradition of my own, one that consisted of a text from Benny with an invitation which I'd always refused and a call left unanswered from my brother.

I had never wanted to spend the holidays with someone, until now.

"You'll come with me, won't you?" She looked incredibly worried for someone who had resembled an elf on a sugar high only moments ago.

"If I don't want to go?"

"Then we'll stay here," she said with such conviction that I knew she'd do it too. I knew she'd stay with me instead of being with her family and that thought alone was enough for me.

"We'll go," I said, getting up and dropping a kiss to the top of her head before making my way right to the gym.

That was then, and this was now.

Exactly four hours later, my muscles were screaming at me for the abuse they'd received and Lucky leaned against the door, staring at me with a small smirk on her face. I knew she was remembering everything that had happened in this room, just like I did every time I came in here. I couldn't get through a fucking session these days without a hard on.

"Time to shower." Her voice was thick with the need I could see all over her face.

Without a single word I walked straight for her and picked her up in my arms. Her legs wrapped around my waist like it was muscle memory.

"You're incredibly sweaty," she said against my lips, "and

I already showered." She gave the wet strands of my hair a solid tug, the effort making me grunt.

"Shame you'll have to start all over again," I nipped at her bottom lip.

"Shame," she breathed before crushing herself to me.

Her family didn't say a thing about how we were entire two hours late.

They did a massive seafood spread with Lucky's famous Chilli Crab as the star of the meal. I had ended up sitting with her Dad, James, his wife Sophie and two of her sisters outside in their sheltered outdoor space, complete with heaters and a fire pit. It was a mild enough day that we'd be eating outside. Everyone else was in the kitchen, working on all of their designated roles.

Riley and Oakleigh were in charge of the barbeque, where they tended to all the shellfish. I remembered they had always enjoyed helping Lucky's dad when we were over for barbecues and it was clear he had passed over the right to them. Philip now sat across from me, his grandson in his lap who was giving him the third degree on the exact layout of Santa's workshop and why, exactly, there were no photos of it if you could buy the man's wardrobe online.

James covered his mouth as his wife smacked his arm playful. "It's so nice to have you here, Cole," Sophie said after her husband had gotten himself under control.

"Thank you. Nice to be here." I smiled politely, running a

hand through my hair.

"Weird having you in our backyard again," Oakleigh said from a few paces away where he and his sister were mid argument about when they should flip the lobster tails.

"Yeah," I said, taking in the yard that hadn't changed at all since the last time I saw it. "Sort of."

"Not in a bad way just—*Ow*. What the hell?" he groaned, rubbing at his side as Riley glared at him.

"I'll put Arthur in your room if you don't stop being an ass."

"I'll shave him if you do," he threw back at her.

The comment drew a chorus of threats to Oakleigh's well being should he harm a single hair on the cat's head.

Arthur was confined to the basement where Riley was sleeping along with the triplets and all the kids. Oakleigh would be in his own room and James and his wife would be in another. Lucky and I would be in her room.

The sleeping arrangements were planned meticulously.

Every year there was a rotation on who shared with the triplets and the kids. Both Addie and May had married military men and they had been stationed overseas for the last three years in a row. Lucky explained everything to me at such a rapid pace I was shocked I even retained the information on our drive over. Being all together helped make the holiday's easier for them.

The more the day tracked on, the chaos and banter of Lucky's family increased.

"It's not your typical Christmas Eve dinner," Lucky's mum had laughed as she walked behind me, squeezing my shoulder, "but it became tradition when Lucky went off to school."

"It's great, Mrs. Peters," I murmured. "Thank you."

"We're so happy to have you here, Cole," she said, smiling down at me, "I'm so glad you and Navy reconnected. I always thought the two of you were just the cute—"

"Okay!" Lucky yelled from across the table, startling her dad and making him throw his spoonful of potato salad across the table.

"Fish sticks," he grumbled, trying to reach across the table to wipe away some of the dressing that landed on the tip of Kate's nose. "Sorry, Katie," he mumbled just as he put his hand right into Sophie's plate. "Oh, frankfurts!" he yelled with vigour.

Lucky's hand shot up to cover her mouth just as she took her seat, moments before everyone at the table broke out into uncontrollable bouts of cackling laughter. With every single hiccup and snort it was hard not to join in and surrender to the chaos that was the entire Peters family.

It was then that I'd noticed what sat behind Lucky. Faded and leaning against the fence at the back of her yard, shrouded in overgrown trees and leaves, sat her pink Barbie pool. I felt my face slack a little at the sight of it, at the onslaught of memories that smacked into me.

"You kept the Barbie pool." The words were out of my mouth before I could stop them, my eyes still on the shell shaped thing.

"Oh, yes," her dad muttered, still cleaning the chilli crab sauce from between his fingers. "Luck wouldn't let us get rid of it." He nodded towards his youngest daughter. "So there it sits."

I looked at her, eyes wide and worried. How she was waiting to see how I would react to the truth I'd already been well aware of. Lucky had held onto the pool the same way I had held onto my hate for her. Like a lifeline to something that neither one of us had ever wanted to let go of.

It was incredibly hard to take my eyes off her from that moment onward, and that was pretty much how the rest of the evening went. Looking at Lucky and always one oddly replaced word away from swearing in front of the children.

All I'd wanted was to get her upstairs, alone and naked. To have my fill of her. I did exactly that with my hand over her mouth, taking my time between her thighs. It was only when she convulsed beneath me that I removed it. She reached for me but I knocked her hands away.

"Whether I come in your mouth or in your pussy, I don't want to have to be quiet about it. I'll be fine."

"Wow, someone's in the Christmas spirit," she mumbled, still soft and pliable from her orgasm.

"Never say I didn't give you anything." I grinned at her from where I hovered above. I settled into the valley of her open thighs and placed soft, unhurried kisses along her jaw.

I was fucking obsessed with this woman.

The feel of her, the taste of her, the sound of her.

She ran her hands up and down the length of my back. "Tell me something," she whispered.

"Mmm," I replied, half hearing her, half not.

"Something extra special," she continued, "for Christmas."

"Hmm," I pulled back, looking at her, "so you want this to be your Christmas present?"

"Is it Christmas present worthy?" She tilted her head to the side and lifted a brow.

"You'll have to be the judge of that." I grinned down at

her, knowing I was about to blow her mind and weirdly giddy about the entire prospect.

I didn't get *giddy*.

The longer my grin stayed in place, the more concerned Lucky got. The point where her confusion turned a little to this side of fear was when I moved my hand to cover her mouth again.

"What I tell you can't leave this room," I said, tilting my head to the side and revelling in the way I had her pinned beneath me, completely at my mercy. The hint of fear in her eyes as I still tasted her on my tongue, felt her wet heat pressed against me.

"I have a hobby, one that I started because of you," I started, grinning wider as her eyes flared a little. "I promised myself I wouldn't think of you again from the moment I left you standing in that hallway at school. Even your name, just a thought in my head, made me want to…" I didn't finish the sentence, not because her eyes shuddered in pain but because the feelings linked to those thoughts no longer meant anything to me.

"But you didn't let me go. No, how could you?" I asked, dragging my nose along the column of her throat and planting a kiss in the spot I loved between her neck and shoulder. "That wouldn't have been your style at all." I bit down and she whimpered into my palm. "Mmm." I soothed the bite with a swipe of my tongue. "No, you needed to be everywhere I looked."

I pulled back to look at her, her eyes shined with a sheen of unshed tears. "*Everywhere.*"

She closed her eyes, one tear escaping down the side of her beautiful face. I couldn't help myself, I leaned down to stop it with my lips before I kept going, speaking against her skin.

"Investing in the entertainment business had always been my plan. It was smart, and when done correctly, it was full proof. It's simple, all you need to do is know what people want. Where will people go even when they don't have the money to spend? What is more important to people than food on their table?" I remained hovering above her and pulled my hand away so she could answer. "Do you know, Lucky girl?"

"No," she breathed into the space between us.

My eyes watched as her lips formed the shape of the word. I captured her mouth in a kiss, slow and gentle, taking my time devouring her and feeling every single one of our movements together pierce my soul.

"Appearance," I said. "It doesn't matter if the fruit is rotten on the inside, so long as it looks delicious enough to eat." I settled in, loving the way I had her full, unwavering attention. Pressing my body closer to hers I felt the rapid beat of her heart against my chest.

"So the fact that *you* went into hospitality, that was just sheer luck. But you had started to make waves early, as early as your third year in culinary school. I knew where you were heading and I thought about what I could do to beat you there. If we were to ever cross paths, how could I best you before you even saw me coming. It took a year or so, I'll admit, before the articles took off. I was pleasantly surprised they were received so well. It had all come together too easily."

Lucky had gone still beneath me, her breaths were shallow and her eyes were no longer on me, but rather tracking the movements of the fan above.

"I sat in your restaurant and watched you cook my meal.

You looked out at the full tables a couple times, like you felt me watching. I think you did, but even though your eyes moved over me they didn't *see* me. But I saw you."

"Please—", she whispered between us, her eyes finally moving back to mine.

I was dragging it out, sure, but this part was almost as important as the ending.

"Patience, Navy Grace." I placed another gentle kiss on her lips, "The end will be worth it."

She just looked on, waiting for me to continue.

"I ate everything you cooked for me, and I wrote two reviews. I wrote the real one, and the one I would use to end you. That was all it would've taken, a simple publication and you'd have been dust, my love."

"Oh my god." Her eyes turned to saucers, the truth to what I was saying finally hitting its mark. "*Oh MY—*" she yelled, my hand clamping down over her mouth halfway through.

I didn't really care if someone walked in to see Lucky pinned beneath me in nothing but her naked glory, but I felt as though she wouldn't be as into it.

She continued to scream into my hand, her words muffled and unintelligible. She yelled and flailed and when she'd finally exhausted herself, her hands clutching onto my forearm like she was worried I'd bolt, I lowered my hand again.

"You're *Acquired Taste*. You're him, oh *my god*. Cole, what the *hell*? I—I need to meditate, or go for a run, or do a paint-by-numbers." She was so frantic at the news, I knew the smugness I felt was all over my face.

"That's what you're saying, right? That you're...him?" her voice hesitantly hopeful.

"One and the same." I still had a stupid grin on my face.

The weird part was it was starting to feel more and more natural. She squealed.

Squealed.

Wriggling out from beneath me, I let her push me down and onto my back as she straddled me. Slowly, her grin started to fade and she observed me quietly.

"Why didn't you publish it?" She wasn't sad. She wasn't hurt. It was curiosity that laced her words.

"I'd never posted a review that wasn't anything but true, and I wasn't going to start then."

"So you actually experienced what it was like to dine at *Seven?*" Lucky's voice was bittersweet.

"I did."

"And you liked it." A statement, but one made with hesitation.

"I gave it five stars." I reached up to drag my fingertips in a line from her bellybutton up to the hollow of her throat, the movement causing her nipples to tighten into stiff peaks and my mouth to fucking water at the sight.

Her breathing hitched, but I don't think it was because of the path I made across her golden skin. It was my confession. She reached between and moved my boxers down, freeing my cock and lifting up on her knees. The swollen tip of me was nestled against her entrance, the need to just thrust into her all consuming. She leaned down towards me, our noses almost touching as she covered my mouth with her hand.

The shock only registered for a second before she spoke against my lips, "My turn." She smirked before impaling herself in one, fast motion.

I couldn't stop the roar of overwhelming pleasure that burst out of me, my eyes rolling into the back of my head at being enveloped in the perfect warmth of her wet heat.

"Merry Christmas," she moaned, her hips moving in just the right tempo, her hand still firmly over my mouth and my fingers digging into her hips so hard it had to have hurt.

Merry Christmas indeed.

43

Lucky

When Cole had said he knew everything, he meant it. Everything about me, everything about investment, everything about *everything*.

After his confession that rocked my fucking world, I'd told him about the proposal. Every single little detail and he'd listened so perfectly I cried. He knew so much about so much and he was choosing to use that knowledge to help me. He didn't even blink an eye every time I insisted we review the proposal from the top over and over again.

It had all started the day after Christmas when we'd arrived home and spent the day on the couch ticking off movies seven, eight and nine of my 'Lucky's Must Watch Christmas Movies List'. He'd asked me to tell him something during the credits of number eight and once I'd started talking I couldn't stop.

After my word vomit, while I was mentally trying to figure

out how I'd be able to move all my things out of his closet in a single trip down the elevator he'd told me he wanted to help.

"I can't ask you to do that." I refused to look at him.

"You didn't ask." He combed his fingers through my hair in a way that was too casual for the offer he'd placed on the metaphorical table between us.

"Isn't it a conflict of interest?"

"Let me help you."

It was terrifying, to firstly share your biggest dream with another person, but then to have them offer to help you, like your dreams were worth a damn. God, that was *terrifying*. That meant there was more than just my time on the line if things didn't work out.

"Don't think so much," he mumbled against the top of my head. "I can hear your brain freaking out."

"Have you ever thought about making motivational cards? You know for, like, your desk? Or the fridge?" I didn't need to turn around to see his scowl.

"Lucky," he said again, his voice softer than before. "Let me help you."

As if it wasn't one of the hardest things I'd ever done, I closed my eyes, breathed in deep, and decided not to think for once.

"Okay."

His smile was radiant at that single word.

We worked through New Years, where we'd celebrated by Cole pressing me up against the glass wall of windows of the penthouse. He had pushed into me with a blinding madness at first but he'd slowed after a moment. His hips had rocked slowly, making sure I felt every single drag of him as he worked me into a frenzy. His pace had been tortuous, and I had come so violently I genuinely thought the building had been shaking around us.

He would work through the day, and then he would work again with me when he got home. He was driven and calculated and it was easy to see how he had achieved everything he had.

"You're incredible," I said, watching him one of the many nights where he had a furrow of concentration on his brow.

He was hunched over the projections for the success of the business based on historical data of the restaurant type, cuisine and location. It was an effort for him to pull his eyes from what was in front of him to look at me

"Hmm?"

"You're incredible," I repeated. I'd tell him every single day.

Cole slowly lowered the paper in front of him and I saw the moment the weight of his stare changed.

"I'm so completely impressed by you, Cole Thompson," I said, willing my voice not to waver. For the words to sound as strong as I felt them in the very core of me. "You're beyond anything I could have ever imagined. And I'd imagined so much for you, believe me," I laughed, but his expression stayed the same. "I had imagined *everything* for you and I'm grateful I got to see how much more you achieved with my own two eyes."

He'd kissed me that night like he'd been a drowning man and I'd been the one to save him when I'd always know it was the other way around.

It was the middle of February when I sat across from Cole in his office that had become another of my favourite places to be in this apartment that had become ours, staring at the folder that sat on his desk between us. He'd poured us both a glass of whisky and we sat drinking in comfortable silence.

Me staring at the folder and him staring at me.

There was an element of feeling lost as I lay in bed that night, Cole's soft snoring sounding behind me, his arm keeping me tucked against him. Everything that I was now sat in a forty page document in Cole's desk and I had to hope that the investors we were meeting with next week saw the same amount of value in it that I did.

44

Lucky

I'd spent the day with Melody which was something I felt like we'd hadn't done for a very long time. In actuality it had probably only been a few weeks, but in the measurement of time used where our friendship was concerned? It might as well have been years.

It was exactly what I'd needed. She was still tight lipped on her budding romance, but I didn't want to push her, knowing how she was with opening her heart. I'd just held her close and let her know in that gesture alone that she deserved whatever it was and when she was ready to share, I was ready to listen.

The elevator's arriving *ding* echoed in the foyer as I strolled in, a smile on my face and feeling like a version of myself I'd never thought I'd see again.

"Hey, Visi," I cooed to the statue I'd dubbed 'Mr. Invisible'.

Trying out a shortened version. I liked it.

I headed straight for Cole's office, where I knew he'd be even on a weekend. I'd been thinking long and hard about what to cook for dinner. We'd talked, or more so *I* talked and Cole looked at me with that unreadable expression on his face, that I wanted to start doing a Sunday night dinner tradition. Once it was established, I wanted to invite Benny over and then maybe my family. I'd compromised immediately on the latter without him even needing to say a word that we would have them visit in groups of two, children and the triplets excluded.

Not stopping to knock, I breezed through the doors to his office with every intention of letting him know that nachos was the perfect meal choice for such an important impending tradition along with the equally as thrilling fact that I'd found twenty bucks on the side of the road while I was out when the look on his face stopped me dead in my tracks. He was already looking right at me.

"..to be delayed for at least two weeks. Please let all parties know that we intend to move forward just as soon as it's cleared up."

My stomach sank. I didn't even know what the conversation was about that I'd walked into, but my heart felt like it was trying to claw its way out of my chest.

"What—" my voice cracked. "What's happened? Are you okay?" I let my eyes roam over him even though I knew the likelihood of it being any sort of physical ailment was slim to none.

"Lucky." He stood from his chair slowly, like he was worried he'd spook me and I'd spin where I was and run for the hills. He wasn't all wrong, I was seriously debating it right now regardless of the fact my knowledge on the context of what was happening was literally zero.

"Who was on the phone?"

"Just list—", he started, rounding the desk towards me.

I stepped back on instinct and the act made his jaw tick, "Who were you on the phone to, Cole?"

He stopped a good distance from me, still much closer to his desk than to me where I lingered near the door of his office. "Have you seen the news?" He was using a voice devoid of emotion to ask me that question. The very same thing that told me the exact opposite was happening behind the cool mask of indifference he wore.

I shook my head, immediately fumbling to open my bag. I grabbed my phone with shaking hands and opened up the web browser. I didn't really know what I was supposed to be looking for so I just Googled my name. I'd never hated it more than I did then. My stupid, *stupid* name.

It was just article after article.

Lucky Peters, owner and Head Chef of the now closed, world renowned 'Seven' has much to pay for, says disgruntled ex employee.

'The' Lucky charm of the culinary world exposed as verbally abusive in the workplace.

Navy 'Lucky' Peters, took everything and left over eighty employee's jobless, penniless and without reference or hope of rehire.

Star Chef Lucky Peters, refused to pay much owed severance to long standing employees of her fine dining restaurant 'Seven'.

Interview with investor of 'Seven' and what really happened behind closed doors.

You'll wish you never ate at 'Seven' when you learn the truth about prized Chef, Navy 'Lucky' Peters.

I was going to throw up. Oh my god, I was going to *throw up.*

I dropped my bag to the floor, only barely aware that Cole was slowly moving closer to where I stood. But the thing was, those headlines weren't even the worst part.

They weren't anywhere *near* the worst part.

Thompson & Co integrity questioned as tentative ties made with fallen-from-stardom chef Lucky Peters.

Famed chef Lucky Peters rumoured to be involved with Founder and CEO of Thompson & Co. What does this mean for the future of T&C?

Billions of dollars hang in the balance as businesses fear integrity of Thompson & Co

What does it say about a business that backs the fraudulent behaviour of a chef has-bin? Do you really want to put the future of your company in their hands?

If Lucky can do it, why can't Cole? Know who you're working with and why it SHOULDN'T be Thompson & Co.

Are the romantic notions of Thompson & Co's founder Cole Thompson a representation of the standing of his company? Don't hang around to find out.

They were destroying him.

Article after article, news headline after news headline, they were absolutely ripping him apart. The more I read the worse it got and I couldn't pull my eyes from my phone screen.

I had done that. *I had done it.*

My phone was gone from where I'd clutched it in a white knuckled grip. It had been an anchor, dragging me down into the darkest water, the light above getting dimmer and dimmer.

I hadn't realised I was crying until Cole's rough hands gripped either side of my face, until he forced me to look at him. Those beautiful green eyes, the very same ones that changed in different lights, with different emotions. They were now encompassed in all consuming fury.

It wasn't directed at me, but for the first time I wished it was.

I couldn't hear a single thing he was saying. His mouth was moving but I could only feel the vibrations of his booming words between us. His body was rigid and barely able to contain the rage that I knew was pumping through his veins. His grip on me, though firm, remained gentle and that was what broke me even more.

I wasn't sure what had happened, who had said what. How

the truth had gotten out or how it had spiralled so quickly into branches of lies.

"Lucky, are you fucking listening to me? *Lucky*—", Cole gave me a small shake where his hands still held me.

I closed my eyes and did my best to remember the way his skin felt against mine. What it was like to feel the warmth of him near me, how it radiated off him like he was my own personal sun. I catalogued the smell of him that always made me relax, knowing that there was safety in it. Security. That this man would have moved through hell or high water for me. This man who had been broken by me, by my ignorance all those years ago. By my inability to look beyond a child's mind, a teenage grudge.

I hadn't been able to do anything for him then. But that was then. This was now.

I'd thought that finally relying on someone for help was the hardest thing I'd ever done, how fucking blissfully ignorant I had been only a week ago to think such naive thoughts.

Wrapping my hands around his wrists was the first step I made in entering into my own personal hell for the second time in my life. The only difference being that this time, it was my decision. I squeezed my hands where I held him, holding on for one second longer before I pulled his hands from me.

I took a step back, then another. Willing the distance between us to shelter me from what I was doing. I palmed the tears from my face, slapping them away in a frenzied need to do this without cracking. Without it looking like it was killing me.

Because it was. It was *killing* me.

"I need some space." My voice sounded much like how I

felt and that wouldn't do at all. It sounded broken and tired and on the verge of giving up.

I didn't insult him by thinking he'd misunderstand what I was saying, he knew what I meant and for the very first time in my entire life I was glad I couldn't read his emotions on his face. I was glad for the blank, bored expression he gave me.

"This was…this was not the way to do this," I swallowed, keeping my eyes on his chest.

"Do what?"

"Rebuild my life." *Lie.* "I never wanted this life with you." *Lie, lie, fucking lie.*

"Mmm." His expression didn't change.

"We got carried away, don't you think?" I dared a look at his face and willed myself to believe that the lack of his emotions was real. "This was a mistake. For both of us. I think everything," I gestured to my phone he still held, "just highlights that even more. We weren't a good fit before and we certainly aren't a good fit now."

I took another step back until I was in the hallway looking at him where he still stood, in the middle of his office. "This was always meant to be temporary, wasn't it?" I turned and I ran. I ran knowing that he would chase me. I knew he would because the Cole I knew would never let me go. He'd never let me leave and he might not believe a single thing I said but I'd give him no reason to think otherwise.

I collided with the closed elevator doors, the call button making them open straight away having only just brought me here minutes ago.

Minutes.

That's all it had taken for my entire world to fall apart for the second time.

I slapped the button for the ground floor just as Cole rounded the corner. The sound of my name was a furious, vicious roar as he came straight for me. It was the first time I'd ever experienced real, honest terror in his presence. But the doors closed before he could get his hand between them to stop me.

He'd wanted to break me. That's what he'd always said. I think it's what we'd both always believed would happen. It didn't surprise me though that in the end he didn't need to.

How could we have known that I would have been so willing to break myself in order to keep him whole?

45

Lucky

There were two sides to having a big family.

The down side was that there had never been a moment of real, true privacy growing up. Even when you thought you were alone, you weren't. Everything was shared, everything was structured and I'd never had a new pair of shoes until I was old enough to earn my own money and buy them for myself.

The upside came in times like this. How I'd been home for only twenty-four hours, all of that time I'd spent in my room, and I'd had a visit from every single member of my family. I'd been held by eight sets of loving arms. I'd been told my worth by eight different voices. I'd been reassured about the love that was held for me in eight different hearts.

I'd been unable to do anything, going in and out of consciousness with no intention of moving and at a complete loss. I felt stupid now, thinking about how I'd sat down to start the new proposal. Thinking of the finished presentation that was still at Cole's penthouse, how it had felt to pour my soul into it. How incredible it was to have someone tell me it was a work of art.

It had taken me another couple of days before I could get out of bed. I stood under the shower spray for only a couple minutes. Compared to the one in Cole's bathroom, it was sort of like being sneezed on repeatedly.

The water turned cold before I'd even managed to wash out the shampoo. I stepped out and realised I forgot a towel, settling to dry myself off with the hand towel while doing my best not to think about the severe lack of Felix's happy, leafy greenness.

The prospect of going back to my room was too tempting, so I did something I never did. I went for a run.

I didn't run so much that I didn't even own a pair of running *shoes*. I settled for lacing up my Converse, pairing them with a set of pyjama shorts and an old oversized shirt I was pretty sure belonged to Jamie and set off.

I'd left my phone along with pretty much every single one of my other possessions at Cole's when I left him. So, when I'd gotten home to find a less than impressed Melody sitting in my kitchen next to my father, her eyes glassy with both the devastation I knew she felt on my behalf and the anger at likely having not heard back from me on what I could only imagine was a legendary amount of calls and texts.

It only took a single look from her, the one that asked every question I couldn't answer without fearing I'd rip the stitches that I'd carelessly threaded to hold myself together over the last few days.

I shook my head at her, clamping my bottom lip between my teeth to stop its tremble and allowed myself to slouch into her embrace.

"Melody, you'll stay for dinner?" my dad asked her, being less than subtle at the way he pretended to read his paper while he was really looking at the two of us with nothing short of concern in his stormy eyes.

"I'll be staying." She nodded, but kept her eyes on me.

That was last week and I'd gone to sleep every night in the comforting embrace of my friend, her slender arms strong as they held onto me.

"You're not a receptionist Lucky, you'll hate it," Jamie said from the kitchen of his townhouse while I draped myself over the back of his couch like a ragdoll cat.

"It's true," Soph said, scooping another spoonful of ice cream out of the carton and placing three little slices of pickles on the top. "You're not a receptionist. You're a chef."

I couldn't stop the look of disgust on my face, watching her shovel the concoction into her mouth, her eyes fluttering closed in delight.

"That's disgusting," I whispered in horror.

My brother looked up from where he was chopping the ingredients for the dinner he was cooking and over at his wife.

"That's not even the worst combo she does. She's been putting chocolate sauce and soy sauce on a plain potato chip."

"James, you're not supposed to tell everyone about the cravings. They're sacred between you, me and the bean."

"They're terrifying," he corrected her.

"And I'm not a chef...anymore," I corrected her statement from earlier.

"You'll quit on me within the week," Jamie said, waving his knife in my general direction.

"I need a job, Jamie." I hated how small my voice sounded, and I hated the looks of pity that both Jamie and Sophie gave me.

"Has Cole—"

"He has nothing to do with this," I cut him off. "It wasn't ever meant to be anything serious and the fact that he got hauled up in the mess was the reminder we both needed. It was a job, nothing more."

Jamie looked at me like he was entirely unconvinced that a single word out of my mouth was true. So I gave him what he so clearly wanted. I gave him something truthful.

"I need to move on with my life, James. I need to move out of home, be an adult again. Have a life again."

"But your life is—"

"If you won't help me that's fine, just say. But I've made up my mind."

"Well then." He frowned, moving his attention back to the chopping board. He was holding his knife wrong and it took everything in me not to correct him. "Once you've made your mind up there's no stopping you."

"So?" I prompted.

"Come into the office on Monday." He sounded reluctant to give the offer, like he was supporting me in my endeavour to give everything up rather than supporting me in my endeavour to find a different path.

We didn't talk much after that and I'd gone back to my parents place feeling more pathetic than when I'd left earlier in the afternoon. Melody showed up like clockwork, wrapping her arms around me and doing her best to fill a void that wouldn't heal upon the notes of peonies and sandalwood that were the perfect combination of scents to explain my best friend.

My heart yearned for mint. For fresh, woodsy air and clean laundry.

"You okay, Luck?" she murmured from behind me, our heads sharing the same pillow.

I didn't want to lie to her, it was all I had been doing for the last two weeks. Lying to her, to myself, to my family.

"This is how it needs to be," I replied.

It had taken me a long time to fall asleep, waking in the middle of the night to find Lid gone. I'd fallen back asleep and found her back beside me in the morning when the sunlight had stirred me awake. She was on her phone, locking it immediately when she clocked my open eyes.

It reminded me again that I still didn't have a phone. I didn't make any attempts to get my things back from Cole, I didn't make any attempts to buy *new* things. Phone included. I just didn't want to.

"How bad?" My voice was still gravelly with sleep.

She looked at me, her curls in wild disarray around her face, eyes full of pain for me.

"Pretty bad, Luck."

That was how it went for the week that followed. I didn't look, but I knew that the headlines kept rolling out. There were less of them than there were initially but the news hadn't died down yet.

    Jamie was right, I hated being a receptionist. But it's what had to be done. This new life. This new path. Once I sorted myself out, once I settled on a new plan for my life then I'd look at the damage that had been done and I'd see how I could fix it though I doubted very much that there would be very much left to save.

46

Cole

I'd gotten as far as the lobby. I'd watched her get into her car and drive away from me and I'd never been so fucking angry in my entire life.

It was written all over her face, why she'd left. Her beautiful, infuriating face. That she had the audacity to think she had any sort of right to decide whether or not I deemed her worth the backlash in the news. Deemed her good enough. I could see it in the way she held her body. The way she had wiped the tears from her face like they were betraying her.

It had taken every single ounce of my self control not to go after her. I could do nothing about the roaring profanities that echoed around the lobby of the building, giving Abe the fright of his fucking life.

My chest was heaving with breaths that couldn't pull enough oxygen into my system. My hands pulled at my hair in a pathetic attempt to grab onto something that wouldn't slip through my fingers. To give myself some relief even just for a second.

But I'd never been as full of potent anger as I was then. I'd forgotten what it had been like to have something to lose, *someone* to lose. Forgotten what it was like to have someone force that loss on me. To take away my control.

So, I didn't mind at all when it was my darkest impulses that urged me to call those very same people who I kept close in case I ever found myself in need of the less than savoury favours.

"Mr Thompson," the deep gravel of the voice on the other end greeted me with bored politeness.

Acer was a businessman. He acted as businessmen did, and handled things in only ways that businessmen could. From things that happened in the light of day all the way to transactions that had no paper trail. That never existed, even to the eyes that witnessed it all.

"I need you to do something for me." I let myself completely fall into the darkness and I revelled in it.

I'd had eyes on Lucky from the moment she walked through the front door of her parents house. It was less than ideal, but it turned out that until I had gotten the situation under control it was a necessary circumstance. Then, and only then, I would bring her home.

I still had her phone, so I could only assume that she hadn't seen the way things had continued to unfold and for that I was glad. There was a time where I'd have been over-fucking-joyed for everything. I might have, at the very least, told myself I was satisfied by every mark against her name.

Now, I considered it a small miracle that I hadn't fucking killed anybody yet.

Yet.

I had a team of people working meticulously on removing article after article. It was a slow and incredibly expensive process, especially considering that for every one you brought down, another two popped up in its place. The news had gone fucking *mad* for this story.

I should have known. Anything on the infamous and so beloved Lucky Peters, especially something that painted her in the exact opposite light that had been cast on her for the entirety of her rise to stardom and her time in the limelight was like cocaine to every starving journalist out there.

Every single outlet that had shared anything to do with *Thompson & Co.* had been sued on the grounds of false information and defamation. It only took eight days for them to stop posting about me or the company. Once that was done, I could shift my focus to the people responsible for everything.

The person who had started the media upheaval. Who had taken my control from the situation and as a result, cost me Lucky. Temporary as it was.

I had to give it to him though, he almost fooled me.

That's what led us here, exactly three weeks since Lucky had run from me. Each and every day was marking a tally on my soul, a promise to show her just how much she'd never be able to run from me again. She could try, I might even enjoy the thrill of having to track her down and she might even succeed for a little while.

But I'd always find her.

Those were the thoughts that ran through my mind as I rolled up the sleeves of my crisp white dress shirt, in a concrete box somewhere very far away, where no one would hear him scream.

"So," I said as I sat down across from Greigory Ashford, his left eye swollen completely shut, dried blood coating so much of his face I had to assume whoever had warmed him up had broken his nose. Shame I hadn't arrived earlier. "Greigory," I sighed his name, so exasperated with this stain of a human it was grinding on my nerves already.

"Cole, Mr. Thompson—" His words were hindered by the swelling of his face. "I didn't—"

"Shh," I hushed him, my voice soft. "That's quite alright," I cooed, leaning towards him, resting my forearms on my knees. "I just thought it was time we had a little talk."

"I—I'll tell you anything," he fumbled over his words, his chubby wrists straining against the ties that held him to the chair.

"I know you will." My gloved fingers gently coasted down the side of his ruined face. "I'd like to know every detail of what you did, and I'd like to know from the beginning."

He nodded his head with vigour, the lax jowls of his cheeks moving so intensely I actually found myself feeling... uncomfortable. "Yes, y–yes, I'll tell you everything and then you'll let me go?"

"Oh yes, I'll release your bindings." I let a little of my mask slip, revealing to him the hint of a smile that he might have only ever glimpsed in his nightmares. "Scouts honour."

I gave him a two finger salute before leaning back in my own chair, my legs splayed out before me like I was casually lounging at home.

But I wasn't, and it would never be home so long as Lucky continued being a self proclaimed martyr. It seemed that there were a few people on my list that deserved punishment.

She'd run from me.

Run.

From.

Me.

The knowledge made my hands clench into fists where they still hung loosely at my side. Greig had started to speak and I hadn't heard a thing he'd said.

"...hard to find the people who were angry with her. No one really had anything bad to say about her. There was one though, all it took was just one person to start talking and I was sure more would be published. I t–took what they wrote in an email and a–a–added to it. It hadn't been bad–d–d enough. G–god," he cried, losing his composure, "please let m–me go. *Please.*"

Mmm.

"What else, Greig?" I'd lost my patience.

"I f–fabricated a few stories, tied them t–to people who worked for Lucky and shot them out to some contacts in the n–n–news."

"Your contacts?"

"M–mother's."

That, I didn't see coming.

"And you sent them out under your name."

"N–no. Mother sent them out."

Another name for the list.

"And Mr. Monteith?"

"It wasn't h—hard to convince him."

"I see," I said, standing slowly and walking toward a table of perfectly organised and laid out tools. This was a little more than I expected, but then again, I'd known the people who helped me with the darker side of my business were nothing if not thorough.

I made a mental note to send Acer a thank you card.

The thought made a genuine smile tug on the side of my face. The relationship I had with him was one of pure business though he had never been afraid to ask me for things in return for my help outside of our financial agreement. This little table of goodies told me everything I needed to know about this particular setup.

He wanted something from me.

I picked up something that resembled pruning shears and moved back to where Greig sat. He'd still been speaking but, again, I'd been so in my own head I hadn't heard a thing he said. That didn't really matter though, I'd heard enough.

The dark patch on his olive green trousers and the acrid smell that surrounded him told me everything I needed to know about how he was feeling and what he was pleading for.

"Shh, shh, shh," I soothed him again, a pathetic whimper escaping him. "I'm just going to cut your binds."

"L—like you said?" he asked, his face now coated in equal parts sweat, tears and blood.

"Just like I said," I purred to him. With the snap of the last tie that secured his ankles in place, I stood back to my full height and dropped the tool to the floor.

I spared only a second for the regret I had if Benny ever found out, but it was quickly overruled by the knowledge that it was because of this man that Lucky had been hurt.

I'd seen the look on her face, the exhaustion, the defeat. It was the second time I'd seen her break and both times had not been at my hands, at my will. The first time, I had relented. I'd solved the issue without dirtying my hands, not directly at least.

This time would be different.

Greigory looked up from where he still sat, either from fear or true inability to move, and the moment he saw my face he began to wail. The sound of pure, undiluted terror that erupted from him was music to my ears.

It was fucking *beautiful.*

In his hasty efforts to get far from me, he scrambled back, chair tipping backwards and sending him sprawling on the floor. I watched him go, mildly amused at the way he behaved so much like a child. Without sense and completely lost without anyone to guide him.

The moment he saw the door, white and almost blending in with the walls either side, he started for it on all fours. Crawling, he shot me look after look over his shoulder, his piercing cries and pungent odour filling the entire room now. I had no doubt he pissed himself again.

I followed after him slowly, lazily, and I couldn't help the grin that split my face when he realised the door was locked, and no one was coming to save him. I knew that what he saw was only the side of myself I let out when no one was looking. No one but Lucky.

I was right behind him, so close I knew he could feel my presence though he hadn't heard me approach.

The silence pressed in around us as he went quiet. His body trembled with crashing waves of terror.

COLE

"I did tell you, Greig," I taunted him. "Your first mistake was letting Lucky's name ever leave your mouth. I might have let you go then, but then you touched her," My smile grew, too big for my face, too much teeth showing to be anything but fucking monstrous, "and since then you've been nothing but very, *very*, dead."

I didn't take note of the way Greig's blood had dried on my hands as I knocked twice on the very door he tried to escape out of, letting the men outside know I was ready for my next visitor.

Her muffled screams reached me well before the door clicked open, the piercing shrill of them grating along my eardrums made me want to crack my neck repeatedly. I felt nothing at all as she pleaded and sobbed, nothing as she began to scream louder against the gag in her mouth when she no doubt discovered what was left of the previous inhibitor of the chair she was being secured to.

The tools before me painted a vivid picture of what her future could have held but the longer I was here, the more time Lucky and I would be apart.

I picked up the gun before I strolled back to my own seat, right across from the girl. Leaning back, I lifted the gun to scratch my temple before dropping to my side. It was only then, once I took her in, my head tilting to the side in quiet observation that my smile returned. Feral and empty and terrifying.

"Hello, Chelsea." My voice was velvety soft eliciting goosebumps across her exposed skin. "Or should I call you Becka? Your name *is* Becka, isn't it?"

Becka's tear streaked face and stared back at me, eyes red and swollen.

"You've done something, Becka. Something very, very bad." I leaned forward so my forearms were now resting on my knees, the gun dangling in front of me. "Do you know what I'm talking about?"

She began to cry harder, pulling frantically at the binds and shaking her head rapidly.

"Tsk, tsk," I tutted, my bottom lip jutting out in a pout. "You're lying to me and you should know," a heavy sigh escaped me, "I really don't like liars."

The screams that tore from the back of her throat were jagged and brutal, the sounds vibrating through the walls around us and echoing back. I closed my eyes against the instant headache the sound produced before getting to my feet.

My exhaustion hit me all at once. The effort of having to move through every single day without Lucky. Of knowing where she was, what she was doing, how she was fucking hurting and not being able to have her. Hold her. *Help* her.

"I was going to drag this out," I told her, "but I'm fucking tired." I lifted the gun, pressing it against her forehead right between her eyes. "Bye-bye, Becka," I grinned at her before pulling the trigger.

47

Lucky

I walked across the street like I was being pursued by a creature of the night. My heart beat was frantic and I could feel a sheen of sweat coat my upper lip.

However, it had nothing to do with the moon that hung full above my head or the sirens that polluted the air in the distance.

It did, however, have everything to do with the building that loomed behind me.

It had to do with the polyester mix of the collared shirt that fit me perfectly. The way my hair was out and flowing, the locks carefree without the stress of wondering if a strand would cascade into a dish mid preparation.

Bessy's stationary presence in front of me had been a siren call the entire day as I watched her waiting faithfully through the window of the front of Jamie's office building. The sound of the door thudding shut as I slid into the warm embrace of my acorn and four leaf clover seat covers was what I would have imagined walking through the pearly gates with a choir of angels at your back felt like.

What sliding into cold sheets and finally finding the warm body within them felt like.

"You suck, Lucky. Don't do that," I scolded myself as I slumped forward and let my forehead fall against the steering wheel.

It was weird, how I was feeling, because I had put myself in this situation and yes I was so desperately unhappy that it was difficult not to burst into tears every morning when Stacey, the other receptionist, asked me how I was that day.

I'm fucking *great*, Stacey. I'm a washed up celebrity chef who lives at home with her parents and on the cusp of what I had really hoped was my comeback I was bent over by the media practically anointing me as Satan's spawn tarnishing any last shreds of dignity I had. Oh, and did I mention I also gave up the love of my life so that I didn't ruin *his* life for a second time in twenty eight years?

So yes, Stacey, I'm just doing so well I struggle not to break into song on an hourly basis.

I didn't say any of that. I always just said 'Great!'.

I now hated the word.

I'd officially been working for Jamie for two weeks. Two whole weeks and every second of every minute dragged so thoroughly it was like my legs were made of lead. I loved my brother for giving me what I'd asked of him, but he was right. This was absolutely not for me and if I had it my way I'd haul ass so fast that I'd break the sound barrier.

The reality of my situation was that I needed to start a new life. I needed a new path and new hobbies and new things that made me want to get out of the bed in the morning, and the only real way I could think to find those things was to first get out into the world on my own again.

A scream lodged in my throat when the passenger side door of Bessy swung open and my behemoth brother folded himself into the front passenger seat, his shaggy blonde hair pressed right against the roof.

He turned to look at me and my tear stoked face before he tried to settle in further. I assumed he thought he looked relaxed but it was sort of like trying to stuff a sleeping bag back into the case once you pulled it out. It just didn't look *right.*

"Hey," I croaked, leaning back into my seat and staring at the dark street in front of me.

"Want to tell me what's on your mind?" Jamie's voice was soft and casual but there was no mistaking the concern.

"It can't be legal for me to drive with you as my passenger," I offered up to him.

"That's not what I meant."

"I know what you meant," I mumbled back, reaching up to dry my face. "I'm fine though, just a big day."

"Am I working you too much?" He lifted a brow at me.

"Like a dog. I have the right mind to contact HR."

"That would be Sophie."

"I would just need to cry in front of her once and she'd steam roll you without question." I smiled genuinely at the thought.

Soph was due next month and aside from her nauseating food cravings, she was doing great in the last stretch of human growing. She'd also adopted the viciousness of a jungle cat in her approach to literally anything mildly upsetting.

"Still no phone?" he asked, knowing I hadn't bothered to replace the one I'd left at Cole's all those weeks ago.

"There's no point."

"Have you even looked at all that's been happening?"

"I don't want to talk about it," I said firmly, hoping he'd drop it.

"But, Luck—"

"James." I shot him a look and wished I could've stopped the quiver of my bottom lip. "I can't talk about it, *please.*"

He frowned at me like he thought I was being stupid, but I'd made a point to completely remove myself from anything news related.

The radio was on? I turned it off.

News? Off.

Dad's paper? I turned around and headed the other way.

Anyone in my family speaking about it? I'd ask them to stop or I'd just turn around and walk away.

I hadn't heard or read a single thing about my further demise since I ran from Cole's. I'd also not read a single thing about what was amounting to be his demise either.

"Have you spoken to Cole?" Jamie asked tentatively like he could hear the thoughts in my own head.

"No." I really didn't want to speak about it, mainly because I was so *sick* of crying. I had cried a lot over the last six weeks, and some of those episodes were from the painful reality that since I ran from him where he'd stood in his office, seeing him coming after me with so much devastating rage before the elevator doors closed between us, he hadn't reached out. He hadn't tried to call or show up or *anything*.

He'd done *nothing*. And it wasn't like I thought I deserved more than that. I was actually more hopeful that he'd been able to nip the slander of his company in the bud, make a statement or something and the very real absence of me would put any further speculation to rest. That he would be saved and any backlash would fall on me.

It still didn't hurt any less, that in mere seconds he had disappeared from my life like he'd never even been mine in the first place.

"Lucky, I really think—"

"Jamie, for the love of god, can't you see I *can't?* I know what they're saying even without reading it and maybe one day I'll be able to look at it but you can't begin to understand what it's like to read the things about yourself that you fear most, the very worst things that you believe, and see it all plastered everywhere. See people *agreeing*. See people you love getting hurt because of you. I—I will not be the person that does that to him. I refuse to cause him that sort of harm. He's better off."

"Does he get a say in that? You haven't said anything about it publicly, Luck. You're not even *trying*—"

"What could I possibly say? Sure, some of the things they've said might be lies, but the very root of their stories are all true. I was the catalyst. I ruined those people's lives. I'm a fraud."

"You're not a fraud Navy Grace, but you are seriously feeling sorry for yourself."

"You're an asshole." I scowled at him, blurry as he was between the tears. "I am doing my best."

"You're not doing anything at all." He sounded angry but I knew my brother, and it wasn't me he was angry with, he was angry *for* me.

"I'm doing my best."

"And your best is sitting in your room from the moment you get home to the moment you leave, only to come to a job you hate, not eat anything and then sit in your car and cry for twenty minutes before you drive home, avoid everyone, sleep for too long and then do it again?"

Well, fuck me.

"I'm doing," my voice cracked with the pain I felt in every single part of my body, "my best." I reached into my bag for a tissue to blow my nose. "This is all I'm capable of doing right now. I know I have to do more, I know it won't blow over any faster if I stay silent, but I have nothing to say right now. Nothing to defend. I hate myself almost as much as I'm sure everyone else does."

"No one hates you, Lucky." His voice had returned to its softer tone, if not still firm.

"I don't need you to lie to me. I've been here before," I reminded him. Knowing that this version of myself wasn't all too dissimilar to how things had looked when I lost *Seven*.

"That's what worries us." He wouldn't look me in the eyes then, and I know he was speaking on behalf of everyone in my family, Liddy included, in their little group chat that I knew they started to keep tabs on me called *'Lucky isn't in this one'*.

"I'll be fine, Jamie. And you need to focus on your own family. Your wife is going to push out an ice cream coated pickle if she doesn't slow down on that weird train."

He finally cracked a smile. "Did she ask you to pick her up some more?"

"I literally have a jar of pickles in my bag. I'll drop them off on the way home." I lifted the jar in question out of my backpack which finally earned me a booming laugh that sounded so much like my own. "Get out of my car before you damage it, you giant human."

"Not my fault you came out the size of a thumb tack." He opened the door, letting in the fresh spring air that came with the turn of the season.

"I don't know how you didn't break our mother in half," I shot back.

"Luck," he scrunched up his nose.

"You just better hope that child of yours doesn't absolutely *demolish*—"

"*Okay,* gah—you really paint a picture." He hoisted himself out of the car with a grunt before turning back and leaning down to look back in, "I just want you to be okay."

"I'm working on it." I gave him a small smile I didn't really feel.

I pulled away from the curb and drove in silence all the way to Sophie, dropping off the pickles along with the ice cream I'd picked up on the way.

"You sure you can't stay?" she asked, holding the food close to her chest.

"Lid's coming over again, so I don't want to leave her hanging." I gave my sister-in-law a kiss on the cheek before planting one on her round belly.

It was already half-past-nine at night when I finally pulled Bess into the driveway of my parents' place, the house already dark. It was just me and them at the moment, no one usually stayed through the week unless they were under the age of five but tonight was a free night.

"I'm home!" I called out, letting the front door click shut behind me, snapping the lock back in place as I waited for a response to come, but it never did. "Hello?" I called again, heading for the kitchen to drop my bag off.

They weren't here. They'd left a note on the counter letting me know they'd headed away for a last minute trip with their friends. If the note was to be believed they were staying in a lighthouse that had been converted into a rentable accommodation.

"Go figure," I mumbled, heading for the house phone and dialling Melody's number.

"Luck." She sounded out of breath, picking up on the third ring.

"Am I interrupting something? And how did you know it was me?"

"Meredith told me they were heading out of town and I have your home number saved. Duh?"

"She told you?"

"Yeah she called me this afternoon, said she tried you at work but Stacey said you were at lunch."

"She never said anything." I frowned, trying really hard not to think about how useless Stacey was on a good day.

"I, uh—" She disappeared from the line for a second before coming back. "What did you say?"

"I said nothing, but *you* are absolutely having sex." I grinned into the phone. "You're having sex on the phone while you're talking to me. That's a new level, Lid."

"I'm not," she breathed.

"Okay, as much as I love you, I don't need an audible front row seat to you getting railed. Are you still coming over?"

"I, uhh, yes. *Yes*," she said with more conviction, the exclamation could either have been to my question or something happening in her immediate vicinity. I was going to wager on the latter.

I suddenly felt incredibly selfish. She'd been spending more nights here in my bed than at her own house.

"Hey, don't worry about it," I said, twisting the wire of the phone around my finger. "I'm good on my own."

"What? No, Lucky, I'll be there."

"I want you to stay where you are and enjoy yourself. This is good, Lid. Enjoy it. I love you."

"You sure?" Her voice was clearer now, albeit concerned.

"Absolutely. I'll talk to you tomorrow though, okay? Maybe we can do lunch."

"I like lunch, and I love you too."

"Lube up, sister." I sent a flurry of kisses into the phone before I hung up, feeling the smile start to fall from my face.

I pulled out old leftovers that should probably not be consumed from the fridge for dinner and did a final check of all the doors in the house while eating it cold. Trudging up the stairs, I brushed my teeth for the shortest amount of time that would still get them acceptably clean before passing out in my bed the moment my head touched the pillow.

The blissful oblivion of sleep was my favourite place to be lately and the hardest to pull away from. I'd pull myself up and out of this, I knew I would. The only problem was that I was just so *tired.*

I just needed to sleep first, then I'd wake up tomorrow with a new perspective and I'd get my shit together. I'd said the same thing to myself every night for the last month but this time I meant it.

I meant it.

48

Lucky

My dreams had been haunting.

They were humiliating and terrifying and the wires of all the very worst things to ever happen to me were crossed over and over again. I'd wanted to wake up, but the heavy blanket of sleep had been too much to climb out of, only managing to resurface when the sound of my bedroom door opening and closing pulled me from the restless onslaught of nightmares.

It took me a second to think through why that should be worrisome to me and in my sleep riddled brain I'd finally concluded that it must have been Melody. It felt like only seconds between hearing the sound and calling out but it could have been longer. Minutes. Hours.

"Lid?" I called out from between dry lips into the room that was undoubtedly filled with the presence of someone else.

It was familiar and foreign all at once. Like I knew what it was like to be blanketed in the shadows cast by this person, but that wasn't how I'd ever felt in the company of my best friend. It was like the walls had pushed in, like the temperature had dropped, like I wanted to scream and cry and laugh. The only conclusion I could come to was that it had to have been lingering emotions from my dreams.

"What are you doing here?" I mumbled groggily, snuggling deeper into the covers, determined to settle down, to slow my heart beat.

Melody didn't say anything and I sort of half wondered if I'd fallen back to sleep momentarily and missed her reply. I was about to turn over and see what she was doing when the mattress dipped and the covers lifted, letting cold air into the cocoon of warmth I'd created.

"Sweet baby cows, Melody, you'll let out all the heat." I frowned, working to peel my eyes open so I could send her a tired glare. I shouldn't have worried about the struggle though, because they almost flew out of my head in the next second.

It was his scent that hit me first.

I'd have to be dead not to know him that way, and even then I think it would still pull my restless spirit from wherever it wandered.

The desperate need to scream consumed me. It was like all the air got pulled from my lungs and I couldn't move. I couldn't do anything but stare at the wall in front of me as I felt him shift behind me.

He loomed like a creature from nightmares, stalking me. But this nightmare was so different to the ones that had plagued me, this one I had yearned for as it slipped through my fingers again and again.

I felt the way his arms reached for me in the dark and I couldn't stop the shaking of my body or the torturous need that was clawing its way out of me, shredding my insides bit by bit.

I still couldn't move my eyes from where they searched the wall, like it would have the answers on what to do, on *why* he was here. To taunt me? To break me further?

His arms wrapped around my frame and pulled hard against his muscled chest, the searing heat of his body burned against the coolness of my own.

It was like I was someone else, watching it all happen from somewhere else. The way my body jolted with a violent sob as he buried his nose in my hair and inhaled deeply. How I could feel his legs against my own where he entwined them, wrapping himself around me so completely it was hard to know where he began and I ended. I wanted to fall into him, but the tiny remaining splinters of my sanity demanded I did no such thing.

Demanded I keep myself safe.

The need to speak, to fucking *wail* was almost painful but I was trapped within my own body with nothing but silent, vicious sobs to show for what this was doing to me.

He ran his nose along the length of my neck before following the scorching path he'd made back with his mouth, sending jolt after burning jolt through me.

"Mmm," he hummed, his grip on me tightening and I closed my eyes at the timbre of his voice. At the way I felt the vibrations against my skin, felt it rattle my bones and shake me from my silence.

A feeble cry fell from me as the first of the hot, heavy tears cascading down my face. He moved us fluidly, my body limp and pliant, until I was on my back and he hovered above me, his body not pressing against mine but rather caging me in.

"Eyes on me." His voice was raw and gritty. The words trailed against my skin like sandpaper, coarse and brutal and all I wanted was for them to hurt more.

I couldn't look at him.

I *wouldn't*.

I didn't want to see his face. I didn't want to play this game. The very last image in my head of this man was the blazing rage that had poured from him before the doors of the elevator closed between us. I had convinced myself that look was something other than it was.

That it was hate and loathing and disgust.

"Eyes. On. Me," Cole bit out every single word, his voice strained.

It wasn't lack of care that kept my limbs heavy, but this deep-sated exhaustion. I could feel the tracks of tears continue as I finally complied with his demand.

It would have been less painful to be strung up and quartered than see him there above me. His face was closer than I'd thought, his features mostly covered in shadows but the gleam of his eyes still bright, still sparkling in their undiluted, untamed, jade tinted anger.

He looked tired.

There were shadows under his eyes and his hair had grown out. He somehow looked *bigger* than the last time I saw him. His shoulders wider, muscles more defined.

I couldn't stop the crashing emotions that consumed me. My eyes fell shut once more as I let loose the pain of my shattered heart. My arms finally moved, lifting up to push at his chest before I pulled them back into me, the heat of his exposed skin searing against my palms.

I thrashed beneath him, wanted to curl into myself, to roll onto my side and hide. To fall through the bed we were on, through the house, into the earth itself and never stop.

I wanted to hide and never be found.

I could hear the sounds falling from my mouth. Rasped, guttural broken things that said everything about what I had held in. What I had been holding onto. Not just with the fracturing of my new dreams, the shell of which had still been soft and delicate, but with the brutal reality of how it sounded to love with a broken heart, to walk around with a damaged soul. It wasn't beautiful or romantic, it was brutal and painful and haunting and *heavy.* It was under the weight of his gaze that I let myself fall into the raging tide of emotions that consistently swirled inside of me.

I hadn't forgotten Cole's looming presence over me. In part, I thought that perhaps it was a figment of my imagination, the culmination of a heart being broken over and over again and dreams being shattered in equal repetition.

"Shh," he whispered against my ear, the sound jolting me into the room around me and out of my mind.

My hands lifted up to find the warm, hard expanse of his chest again.

"No," my voice was just as quiet. "No, no, *no no no no*," I whimpered, pushing against him to no avail. He just pressed in closer to me, nestling between the valley of my legs, getting closer and closer until my hands had no choice but to fall away as he barely pressed his chest to mine.

"Shh," he repeated, the palm of his hand reaching up to press against my cheek, wiping away the tears that cascaded down my face. "Lucky." His voice was hard and heavy, like he was at a war with himself on which emotion to let win. His anger or his concern.

"Please," I whispered, wriggling under him. "*Please, go.*" I hated the words even as I said them. They were the total opposite of every thought in my head, every desperate want of my own body. My head and my heart had been on different sides of the battle ground that was my life in the weeks that had passed.

His nose dragged up the side of my neck, inhaling before a shudder wracked his body. "I can't do that, Lucky Girl." He continued his path up the length of my jaw, ghosting over my lips until his nose brushed against mine.

"Why?" I asked against the darkness of my closed eyes. They'd fallen shut at some point as he burned a path into my skin with his touch, both at the relief of finally having him near and the pain of knowing that he would need to leave. That I would need to let him go again, as much as I was able to.

He said nothing, but didn't move any farther away.

"*Why?*" I asked again, not caring about the desperate sound to my voice or the fact I knew he'd be able to read everything off my face no matter how hard I tried to hide it.

He didn't respond to me, at least not with words.

It was in the silence of the room, in the way every single cell of my body was focused on all the parts of him that were touching the parts of me. That he was *here* of all the places he could have been.

He was finally *here.*

My eyes refused to open because the truth was I was tired. I was so tired of feeling too much while trying to feel as little as possible, at being reminded of what it was like to be near Cole. To be near him but not able to have him.

"I don't want you here," I pushed the words out of my mouth. They were threadbare and pathetic, but I did it. Did I hate myself for it? Did it soften the debilitating feeling of selfishness that came with the relief of having him close again? Both, I think.

I had hoped maybe he wouldn't speak. Maybe I'd eventually feel the weight of him gradually disappear like a phantom in the night and I'd realise I made it all up. That I'd conjured him out of the shadows and the potent, searing *want* that refused to leave me be.

"Cole," I tried again, his name grated on every nerve in my body causing flares of pain and panic and *need*.

"There are a few things we need to clear up, don't you think?" His words pushed past my own, his tone light and conversational like he hadn't heard me at all.

I'll just wait for him to disappear. He'll go away, he'll go away, he'll—

"Eyes on me, Lucky."

I could feel the way his chest vibrated against mine, felt his words down in the very marrow of my bones.

I didn't want to. *I'm so tired.*

That's what I thought as my lids lifted, aching and scratchy. God, I *knew* those eyes. I knew them, I knew them, I knew them. But they shouldn't be here, because him being here meant it was all for nothing.

I'll just wait for him to disappear. He'll go away.

My eyes started to close again, drooping ever so slightly, the call of the sort of oblivion that sleep could give me so loud and inviting and safe.

"If you close them, we start again. Do you understand?" His voice was strong, the vibrations cutting through me again, tethering me to him like he'd reached into the very centre of me and tied ribbons to my soul that bound it right to his.

I wanted it, *God*, I wanted it. *Selfish, Selfish, Selfish.*

I nodded my head anyway, because I could see everything in his eyes.

"I need your words, Lucky. Do you understand?" Cole moved his hand slightly so his thumb rested along the line of my jaw, manoeuvring me so that I was looking right at him, so that there was nowhere I could hide from him.

It flooded me all at once; the fear, the relief, the excitement, the gut wrenching sadness. It stole the breath right out of my lungs.

"Y—yes," I choked out, scared to even blink at this point.

"Good." He sounded pleased, but his face didn't change at all. "The first thing we need to discuss," he started to speak and I kept my eyes locked on him, the tears continuing to fall, "is that you seem to have a bad habit of running away. Wouldn't you agree?"

This version of Cole I was familiar with, he was darker now, more unforgiving. This version terrified me.

"I—" My brain wasn't working. I was sure the moisture on my face was just my brain leaking out of my nose after finally giving up on me. "I couldn't—" I started to explain but he cut me off.

"Do you or do you not agree?" His tone was sharp and commanding, just as he leant down to let his lips graze my jaw, cutting off the path of another falling tear.

"Yes," I gasped out, my eyes fluttering with the need to close.

"Mm," he hummed in acknowledgement. "See, that's a problem for me, Lucky Girl." Cole spoke like he was pondering an article in the daily paper, not like he was keeping me barely put together through his touch alone.

"It's a problem because of the second thing we need to discuss, and that would be—" He placed soft, gentle kisses down the length of my throat which pulled another shuddering sob from me.

"Cole," I cried, wanting so badly to reach out and sink my hands into the dark, tousled strands of his black hair.

"Patience, Navy Grace," he cooed, moving to hover above me again, and I saw it then. The way he was being split in two, the way his arm had started to tremble as he held himself above me, the way his thumb started to move in slow, soothing circles on my jaw. Another tremor moved through my body as I kept my eyes locked on his.

"Point number two is that, despite what you so obviously think," this time when he spoke, his voice wasn't so put together, it sounded like he was coming apart at the seams, "is that you're *mine*," he growled the last word like the thought of me alone drove him mad.

I watched him watching me until the tears were no longer from the pain of what my reality had been for the weeks that had passed since I'd seen him last, but because it was too much. His hands, his mouth, his eyes. It was all too much.

The relief of my body giving out on me and causing my eyes to close was like I'd been released from shackles that had rubbed my wrists raw and left nasty scars. I wanted to will myself to move, to sit up and push him off and demand he not take another step closer because I was losing this battle, the whole fucking war.

"Please." It was my final try, my final plea but really I wasn't entirely sure what I wanted anymore. For him to leave? To leave me be? To never let me go?

"There is just one last thing we need to cover," his voice was so quiet now, I had to strain to hear him. "It's more of a question I need you to answer. Simple enough, I think."

"I don't—"

"I would be very careful on whether or not you let that lie leave your mouth," his voice hardened again in an instant, cold and calculated, contradictory to his warm, strong body or the scent of him that always made me feel safe.

"You'll be coming home with me tonight, Lucky. I was patient, I gave you time to come back on your own but that stubborn streak of yours was always going to get you in trouble," he whispered, planting a small kiss onto my cheek. He lifted his hand and let his pointer finger start at the edge of my eyebrow and lazily make its way down the side of my face as he spoke.

"Will you ever run from me again?" he asked the question like a musing, like he was picturing that exact thing happening.

My body started to tremble again, my mind struggling to catch up with what was happening, what he was saying, what he was doing.

"Answer me, Navy Grace. Will you ever run from me again?"

I opened my mouth to speak but nothing came out. My tongue darted out to wet my cracked lips and I swallowed once, twice, before trying again.

"No," I whispered between us, feeling another set of rallying emotions ball in my chest, trying to cleave me open from the inside.

"Mm," he hummed against my cheek, lowering himself until his mouth was at my ear and his hand once again rested on the side of my face, firm on my jaw so that I couldn't look away from him, "I don't believe you." He bit the words out like they were foul, bitter things.

It felt like we'd been here before. Him, this immovable force and me, pushing at him. Thrashing and scared and so fucking lost it was terrifying, and just like last time it was his words that made me still, that took the fight right out of me.

"You. Fucking. *Left. Me*," his voice broke on the last word and I could feel that tether between his soul and mine so acutely it hurt. He loomed above me like some imposing god who had been wronged. No, not like a god, but like the Devil. Like he hadn't just emerged from the shadows that he was so comfortable in, but like he had *become* that darkness.

I tried to speak, to tell him, to explain but my throat wasn't working, no sounds were coming out against the onslaught of emotion pouring from the man above me.

"You *lied* to me." His breathing had picked up and his body trembled.

I realised then that it wasn't from anger like I'd thought though, it was from pain.

"You lied to me and then you fucking *ran*," he seethed and then like it was one of the hardest things he'd ever done, his grip on me lessened. It seemed, for a second, that he might be trying out what it would be like to let me go, to let go as I'd pleaded time and time again and the mere reality of it terrified me. Facing the possible truth of it *terrified* me.

I dragged in breath after breath, trying to see through the building panic.

"I left for you." I forced myself to lock eyes with him again. To let him see everything, forcing every emotion onto my face that I could, not even caring as the tears filled my eyes again and began to spill over. They hadn't stopped in the last six weeks, why would it matter if they stopped now? "To protect you," I rasped.

"To *protect* me?" He sounded incredulous. He sounded fucking furious and like he'd never heard such a stupid sentence in his life.

"I—I refused to be that person again," I said, the words no louder than a whisper, but not due to the hold he had on me.

His hand slipped to the back of my neck, a move so *him* that it made my heart pang with pain, with want and desperate debilitating *need.*

"I didn't know when we were kids. I *didn't know*—" A sob wracked through me before I could swallow it down. "I didn't want to take anything from you ever again. *Ever.*"

His face changed in an instant from the mask of rage to one of blank nothingness.

No. Not nothingness. Cole was looking at me without the pretence of anything to cover what he was feeling. He was looking at me with *everything.* The tick of his jaw and the storm in his eyes told me everything he wasn't saying. He was letting me see *everything.*

"But you did," he whispered back and the crack in his voice sliced through me deeper than anything else ever had. "You took *you* from me. You *left.*"

"I was trying to protect you." I dug my nails into his forearm deeper, desperate to hold him close, to keep him near.

"That wasn't your decision to make." He gritted out. His

voice was still quiet but growing heavy with the weight of the emotions he let me see, that he'd finally let loose. "You don't *run*. Not from me. Never from us. That's not how this works, Lucky. Tell me you understand," he demanded.

I couldn't say no anymore.

"Okay," I choked out, releasing his wrist and sinking my hands into the silken strands of his hair.

"Dammit, Lucky. *Tell me you understand*," he said again, like he was the one begging. Pleading.

"I understand. I do, I'm sorry," I said the words with as much conviction as I could.

"Promise me," he said, just like when we were young and he had been the centre of my whole entire world. I felt my heart break apart only to come back together in a completely different way, irrevocably changed.

"I promise," I said, gripping his hair in my hands tighter. "I love you."

Cole's eyes took on a sheen I'd never seen before. "Say it again."

"I love you," I breathed, "I love you, *I love you*." I repeated the words over and over, reaching for him, pulling him to me until the hardness of his muscles started to soften and I felt his body shudder before he finally pressed his lips to mine.

"*Lucky*," he spoke my name against my lips like a prayer, or a plea or a curse or maybe like all of those things tied together. Cole's arm snaked its way under my shirt, his rough broad hand pressing tightly against the skin of my back, moving us to our sides and holding me flush to him.

He kissed me like it was new, like the texture of my lips was fascinating to him, like it was something he never wanted to stop doing. He kissed me lazily and fiercely and desperately.

Moving from taking his time, to being worried I would slip through his fingers, and all I could do was hold him close.

I let my fingers feel the strands of his hair, the *realness* of him beneath my touch, his body moulding against mine.

I wasn't sure of the hours that passed when Cole finally spoke. His voice husky and warm. "Tell me something," he said as I traced a finger across his features. It wasn't new, the way I let my fingers map out his eyebrows, the line of his nose, the shape of his lips. But now I did it for a different reason than I did before.

"I'll never run again," I said, determined to make him believe me, no matter how many times I needed to say it.

After a few minutes under the weight of his stare the side of his mouth pulled up.

"What?" I couldn't stop the pull of my own lips.

"It doesn't matter if you're lying, if you do run." The hand pressed against my back began to make soothing circles again and I let myself settle further into the spot between his collarbone and jaw.

"I won't." The words were muffled from where my smile pressed to his neck, "But, why?" I asked, my curiosity winning.

"There's nothing that would keep me from you. Nothing that could happen that would stop me from needing you like this." He reached for my hand and placed it on his chest, "No matter where you go, I'd follow. I'd follow you anywhere."

I pulled my hand up between us, pinky finger extended, "Promise?" I whispered, never letting my eyes leave his.

Cole lifted his own hand, hooking his pinky finger with mine but instead of pressing his lips to the pad of my thumb he leaned down and spoke the words into my skin. Pulling me tighter, holding me closer, enveloping me in everything that was him, "Promise."

49

Lucky

Four months later

Today was going to be the day I wasn't going to be able to hold it in.

I was going to throw up.

Right here, right now, all over the newly carpeted floor of the courtroom, I was going to throw up. I thought for sure the very first day of the trial it would have happened, but I'd held it together which was both reassuring to my own standards of bravery and also, admittedly, very surprising.

This was the last day.

The verdict had been made and now, I was going to throw up.

I'd prepared as much as I could for it, opting to wear a skirt suit which I wasn't sure had turned out to be a good idea or not.

In the mirror of my bedroom? Sure, I looked like I strolled out of *Legally Blonde* and was two shakes shy from kicking your ass. In reality though, my whole body was sweating, my blouse was chafing my armpits in a super uncomfortable way and my legs kept sticking to my seat.

My upper lip was comparable to a waterfall at this point, and I kept on seeing Melody from the corner of my eye waving her hands like a barely subdued lunatic trying to stop me from rubbing off the makeup she'd spent hours doing for me.

"This isn't necessary," I'd complained for the seventeenth time that morning when she came over to help me before scurrying off to the courthouse.

"Yes it is. This is your armour."

"I'd rather just wear the chain link."

"I know you would, but *this* armour says 'business woman extraordinaire, who you can kick while she's down but will always get up and thrive'," she'd said that while swiping a light layer of blush across my cheeks.

Of course, I had burst out into tears because what would a day in my life be (when reflecting on the last two years) if I didn't cry at least once. So there I was, sweating like an Olympic runner, no make up on the bottom half of my face due to extensive wiping and enough sweat between my thighs to fill a paddling pool.

The hardest part had been the testimonies that were made against me. I couldn't rightly fathom how so many people could sit on the stand and lie. They weren't even little white lies, these people had fabricated stories upon stories about me. One of them even called me Lyndsay. *Lyndsay.*

When I tried to recall the last seven days I mostly came

up blank. It was like everything around me was happening in both slow motion and on fast forward. People's mouths were moving, the Judge was speaking, the lawyers that sat on either side and behind me leaned in periodically to say something to which I nodded. And yet, all I could remember was the feeling of Cole's eyes on the back of my head.

It was like the biggest sense of deja vu I'd ever had in my entire life.

I used to sit through day after day, class after class, feeling the weight of his gaze on me. Then, it infuriated me.

He had been so many things to me in my youth. A haven, a best friend, a protector. And then he'd become the culmination of all the worst things of my childhood. He'd become the aggressor in my life, the person who I'd wanted to hide from, the person who'd hurt me.

Now, I clung to the feeling of being cloaked in his attention, knowing that no matter what was happening around us, he was there. Silent and watchful.

Safe. My haven.

The courtroom moved to stand as the judge swept into the room.

"Oh, god," I mumbled as I stood with the lawyers on either side of me, the rustle of everyone's clothing as they got to their feet like static in my ears. "Oh, shit." I clenched my hands at my sides.

"Miss Peters, we couldn't be more confident in the outcome of this case," Larry, one of the lawyers on my team to my right said. Nodding his head in aggressive agreement to his own words.

"Thanks, Larry." I gave him my best smile before chancing a look behind me and finding Cole immediately.

He stood tall and imposing, towering over the room that was filled to the brim with people who had waited out from the early hours of the morning to get a seat and see the trial first hand.

The entire trial had been publicised which was both humiliating and completely out of my control. Cole said it was actually a good thing, that when the verdict was ruled in my favour it would show the rest of the world that believed the 'astounding bullshit', as he'd put it, was false.

I tried to believe him.

His expression was blank, jaw tight and eyes conveying everything he was feeling right to me. He'd left those walls down since the night he showed up at my parents house and pieced me back together, bit by bit. He'd let me see everything he was feeling, even when there was nothing there, when his eyes were like pits of darkness and his beast was raging.

He always came back to me, though. Always.

This wasn't what I'd expected from him here. I'd seen Cole at his job, he was so personable I had to try and keep the shock clear off my face. The man knew everyone's name, *and* their kids' names. He smiled and laughed and I was sure he had been abducted somewhere between the car and the doors to his building, but I'd learned that was the way he was at work, the way he had to be.

It made a lot of sense, actually, how he was so successful. Imagine if that had been *my* greeting when I turned to find myself standing in his kitchen. I certainly wouldn't have attempted to run for the hills.

If you told me a year ago that he would have knelt with me in the ruins to put the pieces of my life back together with me, that even when I couldn't do it myself he'd bare the weight of both me and my shattered dreams, that he'd be the strength for both of us, I'd have figured you were spinning a fantastical yarn, yanking my chain. Telling tall tales, if you will.

I couldn't have been more wrong.

I was glad it was him who was here with me. I'd ended up asking my family not to be here for this. I'd worked hard to always keep them out of the limelight, and plus with little Jack, my brother's new baby, up and out into the world now, it made sense that they all stayed home, but I knew they were watching.

I let my eyes flick across Benny and Lid's faces, landing briefly on Felicity who offered me a reassuring smile before turning back to the judge, just as the jury was led back into the courtroom. Since she'd come back from her final exams I'd realised that she was, in fact, a good egg as I'd pondered on our very first encounter.

"Have you reached a verdict?" The judge's deep, baritone voice echoed around the silent courtroom, making my stomach cramp in anxious knots.

"Yes," said the elected speaker, an older woman dressed entirely in purple.

"Is the verdict unanimous?"

"Yes, your Honour."

I wondered if it's possible for someone to pass out while still being awake. My heart was beating so fast that all I heard was the blood rushing in my ears, all I could do was focus on keeping my legs locked beneath me so that I didn't collapse directly onto Larry.

"Not guilty," the purple lady said.

And the courtroom erupted into deafening yells. Every single person was on their feet. They were yelling, applauding. I was pretty sure I could even hear Melody wailing from behind me.

"*Order!*" The judge smacked his gavel. "*ORDER!*" He smacked it again and again, hardly being heard over the unruly crowd, over the press who were up and against the barricade.

All I could do was just standing there in a state of total shock, unable to feel the tips of my fingers or blink properly.

It felt like forever but finally the noise dampened down, the judge delivered a stern warning and people took their seats once again.

Oh my god.

"On the charge of financial negligence, we find the defendant: not guilty."

Oh sweet fucking turnips.

"On the charge of fraud, we find the defendant: not guilty."

"On the charge of workplace misconduct, we find the defendant: not guilty."

Not guilty, not guilty, not guilty.

"The defendant has been found 'not guilty' on all charges. This trial is now concluded. The defendant is free to go, and the court is adjourned." The judge whacked his little hammer for a final time and then all hell broke loose all over again.

The room broke out into cheers, deafening cheers, but it all fell secondary to the sheer shock that still rooted me to the spot I was in.

I think it's hard to ever realise how much the words and thoughts and feelings of other people can affect you. I had an entire year and a half before the world started talking about me, and then six months where they wouldn't shut up and it became harder and harder to separate myself from the things they were saying. Even though I knew that I hadn't, in fact, demanded the vegetarian and vegan staff in my kitchen all eat a slice of bologna.

Larry gripped me in a tight, celebratory hug which happened so quickly I didn't even have time to react, I'd say his fast detachment had to do with the eyes I still felt on me.

The last day I'd ever seen Cole in the classroom of our senior year science class he'd told me that he knew I always looked for him in a crowded room. He'd said that it was because I wanted to make sure he saw me winning. That I wanted to be certain that he had a front row seat, but that had never been the case. Not even close.

I looked for him because I could *feel* his eyes on me, and every single time I sought him out I had hoped, for a second, that the look in his eyes would be the same as it had been before he'd broken my twelve year old heart. That he'd look at me with awe. With happiness. With *love*.

I wasn't so naive now, I knew that those emotions were too, for lack of a better word, plain, for what he felt for me. That they were too *light*.

Once again in a room full of crowded people, I looked for him. Melody was glued to Benny and Felicity in a hug that saw her hands not even touching as they were wrapped around them both, Cole's spot that had been between them now gone.

I searched for him, trying to see around the press that were asking me questions and yelling over one another, around the lawyers ruffling papers and asking me questions too, I couldn't hear either. My search began to border on frantic, and then I saw him.

I should have known, really, that he was always most comfortable in the shadows, which is where I should have looked for him first.

Cole stood to the back of the room, in a corner far from where the people who had been able to witness the trial in the courtroom had huddled together against the barrier. He wore black slacks with a black dress shirt and black blazer. Needless to say he'd cut a rather impressive picture and I'd pounced on him with incredible speed when he'd walked out of the walk-in-wardrobe, still fastening his cuff links.

I could see his eyes darken as he looked at me, and I knew for a fact that *he* knew exactly what I was thinking about. I didn't even try and hide the small smile that crept across my features as I moved past people to get to his side, focused on no one but him.

As soon as I got within arms reach, he wrapped an arm around my waist and pulled me to him. We'd already started to garner the attention of the people around us, like flies to honey, but still, all I could see was him and all he was looking at was me.

I think this version of us was my favourite. Not me searching for him in a room full of people, or him looking for me, but rather being beside him.

He leaned down to place a gentle kiss on my cheek that was at complete odds with the look on his face. "I think it's time I took you home, Miss Peters."

Cole took my hand, leading me out the doors of the courtroom, tugging me after him and away from everything that had transpired over the last two years that saw us standing there today.

I gripped his hand tighter and let the smile almost split my face in two before finally giving him a reply just as we slid into the back of his car, "Must be my lucky day, Mr. Thompson."

Epilogue

"Why won't you let me read it?" I whined like my life dependent on it, jumping like a maniac at the laptop that Cole held above his head.

"Because." There wasn't a single inflection of emotion in his voice.

I started hammering at his abs, which just somehow continued to get *harder*, over and over again until he pushed me away with a hand on my head and stepped away from me slightly.

"This. Is. Not. *Funny*," I growled, still attempting to swing at him.

"Oh no, I'm taking you quite seriously right now."

"*Cole*." I gave up, flopping to the floor of the lounge room. "I won't say anything to anyone."

"That's not true," he said, sitting back down on the sofa before resuming his previous work.

"That was *one time*. How can you even be angry at that. Liddy loves your *Acquired Taste* articles more than I do!"

"That's also not true."

"Okay, that's not true. She does love them though," I

pointed out, turning my head to look at him.

"She still might conveniently disappear one day," he muttered under his breath.

I chose to ignore him. "Please?" My bottom lip jutted out and my eyes went as wide as I could manage.

Cole flicked his gaze to where I was sprawled on the floor for about a third of a second before focusing on his laptop again. "Nope."

"You hate me," I grumbled. "That's it, isn't it? You despise me."

"Obviously."

"You want me gone. Out of here. Never to return."

"Desperately."

"I'll go to *Helga's* with Melody without you," I threatened, eyebrows lifted in seriousness.

"*Please.*"

"Hey!" I sat up quickly, crossing my arms and glaring at him but he was already looking at me, a twinkle of mischief in his eyes that did things to me below the belt that I seriously couldn't consider at this moment in time.

I needed to be out the door – I checked my watch – ten minutes ago. "Crap."

I got up and ran from the living room straight into our bedroom, changing quickly into a casual set of hospitality blacks and combing my hair back into a tight, neat bun. I turned from my reflection and headed back into the bedroom, checking my watch for a second time to see that I'd lost another minute of time.

After all this time I should have suspected it, really. It wasn't a clear and open doorway that greeted me, but rather a very hard, very solid man-chest.

EPILOGUE

I immediately started to fall back, my hands snapping to cover my face just as my eyes began to water. I didn't hit the ground. Instead I was pulled against the offending man-chest in question.

"For the love of Mary, Joseph and the Carpenter, Cole! You're so *hard*." I could feel the involuntary tears rolling down my face, the relentless stinging of my crushed nose. "*Why are you so hard?*"

"You weren't complaining this morning." He even had the audacity to wink at me, all before the smile fell off his face and he reached to pull my hands from my face.

"Ow, ow, *ow*." I hopped from foot to foot, clenching my hands in his shirt while he gently prodded the throbbing bridge of my nose. "Is it broken?" I had my eyes clamped shut tight, but I couldn't miss the laughter in his voice.

"Not broken, but it might be bruised. That one felt bad."

"Of course, it *felt bad*. My nose was almost joined in holy matrimony with my brain. You need to make more noise."

"I make plenty."

I rolled my eyes and tried to shove away from him but he kept me close against his chest. "Cole, I'm going to be late," I sighed, even as I wound my arms around his waist and pressed further into him.

"It's your restaurant. If you can't be a little late, then what's the point?"

I gave him a little pinch to which he gave my ass a gentle tap.

Clover had been open for just over a year now, and it was everything I'd hoped it would be. It was the result of everything I'd dreamed, everything I'd worked hard for and also the visual representation of what I had learned in life, what I had learned from Cole.

I'd been so focused on this path of being lucky. That it was something inherent to my being. Something I was born with, not something I made happen. I'd never been able to see it any other way. That all felt a little stupid to me now.

I'd taken a lot of time away from cooking in a restaurant. I'd released a cookbook which had been in the best seller list for fourteen weeks. It broke records with over two million copies being sold in the first eight weeks of its release. I'd been a guest on TV shows and a speaker at events, and it felt good to get back out into the public, to get into the world and find who I was as a person again. Or at least do the things I *thought* I enjoyed before.

I wanted fresh cool sheets and a warm body between them. I wanted suggestive bath mats and Felix, the happiest plant in the entire world. I wanted to sit in Cole's art gallery that he had completely transformed.

It was now filled with us. Pictures and pictures of us on our wedding day.

"But this was..." I'd started when he had led me in there after I'd been away on one of the many business trips I had been taking.

"It was a version of myself that I no longer recognised. I didn't need any of it anymore."

"But you said..."

"Once, yes," he cut me off, knowing what I was going to say. "I'd needed it to help me *feel*. To remind me, maybe, that I wasn't empty." He didn't say the words in anger or to extract pity from me. He'd said them like they were just a simple fact.

An undeniable truth.

EPILOGUE

I'd reached my hand up to his cheek which he held in place with his own hold on my wrist.

"And now?" I'd asked him, with tears in my eyes.

"Now I suppose it does the same thing." He leaned his forehead down to mine.

"I love you," I whispered to him, completely unsure with what to do with all the feelings coursing through me. My entire body was swelling with them and I'd honestly wondered for the first time if someone could die from feeling this much.

"You're the light in my darkness." The words were scratchy, like he had pulled them from the depths of his soul, just so I could hear them. "I see clearly because of you."

That memory of that night was something I thought of every single day. It was also the moment I decided I wouldn't be going anywhere anymore. That the world didn't hold as much for me as it had before. There was no pull to go out and find anything more, I had everything I needed right in front of me.

I eventually pulled away from him, and my thoughts, tilting my chin up in a silent request for a kiss. "They might not fire me, but Melody will hand me my ass," I grumbled, reluctant to let him go.

"Do I need to kill someone else for you?"

"Ha-ha," I rolled my eyes dramatically, "that joke doesn't get any funnier you know."

"Not joking," he said, tone flat and eyes serious.

"Not funny," I delivered as sternly as I could manage.

His face didn't change for a whole minute before the corner of his mouth tilted up in that mischievous way of his. "Okay, no one dies today." Cole leaned down to plant a chaste kiss at the corner of my mouth, earning a reluctant smile from me before I peeled myself away from him.

Melody was the manager of *Clover*, and a third of the reason I was brave enough to give having my own restaurant again one more shot. The other third was Cole, and the last third had been all me, as hard as it had been.

With another pat on my ass I walked away from Cole, every step like treading through quick sand.

"Don't be too late, Mrs. Thompson, and I might very well let you read that review."

I stopped at the threshold of our bedroom door, taking a moment to appreciate the way he looked. Tall and broad, his hair the perfect mess of black. His arms were folded across his chest and his feet crossed at the ankles as he leant against the doorway to the bathroom.

God, he was beautiful.

"You promise?" I asked, dragging my eyes back up to his with extreme effort.

"Promise," he said with a wink that told me he was promising a lot more than a sneak peek at his next article and it made goosebumps break out across my skin, every hair on my body standing on end.

It had been two years of this now, and I couldn't ever see it ending, couldn't ever see my life without it. This unquenchable yearning to always come running back to Cole as fast as I could instead of in the other direction. Like a thread tied to the very centre of me, leading me back, leading me home.

Cole believes that you make your own luck, that you have to prepare and strike when opportunity presents itself, and maybe that's true sometimes, but not always. Because there was no way I could have prepared for *him*. No way I would have known *how* to prepare for him.

It was fate and chance and, well, it was just my luck.

Acknowledgements

Woah, this book was an absolute wild ride. At about the halfway point it just started pouring out of me, and when the first draft was finished at over 150,000 words I could have collapsed.

I am SO in love with this book and the characters. I always say that my characters write themselves after a little loving push from me and that was the case yet again.

But just like the other stories I've written, they become what they truly are because of my editor and most incredible friend, Joeli.

I think I say this every time, that I am obsessed with you to the very core of me and that in my own stroke of luck, I managed to weasel my way into your life. My second biggest stroke of luck is that you agreed to keep me around.

When you messaged before the final round of editing with your warning that you were going to be particularly brutal with your cuts, I had all the faith and as always, the end result is more than I could have imagined and that lead me to the last part of this acknowledgement: to the people who will read this book.

I hope you love it in the very same way I do and if you can take nothing else from it, know that you make your own luck in the world and whatever it is you're reaching for is completely and totally possible.

Love, C.

About the Author

Celine L. A. Simpson is an Australian romance and fantasy author, a dog mum, Punk Rock enthusiast, and owns at least 6 dungarees that she consistently pairs with Converse.

Most commonly known for her Romance publication Music to my Ears (2021), she was raised on the Mid-North Coast of Australia and graduated from La Trobe University with a Bachelors Degree in Creative Arts, majoring in Creative and Professional Writing. Growing up with a passion for reading, she began writing at an early age, moving into content creation as a career path before writing and publishing her own novels.

Also by Celine L. A. Simpson

Convincing Florence
Florence wasn't a people person.

Flossy learnt right from the get-go that to expect anything from anyone (apart from her grandmother) would only ever lead to disappointment. That all the minutes and seconds of her life constantly intersected with the hard and tough minutes of everyone else's, right from the moment she entered this world and let loose a wail of arrival.

It was the friends who couldn't be bothered to return the friendship, the dates that were only ever interested in one thing, and the general strangers who were never interested in returning her smile.

Florence loved two things. Her job at the library and her grandmother, Dot.

Apart from them?

People sucked.

Nathaniel Connors loved a challenge.

Tall, dark, and handsome; Nathaniel Connors sailed through life on a dimpled smile and buckets of charm. But when Florence finds him in the library, breaking more than one rule, she might have been the first person who didn't give him the time of day.

If there's one thing that Nathaniel needed to do now, it was to convince Florence that he was worth her time, and that there were people who were worth her while.

She was sure he'd fail.
He knew he wouldn't.

Challenge Accepted.

Music To My Ears
He had one of those side, half smiles that you read about...I always thought that was absolute nonsense - no single smile could make you want to cry out for mercy, but there you have it.

I did manage to, however, maintain enough of my dignity to cry on the inside.

Allie could sum up her entire life in two whole minutes. She lived walking distance to everything; work, her best friend's place and perhaps most importantly, the 24-hour corner store that was only a 1-minute walk away. Allie frequently sought comfort from the bottom of premixed brownie boxes at all times of the evening when she perused the baking aisle alone, until one night...

Wyatt Smith was the front man of the most popular modern rock band to date. Lady Luck travelled the world, their look and their music was recognised by everyone, everywhere. That was until he found himself the midnight errand boy for a runaway baking ingredient where he met Allie. And she had absolutely no idea who he was...

It's true that when someone catches your eye you start to see them everywhere.

But what happens when you do see them again?

Sometimes it's easier to put feelings in boxes, and sometimes it's easier to run away when the going gets tough. But sometimes you find someone to help you unpack, someone who will stand beside you, feel the fear, and take that leap of faith with you.

Terraleise (The Lost Child of the Crown #1)

Terraleise turns 18, only to discover she is now gifted with the elemental power of Earth. The thing about elemental gifts is that only those with royal blood possess them.

Terraleise is thrown into a life she never dreamed to be a part of, discovering all of the secrets entwined with her past, and her future. The heir to a kingdom overthrown by a corrupt branch of her own bloodline, Terra will see what it means to have courage and be brave, learning that the fate of the four kingdoms of Vaashaa rests on her shoulders.

Finding a life to fight for only to be faced with sacrificing it all, Terraleise will have to risk her love and her life to keep the world from falling into darkness. Will the Lost Child of the Crown find her rightful place?

Heir of Vaashaa (The Lost Child of the Crown #2)

The land is dying and the promise of war is thick in the air. With Terraleise still held captive by the enemy, Silas is forced out of his grief to move forward, to march on and ensure Terra's sacrifice, her life for his, doesn't go to waste.

The threat to the World of Vaashaa is more horrific than anyone could have ever anticipated. A long-forgotten darkness has crept back into the hands of the wrong person and time is running out to stop it. The Kingdoms of Vaashaa will have to come together to save their world from the bleak future it is heading towards, all while hoping for aid to come from the truths laced within myths and legends.

There is only one who stands to be a force between the darkness and the light, only one who can save them all. Will the Heir of Vaashaa rise from the ashes?